Praise for Traci Hall and her Scottish mysteries!

MURDER IN A SCOTTISH GARDEN
"Inquisitive and down-to-earth, Paislee makes a charming sleuth in this suspect-packed mystery."
—*Kirkus Reviews*

"In her second Scottish Shire mystery, Hall capably juggles multiple story lines and vividly evokes the Scottish backdrop."
—*Booklist*

MURDER AT A SCOTTISH SOCIAL
"Witty characters match the well-crafted plot. . . . Cozy fans will want to see a lot more of the compassionate Paislee."
—*Publishers Weekly*

MURDER AT A SCOTTISH WEDDING
"Down-to-earth characters and two mysteries to solve add up to a solid read."
—*Kirkus Reviews*

"Intriguing. . . . Fans of all things Scottish will have fun."
—*Publishers Weekly*

T0204931

Books by Traci Hall

MURDER IN A SCOTTISH SHIRE
MURDER IN A SCOTTISH GARDEN
MURDER AT A SCOTTISH SOCIAL
MURDER AT A SCOTTISH WEDDING
MURDER AT A SCOTTISH CASTLE
MURDER AT A SCOTTISH CHRISTMAS

And writing as Traci Wilton

MRS. MORRIS AND THE GHOST
MRS. MORRIS AND THE WITCH
MRS. MORRIS AND THE GHOST OF CHRISTMAS PAST
MRS. MORRIS AND THE SORCERESS
MRS. MORRIS AND THE VAMPIRE
MRS. MORRIS AND THE POT OF GOLD
MRS. MORRIS AND THE WOLFMAN
MRS. MORRIS AND THE MERMAID

Published by Kensington Publishing Corp.

Murder at a Scottish Christmas

TRACI HALL

Kensington Publishing Corp.
www.kensingtonbooks.com

I'd like to dedicate this book to my mom, Judi Potter, who is the best mother a woman could ask for—though I seem to write mums who aren't so nice, she is the gold standard of motherhood and my closest friend.

I've completely stolen my own idea for Paislee's Thursday Knit and Sip nights and started a virtual club. I'd like to dedicate this episode of Paislee's adventures to them—Kathleen, Katherine, Rocki, Kris, Destini, and Judi. We don't do a lot of crafting but it's sure fun to blether.

Chapter 1

Paislee Shaw enjoyed the bounty that Christmas brought into Cashmere Crush, her specialty yarn and sweater shop, but if she had to listen to "Jingle Bells" one more time, she'd go completely mental. A cappella, pipes, fiddle, and every variation in between— Brody and Grandpa even did a rendition using spoons until Paislee had threatened to toss the silverware into the sea.

On November 25th, Nairn kicked off the holiday season with a festive Christmas tree lighting ceremony. Tourists mobbed their quaint Victorian shire, something Paislee and her bank account were grateful for, aye, but today, December 20th, she wasn't prepared and out of sorts. She'd told Lydia that she wanted to be in her own home for Gran's favorite time of year. Was it too much to ask?

It appeared so, as it hadn't happened. Lydia warned her repeatedly to squelch her high hopes.

Cross, Paislee sipped her tea and scowled out the window of her bestie's flat. It had all the amenities as well as a view of the Moray Firth. It was a lovely space but wasn't theirs.

She, Grandpa, Brody, and their pup, Wallace, had been displaced from their home when the water pipes had burst over her head as she'd been about to kiss Hamish McCall. In truth, they *had* kissed, but she denied it and hadn't let it happen again. She could take a hint from Above. She wasn't done being a mum yet. Was it any wonder she was a wee bit moody?

"Mum!" Brody shouted from his bedroom. "Can I stay home today?"

"No, son." It was Friday and he'd be off for holiday as of this afternoon. Paislee was closing the yarn shop from December 24th through January 3rd to spend time together. "You've got early dismissal after your party." She winced as she remembered the manic excitement in the school halls the last day before winter break.

"Lame."

"Enough sass, Brody, or you'll be with me for the weekend instead of snowboarding."

Silence. Brody's best mate, Edwyn Maclean, had invited Brody to the mountains for Saturday and Sunday, and Christmas was on Wednesday. Paislee planned on using the time he was away to get his gifts together. As in, buy them.

There were only twenty-four hours in her day, blast it, or else she might not be last-minute shopping for his special trainers, new football, and video games, but between stocking luxury items at Ramsey Castle in the new gift shop, managing Cashmere Crush, Brody's exams in school, and saying aye or nay to paint samples for her kitchen, which, please all the angels and saints, would be done for Christmas . . . she hadn't had two seconds to buy presents.

It was enough to make her cry—but, she didn't have time for that either.

"Grab your coat. You have your gift for Jenni?"

Two days ago, Brody'd asked Paislee to knit a scarf and slouchy cap in Jenni's favorite bright green. He thought cashmere, though she countered with merino wool, which was just fine for the lass. A project like this normally would take eight hours, but Paislee had a scarf in that shade already completed so had stayed up late to create the matching cap.

Jenni had hinted that she'd gotten something for him too and her son had been surprisingly astute, knowing he'd need to reciprocate.

"It's in my backpack." Brody was growing out his auburn locks, which Paislee thought messy, but not worth the argument. "Should I bring Edwyn's?"

"Nah. Keep it for tomorrow."

Wallace raced from Brody to Grandpa sitting at the kitchen counter, to Paislee. The dog had just been groomed and sported a jolly red collar around his neck. His near-black eyes sparkled.

"I'll take Wallace doon," Grandpa said, noting the clock, which could be her mortal enemy. "You'd best hurry. Traffic has been crazy with all the tourists."

"Thanks, Grandpa!" Brody patted Wallace and tossed the pup a treat shaped like a snowman.

"Thank you!" Paislee slipped on her coat and grabbed her handbag, studying her grandfather who hadn't dressed yet for his part-time shift at Cashmere Crush. His silver-gray hair had turned lighter in the last few months, matching his beard, but his tall frame was straight, his color excellent. He adjusted his black-framed glasses and blinked at her like a sleepy cat. "Call me if you want a ride tae the shop. It's supposed tae snow over the next few days."

"I can walk." Grandpa tied the belt of his flannel robe.

Paislee shook her head—if she was stubborn, Grandpa was the source. "Fine! Text me before you leave."

"Dinnae fash," Grandpa said, shuffling across the floor to the kitchen and the electric kettle.

Was there ever a sentence more annoying than *don't worry*? Paislee and Brody rode the elevator to the lobby, nodding at the security guard, Max, who opened the door leading to the car park.

"Happy holidays," Max said.

"And tae you," Paislee replied.

Brody didn't answer so she bopped him lightly on the back of the head.

Her son grinned at Max. "Happy Christmas!"

The security guard handed over a candy cane that Brody stuffed into his pocket. "Ta."

The air had a crispness to it as they walked to the Juke. Though chilly the sky was a clear blue. She drove Brody to secondary school, the radio on low playing Christmas classics. Lights of red, green, blue, and gold adorned the roof and windows, which added to the holiday atmosphere.

Despite his original protest, Brody fidgeted with happiness on the passenger seat as she stopped in the drop-off queue, and he spotted his mates. "Have a good day, hon!"

"You too, Mum." Brody waved and hurried toward his friends huddled by the front door. Shrieks of joy wafted toward her.

Smiling, Paislee headed toward the shop, prioritizing her list. She was currently working on three projects in various stages of completeness; the thick vest in navy blue should be at the top as it was scheduled for pick up this afternoon. She'd made progress on two others last night at her Thursday evening Knit and Sip and would call her customers to let them know as soon as she finished, possibly tomorrow.

The ladies had all been in a festive frame of mind as they'd laughed and enjoyed time with each other before the holiday. Her best friend, Lydia Barron-Smythe, didn't knit but she created amazing appetizers and kept the conversation rolling.

Though it was out of her way, Paislee decided to drive by her house. It was a standalone two-story building of stone, and she missed it with a pang. Several work lorries were in front, the door ajar. Ladders and buckets cluttered the brown grass.

Once there, her plan to get out of the Juke and check the progress for herself was thwarted by a call from Grandpa. She answered via Bluetooth. "Hi!"

"Hello, lass. I hate tae whinge but I think ye'd better come back."

"Are you all right?" Paislee pulled away from her home with a sorrowful glance in the rearview. All she wanted for Christmas was her house. To bake Gran's cakes and pies in her own kitchen. In the ceiling debacle, Gran's index cards of recipes had gotten damp, but she could still decipher the neat block print—no sloppy scrawl for her schoolteacher granny.

"Elspeth called and she and Susan both have colds. She cannae come in today. I'll help oot."

Paislee was cautious with her older part-time helpers to make sure they didn't overdo or work too hard. Elspeth Booth had retired from her office position at the church with Father Dixon and excelled in needlepoint. Her sister Susan, blind, had been matched with a guide dog around Thanksgiving. This meant a full eight-hour shift for her grandfather rather than just four.

"Will it be too much, Grandpa?"

"Dinnae be daft," he replied, reminding her of his grumpy moods when vexed.

"On my way." Paislee ended the call and dialed Lydia.

"Lydia here," her friend answered in a cheery tone.

"Lyd, I just drove by the house. There are still ladders and trucks, and—"

"I advised you tae be patient! You promised tae wait." Her best friend sounded peeved. "The foreman is trying for Hogmanay, but it might be February."

New Year's Eve? Her eyes stung and her throat tickled. "I need tae make Gran's cakes! Her pies. Father Dixon is expecting a dozen assorted pastries for Christmas Eve dinner at the church, not tae mention three hundred mini black buns." Her pulse raced as she considered all she had to do that wasn't even shopping for Brody.

Paislee knew what she wanted to buy for Grandpa too—a fishing pole and hooks—and had been paying monthly toward a getaway for Lydia and Corbin to Italy at an exclusive spa for a week of their choosing, since Lydia wouldn't accept rent for the flat, insisting rather that Paislee put her money into the new kitchen.

"You can bake those cakes at my flat just fine," Lydia said with heat. "Why so many of them?"

"Father Dixon hands them out as gifts after Christmas Eve and Christmas morning mass, so that each of his parishioners will have a treat. The older ones, especially without family, look forward tae it."

"That is sweet," Lydia agreed, settling down. "And you just stepped intae the role?"

How could Paislee say no to Father Dixon? "I enjoy it, and it connects me tae the community, like Gran always wanted." Baking her granny's recipes as she would have done also brought her closer to the grandmother she loved so much.

"How long does it take?"

"I have two tins that bake ten buns at a time. This weekend Brody will be away with the Macleans at the mountain tae snowboard, so I'll get it done then."

"Perfect." Lydia cleared her throat. "So, since you see the reality of your kitchen, please have Christmas with me and Corbin."

"At Smythe Manor? No, thank you." Paislee'd had enough of the wealthy Smythes at Lydia's wedding to last a lifetime.

"Actually, because we must have Hogmanay with his family, we're going tae be with mine in Edinburgh. Talk aboot magical. The castle is covered with lights and Brody would have a jolly time. Please?"

"Sorry, Lyd." She hadn't been a total scrooge and had decorated a Christmas tree in Lydia's spacious lounge, for Brody's sake. "I'm holding out for my place. If that doesn't happen, the Shaws will celebrate Christmas at the Muthu Newton Hotel. Hamish suggested it and sent over the menu. They have a lovely prix fixe dinner that would be something different tae keep me from pouting."

"At least you're owning it, Ms. Moody," Lydia said. "I think the hotel is a grand idea. I've eaten there before with the agency, and the food was verra tasty. Would Hamish join you?"

Paislee blushed. "We talked about that, aye."

"And I'm just now hearing of it?"

Lydia wanted Paislee knee-deep in romance; Paislee was careful what she shared so as not to get Lydia's hopes up, or Hamish's for that matter. "We've been texting for the past few weeks. Poor man feels terrible for what happened, but he wasn't responsible." No, the collapse of the ceiling had been nobody's fault, just the dubious charm of an old home.

"This is wonderful strides forward, Paislee. I feared you'd permanently pushed him away. Nope, he cares for you."

Paislee understood how special Hamish was to "date" at her speed. "I'd invited him for Christmas but my house refuses tae get finished, Lydia."

"Home projects tend tae drag. I dinnae think they've even begun painting, but I'm not tae blame."

"In this instance, you might be," Paislee said. Lydia had ordered premier appliances within Paislee's budget, and Paislee knew that Lydia had put in more besides, but the refrigerator had been on back order for a month. Over thirty days in flux, wondering if they'd have to find something else, and how much time that would tack on. There'd been a shortage of manual laborers, and then the company her insurance had hired had quit, so they'd had to scramble, and here it was four months later, and she still was out of her home. February? *Och.*

"I want you tae have the best," Lydia said. "I'm absolutely chuffed for you tae see it all finished. I've chosen everything with you in mind."

Paislee had given Lydia artistic free rein and promised not to peek until it was put together and complete. This morning she'd been beyond tempted.

She pulled up in front of the modern condominium and stopped. Grandpa exited the lobby and climbed in. "Heya. You're right. Smells like it might finally snow," he said. It had been too cold for the white stuff though the mountains were covered.

Lydia, on speaker, greeted Grandpa with her customary enthusiasm. "Angus! You're working early?"

"Aye, Lydia, lass. Elspeth and Susan both have colds, and the shop is bursting with people wanting tae buy scarves, jumpers, cardigans, tams, gloves . . . Paislee needs me."

"I hope they feel better," Lydia said. "Selfishly, I hope we dinnae get sick but 'tis the season, eh?"

Grandpa chuckled. "Nothing a dram with honey cannae fix."

"It's a little early, Grandpa," Paislee teased, heading toward Cashmere Crush.

"Come tae a party on Saturday at our house," Lydia said. "Both of you, since Brody will be with Edwyn."

"I can't! I'll be baking all night and Sunday too."

"I adore Agnes's black bun puddings," her bestie said. "Will you save me one?"

"Promise. I was hoping tae see you Christmas Day, but it will keep." Paislee would bake extra for all that Lydia had done.

"We'll be back on Boxing Day—after a morning of serious power shopping. Mum and I load up on the best deals."

The day after Christmas was full of sales. "We'll be here. If I don't see you before . . ."

"That would be too strange," Lydia declared. "But tonight, we have dinner with Corbin's friends, Saturday you're busy, and Sunday we're hitting the road tae my parents'. I love the holidays and I hate the holidays."

Grandpa chuckled. Paislee arrived at Market Street, turning slowly into the alley. She passed the corner ice cream parlor which didn't open until eleven, the office supply store, the medical center, the dry cleaner, and the leather repair shop. Cashmere Crush was located at the far end of the block and just over two miles from Lydia's condo. "I hear you! So—we'll celebrate together the evening of the twenty-sixth."

"Just wait until Brody sees what we got him for Christmas," Lydia said. "He'll be the envy of all his mates."

"Lydia, you've done so much already!" Paislee turned off the engine.

"Hey, Brody is my family. Corbin having so many nephews and nieces really opens my eyes for available prezzies."

"You spoil him. And us—thank you." It was a losing battle, so Paislee didn't fight. "Bye for now!" She ended the call.

Paislee and Grandpa exited the Juke, climbed the cement steps where she fumbled to get the key into the lock because her hands were cold, then hurried into the shop. It smelled like pine, balsam, and peppermint. She flicked on the light and despite her Christmas music fatigue, the red, green, white, and gold decorations everywhere lifted her spirits. Battery-operated candles glimmered on the two high-top tables, in baskets of fresh evergreen and pinecones. She'd knitted holiday wreaths for sale that flew off the rack.

Grandpa switched on the electric kettle in the storage room. "I didnae get a chance tae finish my second cup of tea. Maybe I'll add some whisky." He glanced at Paislee as if to see her response.

He was a grown man in perfect health, so if he wanted a splash to warm his bones, she wasn't going to judge.

"I'd love a cup, straight up tea." Paislee shrugged out of her coat and hung it on a hook in back where customers couldn't see it, along with her scarf. Her hat was next, her fine hair springing with static electricity.

Grandpa prepared their tea and Paislee walked to the front door, peering out the frosted glass window.

Amelia, her Saturday helper who was full-time at the Nairn Police Station as a receptionist, had painted a chubby snowman with a knitted scarf and matching tam. Green elves frolicked with roly-poly puppies in holly leaves around the edge of the window and they'd gotten many compliments on how festive it was—it surely drew folks in. Amelia had confessed to dabbling in comics as a teen.

Paislee unlocked the door, though it was only half past nine and they didn't officially open until ten. She returned to the register counter and pulled her most immediate project from the shelf, a navy-blue fisherman's pattern vest with thick braids.

"You should make an ugly sweater," Grandpa said, putting her mug down on a cocktail napkin from the previous night's Knit and Sip, with pretty snowflakes on a silver background.

"What?" Paislee prided herself on quality bespoke items.

"You know what I mean. They have contests and everythin'." With a wince, Grandpa stretched out his back, and then blew on his hot tea. The mug he'd chosen had a very jolly Santa playing drinking games with his reindeer.

Paislee, perched on a stool, settled the vest in her lap and gathered her needles and yarn. "I am not joining the ugly sweater craze. It's a fad I hope will disappear."

"I wouldnae be so sure of that. James thinks they're a riot. Told his grandkids that's what tae buy him for Christmas."

James Young was the leather repair shop owner next to her prime position on the corner of Market Street. She'd had the opportunity to switch to the opposite end of the block, where the bakery used to be, but had stuck with her instincts and stayed to sock away money for her house expenses. Even with her insurance, and Lydia's bargaining, it cost a pretty penny.

Now there was an ice cream shop there called Scoops, which always had customers, despite the cold weather. The owner was a man in his forties who had retired from the military and spent his days making people happy. He had a dozen homemade flavors, and hand-rolled his own cones. Paislee's favorite so far was one called Holly Berry, which had huge pieces of real raspberries. With a fudge drizzle? Well, it was the holidays.

"Grandpa," Paislee said as she knitted the not-ugly-if-she-could-help-it vest, "Lydia is really being a stickler and not letting me see inside our house. I'm ready tae sneak down the chimney."

"I've got the key, lass. No need tae risk your neck." Grandpa raised his mug to her as he reclined on a high-back chair in front of a tall shelf with beige, brown, and orange yarn. "I'd hold the ladder for you, if you wanted tae do it anyway."

"Thanks." Paislee grinned at him, this unexpected gift of a grandparent. "I promised Lydia I wouldn't peek inside, but I really want tae have Christmas dinner there. Just us, and Hamish agreed tae be our first-footer for good luck, but she told me this morning that they haven't even started painting."

"Ah." Grandpa slurped his tea. "So, is that why ye've been so crabbit?"

"Oh!" Paislee blinked at his assessment. "Have I been?"

"A wee bit grumpy," Grandpa confirmed. "I figured it was because ye've been so busy."

"We have been, true, but I know a slump will come in January. It's the season, and not anything tae worry about." Paislee continued with the next row, remembering her first years in business and how she'd fretted, learning to save for a rainy day, or an unexpected business expense. "Gran taught me that."

"She was a wise woman."

"Aye. I miss her." Paislee's nose stung but she didn't cry, sniffing the tears away.

Grandpa peered at her over his mug. "Agnes was a one for Christmas." His gaze softened with memories. "I was raised Church of Scotland, Agnes was Catholic tae her core. Her family celebrated proudly and openly since the law changed in 1958. We Protestants observed in a similar fashion, but yer granny was just a touch extra aboot it all."

Paislee laughed and sipped her tea. "Extra is a brilliant word for it. Christmas carols, fruit pies, wreaths, blankets, cakes, her famous black bun pudding. If there was a place tae put some tinsel and evergreen boughs, she found it."

"That she did." Grandpa chuckled and settled back in his chair. "Workin' with the weans at school encouraged her holiday creativity."

"What did Gran's parents think about you being Protestant, since they were Catholic?"

Grandpa's brown eyes twinkled behind the lenses of his glasses. "Her dad had died young, and I think your great-grandmother was so glad Agnes had deigned tae marry after bein' a staunch supporter of women's rights that she welcomed me with open arms. Agnes had her degree from university in London and had seen the world. Now, her sister wasnae as welcoming." He shrugged. "Besides, I converted. I'm not a stickler for the details. I know what I believe."

Paislee had been raised Catholic, though Da hadn't been strict with it, nor her mother. The main differences between the religions were that Catholics believed in Saints, and in Mary, Mother of God. They thought a priest should be celibate and that the Host became the Body and Blood of Christ when consecrated, and non-Catholics couldn't take the Host. Protestants believed that the Bible was the ultimate Word of God.

Like Grandpa, she didn't care so much about the particulars of people's religion but was a definite fan of being kind. "Gran would say tae just be nice," Paislee said. She tugged on the ball of yarn, which had stuck.

"That she did," Grandpa said. "And she was the first tae offer help—it wasnae just talk with her."

"Father Dixon is a true pillar in our community, which reminds me! We have blankets for some of the families at church. Let's drop them off after work today."

"Blankets *and* black buns? Just like yer granny." Grandpa drained his tea and stood, rubbing his hands. "I'm ready. I know it's not what you wanted, but should we make a wee Christmas dinner at Lydia's?"

Paislee focused on her knitting project, the wool smooth beneath her fingers. How to explain that it would feel like settling? "Well, since it looks like we really can't have dinner at our house, it might be a treat tae eat at the Muthu Newton Hotel."

"Fancy!" Grandpa grinned. "Ye've been spendin' too much time around Ramsey Castle and the Leery Estate—wantin' posh Christmas dinner at a hotel."

Paislee rolled her eyes, her mouth twitching. "It was actually Hamish's idea."

Grandpa reached for the shop phone. "I'll make reservations, if it's not too late. How many?"

"If Hamish comes, that would be four." Paislee lowered her vest and needles. "I don't need another thing tae add tae our list, like braving the market for a ham. A dinner out will be nice. You realize I haven't shopped for Brody yet?"

Grandpa exchanged the landline for his mobile and typed in the name of the hotel as Paislee didn't have a physical business directory. He called but there was no answer.

"That's the way of things when yer a parent, Paislee. Your gran would be up tae the wee hours makin' sure every last package was wrapped just right. Come midnight, I'd eat a bite oot of Santa's biscuits tae prove the man in red had stopped by. Your da and auntie always checked the plate."

A steady stream of customers halted conversation, laughing and cheery people eager to enjoy the holiday.

As it turned out, Grandpa's sniffer was right, and the gray sky brightened with snow, which fell in huge fluffy flakes.

Amelia Henry popped in during her lunch break at the police station, red-cheeked from her walk. "Paislee! Angus . . ." The blue yarn of her cap matched her eyes and snow fell from the brim. "It's spectacular, eh?"

"There's something special about the first big snow of the year," Paislee agreed.

"Last night you'd mentioned that you're still shopping for Brody," Amelia said. "My brother McCormac just came tae town from Belfast. If he'd told us, Mum and Da wouldnae have gone tae Glasgow tae be with Michael. He's never been the best communicator. Anyway, he's got a friend who knows someone with the sweetest little puppies!"

"A puppy?" Paislee asked, alarmed. Puppies required a lot of work.

"Look!" Amelia whipped out her mobile to show a selection of tiny pups with assorted red or green bows. Fur shades ranged from white to sable to black.

"They are adorable," Paislee said, thinking of how often a puppy, even a cute one, needed to go outside or be trained on the potty pad.

"McCormac can get a deal fer ye, if you want one for Brody." Amelia pocketed her phone. "Breeding certificate and everything."

"That's okay, Amelia. I'll stick with the trainers—they only cost a hundred pounds."

Amelia laughed. "Fair enough. See you tomorrow morning for my shift." She tucked her black hair with cherry-red tips beneath the cap. "I told McCormac I'd ask around. Knowing him, he's gettin' a commission."

Paislee didn't know much about McCormac Henry other than he was a black sheep in a family of black sheep. "How's he doing?"

"I think he's all right," Amelia said. "He seems in a guid head space. Nice car, nice clothes. Not strung oot. Makes me believe in Christmas miracles." She smacked her palm to her chest, chuckling at her own jest.

"That's brilliant. Too bad for your folks. Can he stay at their place, or is he staying with you?"

"McCormac's got a couple of ladybirds he'll spend his time with." Amelia scrunched her nose. "He'll stay with me a few nights oot of obligation, but he says he's fine. My brother usually needs somethin', so I'm really happy tae see him, actually."

"With your parents gone, what will you do for Christmas dinner?" Paislee kept her gaze on a young woman checking out a knitted wreath.

"I dinnae ken." Amelia shrugged. "Probably head tae the pub."

"Well, Grandpa is going tae make a reservation at the Muthu Newton . . . Would you and McCormac care tae join us? Hamish will be there too."

"We'd love tae!" Amelia winked at Paislee and echoed Grandpa with a lifted pinky. "Fancy."

Chapter 2

Christmas Day dawned with a bright blue, clear sky visible to Paislee from the window of the master bedroom. She was tempted to stay in bed under the cozy comforter for another hour as she didn't hear anyone stirring.

Paislee, Grandpa, and Brody had gone to midnight Mass, and she was quite proud of how Gran's mini black-bun loaves had turned out; the treat was like a fruit cake baked in a pastry with lots of room for error. It was worth the burn marks on her fingers (from being too hasty in taking them from the oven) to see people's eyes light up. Gran's baking was famous in the parish.

They'd gotten home around one thirty. Though Brody knew darn good and well there was no Santa, he went along with the ruse for the filled stocking. She'd done one for Grandpa too and crawled into bed by two. It was now eight.

There was no more sleep for her racing mind, so Paislee disentangled her legs from the blankets and shrugged into her robe. She'd come to peace last night with the fact that her house wasn't done, and so be it. No more bad mood. Gran wouldn't have liked her whingeing.

She entered the living room. To her surprise, Grandpa and Brody had filled a pretty red stocking for her. The small tree near the picture window overlooking the water glittered with lights. Wallace's stocking was green with a paw print on it.

Paislee walked to the window and in the distance, sleek dolphins jumped and twirled. "Good morning!" She bowed her head in true thanks for all of her many blessings, despite the hurdles.

"Mornin'," Grandpa said from behind her.

"Hi! Shall I make tea?" She gave her grandfather a hug. "Thank you for all your help with the shop, and the baking. Everything."

His cheeks turned pink. "Och, well, yer welcome. You're happy? No need tae break intae our own house?"

"I've been feeling a wee bit sorry for myself!" She extended her arms to her sides and shook her hands. "No more! I swear I heard Gran's voice last night telling me quite sternly tae count my blessings."

Grandpa laughed and they settled into the morning routine of preparing tea. Paislee's phone rang and she answered, expecting it to be Lydia. "Happy Christmas!"

"Ach, Paislee. I'm in the car on the A83 tae Inveraray. Mum was in an accident," Hamish said in a rush. "I'm almost tae the hospital."

"Oh no!" Hamish was an only child, like she was. Unlike her, he had a wonderful relationship with his mother. "Please, keep me updated, all right? I'll say prayers for her recovery. What happened?"

"I cannae believe it," Hamish groused. "Mum's being x-rayed tae see if she broke her leg while ice-skating. Rain check for dinner?"

"You got it," Paislee said.

After another round of well-wishes, she ended the call and told Grandpa that they'd be down a person for their holiday meal at the hotel.

"Poor fellow." Grandpa sipped his hot tea. "We could use a dose of guid luck, eh?"

"Well, our dark-haired gentleman will be in Inveraray, and we can only hope he'll be home in time for Hogmanay. How long does a break take tae heal?"

Grandpa shrugged. "Depends on the location and whether or not it requires a surgeon."

Brody and Wallace burst from his bedroom and banished all gloomy thoughts with the exuberance of youth and Christmas morn. "Happy Christmas," they all said in unison. Wallace chuffed and raced around the tree.

Her son went straight for Wallace's stocking, pulling out a giant bone that was vet approved for the tail-wagging pup. Next, Brody grabbed his own stocking and sat cross-legged on the floor, diving in for sweets, playing cards, comics, and fishing lures. With a roll of his eyes, he reached deep for the orange and apple Gran had always included.

"Tradition," Paislee said. "Santa wants you tae have healthy teeth."

Grandpa snickered and showed that he'd also received an apple and an orange. "Santa knows best."

"Can we let Santa know for next year that we'd prefer oranges covered in chocolate?" Brody grinned at her. "My teeth are fine."

Paislee sipped her tea. "I'll see what I can do."

Grandpa handed out presents and they slowly opened gifts. She'd made an egg and potato casserole for breakfast, acutely aware of the passage of time. Brody would be a teenager next year. He'd possibly move away for college. Get married, if he wanted, maybe have children. Football was his love, and who knew where that might take him?

No matter how hard Paislee tugged, she couldn't stop the clock.

At two that afternoon, Paislee wore her new dress from Grandpa, something fitting for her forays to the castle, he'd said, in a light blue fabric that was very soft. She admired her handsome son as Brody complained about having to tog up twice in two days. She'd bought him a new jacket for church with matching slacks and shoes.

"Why cannae we stay home?" Brody asked. He'd been chuffed about the video games and wanted to play them.

"Tomorrow—we have no plans tae leave the house, promise. Aunt Lydia and Uncle Corbin are coming over." Paislee ruffled her son's auburn hair, realizing with dismay that they were almost nose to nose. Then, she'd be looking up at him, heaven help her.

"A whole day tae do nothing," Grandpa said, clasping his hands.

"I'll put some nibbles together for Corbin and Lydia, but we'll take it easy." Her phone dinged a text message.

"Who's that?" Brody asked. "Aunt Lydia?"

"No." Hamish, the headmaster at Fordythe Primary where her son used to attend, was sharing that his mother would need help for the entire school holiday. Poor thing had broken her leg in two places in a skating accident that she claimed was her own bloody fault. Surgery scheduled for Monday. "It's Mr. McCall. He's with his mum in Inveraray."

Which meant Hamish, handsome and dark-haired, would be gone through the New Year. Paislee sighed. She'd take no luck at all, to the bad spell she'd been having.

Grandpa patted her shoulder. He looked quite dapper as well, with his new cashmere sweater and trousers. Like Brody, he wore the same jacket he'd donned for church the night before.

Paislee drove, comfortable in the snow since she'd done it all her life. They arrived at the Muthu Newton Hotel, made famous by Charlie Chaplin, who would vacation there with his family. They offered a prix fixe Christmas dinner from three o'clock to six, which suited Paislee fine. No cooking, no cleaning up.

Paislee and her family exited the Juke. The snow reached the toes of her boots. Outside the hotel was a lighted sleigh with six reindeer and a Santa. She, Brody, and Grandpa posed by the cheerful sled, and she snapped pictures, sending them to Lydia.

"Brilliant ride." Brody pointed to a Mercedes SUV with large tires and metal trim that might be something Corbin would drive. "That's the latest model GLS-Class 450."

Grandpa tugged his beard in admiration. "Splendid vehicle."

"I'd need a stepstool tae get in," Paislee demurred. Lydia, tall to Paislee's average height, had shared what the monster vehicles cost, because Corbin liked them too. Added with the price of petrol . . . Paislee preferred something more manageable in value and size.

The three went inside the swanky hotel. The lobby was crowded, and savory food warred with cologne and perfumes, as well as holiday greenery. Her head ached.

"Paislee!" Paislee was greeted by Amelia and a taller, masculine version of her. Black hair, blue eyes, pale skin. A full mouth and quick smile. "This is McCormac," she said, tugging her brother's arm.

The handsome man leaned in to kiss Paislee's cheek, but the firm buss landed on her mouth instead with a flick of his tongue to her lips. The cheeky gent winked when she began to protest. Nobody else had noticed the inappropriate action.

The hostess, a short woman in a red velvet dress with a white apron, wished them a Happy Christmas. "Is this your entire party?"

"Aye," Paislee said. She turned to Amelia, hiding her indignation. "Hamish's mother broke her leg ice-skating, so he's in Inveraray tae care for her."

"Rotten luck." Amelia's expression implied more than just about the broken leg, but Paislee's lack of a dinner companion too.

"We're in need of a first-footer," Grandpa said in all seriousness. "Perhaps a dozen of them."

The tradition of a handsome dark-haired man to be the first through your door with whisky, black bun, and gifts was meant to bring luck and prosperity for the coming year. Amelia elbowed her brother. "What do ye say, McCormac? Can you stop by Paislee's for Hogmanay?"

"Aye, I'll see what I can do." McCormac was dressed quite well, his black hair stylishly mussed. Suit jacket and nice leather boots. Paislee had just turned the dreaded thirty and he was probably close to her age.

"Don't put yourself out," Paislee said.

The look he gave her was charming, but instead of flattering her, Paislee wanted to wrap her scarf tight around her body and step into the restroom to wash her mouth. A playboy, as Amelia had mentioned, with plenty of girlfriends.

There was no accounting for taste.

"This way," the hostess said. The table for six was now five, and the woman removed the place setting. "Have a seat—the holiday dinner menu is a choice of roast turkey, beef Wellington, or smoked salmon. I'll be back shortly."

"I'd like a double whisky," McCormac said before the hostess could leave.

"I'll be back tae get your drink orders, sir."

"Well, when ye come back bring my whisky, would ye, hen?"

The hostess left with a stiff nod.

Brody looked from McCormac to Paislee and bowed his head to hide a snicker.

Amelia didn't notice anything wrong with what had just happened and might be used to McCormac's behaving the bampot. They took off their jackets and settled in.

"What will you have, Brody?" Paislee was glad that he'd grown into an adventurous eater, in part due to hanging out with Edwyn.

"The salmon," her son said. "You?"

"I might have the beef Wellington. That's pure decadence."

"I was thinking the same," Grandpa agreed.

Paislee glanced at Amelia and then McCormac. McCormac tapped his fingers to the table, pulling his phone from his suit pocket.

"I cannae stay too long," McCormac said. "Sula is expectin' me for gifts."

"McCormac! It's Christmas," Amelia said. "Dinner will be over in two hours. I hardly ever get tae visit with you."

"Dinnae fash," he said. "I'm here, eh?"

Amelia raised her brow at her brother.

"What?" He narrowed his eyes at her.

Amelia bowed her head and sighed. "Nothin'."

The hostess came back with McCormac's drink and handed it to him. He sipped and thanked her, oblivious to the rest of them.

The waiter followed and took their drink and food orders, shaking his head at McCormac for being rude, but then focused on the rest of the group.

"And dessert is included in the meal," the waiter finished. "I'll be back soon with your drinks and starters."

"Thank you," Paislee said. For fun they'd ordered deep-fried haggis and a selection of artisan breads.

The drinks arrived first.

McCormac, Amelia, and Grandpa had whisky and Paislee decided on a local cider. Brody had Irn-Bru.

"Tae friends," Amelia said, lifting her glass. "Thanks for letting us join your party."

"Anytime. And I'm serious about an invite for New Year's dinner," Paislee said. She'd mellowed regarding McCormac, who'd been thoughtful of Amelia during the ordering process and put the rude kiss down to drinking. "I hope tae be in our house."

McCormac shrugged. "I'll be makin' the rounds, but aye, I'll drop in—for the whisky, eh?" He chuckled.

Paislee was familiar with the tribute expected but decided that he wouldn't be getting the good scotch, if he actually showed.

Amelia deep-sighed.

"Sis, did ye tell them what I got ye for Christmas?" McCormac finished his glass and shook the empty at the passing waiter.

"Nah—I was totally surprised with this adorable puppy!" Amelia showed a picture of a white fluffball. "The only white Pomeranian in the litter. I fell in love."

"Sweet!" Brody stood to get a closer peek. "What did you name her?"

"Snowball, of course," Amelia said.

"Yeah. She's cute. Or you could name her Storm, from *X-Men*."

Brody and Amelia often discussed video games, as when Amelia wasn't working or knitting, she was gaming.

"She just seems like a Snowball tae me," Amelia said. "Mibbe she can have two names? Snowball Storm Henry."

Brody and Amelia high-fived and he returned to his seat.

"She's so pretty!" Paislee said when Amelia passed down the phone.

Grandpa nodded and made appropriate noises of approval.

McCormac gazed at Paislee. "Want tae get your boyo here a puppy for Christmas? I'll give ye a guid deal, but I only have one left. Papers included."

"Please, Mum?" Brody clasped his hands together.

"No." Some decisions were tough to make but this one was not. They barely had time for Wallace, and taking a puppy down the elevator to the dog park in the middle of the night? No way.

Brody saw how serious she was and didn't press.

Luckily their dinner arrived, and all talk was on the amazing food before them. Paislee hadn't had beef Wellington like this ever. The golden pastry baked around a roll of beef tenderloin, mushrooms, and ham, was so light and flaky that it melted on her tongue. Roasted potatoes on the side, and savory gravy with thyme.

"Can you make this, Grandpa?" Paislee asked.

Grandpa scraped a bite of pastry through the gravy with a contented sigh. "Some things are best left tae the professionals."

McCormac finished his smoked salmon and by half past four, had consumed three drinks and was antsy to go. "I'm bringin' Lyla a puppy for Christmas too," he said as he pushed back his chair.

Amelia hadn't finished her turkey yet or been served her dessert. "Lyla? What aboot Sula?"

"Dinnae fash, sis. If a lass wants tae be with me, they know they gotta share. There's plenty tae go around." McCormac's phone dinged, and he swore, exasperated. "Mates found oot I'm in town and willnae stop pestering me. Hank and I are gonna talk."

"Hank is his best friend," Amelia explained. "And Porche's brother. Porche is his ex. It's complicated."

"And none of their business," McCormac griped, jerking his thumb toward Paislee and Grandpa. Brody was focused on his salmon, having eaten the green beans first.

"Sairy!" Amelia said.

McCormac gritted his teeth at another string of notifications.

"Is something wrong?" Amelia asked.

"Hank's a dobber, that's what. I dinnae need his permission to make new friends. He doesnae like Dougie, but too bad," McCormac said. "Dougie knows how tae get things done."

His phone rang and McCormac glared at Amelia even as he hung up on the caller.

"What now?" Amelia arched her brow at her brother, her annoyance plain. "We still have dessert that is part of our dinner."

Paislee could see that McCormac was ready to go so she patted Amelia's hand. "We can take you home. Enjoy your meal."

"Yeah? Grand." McCormac opened his wallet and dropped cash on the table. "I owe ya, Paislee. Never mind—we'll be even after I visit yer place on New Year's. Ta!"

He left in a rush.

Amelia sat back and shook her head. "Sairy aboot that. McCormac can be so . . . intense."

Drugs? Drinking? Paislee smiled at her friend. "It's the holiday. It makes everyone manic. Your puppy sure is cute though."

"I've never had a pet in my life, but why not?" Amelia sipped her whisky, more relaxed with McCormac gone. "How hard can it be?"

"I'll give you the name of my vet for when you're ready," Paislee offered. "She's really great with Wallace."

"The package came with the first vet visit paid. Trust McCormac tae give the gift that keeps on giving. I got him a gift certificate tae the golf course."

Grandpa hooked his arm on the armrest. "That sounds nice."

"Not on the same page though. McCormac said these puppies are purebreds and worth thousands of pounds. He's probably exaggeratin'." Amelia wiped her mouth with the cloth napkin and then dropped it over her plate, signaling that she was finished.

Brody gasped, eyes round. "I was gonna ask if I could give one tae Jenni, but that's a lot of money."

"Aye. Also," Paislee said, treading delicately, "you should make sure that when you give someone a puppy, it's a present they want and can take care of. There are all kinds of additional expenses."

"But they're so cute!" Brody shifted on his seat. "Jenni would love it."

"We can talk about it later."

"I dinnae have that kind of money, so it doesnae matter," Brody decided. "Where is dessert?"

The waiter arrived with a selection to choose from of mini cheesecakes, cranachan, and peppermint brownies.

Paislee was so full, but somehow managed a bite and then passed her cheesecake to Brody.

The bill came and Amelia paid with the cash that McCormac had dropped on the table; even with a very generous tip there was still money left over.

"Well," Paislee said, uncomfortable until she recalled his cheeky kiss and disregard of the rest of them at the table. "That was nice. Thank him for us?"

"Aye. It's so guid tae know that he's doing well," Amelia said. "He's been in Ireland for over a year, sorting himself oot. Had a bad breakup with one of his girlfriends, Porche. Not Sula. Sula's a sweetheart—we've known her our whole lives. Lyla's just a fling."

"Yes, thank your brother for dinner for us," Grandpa said.

"Was that his new car parked next tae the sleigh?" Brody asked.

"Probably." Amelia smoothed a cherry-red tip of hair. "McCormac drove us in his Mercedes that had all the bells and whistles. He's a salesman at a luxury dealership in Belfast."

"That seems like a cool job." Brody zipped his coat.

Paislee hoped this wouldn't become a career choice in the running, flashing money around like a numpty. "Please come for New Year's. I'll be making dinner in our kitchen, wet paint or no."

"I accept," Amelia said. "With thanks. Our parents are in Glasgow until the middle of January visiting my other brother, Michael."

They all headed to the Juke. When Paislee dropped Amelia off at her flat, they were too full to go inside and meet Snowball, but Paislee invited Amelia to bring her pup along for Hogmanay, since they'd be at the house with a back garden.

"Happy Christmas!"

Chapter 3

Boxing Day

Paislee, true to her word, had spent the morning in her pajamas and thick robe, reading her book, while Grandpa watched telly and Brody played his new video games.

She was curled up in the coziest armchair, immersed in Shetland. Ann Cleeves had written a spectacular series that had been turned into online streaming, but she preferred the books.

Everyone had been on their own for food as there were plenty of options, from cold cereal to quiche—not to mention treats like candied almonds or chocolate-covered pretzels. At three in the afternoon, she still hadn't changed out of her jammies and noted the clock and passing time with dismay.

"Is it wrong that I just want tae stay right here for another day or two?" Paislee had a few chapters left of the novel. "Do you think Lydia and Corbin would mind if we ordered takeout and hosted them in our slippers?"

Grandpa grinned at her from where he'd stretched out on the sofa, Wallace at his feet, and brushed cookie crumbs from his beard. "Feels decadent. What time will they be here?"

As if thinking of Lydia had summoned her bestie, Paislee's

phone rang. She reached for the mobile next to her cup of tea, and saucer with a half-eaten scone, placing her novel in her lap.

"Happy Christmas, love," Lydia said, sounding way too chipper for the low energy vibe the Shaws were feeling.

Still, it was always nice to hear from Lydia. "Happy Christmas! How was Edinburgh?"

"Fine, fine. Mum and Da are guid, and so is their Baxter." The Barrons had a darling wee dog that was all fur and attitude.

"Amelia got a puppy from her brother for Christmas." Wallace jumped down from the couch to sniff Grandpa's beard, and the floor beside him, better than a vacuum. What crumbs? "A designer breed with papers he can give you a deal on, if you're interested?"

"No, no. I plan on traveling and dinnae want a pet just yet. Someday when Corbin and I are old and gray, we may consider an independent cat, but for now, we have places tae go!"

The Barron-Smythes loved to travel, and Paislee hoped they enjoyed the gift she and Grandpa had chosen for them. One had to be creative for folks who had everything. "You ready tae come over?"

"Well, aboot that . . ."

Paislee crossed her fingers that they'd cancel and could reschedule for the next day. She could get used to this decadence of nothing pressing to do. "Yes?"

"I was hopin' you could meet me at your place," Lydia said.

"Now?" Paislee heard her tone and cleared her throat, reaching for her tea to sip. Leaving the flat meant getting dressed and going into the snowy weather instead of finding out what happened next in her book. "I thought you and Corbin were coming here?"

"There's a problem."

Paislee stood, the novel falling to the ground. She brought her fingers to her thumping heart. The roof? The carport? "A problem?"

"Just come!"

Lydia's voice sounded strained to Paislee. What if Corbin's family had been acting up again? "Are *you* okay?"

"Of course," Lydia said. "But, get Grandpa and Brody too."

Wallace joined her and sat at her feet, his eyes shining. He was up for an adventure, unlike the rest of the lazy Shaws. She could just imagine Brody whingeing now. "I—instead of coming over here? But—"

"Dinnae argue . . . hey, didnae you want tae see me and Corbin today?" Lydia applied the tiniest hint of guilt.

"You know we do!"

Brody had left his room for snacks. "Who is that?"

"Aunt Lydia."

"Hiya!" Her son shouted to be heard as Paislee held the phone to her ear. "I cannae wait tae show her and Uncle Corbin my new game."

Maybe it was just her and Grandpa who wanted to burrow down. "Well, you'll have tae pack it up and bring it with us, me lad. I guess there's a problem with the house. Problem." Paislee took a breath. The day had been just perfect until now.

"Be there in thirty minutes. And dinnae forget my black bun." Lydia hung up.

"Bossy!" Paislee stooped to pick up her novel and placed it by her tea. She dropped the mobile into her robe pocket, then gathered the dishes to bring to the sink. Brody had ducked into his room . . . Paislee hoped to get dressed.

Grandpa turned the telly off and stood, adjusting his glasses. "There's a problem at the house?"

"Aye. Lydia asks that we all come. Maybe the roof collapsed, and we'll need tae get the rest of our things?" Paislee's stomach ached. The cost of that made her head spin. "The chestnut tree in back was overgrown. I should've had it trimmed."

"Dinnae borrow trouble, lass," Grandpa opined in a neutral tone.

"We need McCormac tae change our fortunes—but at this rate, the house won't be ready till next Christmas." She hated to think what fate might do to keep her and Hamish apart for another whole year.

Bundled up in a scarf and hat, Paislee decided to leave Wallace at home with a chew toy and her family piled into the steadfast Juke. Despite the cost of home repairs, Paislee had put away a wee bit each month for the brakes to be replaced, but if something else went wrong at the house, what would she do?

She was maxed a hundred percent on her credit cards and the boon of business would slow for January and February—the flip side meant she'd have time to create new inventory.

Brody wore a pensive expression and Paislee regretted her outburst. She looked behind the passenger seat as Grandpa buckled up, and patted Brody's knee. "Things will be fine, hon, all right?"

"Aye." Brody's mouth twisted in doubt.

Note to self: Don't be a Negative Nelly.

They arrived at the house as a light dusting of snow drifted down from a charcoal sky. At four in the afternoon, it was getting dark, but the holiday lights in the neighborhood were cheery. Their home was the only one not lit up, though the snow layered over the exterior gave it a fresh appearance. There wasn't a single work lorry. Doors and windows were shut tight. The carport held Lydia's Mercedes, which was scooted over enough for her to park too.

"Roof seems fine," Grandpa said as they climbed out.

"Maybe the back garden?" Paislee mentally shuffled through the items in the yard. "I never liked that shed anyway, if it fell. Or the clothesline? It would be easy tae replace and not so costly." There, she thought, that was positive.

Brody, rushing ahead, opened the front door. Lydia and Corbin crowded the narrow hall with locked arms and silly grins.

"Happy Christmas, Shaw family!"

Paislee squinted at her bestie, who had a mischievous glint in her gray eyes. Lydia and Corbin wore matching plaid shirts and red Santa hats.

"Come in," Lydia said, stepping backward a few paces so the three could enter but not get far down the hall, Corbin at her shoulder.

Paislee, joined at the hip to Brody, slowly looked around. The foyer gleamed with polished woodwork on the staircase and trim, the walls freshly painted a soft ivory.

Her favorite pictures of Gran and Brody and current photos with Grandpa, Wallace, Lydia, and Corbin hung in brand-new frames that screamed artsy. The foyer table had been repainted a distressed driftwood style that updated what she'd had. Shelves for boots and bags had been created to maximize the narrow space. Hooks on the opposite wall of the staircase gave more room for outdoor garments than the old, crowded coat tree. The iron Scottie doorstop had been repainted and sparkled like coal.

Brody put his hand in hers. "Whoa!"

"Nothin's wrong?" Grandpa asked, scratching his beard. Snow melted on the brim of his cap.

Lydia placed her palm to her heart. "I hope not! We paid the workmen extra so you could move in by New Year's. I ken it's important, Paislee. Ready tae see the kitchen?"

Paislee nodded, a wee bit in shock. "Aye." Hand in hand with Brody, she eyed the ceiling, which was smooth as an eggshell with nary a crack or stain. They followed Lydia down the hall, Grandpa at her heels.

The warped wooden floor had been replaced with sturdy hardwood planks, and a circular rug in soft grays and beiges, with pops of teal, was in the center of the kitchen. Her favorite table, refinished and shiny, atop it. Paislee blinked tears and somewhat numbly took in the stainless-steel refrigerator, the matching stove with a gas hob, the washer/dryer combo hidden behind a cabinet door, all in muted grays and beiges with teal accents.

Brody ran to the fridge and opened it. Lydia had stocked the appliance with orange marmalade, Irn-Bru, and pinot grigio from Germany. In the center was a bottle of champagne with a red ribbon.

"There's an ice maker, too. Water from the door. Plenty of room in the freezer for ice cream." Lydia spoke in a rush of words as if she was nervous.

The pantry had been painted and had wood shelves rather than mesh, with two hinge doors so it could be closed—it used to be open for all to see whether she was tidy. Grandpa's favorite whisky was on the top shelf.

Paislee trailed her fingers over the countertop. The biggest change was the placement of the sink against the wall that connected to the covered back porch, and a rectangular window to let in light. Stools were snugged under the short counter where an electric kettle and tea station had been compiled.

Grandpa peered out to the snowy night, bending over the double stainless-steel sink. "Never thought of this but it makes sense, eh? This corner was always dark."

Everything had been finished in a way that was stylish and yet so comfortable.

"Do ye hate it, Paislee?" Lydia asked, her voice raised. "Why arenae you saying anything?"

"Are you crazy?" Paislee shook her friend by the shoulders. "This is the kitchen I've always dreamed of. Thank you, Lydia." She reached for Corbin's hand. His grin was as wide as the new window. "Thank you."

"You're so welcome." Corbin got out the champagne and popped it open.

Lydia retrieved crystal flutes. "Tae new beginnings," she said. "Brody, love, your present is upstairs in yer bedroom."

Paislee watched as Brody raced by her and up the stairs, the third and fifth creaking, and allowed a tear to fall.

This was home.

Brody shouted from the top landing. "Thank you!"

"What did ye get him?" Grandpa asked.

"A new TV." Corbin shrugged.

Paislee arched her brow.

"The other one was old. This is a wee bit bigger." Lydia pinched her finger and thumb together.

Corbin laughed and poured the bubbling champagne like an expert. "Just a bit. And mibbe a new gaming system."

Paislee swallowed her tears, humbled by the thoughtfulness of the gifts. "How can I thank you both?"

"We are family!" Lydia wrapped an arm around Paislee, squeezing. She smelled of subtle floral perfume. *"Sláinte."* The four adults clinked glasses.

"When can we move in?" Paislee sipped the bubbles, which tickled her nose. It would be fun to unwrap each new feature of this space.

"As soon as ye want," Lydia said. "But also take your time moving oot of the flat. There is no rush."

"We Shaws went together for a gift for you too." Paislee had put the certificate in her bag just in case, next to the black bun with a red-and-green bow. She had three more at the flat for Lydia and now she wished she'd brought them all.

"We have," Grandpa said. "But it cannae compare." He'd been a big help with finding something unique. The spa in Italy had five-star reviews for pampering their guests; Lydia and Corbin deserved every hot stone massage or chocolate facial they desired.

"No offense, but I'm lookin' forward tae the black bun," Corbin said. "Lyd's raved aboot it for days."

Paislee placed it in the center of the table. "We can open it now if you want."

"Um, no, because then we'd have tae share," Lydia teased.

"I have more for you." Paislee gave them the gift certificate to the first-class spa. It was evidently a hit, as Lydia squealed and hugged first Paislee then Grandpa.

"This is perfect," Lydia exclaimed, truly pleased. "Thank you!

I've heard so much aboot this place but it's impossible tae get a reservation. How did ye manage it?"

Paislee pointed her flute toward Grandpa. "He oozed charm and had the receptionist believing you both walked on water—right up there with Mother Teresa. He wasn't wrong, was he?" Her kitchen was spectacular and worth the angst.

Grandpa's eyes twinkled and he wiggled his pinky as he sipped champagne.

"Thank you." Corbin refreshed their glasses and they clinked again.

Paislee glanced above her at the new ceiling and thought of handsome Hamish, with his dark hair, and how good a sport he'd been about being drenched when the pipes burst. Please God, that was in the past.

"And Corbin is here, Paislee, an ebony-haired man, quite handsome if I do say so myself." Lydia nudged her arm to her husband's with a wink.

"Not Christmas but close enough," Grandpa said. He retrieved The Macallan from the pantry.

Paislee located the silverware drawer and the plates, while Lydia exchanged the champagne flutes for whisky tumblers.

"I've three more at the flat with your name on them so we can share this now, all right?" Paislee hoped a dram, the pudding, the dark-haired man, and a new kitchen would change her fortune. She was willing to give anything a go.

"Happy Christmas!"

And it really, truly was. *Amen*.

"This is so good, Grandpa!" Hard to believe it was Hogmanay already. Paislee dipped her spoon into a hearty bowl of lentil stew that Grandpa had made with a ham hock; Brody could hardly sit still as he and Grandpa talked about the upcoming fireworks at midnight. Nairn had a spectacular event planned at the bandstand.

Paislee partially listened as she mentally went over the guest list for tomorrow's New Year's Day buffet. She'd invited Amelia, and accidentally DI Zeffer because he'd been in the police station when she'd stopped in to make sure that McCormac was coming too.

Zeffer didn't believe in the first-footer tradition, but she didn't pay him any mind. She needed a handsome dark-haired man and Zeffer, while attractive, had russet locks. Corbin's arrival on Boxing Day had been good, but Paislee wanted to double down and ensure a change of fortune for the New Year, which meant possibly Hamish, if he could get to Nairn in time, with Amelia's brother McCormac on standby.

The Macleans, blond, would be feasting with Bennett's parents in Dundee. Lydia and ebony-haired Corbin were at Smythe Manor.

She'd also invited Elspeth and Susan—the sisters were feeling better. Susan was bringing her guide dog, a labradoodle named Rosie. Paislee had yet to meet Amelia's cute Snowball. Meri was a yes.

"Did you hear that, Mum?" Brody asked impatiently.

"Em, no." She ate another bite of soup.

"Grandpa said that Gran's family were rebels." His forehead scrunched, moving the fringe across his brow.

"Rebels?" Paislee shook her head, lost.

"They could have been *killed* for goin' tae church." Brody looked at her as if expecting her to deny it.

Paislee turned to Grandpa, who had started the conversation, and gestured with her spoon for him to explain Reformation to a twelve-year-old who just cared about comics and football.

"The Reformation began in 1560," Grandpa said. "Agnes used tae joke that you couldnae take away the Scots' right tae party. Since our genetic ancestry is a mix of bold Viking and passionate Celtic, that means chasing away the winter darkness with bonfires and bright lights, drinking, and food."

"Community," Paislee said.

"Fireworks?" Brody got up to ladle more lentil soup into his bowl and brought it back very carefully. Wallace watched patiently for anything to drop.

"How else are we supposed tae bring in the New Year with a bang?" Grandpa asked.

Paislee had the lesson memorized from her school days. Prior to the Reformation, Scotland had been firmly Catholic . . . accepting the dominion of the Pope, crucifixes, stained glass, and the use of icons to inspire prayer. Saints. Mother Mary as a conduit to Jesus and God.

Protestants thought that anybody who believed in Jesus was a saint. They followed the Bible alone, positing that the church had grown corrupt. Mary, blessed by God to bear Jesus as a virgin mother, was not elevated to holy status.

Due to the Church of Scotland, social behaviors in the sixteenth century changed for a stricter society. The art of early Scotland abbeys was destroyed by zealous folks who believed that the only way to God was a conversation with Jesus.

This meant that the rowdy Scots learned manners—a plus, sure, but they needed a way to combat the dark, dreary days and nights through winter, so adopted Hogmanay around the winter solstice.

In a recent poll published in the newspaper, around half of Scots didn't believe in religion at all. Church of Scotland was next, and the Catholic religion after that.

"Is there any more soup?" Brody showed his empty dish.

Grandpa shook his head. "If I hadnae seen you put it doon your gullet, I wouldnae have believed it. Make yourself a piece. There's tuna."

"Nah." Brody sighed. "A sandwich is too much work."

"They'll be plenty tae eat tonight at the festival," Paislee reminded him. "We leave in an hour, so you should get changed—dress warm."

"Can Wallace come?" Brody asked.

"No, son." Paislee ignored Wallace's hopeful gaze. The dog liked to go out with them. "He doesn't mind the fireworks but it's still so loud that he'll be happier snug at home in his bed."

Brody didn't argue. He rinsed the bowl and put it in the dish-washer, the thrill of having the magical appliance not worn off yet. He and Wallace ran upstairs.

"I'm looking forward tae tomorrow's dinner," Paislee said.

Grandpa raised a finger for each item he considered important. "Lamb, turkey, steak pie. The oven is so big it will fit the meat *and* the sides."

"Don't forget the homemade shortbread." She couldn't wait. "Yours is as wonderful as Gran's."

For Christmas Brody had thoughtfully typed up Gran's recipes for her and put them in a file so they wouldn't get lost or ruined if the kitchen ever had another downpour.

"That's a high compliment. Any New Year's resolutions?" Grandpa asked.

"Cut down on chocolate . . ." Paislee shrugged. It was always the same one and she never quite managed it. "You?"

"I havenae decided yet."

Paislee stood and went to the sink, rinsing the pot. "Fair." It was four in the afternoon. "You have a whole eight hours."

"Plenty of time." Grandpa waved her off. "Meet back here in an hour, you say?"

"Aye. Wear something new tae greet the year."

For Hogmanay the bandstand would be surrounded by several heated tents with music and vendors. The odd fireworks might go off all night, but the big display was planned for midnight—goodbye old year, and hello new. She was so ready.

Paislee, upstairs in her room, applied glittery eyeshadow and lip gloss. Her silver mesh shirt was perfect for the party vibe, though nobody would see it under her jacket. Her mobile dinged with a notification, and she read the text from Hamish. He was trying to be home for New Year's Day. He would be the first-footer that she preferred.

A pop sounded from a series of firecrackers. Wallace didn't like them, but he wasn't afraid. Still, they'd keep him home for the night, tucked in Brody's room with his blanket and chew toy.

Paislee texted Hamish back that she hoped to see him—and she meant it. She was glad that his mum was on the mend.

Grabbing her silver down jacket, Paislee left her room. Knocking on Brody's door, she poked her head in. The TV from Lydia and Corbin was almost as long as the wall. He was watching a movie and texting, Wallace at his side. The pup looked up when she entered and gave her a tail wag.

"Who's that? Edwyn?"

"Jenni." Brody blew his hair off his forehead. "She's going tae be at the bandstand tonight too."

"Awesome." Paislee studied his outfit. New jeans, new boots, and a sweatshirt with Jack Skellington on the front. It was his favorite, and she recalled Gran's wise words to pick her battles.

"Her dad's in the band. Plays the drums."

"Hmm. That is very cool. We'll have tae say hello."

Brody scowled at her. "Dinnae be weird, Mum."

"Gotcha." Paislee entered the room to pat Wallace rather than ruffle Brody's hair. "It's my job though, eh?"

"No," Brody said with a straight face. "It's not."

Paislee cleared her throat and averted her eyes so he wouldn't see her emotions. What would she do if they wanted to be boyfriend and girlfriend? "Are you ready?"

"Yeah. I want tae buy some fried dough. And eat ice cream."

"Ice cream? It's freezing outside."

"So?" Brody scooted off the bed, getting Wallace a treat.

"Fine with me." Paislee raised her palms. "Is the phone charged? It's going tae be crazy tonight and I want you tae be safe."

"Aye." He showed her that it was at a hundred percent.

She had to trust that he would be all right and not hold on too tight.

Paislee drove her family and parked behind Cashmere Crush. The festival was only a few blocks away and the lot had been full already when she'd passed. It was snowing as they walked, so not baltic anyway.

Grandpa wore a down coat in navy blue, and she'd knitted him a new plaid cap with a matching scarf. Adorable. Brody's knit cap, also made by her, was in crimson and black, his favorite colors. Her boys would not be cold on her watch, and they were stylish to boot.

They crossed onto the field. Brown grass poked through the trampled snow around the large tents. There were numerous bonfires, and heating lamps, and whisky, to keep warm.

"Brody!" a girl called.

Paislee turned to see Jenni, wearing Brody's gift of the green knit cap and scarf, running toward them.

"Hi Paislee, and Angus." Jenni waved, her cheeks pink.

The girl, twelve turning on twenty, sparkled with joy, and her sunny nature was impossible to dislike. They'd met at Brody's football games. Mermaid-blue hair peeked from beneath her cap.

"Hey, lass," Grandpa said. "Happy Christmas."

"Happy New Year," Paislee added with a smile.

"Happy Hogmanay!" Jenni punched Brody in the arm. "Sam and Anna are here, getting snacks."

"Can I go, Mum?" Brody asked.

Paislee blinked. She'd thought that he would be with them, but she quickly cleared her throat and pulled cash from her jacket pocket. "You have your phone?" She handed him the money as he nodded. "I want you tae meet me at the bandstand"—she read the time on her mobile—"in an hour. At seven. If you're late, then you're with me for the rest of the night."

Brody grimaced and Jenni giggled.

"I'll remind him, Paislee. My da says I have tae check in too. He'll be playin' music at eight in the big tent."

"I'd love tae meet him," Paislee said.

"Sure!"

Brody and Jenni raced off to find their mates, which left Paislee with Grandpa. "Can I interest you in a dram?" Paislee asked. "I think I need it. He's going tae be all grown up!"

Grandpa elbowed her. "Get it together, lass. He just turned twelve. You've some time yet."

Paislee felt as if each day passed in a heartbeat. She couldn't keep Brody a child. He was not really a boy, but a tween.

Grandpa bought them each a whisky. *"Sláinte."*

They clicked cardboard cups and she distracted herself in the crowd of revelers. Arran and Mary Beth, with their twin girls, joined them. Everyone was in high spirits as the Mulhollands all drank warm cocoa with whipped cream.

Amelia crossed the park toward them with McCormac and a young lady she assumed was one of McCormac's girlfriends from the way they hung all over each other. Both ladies had their new pups with them. Tiny things that were more fur and eyes. Snowball was wrapped in a puppy blanket and snugged inside Amelia's coat.

"What a cutie," Paislee said.

"I was afraid tae leave her home alone," Amelia explained. "I looked up online aboot the fireworks, but I cannae tell if she's shaking because of the cold, or a new environment, or the noises." She patted the pup behind the ears. "This way I can soothe her, but she seems all right."

It was sweet how Amelia cared for her new dog. Pets offered unconditional love—Paislee couldn't imagine their lives without Wallace.

"This is Sula," Amelia said, introducing McCormac's friend. "And her pup, Thor. It's a Brussels griffon." The tiny pup had reddish-brown fur and a growly disposition. Sula was a pretty young woman about twenty-five with green eyes and blond hair.

"I told the lasses tae keep the pups at home, but they didnae listen, dafties," McCormac said. He dangled a bottle of beer between his fingers.

Paislee bristled on their behalf. He hadn't asked Amelia if she'd wanted the puppy in the first place. Had Sula known about her gift?

Arran and Mary Beth exchanged a look that long-time married couples could give, and Mary Beth casually stepped between McCormac and the twins.

"You know anybody who wants a puppy?" McCormac asked. "Fantastic price and all the paperwork."

Hmm. Amelia was probably right, and he was getting a commission. "This is my brother, McCormac."

"We have a dog already," Mary Beth said.

"Nice tae meet you, McCormac," Arran said.

Mary Beth nodded and smiled. "Let's catch up later. The girls want tae get their faces painted."

The Mulhollands walked away as a unit. Impressive, Paislee thought, turning her attention back to McCormac. She was tempted to get her face painted too, but that wouldn't be fair to Grandpa.

"What do you do for work?" Grandpa was asking. He must not have heard Amelia at dinner.

"Och, sales," McCormac said. "High-end Mercedes." He showed the watch on his wrist that Lydia might recognize but just looked expensive to Paislee. "It's a Tag Heuer. Got a Rolex too. Cannae afford the best by selling junk, eh?"

"That's his car," Sula said, pointing to the Mercedes she'd seen at the hotel for Christmas dinner. It was parked in the VIP parking, which came with a hefty price.

Amelia smiled with pride at her brother.

Sula patted his back. "You were always guid at convincing people tae do things." She faced Paislee and Grandpa. "I never wanted tae jump into the river from the rope hanging from a tree branch, but he convinced me tae do it."

"And?" McCormac pressed.

"It was thrilling," Sula admitted.

The dangers of a bad boy, Paislee observed. They offered excitement. Flash. But usually didn't last.

A firework lit up with a crack that had Thor whining and burying his head beneath Sula's jacket.

"Told you tae keep him home." The friendly tone disappeared from McCormac's voice as the charm was replaced with anger.

"He's my gift," Sula said, hefting her chin. "I wanted tae bring him. Dougie said it was fine."

Dougie was Sula's brother, if Paislee remembered correctly, the one McCormac had complained his old mate Hank didn't like. McCormac pulled his irritated gaze from his girlfriend and winked at Paislee. "You still need me tae bring ye guid luck tonight?" His tone was naughty, and Sula gasped.

Grandpa bristled. "Watch yerself, lad," he said.

Amelia pushed him away with a grimace. "Shove it, McCormac."

"Actually, I don't need you at all," Paislee said, grateful for Corbin and Lydia. "Amelia, *you* are still welcome for dinner."

McCormac stalked off, followed by Sula calling after him.

He, a grown man, was pouting like a bairn.

"Sairy," Amelia said. "He gets tae drinking and turns into an arse. But not always, right? He keeps ya guessing."

"Not your fault," Paislee said. "How's the visit been?"

Amelia sighed. "I dinnae want tae bore you with it right now. But, not great. He's in town thinking he can toss all this cash around but he's a real numpty, not Joe Cool at all."

"Is McCormac going back tae Ireland after the holiday?" Paislee asked.

"Next week, mibbe . . . he's not forthcoming with details. He's a grand salesman, you know? Gets everyone on board, and then come tae find oot, there's more tae the story. He offered me a sweet price on a Mercedes, though. Can ye see me behind the wheel of a sports car?" Amelia's blue eyes flashed.

The evening passed with merriment and good cheer, meeting old friends, and making new. Sula seemed very young and besotted with McCormac. Hamish texted Paislee a Happy Hogmanay, as did Lydia.

Paislee wasn't much for New Year's resolutions, but this togetherness, this being a part of her community, was something she would do more of just because she liked it.

Dougie Selkirk arrived with his girlfriend, Lyla. Lyla, that Mc-Cormac had given a puppy to at Christmas? Did Dougie know Mc-Cormac had bestowed gifts to his girl? Dougie had light brown hair, square features, and proper manners compared to McCormac's obnoxious behavior. The more McCormac drank the louder his voice rose.

Paislee had met Jenni's dad, Drew Ross, briefly and enjoyed the live music, which was a mix of classic rock and pop. Grandpa, Paislee, and Amelia stayed near enough to the tent to keep an eye on Brody and his mates. The tweens didn't dance exactly but bobbed to the music. Oh, to be twelve. Snowball had fallen asleep inside Amelia's jacket, unperturbed by the racket.

"Uh oh. That's Porche Walsh, and her brother, Hank." Amelia pointed out McCormac's ex, and Hank, making a beeline for McCormac. Porche was lovely, her heart-shaped face framed with a fur hood sure to keep her warm on this chilly night. Hank pushed McCormac, who shoved back. Hank slugged McCormac hard enough the man rocked backward into Sula. Thor barked. Blood spurted from McCormac's nose as Porche pulled Hank away.

"What was that about?" Paislee asked Amelia. It was only ten and they still had two more hours until the fireworks. The heated tents and hot cider kept her warm. Rowdy drinkers could ruin the fun night.

"McCormac messin' around, I bet," Amelia said. "I love him because he's my brother, but he can be a right dobber when it comes tae women."

Paislee had witnessed that firsthand.

At midnight, she, Brody, and Grandpa, with Amelia and Sula, linked arms and sang along to "Auld Lang Syne" as the fireworks exploded above their heads. McCormac, nearest the bandstand, rocked on his heels to see the sky.

It was pure magic, but Paislee grew alarmed as the scent of singed fabric followed a firework whizzing past them to ricochet off the bandstand. McCormac whirled and bumped into them, drunk, laughing. His handsome face was a mess, with a swollen nose and dried blood beneath it. His lightweight jacket was open, and he brought his hand to his heart with a grimace.

Paislee blinked out of her dazzled reverie and moved Brody back to Grandpa, trying to shield her son from the drunk man clutching his chest. McCormac collapsed on his back with a sucking noise. The snow had melted from a multitude of feet, creating slushy mud.

Drunk, or drugs? McCormac was too young for a heart attack, but she pulled out her phone in case she had to call emergency services.

In a medical situation, time was of the essence.

"Dinnae do that, Paislee," Amelia warned. "McCormac willnae like it."

Chapter 4

Paislee knelt by McCormac's side as Grandpa and Brody scooted back. Amelia hovered, worry on her expression. Mud soaked the knees of Paislee's jeans. She scanned the man's body as he groaned. His coat was black leather, open at the chest. His cashmere sweater, also black, was dark over his chest. Was that a hole in the fabric?

She recalled the smell she'd detected right before he'd fallen, and glanced up at the wooden bandstand several paces from them. The fireworks she'd heard speeding by.

Arran, Mary Beth's husband, was a well-to-do solicitor who didn't drink and was as sober as a judge when he joined her, taking in the situation. "Drunk?"

Paislee shrugged and poised her finger over the hole in his shirt. "I heard a firework go by."

Arran's brow furrowed in surprise, and he kneeled on the opposite side of the moaning McCormac. "He's hurt." The solicitor's gaze scanned the length of McCormac's body, pausing at the mud on his palm and stopping at the blood on his face from being punched. "Rough night, eh, but he was partying pretty hard. Did ye call for an ambulance?"

Paislee looked at Amelia who was shaking her head, no. "We have tae, Amelia. I'll take the blame if McCormac gets mad."

At last, Amelia nodded. Paislee pulled her phone from her jacket pocket, dialing 999, and told the emergency operator the location and that a man had been injured. They didn't know how. The operator said an ambulance would be on the way, but the police might be faster as it was New Year's Eve and the roads crowded. There were patrolmen at the park. Paislee ended the call and relayed the information.

"I'll go find a constable," Grandpa said, heading into the crowd with Brody.

Arran removed his jacket and folded it, placing the garment beneath McCormac's head without a thought for the mud. McCormac's breathing grew ragged.

"Is he going tae be all right?" Sula asked. Thor barked wildly from her arms. He hadn't slept through the noise like Snowball. Dogs had different personalities just like people.

"Of course," Paislee said automatically.

Amelia stared at her fallen brother as she crooned to Snowball.

"I wish Dougie was still here. He'd know what to do," Sula said, petting Thor between the ears. "He had tae take Lyla home."

Grandpa and Brody returned right away with Constable Payne, one of her favorite officers at the Nairn Police Station. Dark-skinned and slightly round in shape, he arrived out of breath from the rush and nodded at Paislee, then Arran. "Hiya."

Arran rose and offered a hand to Paislee, pulling her up too.

"Constable! This is my brother, McCormac Henry," Amelia said, stepping forward with a nervous smile. "He was dancing and stumbled. I'm sure he's just pished. No laws broken."

"Most everyone will have achin' heads tomorrow," Constable Payne agreed.

"I called the ambulance," Paislee said. "If it's nothing maybe we can cancel it. The operator sounded busy."

"It's a hectic night." The constable kneeled by McCormac and put his fingers to the man's wrist, and then his throat and finally his chest, touching the hole in the black cashmere shirt. His hand came away wet with something crimson. Not mud after all. There was no mistaking the metallic scent of blood when compared to the fresh earth smell.

Amelia gasped.

"What's that?" Sula asked. She gripped Amelia's arm.

"I dinnae ken," Payne said with concern. He spoke into his radio, but Paislee couldn't make out the words. He settled on his bootheels. "Back up, everyone, and make room."

DI Mack Zeffer arrived, along with Constable Sarah Monroe, the female police officer who was often partnered with Payne.

The DI's glance at Paislee told her he'd noted her presence and would get back to her, indeed. For now, he took charge of the scene. Constable Monroe snapped pictures—all while the fireworks still went off overhead. It was only twenty past midnight. They'd been known to last forty-five minutes to an hour.

Surreal.

Payne ripped open the cashmere sweater and put his hand over McCormac's chest, pressing down. Had McCormac run into something sharp? He'd bumped into the wooden bandstand. Remembering the singed smell, she wondered if he'd been hit by a random firecracker. She'd never have believed such a thing could be possible.

"Who is this?" Zeffer gestured toward the man on the ground. McCormac had stopped groaning and must have passed out from pain.

"McCormac Henry," Amelia said. "My brother."

"I see," Zeffer said. "I thought he lived in Ireland?"

Amelia sniffed and lowered her gaze. "He did. He does. Nothing wrong with someone comin' home for the holidays, eh?"

Zeffer narrowed his eyes at her.

Having Amelia work at the police station, despite her family's brushes with the law in the past, meant Amelia hadn't followed her dream to be a constable, though the previous inspector had encouraged her.

Paislee had offered to help Amelia study, but she hadn't pursued it.

McCormac's face was paler than it had been earlier that day, his eyes closed tight. The blood was disconcerting.

Amelia shivered, so Paislee put her arm around the poor lass. Snowball also trembled.

Sula collapsed against Grandpa in hysterical tears. "Och, Mac, me love! My soulmate. Will he be awright?" Her puppy barked insistently at the commotion.

The ambulance drove slowly through the crowd of revelers. After a quick assessment, the medics loaded McCormac to a stretcher, leaving a pink tinge on the slushy mud. He didn't rouse from his stupor.

"Should I come with him?" Sula asked the harried medic. Fireworks blossomed above in vibrant color.

"No, ma'am. I suggest you meet us at the hospital."

Sula switched from Grandpa to Arran as she continued to sob. Mary Beth had kept her twin girls back from the incident, not wanting them to witness something so disturbing.

The ambulance hurried McCormac away from the park. Brody stood next to Amelia with wide-eyed concern and Paislee, stunned, did her best to answer Constable Monroe's questions.

"I'm going tae the hospital," Zeffer announced, then slid adeptly through the throng toward the nearby station. Constables Payne and Monroe stayed behind. Monroe offered Payne a disposable towel to clean his hands, which he did.

"What happened?" Payne asked.

"It was so fast," Amelia said. "I dinnae ken. McCormac was dancin' and then he fell."

Sula cried into her pup's fur. Arran stepped away from Sula, glancing from the constables to his waiting family. "I didnae see anything . . . I arrived after it happened. Do you mind if I go?" The solicitor handed Monroe a business card. "Here's how tae reach me."

"Thank you," Monroe said. "That's fine."

Arran left and Payne looked at Paislee, who filled in what she'd seen and smelled. Constable Monroe didn't give much credence to Paislee's theory that McCormac was hit by a firework, but Payne jotted it down into his tablet.

The fireworks display increased the tempo of rockets as it signaled a New Year. So far it wasn't shaping up to be any better than the previous one.

"Should I go tae the hospital now?" Amelia asked.

"Ye cannae bring your puppy," Constable Payne said in a kind voice. "Drop the dog at home, but then, aye." The officer was friends with Amelia from the station.

"I'll do that," Amelia said, still somewhat dazed.

"Take a cab, if you've been drinkin'," Payne added. "But it's a guid idea."

In other words, the wound was serious. Paislee said a quick prayer that McCormac would have a speedy recovery.

Sula, who'd quieted a wee bit, wailed. "McCormac! Let's hurry, Amelia. He needs us."

Constable Payne noticed Thor tucked in Sula's coat. "New dog too?"

"Aye," Amelia said. She wiped a tear from her cheek. "I think McCormac has one Christmas puppy left for sale. Interested?"

"My dog would consider anything this small a chew toy," Payne said, patting Snowball's tiny head. His dog was a large bulldog.

He'd brought his dog to the park and the station. Amelia shrugged. "Bruiser wouldnae mean tae, but mibbe."

A pushing match erupted next to them as two men argued over who had the best football team.

"You have this handled?" Constable Monroe asked Payne. He nodded and Constable Monroe wished them a goodnight before breaking up the fight with a strict warning.

"Can I help you with anything?" Paislee asked Amelia. "A ride?"

"Thanks, but no," Amelia said, her brow furrowed. "I came with McCormac and Sula."

Sula inhaled and sniffed. "I have McCormac's keys. We'll run

the dogs home and go tae the hospital together, Amelia. Dougie
will need tae know too."

Payne arched a brow at Sula. "We dinnae need another accident on top of this."

Sula raised her palm. "I didnae drink—I was McCormac's des-
ignated driver."

It was now half past twelve.

"All right." Payne nodded. "Be careful."

"Do you know what happened tae McCormac?" Sula asked,
her voice holding fear.

"They'll fill you in at the hospital." Payne wasn't giving a clue.

"Call me, okay?" Paislee said to Amelia.

"Dinner tomorrow . . ." her friend drawled. "I'm not sure what
tae do."

She'd wanted to uninvite McCormac for his poor behavior but
didn't add that stress to Amelia. "Please come, both of you," Paislee
said. "And Snowball too."

"McCormac will be with me at home tomorrow," Sula declared. "He'll need me while he recovers."

Amelia's dog poked her white furry head from her jacket to lick
Paislee's hand before the ladies left the park. Paislee returned her attention to Constable Payne, but he was looking at something in the
bandstand. Had he believed Paislee's tale of a rogue firework?

"Lass," Grandpa said as his teeth chattered. "Can we go?"

"Aye." Paislee swallowed her curiosity regarding the incident,
gathered her family, and drove home. After realizing there were no
answers about McCormac to be had, Brody talked nonstop about
Jenni this and Jenni that, and how cool her dad was to play in a rock
band.

Once home, her son, in the grips of a real crush, went upstairs
to his room.

"Young love," Grandpa said with a chuckle.

It warmed her heart and yet scared the bejeezus out of her at
the same time.

Wallace barked in welcome and flew down the stairs to the foyer, then raced along the hall toward the back door. Paislee let the pup out and he sniffed around the edge of the trees, not minding the cold. As nice as Lydia's flat was, she didn't miss the elevator and having to take Wallace downstairs—this was much easier.

"I love this kitchen," Paislee said.

Grandpa got out two glasses. "A nightcap?"

"Aye." She'd also limited her drinks to two over five hours, but since she wasn't a big drinker, it was no hardship. She liked the hot apple cider with cinnamon and the hot chocolate with whipped cream.

She gestured to the covered back porch.

"I'll bring the whisky," Grandpa said.

"I'll get the blankets."

Paislee and Grandpa each sank into a chair with an afghan for their laps and watched the snow begin to fall. Wallace raced around the yard marking his territory as if he might never come back again.

"What happened tonight, do ye think?" Grandpa asked.

"I honestly don't have a clue. Maybe McCormac ran into something? I saw him bump into the bandstand."

"Could have been stabbed," Grandpa said.

"Uh, what?" Paislee shook her head to clear it, sure she'd heard Grandpa wrong.

"He's kind of an arse." Grandpa sipped. "Mibbe someone had enough. Or he coulda been robbed? For that fancy watch. Was he wearing it at the time?"

"The watch? No, I didn't notice at all. You miss being involved in things," Paislee realized.

"What?" Grandpa sounded surprised.

"I don't know about the wallet or the watch, but *stabbed* makes more sense than randomly falling against something sharp or hit by a firework." She sipped her whisky. "You should have seen Constable Monroe's face when I suggested it."

"Random acts of violence are rarely random."

"Words of wisdom." Paislee snickered. She inhaled the whisky, enjoying the scent of peat and oak.

Wallace zoomed back to the porch and jumped up on her lap.

She petted him, scratching under his chin and behind his ears as he liked the best. "Good boy."

Wallace rolled over for belly rubs.

She set aside her whisky. "It was a treat tae see the dolphins at Lydia's, but I prefer our back garden—even that old shed."

Grandpa chuckled. "Aye. I do too. Everyone's different, guid thing."

Her phone dinged and she smiled down at the screen, thinking it might be Hamish to say he would be home for the New Year.

Her stomach clenched. "It's Amelia."

Call me.

Paislee had the worst feeling about this. "Amelia wants us tae call."

Grandpa scowled as if to brace himself for bad news.

Paislee dialed and Amelia answered right away.

"Paislee," her friend cried.

"Aye?" She didn't ask how she was—obviously, not great. She put the phone on speaker.

"McCormac was shot in the chest!"

"Shot?"

Grandpa gripped his tumbler. "Shot."

Paislee hugged Wallace. "I heard a whizzing sound."

"The fireworks were so loud," Amelia said. "It covered the noise of the gun."

"How is he?"

"Dead. McCormac is dead."

"Amelia!"

She and Grandpa exchanged a look of compassion for Amelia, who they both liked very much.

"Where are you?" Paislee asked.

"The hospital, with Sula."

"How is she?"

"Cryin' like she's lost her soul mate. I know McCormac didnae love her like that," Amelia said in a low voice. "It was always Porche for him. But what can I do? I cannae be mean tae her."

"No," Paislee agreed.

"She's an idiot, anyway." Amelia gave a little hiccup.

"Why is that?"

"I cannae talk aboot it right now," Amelia said. "She might hear me."

"Later, then." Paislee stroked Wallace's fur. "Do your parents know?"

"Called them at my brother Michael's and they arenae even upset that McCormac was killed, can you believe it?" Amelia's voice was thick with tears.

Paislee couldn't imagine not being gutted by such devastating news. "Maybe they're in shock."

"Naw. They dinnae think he changed. That McCormac deserved what he got, but I saw it for myself."

"Changed from what?"

"He did some time in jail is all. Drugs. Petty theft. It was the crowd he was in, you know? He did his time. Sure, he was tossin' cash around since he came tae town, but I can guarantee the old McCormac wouldnae think twice aboot gifts for the family. And"— Amelia sniffled—"what the heck am I supposed tae do with their Christmas presents?"

Paislee's eyes widened. The only gifts she knew about were of the furry variety. "He gave your parents a puppy?"

"Two, actually. One for Michael, and one for Mum and Da."

Grandpa sat back and shook his head.

"The doctor is being verra rude, and Zeffer was here, questioning me. I can see how little respect the DI has for McCormac, as if he's never made a mistake. Payne isnae like that, all better than everyone."

Zeffer probably had his reasons, but that didn't help Amelia. "I'm so, so sorry."

Amelia exhaled loudly. "How could McCormac have gotten

shot? I just dinnae understand it. Was it an accident, and he was in the wrong place? Or is Mum right that he didnae change, and someone shot him on purpose?"

Grandpa finished his whisky without sharing his opinion.

"A random act of violence," Paislee said, trying to make her friend feel better. "It is unfortunate but they do happen."

"Well, I willnae put my money there," Amelia said. "Zeffer is too interested in me brother. Where's he been, what he's been doin'. I told him aboot McCormac's new leaf, selling high-end cars, and the DI wanted tae know the name of his employer in Belfast."

"Say what you will, Zeffer is very good at getting answers."

Amelia sighed. "That's what worries me."

"Is there anything we can do, Amelia?"

"I dinnae ken!" She cried softly. "McCormac was my favorite, even if he wasnae perfect—and now he's gone. Here comes Sula. I should go."

"All right."

"I'm not sure aboot tomorrow," Amelia said.

"You have an open invitation, if you decide you don't want tae be alone. Sula too. You're welcome tae bring Snowball."

"Thanks. Mibbe you can put your thinking caps on tae find a home for my parents' puppy, and my brother's too. They're at my flat. Mum and Michael willnae want them, though they are pure-breds—tiny Maltese pups."

Snowball was a Pomeranian and Thor a Brussels griffon. "So not from the same litter as yours or Sula's?"

"Naw." Amelia paused and said, "Paislee, you need tae help me find oot who killed McCormac."

Chapter 5

New Year's Day, Paislee woke to hail and freezing rain pelting her window and lay in bed listening to the storm howl. Not the weather she'd have ordered, but nothing would stop her from today's open house. Hadn't she purchased a new welcome mat for outside the front door, guaranteed to be absorbent? And the floors had a waterproof varnish to keep them dry and easy to clean.

After all she'd been through, Paislee was claiming this New Year with a victory yell.

The digital clock on her bedstand read nine. She slipped on her robe over her pajamas and jammed her feet into her slippers, heading downstairs. Brody and Wallace didn't stir. Grandpa's door was also closed. They'd stayed up talking until two about Amelia and how short this life could be, with no guarantee. Poor McCormac, even if he was shady, would never get another chance to be better.

Paislee switched on her electric kettle, feeling like a queen in this updated space with new counters and appliances. Would it ever get old?

"Can you believe it, Gran?" Paislee asked aloud.

Warmth in her heart made her feel as if her granny was listening, and happy for Paislee's good fortune. She would never take her home for granted.

Grandpa came out of his downstairs room, sweatpants and baggy sweatshirt rumpled, his feet bare, and his silvery-gray hair sticking up every which way. He hadn't put on his glasses yet as he crossed the kitchen to the counter where the tea kettle used to be but that was now a cabinet that hid the washer-dryer combo. "Happy New Year's, Paislee. Got tae get the lamb in the oven. It'll take six hours tae roast."

"Happy New Year's!" She rarely saw him so discombobulated, so he must have been worried all night. "Did I wake you?"

"Och, no. I couldnae sleep, afraid I wouldnae hear the alarm." Grandpa patted his hair down. "And I was so tired from last night that I didnae even set it."

Paislee chuckled and returned to the steaming kettle, retrieving a mug with a picture of a fish on it that Brody had made for him. "Tea?"

"Aye. Extra strong," Grandpa advised. "I know how tae roast a brilliant lamb in the old oven, but what aboot this new-fangled one?"

"We have lots of time, Grandpa. Folks will be here at three and it's only quarter past nine. It will be buffet-style so people can nibble something else until the lamb is ready. I just hope we don't have anybody early." Paislee raised her hands. "I am your sous chef, ready tae peel and dice."

"Bless ye, lass." Grandpa lifted his steaming mug of Brodies. "Just keep the tea comin'."

She squeezed his forearm. "I won't let you down."

Over the past week they'd brought things from Lydia's, so they could start the New Year off here. She'd cleaned the flat spotless and left a fresh azalea plant on the counter as a thank-you along with the three black buns.

"Tell me the menu one more time," Grandpa said.

Like he didn't have it memorized! "Lamb. Turkey. Steak pie. Roasted veg. Skirlie. Rumbledethumps. Fresh rolls. Black bun." Paislee narrowed her eyes and then snapped her fingers. "Gran's shortbread."

Grandpa opened the door to the refrigerator and retrieved the huge leg of lamb, placing it on the counter.

"Let's get the lamb in and then worry aboot the rest," Grandpa decided. He located the pans in a deep drawer next to the stove.

Paislee topped off his tea, then checked the pantry for onions they'd need for the skirlie, which was toasted oats and onions cooked in fat. Rumbledethumps also required onion. The delicious dish was potato, cabbage, and onion, baked with cheese. A bag of swede for the neeps and tatties. The potatoes were on the bottom shelf. She couldn't get over how much room she had.

The washer/dryer combo with a working dryer meant she didn't need to hang the wet clothes on wooden racks to dry, which gave her more space. Along the wall where the sink used to be were now the refrigerator, washer/dryer, long counter, cabinets, and then the oven.

At the corner were shelves and another counter with the sink centered beneath the window, and two barstools. Next to that was the back door and a new bed for Wallace.

The kitchen used to be separated from the lounge/living room with shelving, but Lydia had opened it to make the space seem double in size. The round dining table was now to the left of the hall rather than at the end of it, but still a vital part of family meals.

Paislee, standing at her sink, found the sound from the TV in the lounge muted, thanks to the row of hanging plants, which provided a screen. The old couch (with a new slipcover) faced the telly and the swivel armchair was by the fireplace. The walls had been painted a soft ivory.

She could entertain this New Year's Day with ease. She'd borrowed two folding tables from Father Dixon at the church to set up the dishes and food.

Drinks, from Irn-Bru to tea to whisky, would be kept on the round table and the food on the long tables. She'd picked up two hundred sturdy paper plates along with inexpensive silverware at Tesco. Her new dishwasher would be put to the test.

Grandpa finished prepping the lamb and shut the oven door, setting the timer. "How many people are we expecting, lass?"

Paislee pulled her gaze from the window and a squirrel skipping along the clothesline. She leaned her hip to the counter and crossed her arms. "Well, it's an open house, so there weren't exact invitations. I told our business neighbors on Market Street. The ladies at Knit and Sip. Meri is coming for sure. Blaise and Shep are a maybe. Mary Beth and Arran, with the girls, will stop by. When I was at the station tae talk with Amelia, I invited the constables. And Zeffer."

Grandpa choked on the tea he'd been swallowing. "Must've been a weak moment."

Paislee sighed. The invite had been all-inclusive. "We have a few RSVPs but more that couldn't come, like Father Dixon, Lydia and Corbin, Bennett and Edwyn. James is with his family. Amelia a maybe. I don't blame her if she stays in bed all day."

Amelia had asked Paislee for her help to find out who had shot her brother, but Paislee put the request down to shock. Police Scotland did a grand job keeping crime low in Nairn.

"Not a bit," Grandpa said. "Poor lass."

"I haven't heard from her today." Paislee finished her tea but held the empty mug for warmth against the chill of death. It was sad, yet a cycle of this life. "Elspeth will be here, and Susan."

"Margot?"

Margot managed the medical clinic on their block and Susan, Elspeth's blind sister, answered phones there part-time. She'd surprised them all by dating their landlord, Shawn Marcus, who happened to be Lady Shannon Leery's son. "Margot will be with Shawn at the Leery Estate." Paislee had Shannon Leery to thank for her good fortune in having bespoke cashmere goods at Ramsey Castle, so the lady was always in her prayers even when she was annoying.

"Jerry?"

Jerry McFadden had become a close friend over the years as he'd delivered her yarn every Tuesday, so it had been a natural thing to ask him. "He'll be with his family."

"Hamish?" Grandpa asked with a smirk, less grumpy after his tea and the lamb in the oven. He had a list with notes for when the turkey would go in and the casseroles too.

"I haven't heard since he sent a text yesterday hoping tae be here." Paislee eyed the ceiling, which was smooth with no clue to the spot of trouble that had happened when she'd kissed Hamish.

Grandpa saw her looking and chuckled. "All right." He set his mug aside and pointed to the casseroles that could be made ahead. "Let's get started. Did we decide how many people tae feed?"

"I told folks not tae bring anything," Paislee said. "So, we should have sides for fifty people."

"Let's do more than that—seventy-five?" Grandpa suggested.

"That's too much food!"

"We have this grand freezer tae put the leftovers in and that will save us doon the road."

"Smart." She'd actually be able to stretch her food budget by buying things on sale and storing them.

"I'm not just a bonnie face," Grandpa teased. He raised his empty mug. "Tea?"

"On it!" Paislee quickly made them both another round of Brodies.

Several hours later, Paislee's house smelled like a five-star restaurant. Lamb, rosemary, sage, nutmeg . . . turkey, steak, and butter. The scents made her tummy rumble.

Brody, up at noon, had been put to the task of wrapping paper napkins around inexpensive silverware. No plastic, as she wanted to do what she could for their carbon footprint even though it meant more washing. She peeked out the new window.

The snow flurries had stopped as had the wind. A soft blanket of white covered the back garden. Her heart was filled with joy.

"Mum! I'm done," Brody said. "And I'm bored."

Paislee whirled and checked the time. One in the afternoon. She resisted the lecture on only boring people being bored. Grandpa was in his room changing. Wallace snored in his new bed. "We have two hours. You showered already?"

Brody's thick auburn hair was damp.

"Yeah."

Dressed in jeans and a long-sleeved tee, he wiggled his sock-covered feet. What could she have him do? School was off for another week. Paislee went to work on Saturday the fifth. She'd be up at the castle on Wednesday to check her orders, but that was it for her schedule while Brody was on holiday vacation.

It had been all about the house being fixed for so long that now that they were here, Paislee had to regroup.

She grinned. "What do *you* want tae do?"

Brody gave her a sly look. "Jenni invited me over tae her house."

"Nope." Just as serious as she'd been about the puppy, Paislee wanted Brody home on this first holiday in their refurbished kitchen.

"Why?" His lower lip jutted.

"We are having guests."

He palmed the phone. "She'd be a guest. I'll ask her here, then."

"Brody!" Her good mood evaporated.

"It's no fair. All yer friends are coming over. Why cannae mine?"

"What's Sam doing?" She knew that Brody's best friend, Edwyn, was with his family in Dundee.

"I dinnae ken." Brody stared at her. "Well? Can I?"

Paislee tried to dream up a reasonable excuse other than that

Jenni was a girl and she feared where that was headed. "You can't invite people at the last minute. It's rude."

"You said it was an open house," Brody countered.

Dang it. "I don't really know her or her family."

"You met her dad last night. The drummer. Mr. Ross. He said we could call him Drew?"

Paislee raised her hands. "Fine. You can invite them over but just be clear that it's not a sit-down meal. I'm not driving there or back. It's a buffet."

"Casual," Brody said with a grin. "I know." He darted from the kitchen and ran upstairs.

"Well," Paislee said. "That was awful."

Grandpa, in a clean shirt and trousers, beard freshly trimmed, hair shiny, had come out for the end of the conversation. "It's fine. Dinnae worry aboot it. Mibbe her dad will say no." He opened the oven door and peered over his shoulder at her. "In fact, you've got time tae shower. I need you back at your station at two tae help with the baked dishes. You've got mashed tatties in your hair."

"Oh!" Her mobile phone dinged a notification. "Hamish." Her hopes plummeted when she saw that he was still with his mum in Inveraray. "He wants tae see me on Saturday night instead."

The doorbell rang and Paislee patted at her hair. Sure enough, there was something icky in it—she was in her comfy jeans and a sweatshirt.

She opened the door and her mouth gaped.

Zeffer—looking like a supermodel in designer jeans, leather loafers, and, shock of all shocks, a leather jacket over a polo shirt— smiled at her. In his hands was a bouquet of flowers.

Her mouth dried. "Uh . . ."

Wallace sniffed and wagged his tail. Grandpa called from the hall as he wiped his hands on a dishtowel, "Who is it?"

"Z . . . Zeffer."

The man had the nerve to wink at her.

Grandpa joined her. "You goin' tae invite him in, lass? It's pure baltic out there. The open house doesnae start until three."

"Of course! Come in. Please." What the hell was Zeffer doing here?

"I know it's early, but I had another stop tae make this afternoon, so I thought I'd drop off these flowers." Zeffer gave them to Paislee and eyed the new foyer and floor. "I'm curious aboot the remodel and couldnae resist a peek."

Brody left his room and stood at the top landing, peering down at Zeffer. "Hey." Her son scowled. "You here aboot the flashy dead guy?"

Paislee bowed her head. That made more sense than Zeffer simply dropping by with flowers. "Are you?"

Zeffer waved at Brody, who raised his hand back. "No. Your mum invited me."

"Yer early," Brody said.

"I cannae stay." Zeffer didn't budge from the foyer and Paislee reached around him to shut the front door. His boots were dry from where he'd wiped them.

Brody accepted this with a tilt of his head. "Mum, Jenni said that she and her dad are coming. At *three*."

"All right." Paislee glanced at Zeffer as Wallace sniffed his boots, giving the lace a lick. Brody raced back to his room and slammed the door. What on earth?

"Can I get you a drink?" Grandpa asked.

It was a good thing her grandfather was remembering the social graces as Paislee was tongue-tied. She really wished she knew whether she still had mashed potatoes in her hair but didn't dare check.

"Another time," Zeffer said. He followed Grandpa, admiring the artistic framed photos on the wall. "I cannae believe how bright it is in here. It's verra nice."

"Lydia designed it."

"An interior designer as well as an estate agent. Multitalented."

Even though the table had been moved to the left, it was still the focal point of the kitchen. Paislee put the flowers in the sink. The holiday bouquet was fragrant with red-and-white lilies, evergreens, and a plaid ribbon.

"The window new?" Zeffer asked. "Top-of-the-line appliances but with a rustic feel. I'm impressed."

"We're so happy here. Has Lydia been able tae help you find a place?"

"I was waiting tae buy until my lease is up in February."

"That's nice." Paislee glanced at him to catch him smiling at her. Her stomach clenched. Smiling . . . wow. His teeth were white and straight.

"Any word aboot what happened tae McCormac?" Grandpa asked, breaking the spell.

Zeffer's expression closed off. "No."

Grandpa opened the door of the oven. The scent of roasted lamb escaped. What would it be like to have Zeffer just drop by?

Like a friend.

They weren't really friends though.

"Amelia's worried," Grandpa said. "Loves her brother but we could tell he was a blowhard. Really all aboot McCormac."

"He's a luxury-car salesman," Paislee said.

Zeffer didn't say anything, looking out the window to the back garden. Wallace curled up on his soft new bed. "This is great." He gestured to the hanging plants that created a living wall. "I've seen this in magazines."

He read design magazines?

"We just met McCormac on Christmas Day at the hotel," Paislee said. "He laid down a lot of cash but left Amelia with us. He was in a big rush tae get to his new girlfriend's place without his other girlfriend finding out."

Grandpa tossed a dish towel over his shoulder. "Lyla. His ex, Porche, showed up last night at the park too."

Zeffer didn't respond.

"You know McCormac got intae a fistfight with Hank, Porche's brother? They used tae be best friends, according tae Amelia." Grandpa watched Zeffer as closely as Paislee did, but the man didn't even blink. "Porche and McCormac had an ugly split. If I were you, I'd want tae talk tae Porche and Hank both."

Zeffer exhaled and folded his hands behind his back. "I'm not on the clock, Angus. You can tell all of this tae Constable Payne, or Constable Monroe, if they're interviewing folks today, but I think it will be fairly lax. I really like your new kitchen, Shaw family."

Paislee chose a crystal vase off the shelf for the flowers. "Thank you. These flowers are perfect. Where are you going?"

"Tae visit my sister. She's moved tae Stonehaven. I'd actually scheduled a few days off, but with the Henry case I'll be back in the morning. Murder doesnae get a holiday."

"I guess not."

Zeffer reached out and Paislee leaned toward his hand, thinking he'd touch her cheek. He pulled something from her hair instead.

"Potatoes?" he asked, fighting a laugh.

Paislee wanted to melt into the floor.

Grandpa snickered.

"I'll walk you out," Paislee said. "I was just on my way tae the shower when you dropped in . . . *early*."

Zeffer strode down the hall from the front door as if he owned the place, stopping at the foyer table. "I hope you have a happy New Year."

"You too, Zeffer."

"Any resolutions, besides not getting involved in any more crimes?"

"I never said that, actually."

"Mibbe you should consider it for next year." Zeffer stared at her hard as if he wanted to say more, or do more, but in the end, he left, and Paislee felt the void of his absence.

Chapter 6

Paislee, freshly showered and dressed in a fitted top and pants, sat before her vanity mirror and fluffed her fine red hair. Pale blue eyes popped from dark-brown liner and mascara. She couldn't get Zeffer's unsettling visit from her mind.

He deserved a day off and she'd been impressed that he hadn't discussed the case at all. Granted, he'd only been there for fifteen minutes, but it was enough for her to see him in a different light.

She went downstairs to answer the doorbell at three o'clock on the dot.

Elspeth Booth arrived first, with her blind sister, Susan, and Susan's service dog, a labradoodle named Rosie. Wallace didn't know what to make of the large dog who was trained to be at Susan's side. They touched noses and in some mystical doggy language, Wallace seemed to understand that Rosie wasn't a playmate. The sisters brought a plate of homemade toffee squares that Paislee was tempted to hide in the pantry to save for herself, they were that good.

Meri McVie showed up, bringing a bottle of whisky and a houseplant. The piping competition judge had become a dear friend in no time at all. Next came Jenni and Jenni's dad, Drew Ross, with a loaf of fresh bread still warm wrapped in a towel. Margot and Shawn dropped in to say hello after all, staying just a few moments, and gifting a bottle of champagne to celebrate the New Year. Most were very curious to see Paislee's remodeled kitchen.

At four, Amelia and Sula arrived. Paislee noticed that Sula had driven McCormac's SUV and had parked on the front grass as all the spaces on the street were taken.

The ladies brought their new puppies.

"Wallace, be careful," Paislee told her dog. "These are tiny pups." Wallace was gentle with them as they played on the back porch, where Brody and Jenni sat with plates of food. She and Grandpa had connected the tables so that there was room for people to sit and eat on the back porch as well as in the kitchen and living room.

"They're so cute! We'll watch the puppies for you," Jenni said to Sula and Amelia. "If you want tae get some food."

"Thanks," Amelia said. "That's kind."

Amelia and Sula entered the kitchen and Paislee couldn't miss their red-rimmed eyes. Amelia had her black hair down, while Sula's blond was in a ponytail. Sula's mascara had smudged from her tears.

"I was on the fence aboot comin'." Amelia dabbed the tip of her nose with a tissue. "But I thought that a distraction might help."

"I'm glad you're here." Paislee gave Amelia a hug and squeezed Sula's wrist. "Help yourself. Drinks?"

"Not for me." Sula scanned the platters of savory food and chose a cracker. "I can only stay a minute. I'm expected at Mum's, with Dougie—he's a mess and kickin' himself for leavin' early last night. Mum's no cook and this looks delicious, but . . . nothing tastes guid with my McCormac gone." Shadows colored the delicate skin around her eyes.

Amelia patted her stomach. "My tummy is in knots. Hey, who are these flowers from? They're beautiful."

"Zeffer." Grandpa chortled.

Amelia's eyes rounded. "DI Mack Zeffer?"

"Yes, and he didn't discuss the case. Grandpa and I tried our best." Paislee held up her hand. "I think he wanted tae check out the new kitchen. He didn't stay."

"He didnae talk aboot my brother *at all*?" Amelia crumpled her tissue in her palm.

Paislee shook her head. "He's off today, though Constables Payne and Monroe are on duty. Have you heard from them?"

Sula finished the cracker but didn't eat anything else. "Constable Payne said last night when he met us at the hospital that it could be a few days because of the holiday."

Amelia looked out the window to where Jenni held Snowball. "Was this window here before?"

"No, it's new."

"It's great." Amelia sniffed; her words didn't match her expression. "I'll never celebrate New Year's the same way." She pitched her voice low so that only Paislee and Grandpa could hear her. "You're sure Zeffer didnae ask questions?"

"Not a one," Paislee said.

Amelia exhaled loudly and poured herself a dram. "This mornin', I got a surprise text from my mum. She and my brother are on their way. It seems she's had a change of heart. Must've realized when she sobered up that her youngest son is really dead."

Paislee squeezed her shoulder. "I'm sorry. Do you still need help finding homes for the pups?"

"Another surprise! Letitia Henry cannae wait tae see the last gift her precious McCormac would ever give her." Amelia's gaze chilled. "The Maltese pups are so tiny that I figured they'd be cozier at my flat, so I didnae bring them."

"Are you close tae your mum?" Paislee asked.

"No. Mum's got the maternal instincts of a barn cat."

Paislee stifled a surprised laugh. "I'm not close tae my mother

either." Her mum had moved to America after Paislee's da had
passed away, and remarried quickly. They exchanged birthday cards
and Christmas cards.

It was odd, actually, that Paislee hadn't received either this year.
She'd had her mail forwarded to Lydia's but maybe there'd been a
snafu.

Or maybe her mother had realized that there was no point in
wasting a stamp.

"Once I started primary school, I realized me family was not
like other families," Amelia said.

"Poor as church mice," Sula agreed. "Mine was too. It's the
neighborhood. Still are poor, which is why the lads skirted the
rules. By the Grace of God, Dougie stayed oot of big trouble."

"McCormac changed after jail," Amelia said proudly. "He didnae
have tae steal when he could earn guid money with his gift of
blarney."

"How did he end up in Ireland?" Paislee peered out the window. Brody had Thor in his lap while Wallace sniffed the golden
pup all over.

"McCormac was after a fresh start," Amelia said. "He couldnae
be on the straight and narrow path with his old mates holding him
doon."

"It's why he'd befriended Dougie. Dougie's younger so never
hung oot with McCormac or Hank. McCormac and I had just
started dating before he went tae jail. After his release, he went tae
Belfast. Away from Hank." Sula edged from the table to make
room for Arran, who snagged a scoop of skirlie on his plate, followed by steak pie. "For the most part, Mac and I stayed in touch
over text. It's been a verra long year."

"He wasn't back in all that time?" Paislee asked. She was surprised at the lack of contact considering it was less than a day's drive
from Nairn to the Emerald Isle. Seven and a half hours.

"Not really," Sula said. She tossed her napkin in the bin.

Amelia made a point of not saying anything.

Had her brother come home to visit without telling Sula? Paislee imagined him juggling his relationship with Porche, Lyla, Sula, and who knew what other ladies.

Hank, Porche's brother, and McCormac's once best friend, must not have been okay with how McCormac had treated his sister, as evidenced by the fist to his nose last night.

Could Hank have shot McCormac out of anger?

Paislee took a page from Zeffer's book and turned the subject to something else. "Amelia, you should try Grandpa's steak pie, or the lamb."

Sula, pale, checked the time on her phone. "I'm headed tae my mum's." She gave hugs to Paislee and Amelia. "I dinnae ken how it's supposed tae be a happy New Year with the love of my life shot tae death."

The young lady thanked Brody and Jenni for minding Thor and left with her pup.

Amelia sighed. "Poor Sula." Going to the back porch, Amelia gathered the white Pom from Jenni, then tucked her into the soft carrier she'd brought, hiding the sleepy pup out of the way of the people walking around. She washed her hands and sadly picked up a plate.

Amelia's phone dinged. She rolled her eyes. "Just when I was startin' tae get my appetite back. Mum is in Nairn and wants tae see me."

"Invite her tae come over," Paislee offered. In the years since she'd known Amelia from her Knit and Sip nights, she'd never met Amelia's family.

"Are you sure?" Amelia scrunched her nose. "I thought I'd catch an Uber home, but this way Mum could bring me."

"That's fine!" Paislee said.

"We'll probably go tae their house tonight." Amelia put a slice of lamb on the plate, then some turkey, and steak pie. "It's a pit. Da was a hoarder, as was his da, all doon the line. Henrys have been in this area for two hundred years. Mum made do with the junk, but it wasnae easy on her."

"I'm sorry," Paislee said. There had to be a better saying, she thought.

"Ye dinnae ken what you dinnae ken," Amelia said. "In school I realized that other kids were clean. Fed. Different. I wanted tae be like them but my family knocked me upside the head for being too intae myself."

Paislee had met Amelia when Amelia had quit smoking and wanted something to do with her hands so she'd learned knitting.

"How did you come tae work at Nairn Police Station?" Paislee decided to indulge her curiosity while Amelia was in a sharing mood. She scanned the kitchen and lounge. Jenni's dad, Drew, was in conversation with Meri, Grandpa, and Elspeth. Susan was in the armchair with Rosie the labradoodle at her side; Arran and Mary Beth conversed with her. Their twin girls played with toys quietly by the fireplace.

"Given that my family is this side of the law?" Amelia squeezed her forefinger and thumb together, gathering Paislee's attention at once.

"Aye." Paislee topped off Amelia's tumbler of whisky, pouring herself a hard cider.

"I was fourteen when Inspector Shinner caught me with my hands in the cookie jar, so tae speak, and guided me away from that life. He taught me that I had a choice, and I didnae have tae be like anybody but myself. I could choose. It was empowerin'. I miss him."

Paislee added a slice of Drew's homemade bread to Amelia's plate. "That's sage advice. Did he know McCormac?"

"Yep. Inspector Shinner is the one who sent McCormac tae jail. Stealin' cars, can you believe it?"

Paislee could, actually, but didn't say so. Amelia bit into the bread.

"I bet Inspector Shinner would've been verra proud of McCormac for turnin' himself around." Amelia added some skirlie to her plate and a scoop of neeps and tatties. "He was fair. Like Constable Payne, in a way." Her eyes welled.

Paislee wished she could ask, without hurting Amelia's feelings, how certain she was that McCormac's new life was aboveboard. People didn't just get shot in the chest for no reason, but now was not the time.

"I like Constable Payne," Paislee said. "He would help you be an officer. Signs are posted all around town that Police Scotland is hiring."

"Nah, that dream is over. I like my life." Amelia scrunched her nose. "Sairy tae be such a downer."

Meri joined them, the redheaded judge having overheard enough of the conversation to offer a one-sided hug. "Amelia, lass, you have a reason tae be sad today. Grief takes time no matter how strong we think we should be, so dinnae be hard on yourself. It's guid tae be surrounded by friends."

Paislee nodded. "You're very right." She'd suspected that Meri, who she'd just met in September, would be a good fit for their Knit and Sip group, and she'd been spot-on.

A knock sounded at the front door. Paislee peeked out back to see Jenni and Brody playing with Wallace, as Grandpa conversed with the guests in the lounge. Arran nodded at her, his plate balanced on his knee. He'd been a big help last night with McCormac. She left Meri and Amelia with an, "I'll be right back."

Blaise, Shep, and their young daughter Suzannah arrived wearing matching green scarves Blaise had knit herself.

"We can only stay a sec," Blaise said. "But I wanted tae see the kitchen." She pulled her golf pro husband toward the laden table. "We brought a peach tart for dessert."

Suzannah clung to Blaise's leg but was welcomed by the twins and released her grip on Blaise. The couple seamlessly fit into the party as Shep joined Grandpa and Drew while Blaise admired the kitchen, placing her dish on the counter.

"I'll have tae tell Lydia how much I love her design," Blaise declared. "It feels like a bigger house."

"She did an amazing job." Paislee wished Lydia could be here but understood that her bestie had obligations at Corbin's family manor.

The ladies shared small talk and Paislee decided to mingle. Paislee topped off drinks as she circulated, catching up with Susan and her service dog. "Rosie has made a world of difference," Susan said. "In such a short time."

"You've always been independent, Susan. This helps you even more." Elspeth got up and refilled their plates with an assortment of snacks.

An aggressive knock sounded, and Paislee excused herself to answer the door. Grandpa and Shep were talking with Jenni's dad about golf. It seems that Drew was recently divorced and had custody of Jenni. No extra time for golf.

"Hello!" Paislee smiled as she opened the door. She swallowed quickly, taking in an angry-looking woman in her late fifties wearing a black coat. Behind her was a man who resembled McCormac and Amelia.

"I'm Letitia Henry." The haggard woman jerked her thumb over her shoulder. "My son, Michael Henry. Where is Amelia?"

"I'm Paislee Shaw. I'm so sorry for your loss . . . please, come in. You are welcome tae hang your coats on the hooks there."

"I'll keep mine," Letitia said, wrapping the tattered wool tighter around her plump body.

"Me too." Michael shuffled inside, on his mother's heels.

Too close, as Letitia pushed him back. "Oaf!"

"Sairy," Michael mumbled, his face red. He smelled of beer and had a layer of dirt around his fingernails.

"Amelia!" Letitia shouted down the hall from the foyer. As if this was outdoors instead of inside someone's home.

Paislee wasn't sure what to do. "Would you like something tae eat? We're having a buffet-style meal. Lamb, steak pie. There is plenty."

Letitia's eyes were dark brown—unlike her children, who must get the cobalt blue from their da—her hair in coarse, faded brown curls.

Michael licked his lips. "Got anything tae drink?"

Nodding, Paislee said, "Tea, soda. Whisky."

Letitia rubbed her hands together. "I guess we could stay and have a wee bit of somethin'. I havenae felt right since finding oot my son is dead."

"Of course," Paislee said.

Amelia had put her plate down and walked quickly down the hall to the foyer. "Mum!" She hugged her mother, including her brother in the embrace. Michael and Letitia remained dry-eyed.

"Dinnae make a scene, Amelia," Letitia admonished.

"Sairy." Amelia dashed a tear from her cheek.

"Never thought I'd see the day tae outlive my bairns." Letitia patted her wiry hair and scowled at Paislee as if Paislee had any power over such things.

Michael stepped around the women, bumping into Paislee. "Food doon here? I'm starved."

"Michael!" Amelia said. "Dinnae be rude—Paislee is a verra guid friend of mine."

"You own the yarn shop?" Letitia asked. "And you have this nice house? Amelia said you arenae married. You need a man. Michael's single."

Michael eyed Paislee with a grunt. "I dinnae like redheads."

Paislee gazed at the obnoxious man with disdain. Before she could tell him what she thought of him, Amelia elbowed him hard in the small of his back.

Amelia was petite in comparison to him, but he groaned.

Paislee could imagine that Amelia would have to be scrappy to survive in a house full of bullies.

"Dinnae talk smack tae my friend in her own house," Amelia said. "Or you can wait in the car."

"Calm doon, calm doon," Letitia said. "Sairy. We arenae ourselves today. Tried tae see McCormac but he's on ice until after the holiday."

Paislee hoped her expression was neutral and not appalled. "I understand." She led the way to her kitchen, feeling Letitia's eyes calculating the monetary value of the appliances.

Amelia poured her mother a drink after Michael helped himself, filling the tumbler to the rim.

"Ta," Letitia said, scanning the food. "Fix me a plate, pet."

Amelia did, introducing her friends to her family. Everyone was polite and tried to stay away from the subject of dead McCormac. Blaise, Shep, and Suzannah left, then Jenni and her dad. Arran and Mary Beth and the twins followed.

Arran stopped to speak with Paislee in the foyer. "Have you heard anything aboot McCormac?"

"I'm sorry, Arran, but no. You were really a rock last night and I thank you." Paislee helped the girls into their pink jackets.

"You were too. I hate this waiting business. Angus said he was"—Arran turned to mouth—"shot?"

"Aye."

"I dinnae ken if it's appropriate or not, but if Amelia needs a solicitor for anything, have her call, no charge."

"I'll give her the message." Paislee hugged him, then Mary Beth, and last the adorable girls. "Happy New Year!"

Brody, with Wallace, disappeared upstairs to his room to play his new games, and Paislee didn't chide him. He'd been very social and polite, even helpful with the puppies.

She returned to the kitchen. Michael was on his third whisky and second large plate of food. The refreshments loosened his tongue as he sat at the kitchen table.

"Show me your dog, sis," Michael said. "Where are ours?"

"My flat." Amelia unzipped the soft carrier and brought out a sleepy Snowball. "Isnae she cute?"

"She's all right," Michael said. "And they're worth a couple thousand pounds?"

"I dinnae ken for sure." Amelia frowned at his response. "Mibbe."

Letitia studied the puppy, a glass of gin in her hand. Someone must have brought a bottle as it wasn't something Paislee stocked in her pantry. "But ye say they came with papers. The real thing."

"Aye, Mum." Amelia placed Snowball by her feet.

Letitia slurped her drink, her body relaxed. "Give me puddin', on a clean plate, mind. How could he afford 'em?"

"McCormac was selling high-end cars," Amelia said. She chose a smaller dessert plate, also paper, and piled samples of several sweets on it. "He wanted tae spoil us." She gave it to her mother along with a fork and napkin.

"I'd rather have cash than a whingeing dog," Michael said.

Amelia watched to see that her mum liked the choices before focusing on Michael. "McCormac was really guid at his job. Sula, one of his girlfriends, is driving his Mercedes. Brand-new. He offered tae help me get one too."

"Well, we'll need tae pick that up," Letitia said. "Dinnae belong tae her, the silly cow."

Amelia winced. "I guess." She glanced at Paislee as if embarrassed by her family's reactions.

"We're gonna sell the pups," Michael said.

"You cannae do that!" Amelia replied. She sounded horrified by the suggestion. She turned to her mum, who wasn't an ally.

"Aye, we can," Letitia argued. "They're mine."

"It isnae right." Amelia lifted Snowball.

Michael stood, a large mass of bully as he curled his fist. "Aye—gimme yours too."

"I willnae." Amelia snuggled the white pup close to her chest. "Snowball belongs tae me, and you cannae have her for love or money."

"You're bein' dafty," Letitia declared. She looked at Paislee. "Can ye believe what I have tae put up with?"

Paislee was Team Amelia.

Chapter 7

Amelia kept Snowball close to her heart, and away from her mum and her brother. "No. You cannae have Snowball—she belongs tae me, from McCormac."

Meri drew near to Paislee. Luckily Susan and Elspeth were in the lounge area with Grandpa and hadn't heard the commotion in the kitchen.

Rosie, Susan's new service dog, who'd been a gem all afternoon, perked her ears in interest. The labradoodle was waist-height to Susan and a lovely golden color.

"Stop bein' a wean, Amelia Henry," Letitia retorted. "It's money in the bank. Havenae I told you tae not get attached? Dogs and cats are nothin' but a drain on the purse."

Amelia didn't relax and the pup in her arms whined.

"I willnae have that dammed-awful noise," Letitia warned. "Hurts me ears and I dinnae like it at all."

"The pups can stay with me if you dinnae want them," Amelia said, her entire body tense. Paislee wished she could intercept or assist but sensed that if she tried, it would make the matter worse.

"So you pocket the dough?" Michael shook his head. "Dinnae be an eejit."

"If you only want the puppies for money, then I am going tae keep them," Amelia announced.

"You wouldnae dare!" Letitia thundered. "They were a gift from me son, and by God, I will have them."

Amelia realized she'd pinned her mother against the wall, and backtracked. "Yer right, Mum. It's just that they're so young right now, and a lot of trouble with potty training, feeding, and barking. Mibbe let me keep them for you until you find a buyer." Her smile was cajoling as she said, "I dinnae mind because I'm up already with Snowball. You cannae lose at such an offer."

Paislee was getting an interesting peek into the Henry household. Letitia ruled with an iron fist.

Amelia had realized that she had to appeal to her mother or risk the dogs being neglected. Paislee didn't care for people who harmed animals. She adored Amelia, however, so wouldn't kick the Henrys out just yet.

"How much you think we can get?" Michael asked.

"I dinnae ken, really. McCormac gave us the breeding papers and a free consultation with a veterinarian in the Highlands. Snowball is a Pomeranian and Thor a Brussels griffon and the two from your litter are Maltese." Amelia patted her dog behind the ears.

"Fine." Letitia shrugged and brushed her hands together. "But I'm not givin' ye any of my share of the cash, so dinnae waste your breath."

"I willnae." Amelia bowed her head.

"Where's McCormac's stuff?" Michael asked. "That hen's house what's got his SUV?"

Paislee could see that Michael was a chip off of Letitia's block. All about the money.

"Mibbe. He's only been in town a week or so," Amelia said. "He stayed a few nights with me, and then with Sula. He didnae see any reason tae lease a flat since his plans tae return were in flux."

"Tae go where?" Letitia asked.

"Back tae his job. Selling cars."

"In Belfast?"

"Aye."

Michael stood, pushing the chair back a few inches. "I'm ready tae go. You comin' or not?"

"Sure," Amelia said. She placed Snowball in the carrier and zipped the top. "Where's Da?"

"We left him in Glasgow at Michael's place." Letitia lumbered to her feet. "He can find his own way home if he wants tae join us."

Amelia lowered her eyes.

"I'll run you home, if you want tae stay longer," Meri offered to Amelia.

"Och, no." Amelia's cheeks tinted pink. "I'm awright."

Letitia puffed her plump chest like an affronted pigeon. "I can take me own daughter home. Who are you?"

Meri didn't back down. "I'm a judge for the piping competitions, Meri McVie. Amelia and I are friends from Paislee's Knit and Sip nights."

Michael smacked his palm to his thigh. "A bunch of hens together for a blether."

When he said it with such a snide tone, Paislee didn't like it.

Grandpa brought a few cups to the kitchen and tossed the paper plates. "Hello there. I'm Angus Shaw."

"Nice spread," Michael said, putting his empty whisky glass on the varnished hardwood floor.

"Thanks." Grandpa looked from Amelia to Letitia, and Michael again. "Can I get your coats?"

The Henrys were wearing them, but Grandpa was correct in reading the room. They should go.

Michael pulled his keys from his jacket pocket. "We're ready. Just waitin' on the princess here."

"Are ye sure you should be driving?" Meri asked. "The police are out in force, and I'd hate for you tae get a ticket. Happy tae run you wherever you need tae go."

"You can mind yer own business," Letitia told Meri.

"We'll be fine." Amelia checked that Snowball was secure in the carrier and followed her family. "See you Saturday at work, Paislee, if we dinnae talk sooner."

"What happened tae having a holiday?" Michael asked, sounding like he thought Paislee was raking Amelia over the coals. "And our brother dead."

"Please, take the time off you need," Paislee said to Amelia.

"Just shut up, would ye, Michael?" Amelia said, shaking her head. She stopped at the threshold. "Thank you, Paislee. Angus. Bye, everyone."

She didn't say Happy New Year, and Paislee didn't blame her. It took all she had to let Amelia, a woman grown, leave her house with her mother and her brother. As they left, she recalled Arran's offer of legal assistance, which she hadn't relayed to Amelia. Did Arran know something about the Henrys to prompt the suggestion?

Tuesday morning, Paislee startled awake and took a moment to ground herself. She was in her home. Not Lydia's flat. There wasn't a list so long it would wrap around the block twice to be done today . . . in fact, there were no plans at all, except to relax in this wonderful space. Home.

Brody and Grandpa had decided to watch back-to-back movies on the next superhero story, and nobody required her attention.

Grinning, she tossed back the comforter. This was a rare day indeed.

Should she read a novel? Work on a knitting project? Stay upstairs with her laptop and watch romantic comedies?

She slid slippers on her feet and a robe over her flannel pajamas, unable to knock the silly smile from her face as she entered her brand-spanking-new kitchen. The lilies from Zeffer added a sweet fragrance.

Paislee pinched her wrist to make sure she wasn't dreaming. She turned on her heel to admire the sleek appliances, the counters, the washer/dryer, the window over the sink. The kettle with a little tea station.

They'd all gone to bed by midnight last night, tired from the night before. It was a pleasure to clean up with all the modern gadgets. Dishes, even the pans, done. Tablecloths in the machine, and dry already, to be folded and put away.

Heating the kettle, Paislee went to get the paper from the front stoop, then remembered that she'd canceled it while they were away. Like the mail she'd had forwarded that she would need to correct.

She could do those trivial chores today, or she could put a cap on and her wellies and run to the corner market so that Grandpa would be surprised with the paper.

He'd been so great with all of the upheaval, and she wanted to do something nice for him. What were the chances that anybody would be out that she knew this early, at seven in the morning?

She exchanged her slippers for boots, grabbed her coat and keys, then hurried out the door, where she took a breath that was so cold it hurt her lungs.

Paislee blinked, tears freezing her eyelids as she dashed for the Juke. "Come on, lass. I know it's cold. There and back, then you can stay parked for the day."

She drove to the market and dashed in, paying cash for the newspaper, and running right back out again.

"Paislee—is that you?"

Drat. She lifted her head to see Jerry McFadden. Her breath plumed in the cold. "Aye! Happy New Year, Jerry."

He stepped closer and she inched back. He didn't get the hint that she wanted to go, fast.

"I'm sairy that I couldnae make your open house yesterday," Jerry said, seeming to want a conversation.

"It's fine, fine."

"When are ye openin' shop?"

"Saturday. I have today off," she said, hoping that he would overlook her state of dishabille.

"That's wonderful." Jerry smacked his hands together. "And how was yer Christmas?"

"Fine." Her teeth chattered. "Yours?"

"'Twas grand. I met a lady." Jerry smoothed his mustache. He tilted his head toward his pickup. "Would ye like tae meet her? We're on our way tae breakfast."

"No! Thank you!" Paislee kept her head low.

"No?" Jerry asked, confused.

"Not right now, Jer. I haven't even brushed my teeth," Paislee confessed. "I just dashed out for the paper." She would be properly thrilled for him—later. She didn't dare peek toward Jerry's vehicle. "And I'm going now . . . I'd be happy tae meet your friend another day."

"Gotcha." Jerry snickered. "Ta."

"Bye!" She climbed into her car, hoping that Grandpa's joy in the paper would be worth her embarrassment at being caught in her jammies at the convenience mart.

She hurried home, where Grandpa was at the table with a steaming mug of tea. "Hey there, Grandpa."

"Hiya!" He raised his mug toward her phone on the counter. "I wasnae sure whether or not tae be worried—you didnae even bring your mobile."

"Just ducked out for a second." Paislee handed him the rolled paper. "I wanted tae surprise you."

Grandpa brushed his beard with his fingers, a smile peeking through. "Thank ye. You're a sweet lass, Paislee."

"It's nice tae have an entire day tae ourselves, isn't it? Be right back." Paislee exchanged her coat for her cozy robe, and boots for slippers, then returned to the kitchen.

A fragrant mug of tea waited for her as Grandpa snapped open the paper and read the headline. "Well! This cannae be guid."

"What?" Served her right for waking up in such a happy mood.

Grandpa handed her the sales section like it was old times. "McCormac Henry is on the front page. 'Local man shot tae death under cover of fireworks.' Guess everyone took the day off yesterday and they're just now gettin' around tae reporting it."

"Maybe Zeffer will be back tae question us," Paislee said, partially joking. "No matter how much you tried tae engage him with information yesterday, he wasn't biting."

"That man has nerves of steel," Grandpa replied dryly.

In the past they might have disparaged Zeffer, but they'd learned he had a way of finding the bad guy and usually doing the right thing. Like, saving her uncle Craigh and sending him to Key West to drink margaritas in the sun rather than prison.

"I prefer that feisty Constable Monroe," Grandpa declared. "Constable Payne would also be better than Zeffer."

"The important thing is tae find out who shot McCormac." Paislee scanned the sales. "I hope it's not just some random whacko running loose in Nairn."

"McCormac Henry wasnae the most likable of gents. But, havin' met Letitia and Michael yesterday, I see where he gets it." Grandpa lowered the paper to look at Paislee across it. "Why is Amelia such a love?"

Since Amelia had shared some of her personal history, Paislee said, "Inspector Shinner took her under his wing. Gave her the job at the station tae answer phones, and told her she had a choice on how tae live her life."

Grandpa slurped his tea. "You think McCormac really changed too?"

"I don't know, but Amelia believes it, and that's what matters." Tesco had a sale on lean beef that was good for the week. Apples too.

"She believes it because she had the strength tae do it herself," Grandpa surmised. "It's a rare thing."

"You're so right." Paislee heard Brody in the bathroom upstairs—the footsteps, not the new pipes, thank all the angels. "Shall I make us some breakfast?"

"I can do it." Grandpa set the paper on the table.

Paislee covered his hand. "You cooked all day yesterday. Everyone raved about the lamb, and the turkey, and the steak pie . . ."

Grandpa winked. "With your help."

Paislee flexed her sous-chef-sore fingers. "Right again. Maybe Brody can forage in the fridge for leftovers?"

"Why not?" Grandpa returned to the article about McCormac. "You should read this too. McCormac wasnae a guid lad. Not that Arran directly said so yesterday when we talked aboot the incident, but it was implied."

"Arran offered tae help Amelia if she needed it. Why would she though?" Paislee asked. "It was nice of him, but I didn't have the chance tae tell her about it."

"Arran's a canny solicitor with solid old-fashioned shire values. His wife and lasses are sweet too. Really kind with Rosie, Susan's guide dog. They wanted tae play with her but asked Susan before they petted her."

High praise from her grandfather for the Mullholland family.

Grandpa pushed the comics toward Brody's seat and gave the article on McCormac to Paislee. It was a scathing review of his past misdeeds. The editor was a woman and Paislee wondered if McCormac had burned her too, since that seemed to be his style.

To her surprise, Wallace came down the stairs without Brody, who, she surmised as his bedroom door slammed, went back to bed.

"Outside, boy?" Paislee stood and opened the back door.

Wallace raced through the kitchen and out but stopped on the porch stairs, ears up and tail out—it was that cold. She waited with him, arms around her middle, until he did his business in the fastest time ever and they both came back in. She wiped snow from his fur, and he curled up on his dog bed, also content for more sleep.

She added hot water to her mug, but Grandpa's was already full. "Let's have a lazy day, with no stress. Sound good, Grandpa?"

"Aye. We deserve it." Grandpa sipped and stood, going to the pantry for some chocolate biscuits. "I found some boxes in the bedroom closet that have Bruce's name on them."

Paislee lowered the paper and looked at her grandfather, bemused. Memories of her dad warmed her heart. She'd been sixteen when he'd died in a boating accident. Gran had been a rock when she must have been grieving hard, to lose her only son. "You did?"

"I'd like tae see what your gran saved of his life." Grandpa placed his hand on her shoulder. "Mibbe we could go through the boxes together. It seems a verra nice way tae spend the morning. Our Brucie was a handsome lad. A fine man who died much too soon."

"Now?" It wasn't what she thought of as a low-key day, but why not? It would be interesting to hear Grandpa's memories and possibly learn more about her father.

"Aye." Grandpa swallowed the chocolate treat and went into his room, dragging two plastic bins that had her dad's name on them in Gran's neat print out to the kitchen. BRUCE SHAW. "They were next to Agnes's boxes you'd stored."

She'd used the space for storage, unable to utilize her grandmother's rooms for emotional reasons. They'd been Gran's until Grandpa came along after her death.

Paislee opened the first tub and saw things from when her da was a kid. Baby pictures that made Grandpa smile too.

"I remember when Bruce was teethin'. Agnes didnae know what tae do, and when I suggested me mum's trick of a wee bit of whisky on the gums, I thought she'd kill me for giving alcohol tae a babe."

"And?"

Grandpa spread his arms to the side with a satisfied smirk. "It worked like a charm, didnae it?"

They looked through pictures and photo albums. Her da's boyhood memories and then high school. The picture of him and her mum getting married. Bruce and Rosanna Shaw.

"How is Rosanna now?" Grandpa asked.

Paislee had taught herself not to be emotionally tied to her mother, who had abandoned her. "Don't know. Don't care."

Grandpa peered at her over the wedding photo. Mum and Da happy, and young. "That sounds cold."

"I had tae be, tae protect my heart, Grandpa."

The landline rang, and it was Elspeth for a chat, to say thanks, and what a good time they'd had. After that Amelia called about the article in the paper maligning her brother.

"Can ye believe how vicious they've been aboot poor McCormac?" Amelia asked. "Like he never changed at all. He served his time in jail and that should be the end of it."

"It's unfortunate when a reputation can't be overlooked," Paislee said diplomatically. "How are you, and the puppies?"

"Mum insisted that she take them despite the extra work I warned her and Michael aboot. We picked them up and went tae Mum's house last night. I gave them a long list of things tae do for the puppies. All they do is drink gin and complain. Not my favorite, but I was trapped since my car is at the mechanic."

"It hadn't crossed my mind tae ask why you were being driven around! Just assumed it was because you wanted tae be together."

"Dinnae worry aboot it. I hate being stuck is all. Thank goodness for Uber. By ten, Michael was too blitzed tae drive. I felt guilty leaving the puppies there, but I made sure they were in their crates before I left."

"Have you talked with Constable Payne or Constable Monroe today?"

"Payne returned my tenth call, but he doesnae have more tae add, other than McCormac had unsavory associates in his past when he lived in Nairn. Could be tae do with old grudges, but they're gathering information." Amelia scoffed. "He acted like I should know that, but it's different when it's your family, eh?"

"Understandable for you tae be upset," Paislee said. "Arran asked after you, by the way."

"We didnae get a chance tae talk yesterday besides a quick hello," Amelia said. "Nor Mary Beth and the weans. I wanted tae thank him for tryin' tae help McCormac."

"Maybe give him a call." She bit her tongue about his offer of assistance as she sensed it might alienate Amelia. They said goodbye.

Paislee returned to the kitchen table where her grandfather was knee-deep in photos and memories. Drawn to the treasure trove, she turned over a picture of her da at Brody's age. "They could be twins."

"Bruce always had a verra kind heart, and I see that in Brody as well."

"I can't believe Da's been gone almost half my life, and he's never met Brody." Paislee caressed the image of her father at twelve. Freckles and the same cowlick.

Grandpa tapped a picture of Rosanna that Gran must have put in the box. Her mum had to be about twenty, her hair blond and long. "She's lovely," he said.

"I suppose." Paislee had gotten her pale blue eye color from Rosanna, who was smiling and young in the photo. A far cry from the woman who whinged all the time.

When Brody finally came down, he was fascinated by his personal history and peppered Grandpa and Paislee with questions. She didn't talk about her da very much and she hadn't realized how hungry she was for these insights from her grandfather. Paislee listened as avidly as Brody. Her dad had liked to snow ski—something she didn't know—and boat. Loved the water and fishing. The pain of his freak accident where the boat had capsized, and he'd drowned, returned. She and Grandpa held hands and the moment passed.

Brody asked if he could keep one of the pictures and brought it to his room. Connection.

With a quiet sense of contentment, Paislee curled up on the sofa to read a novel as the guys watched movies—the only stress brought on by the characters.

Chapter 8

By Wednesday, January 3rd, Paislee was getting just a wee bit stir-crazy. Spending a day doing nothing at all had been just the mental break she'd needed, but this morning she'd woken with a to-do list she couldn't ignore.

Call the paper and get it delivered again to avoid any more early morning humiliations, and stop at the post office to get her mail rerouted from Lydia's, then a trip to Ramsey Castle to deliver more scarves, sweaters, and coin purses in the Ramsey tartan.

Grandpa and Brody planned another day in front of the telly with pizza; they'd discussed how she might join them this afternoon to knit before the cozy fire.

She'd dreamed of her da last night, thanks to Grandpa bringing out the bins. Would Bruce Shaw be proud of the life she'd created? He'd been one for hugs and teasing.

Downstairs, Paislee found Grandpa on the sofa reading a book on fishing, with Wallace curled up by his side. Her son remained in his bedroom, out like a light. "Morning," she said.

"It's after nine, lazybones!" Grandpa joked. "I've been up since dawn. I'll make a nice mash-up with the leftovers for dinner, since we're having pizza for lunch. What time will you be home?"

"I shouldn't be long," Paislee said. "I'll call on my way from the castle. Want me tae pick up a paper?"

"Aye. I'm right curious if they've made progress on McCormac's death." Grandpa and Wallace got off the couch and meandered to the kitchen. "You think we can have delivery restarted by tomorrow?"

"I'll see what I can do." Paislee poured a cup of tea into a stainless-steel mug and rifled in the pantry for a fast breakfast option.

Grandpa joined her to peer inside as if something interesting or new might appear.

Paislee reached for a box of granola bars drizzled with dark chocolate. "Want one?"

"Aye," Grandpa said. She handed him a wrapped bar and closed the pantry door. "There's no reason I cannae phone tae restart the paper delivery, and then you just have the post office and the castle."

"That's a timesaver, Grandpa." Paislee raised her mug and pocketed her breakfast to eat in the car. "Thank you. I'll give you a ring later."

She darted across the lawn to her Juke, her teeth chattering as she waited for it to warm up. Her phone rang and Lydia's face lit the screen.

"Lydia! How was your New Year?"

"Fine, fine. We didnae have anybody die, Paislee Ann—why didnae you mention it?"

"We haven't talked!" Paislee unwrapped her granola bar as she waited for the Juke to defrost. "How did you find out?"

"One of the Smythe cousins has a friend who was running the fireworks display at the bandstand, and they mentioned that someone had been killed. Just this morning over eggs, or I would have called sooner."

"There is no news tae share. There was an article in the paper listing McCormac's misdeeds, and Constable Payne suggested it might have tae do with the folks he knew before going tae jail. Amelia is gutted, of course, because it's her brother. She was proud of him for turning over a new leaf."

"I cannae believe it." Lydia blew out a frustrated breath. "What if you or Brody or Grandpa had been shot instead of McCormac? Was it a random gunman?"

Paislee swallowed her granola bar with a chuckle. "Getting shot would have been a downer for sure. I don't think it was a random thing—it seemed personal tae McCormac. I heard a sound and smelled something burning that I think was his sweater from the bullet."

"Paislee!"

"The point is that he was a ladies' man. Him and one of his old best friends had gotten into a fist fight at the park, around ten. Hank punched McCormac in the nose hard enough tae draw blood."

"Poor Amelia. How certain is she that he'd changed?"

"Well, McCormac had money that he didn't before and flashed his new wealth around. Treated his family with gifts of expensive puppies. He found his calling as a luxury-car salesman. The new Mercedes."

"A master at malarkey. That would bring in cash all right." Lydia sniffed. "Well, you be careful just the same."

"I will! I love my new kitchen, Lydia. It's perfect for entertaining. So light and bright! Zeffer couldn't believe it."

"Zeffer stopped by—aboot McCormac's death?"

"No." Paislee unwrapped the bar in preparation for the next bite. "Just tae see the kitchen remodel. He brought flowers."

"Did he?" Lydia sounded suspicious. "What does Hamish think of the kitchen?"

Paislee gave an eyeroll, glad her bestie couldn't see it. "Hamish hasn't been by yet. Still in Inveraray with his poor mum. We might go out Saturday night though."

"I'm chuffed that you like it. I was verra worried," Lydia said. "You dinnae like change."

"That's not true! And I love, love, love it." Paislee swallowed her bite and placed the rest in the cupholder. "Can I call you later? I need tae drive tae the post office tae reroute my mail back tae my house. Thank you for everything that you've done, which is over and above bestie duties."

"We're family. Cheers!" Lydia ended the call.

Ten minutes later, Paislee snagged street parking a block away from the post office. It was too cold to snow but there were a few inches of white from New Year's Day. Lights and decorations made the Victorian shire something out of a storybook.

Paislee went inside and joined the short queue. When it was her turn, she smiled at the harried iron-haired matron in red glasses behind the counter. "Morning," she said.

"It is that," the woman said in a curt tone. "Can I help ye?"

"I'm Paislee Shaw and I'd like tae have my mail routed tae my home address." Paislee kept her voice friendly. "I'd had it delivered tae a friend's place but we're back home now."

"ID, please."

Paislee handed her license across the counter and the woman typed in the information.

"Paislee Shaw, you said?" The woman peered over her nose at Paislee, the red frames sliding down the bridge. "There's a flag here."

"A flag?"

"It means we have mail being held at this facility for you. That happens sometimes if the address is in question. Our carrier recognized yer name, or it would have been returned tae sender. It's important tae write the address legibly."

Paislee nodded. The only person she could think to make a mistake like that was Uncle Craigh. No matter. Grandpa would be thrilled to hear from his son.

The woman rose and disappeared behind a door, returning shortly with two envelopes banded together that she gave to Paislee.

"Thank you so much."

"Happy New Year," the woman snapped. "Next!"

Paislee left and glanced at the envelope. It had been addressed in marker that had smudged. From America, yes, but from her mother. Her stomach tightened.

The address mistake would explain why she hadn't heard from her mum. Paislee climbed in the Juke and tossed the envelopes to the passenger side, driving the few blocks to Cashmere Crush. Before she got out, she opened the envelope, expecting the usual scrawl from her mum on a birthday card, and a Christmas card.

To her surprise, it wasn't just her mother who had signed, but her sister and brother with a little note. Paislee sucked in a breath, her heart hammering at the unexpected connection.

Nine and eight. Natalie and Josh. Josh?

Tears sprang to her eyes. Her mother was forty-nine, and while that was late in life it wasn't unheard of to bear children in your forties. She'd known, of course, but this was different. Paislee had felt like her mother's dirty secret in Scotland, but now it was obvious that her siblings knew about her.

Now what?

Was it selfish of her to keep Brody from knowing his family? His grandmother?

Turning off the engine, Paislee cursed under her breath and entered her shop, shoving this new dilemma from her mind. She would rather have another kitchen blowout than deal with her mum, or Paislee's *siblings*.

Packing a large box with cashmere goods, and a dozen coin purses that she made just for the inventory at Ramsey Castle, Paislee locked up Cashmere Crush, climbed into the car and cranked the radio, keeping all thoughts of her mum buried.

The winding roads were clear of snow, though the trees and fields were covered in white. When she reached Ramsey Castle, the gate was open, and Paislee drove to the car park designed for the gift shop entrance. Two vehicles were there already, and she parked next to a shiny BMW.

She exited and gathered the box, hurrying toward the gift shop that had once been a sunroom attached to the castle. Christmas lights outlined the glass panes. Fake reindeer frolicked before the door.

Cinda Dorset, a cute blonde with an upturned nose, was behind the register, ringing up a man buying a jar of honey and a tam in the Ramsey tartan.

"Paislee!" Cinda greeted her with a smile, accepted the money from her customer, and bagged the items. "Sir, this woman is the artist who creates the bespoke knitted guids here. Paislee Shaw. I've put her card in the bag for you."

"Nice tae meet you," the gentleman said to Paislee. "This shop has been full of surprises since it opened. I always stop tae see what new treats are available. My wife and I both enjoy the honey."

He ambled past Paislee with a nod and went out the door.

"He's a sweetheart," Cinda declared. "Lives just up the road. He bought his wife a cashmere jumper for Christmas."

"Thank you so much for all you're doing," Paislee said. "You're a natural saleswoman."

"Do ye think so?" Cinda's smile widened. "I want tae help oot as much as I can."

"Aye! And I appreciate it. I'm sure the dowager countess does too." It was no secret that Sorcha Grant, Dowager Countess of Ramsey Castle, didn't really care for Cinda, but Patrick, Sorcha's second oldest son, was in a relationship with Cinda despite her disapproval.

"Sorcha is . . . not as rigid as she has been." Cinda shrugged. "Could be the holidays."

"Could be." The women shared a smile. Sorcha would get a loyal and hardworking daughter-in-law if she just relented a wee bit. Castles were not cheap to operate and while it may seem glamourous, the truth meant drafty stone walls and the legacy being more important than personal sacrifices.

"Too bad aboot the bloke who was killed during the fireworks!" Cinda said. "Do ye know anything aboot it?" She lifted the newspaper, which had been folded to the article about McCormac Henry's death.

"Not much." Paislee placed her handbag on the counter. "We

were with him when it happened, though. The constables think it might have tae do with McCormac's past."

Cinda tapped the paper. "That's a shame. Hard tae believe the recent tragedies we've had in Nairn."

"True." Paislee scanned the interior of the shop. She had her own section of items displayed enticingly. She couldn't keep up with the coin purses.

"If I could I'd whisk Patrick away somewhere safe, but he willnae leave here, especially not with Robert in Europe tryin' tae drum up a suitable wife."

As the Earl of Lyon, it was Robert Grant's duty to marry well—a woman with breeding and money. Love be damned. Lissia, Sorcha's only daughter, was spending time in a mental facility in London. Perhaps the pressure of the family name had gotten to her.

"The castle must have seemed empty over the holiday," Paislee commiserated.

"Nah. Sorcha's had tae hire four people tae manage the grounds with Finn McDonald retired. She misses him, more than Robert." Cinda put a finger to her lips, as if she'd shared a secret.

"And Lissia?"

Cinda shrugged. "Lissia wasnae right in the head for a while. Love can do that tae a person."

Paislee had never been besotted like that. "Well, I should get going, Cinda. Do you have an envelope for me?"

"Aye!" Cinda opened the cash register. "Here you are. I'm sure we'll need more inventory next month, but I'll be in touch with what exactly. The coin purses are popular. I gave one tae my mum for Christmas and she raved aboot it."

"Thank you!" Paislee put the check into her bag and left the gift shop.

Her phone rang and she hurried to the car to answer it inside via Bluetooth so she could be hands-free.

"Hello?"

"Paislee, it's Amelia. You have tae come over."

"What's wrong?"

"I think Snowball is sick." Amelia sounded panicked. "I dinnae ken what tae do."

Paislee recalled that the puppy had come with a free consultation with a veterinarian in the Highlands. A very responsible portion of the gift. "Did you phone the vet?"

"Aye." Amelia's words sped together. "It went tae voicemail as they are on holiday hours."

"All right. Stay calm. Are you at your flat?"

"Yeah. Hurry! My little Snowball is just wheezing like the poor dear cannae catch a breath."

"I'll be there in ten."

Driving a tad faster but still careful on the slick roads, Paislee arrived at Amelia's within the allotted time. She'd called her vet, Dr. Kathleen McHenry, to make sure she was open and could see Snowball.

She rushed out of the car and into the lobby. Amelia's apartment complex had five stories and was made of brick. Amelia lived on the second floor, and she answered on Paislee's first knock.

Paislee had never been inside Amelia's place, though she'd dropped her off once or twice after a Knit and Sip meeting, or a Saturday shift at Cashmere Crush.

The interior had an overhead light. The space on the left had a couch, a low table, shelves, and a large television with a gaming system attached. By the couch, a small artificial Christmas tree was lit with holiday lights.

To the right was a kitchen area on linoleum, where Amelia had penned in the puppies. Easier cleanup for accidents, as evidenced by the kitchen roll on the small table, next to some spray cleaner.

"Come on in," Amelia said. She stepped over the barricade of bins to pick up Snowball. The white Pomeranian had runny eyes and was lethargic compared to how she'd been on Monday.

"Poor pup! How are the others?"

"Mum and Michael have them, so I dinnae ken. I asked, and

Mum accused me of not trusting them, and tae mind me own business. I feel awful aboot how they acted at your house on New Year's."

"Don't," Paislee said. "You've had a tragedy in your family."

Amelia bit her lip. "It brings me tae tears still. All Mum and Michael care aboot is the money McCormac might have had, or the cash they'll score from selling the puppies."

Paislee patted Amelia's shoulder.

"It's all aboot what they can buy." Amelia snuggled Snowball to her chest. "I dinnae want anything tae do with them. No wonder McCormac went away tae get clean. How could he do guid when they are so bad?"

There was no answer to that question so Paislee bit her tongue.

"I cannae stand it." Amelia peered at her with sorrowful blue eyes over Snowball's white fur.

"Have you heard from Constable Payne?"

"Only because I've been pestering him with texts," Amelia said. "I feel like I'm the one who did somethin' wrong, which isnae fair. I dinnae ken anything aboot McCormac's life in Belfast."

"I'm sorry."

"It's okay." Amelia's shoulders drooped. "I've been going on and on like a wee babe. The vet called—Dr. MacTavish, in the Highlands—he'll meet me at his clinic."

"That's wonderful." Paislee was relieved for Amelia. "Most veterinarians have an emergency number." She'd follow up with Dr. Kathleen later. "Want me tae drive?"

"Yes, please. I'm a nervous wreck. For a dog that I've had for a week! Can ye imagine if I'd had kids?" Amelia scrunched her mouth in horror.

Paislee laughed. "It will be fine."

"I hope so. I love this little pup."

Paislee drove the twenty minutes to the veterinarian's shop in the Highlands. Pretty, with snow-covered evergreens behind the building. The space was in a quiet strip of business offices. She parked next to a Mercedes SUV that probably belonged to the vet—not as fancy as McCormac's but still very nice.

They got out and she locked the Juke. Amelia knocked on the door with a sign that read, DR. MACTAVISH, VETERINARIAN. It gave a listing of hours with a phone number.

A tall brown-haired man with blue glasses in his late thirties met them at the door. He was just buttoning a white coat over street clothes. "Amelia Henry?"

"That's me," Amelia said. "And this is Snowball." She lifted the pup in her arms. She hadn't bothered with the carrier. The pup wheezed pitifully.

"I'm Paislee," she said.

"Come in!" The man ushered them past the threshold and closed the door behind them. There was nobody at the reception desk. A framed certificate with his name was hung on the wall. "I'm Dr. Torrance MacTavish. It's just me this week seeing any emergencies. So far, this pup is the only one. And who do we have here?" The vet expertly cooed to the shaking Snowball, his brown eyes narrowing as he assessed the pup.

"Snowball's my new dog," Amelia said. "Darn. I forgot the paperwork for her. See, I was just so upset. My brother gave me a whole kit for Christmas."

"Dinnae worry aboot that right now," the vet said assuredly. "We can get all of that later. Now, let's see what's going on with this wee dear."

He led the way to an exam room in the back that smelled of sanitizer, pulling a stethoscope from his pocket. A stainless-steel table was in the center, shelves of pet paraphernalia, from leads to collars to crates, along the walls. Stacks of designer dog food were arrayed. There wasn't a window and Paislee hadn't noticed any other dogs. Just because her vet provided boarding services didn't mean they all did.

"You're right tae have brought her in," the vet said to Amelia after listening to Snowball's chest. "She's got some kennel cough that we can treat with medicine. I'm a little worried because she's so young. I'd like tae keep an eye on her."

"Overnight?" Amelia asked, alarmed.

"I'm afraid so," the vet said. This close to him, Paislee noticed a mole on his chin and dark bristles, as if he required a shave.

"If you think it's necessary. But, well, when can I take her home? My brother gave me this puppy for Christmas, and I cannae let anything happen tae her." Amelia's voice lowered. "He died."

Dr. MacTavish stepped back with the stethoscope. "Excuse me?"

"McCormac Henry," Amelia said. "It's been in the news."

"He was shot at midnight under the cover of fireworks," Paislee said.

"Poor lass," the vet said with compassion. "That was yer brother? I've been away from the telly tae enjoy the holiday with me family, but of course, I'd heard. Tragic."

"Aye." Amelia's eyes filled with tears.

"Do they know who did it?" Dr. MacTavish petted Snowball's head. "May I?" He took the pup from Amelia.

"They dinnae." Amelia stuck her free hands in her jacket pockets. "But Paislee is going tae help me find the killer."

Paislee's smile dropped. She'd thought Amelia had forgotten her Hogmanay request.

Chapter 9

Paislee blushed a brilliant redhead blush at the vet's intense look. Dr. MacTavish asked, "Shouldnae the constables be in charge of finding who killed her brother?"

"Aye, and they will!" Paislee said, fanning her face. It wasn't her fault that she'd earned a reputation among her friends for being curious. Sometimes that curiosity paid off and helped solve the occasional crime. Not a big deal.

"We'll see." Amelia scowled. "I just want whoever stole McCormac's life tae be held accountable. Dinnae care by who."

"Completely understandable." Dr. MacTavish checked the puppy one more time. "Let's touch base tomorrow morning."

Amelia's lower lip jutted. "Nobody's here and Snowball will be all alone."

"I'll be here," the vet assured Amelia.

"Do you board other pets?" Paislee asked.

"No, we arenae a boarding service," the vet replied stiffly. "We have kennels in the back for emergencies. This is a small but dedicated clinic."

As in, a one-man show. Maybe that's how all veterinarians started off.

"I just . . . this is my first pet." Amelia looked like she wanted to grab Snowball back from the vet and run all the way home.

"I understand." Dr. MacTavish peered into each of Snowball's ears. The lethargic pup didn't seem to notice. "How old is Snowball?"

"Eight weeks. Wouldn't she be in your system?" Amelia asked. "She's supposed tae have a microchip and everything."

"My assistant manages all of the paperwork like that. You're right, though. I'll have her look this wee darling up when she comes in at ten." The vet smiled good-naturedly. "I have a cot in the back. Snowball must be the runt of the litter."

Amelia patted Snowball gently, oozing love for her puppy. "She's verra tiny. I wonder if Sula's is sick?"

"There are others from this litter?" Dr. MacTavish asked.

"Not the same breed but I think they were raised together. My brother's girlfriend has a Brussels griffon. Thor."

Dr. MacTavish hummed thoughtfully. "Let me know how Thor is doing. I'm already here, so if she needs tae bring him in, just have her call me. I'll keep the phone close by."

"We will," Amelia said. "You have my mobile number too if anything changes."

"Dinnae fash, lass. Snowball is in guid hands." Dr. MacTavish escorted them out the door, having Snowball wave her tiny white paw.

Amelia sniffled as Paislee drove away from the building.

"I hate tae leave her," Amelia said, her throat thick.

"It's for the best." Paislee reached over to nudge Amelia's arm across the console. "Should we get an ice cream?" It's what she did with Brody when he was sad.

"Aye." Amelia didn't even hesitate.

Paislee drove to the harbor shops, and they stopped in for two scoops each. The shop was busy with holiday tourists and heated inside.

"We should have gone tae the new shop! Scoops," Paislee said. "But this was closer."

"It was an ice cream emergency. Grand idea."

She'd chosen peppermint and chocolate with hot fudge over

the top in a bowl. Amelia had gone for cherry mocha and candy cane. Sprinkles too.

"Dr. MacTavish seems nice." Amelia swirled a bite onto her spoon. "I dinnae think McCormac understood that puppies should-nae be taken from their mums so early. Is eight weeks normal?"

"I don't know." Paislee watched her friend closely. "We can ask my vet, Dr. Kathleen. She's very matter-of-fact."

Amelia sighed but her eyes were dry at least. "You might have noticed that my mum was a bit aboot the cash. McCormac knew gifts were one way tae make our folks happy, Da being a hoarder and all. Michael's just like him."

Paislee swallowed a delicious bite of peppermint, sensing that Amelia needed to talk.

"Not me though. If I dinnae need it, I toss it. McCormac was somewhere in the middle, always wanting tae make my parents proud."

"How so?"

"When we were younger"—Amelia gestured with her spoon—"we were encouraged tae behave badly and see what we could get away with. I think he still did that." She focused on her ice cream; her dark head bent. The red highlights for the holiday season were beginning to fade. "How was your childhood?"

"My parents were strict." Paislee had been an easy enough kid, wanting to please her folks too. "I had tae get good grades. Gran was a teacher."

"I wish that mine would have cared at least a little aboot school," Amelia said with a shrug.

"You should be very proud of all that you've accomplished," Paislee said. She didn't add, considering her rough beginning, but it was there between them on the table.

"My folks laughed at me, daring tae get a job at the police sta-tion." Amelia swallowed another bite and licked a sprinkle off her lip. "Told me that it was guid, so I could keep them apprised if the law got too close tae any of the family's shady dealings."

Paislee's eyes widened.

"And then when McCormac went tae jail they didnae understand why I stayed answering phones for the coppers. Mibbe they just dinnae get wrong versus right." Amelia sighed. "Is that even possible?"

There were names for that type of behavior, but Paislee didn't share them. Amoral. Sociopath. She was glad that Amelia did recognize right from wrong and chose to act appropriately.

"Should you call Sula tae see how Thor is?" Paislee asked.

"I'd prefer tae drive by Sula's after this. Do you mind?" Amelia tilted her head. "See how her puppy is, just in case she needs the vet. She's been sending really sad texts aboot losing McCormac and not saying much aboot Thor."

"Sure!" Paislee was curious as to how Thor was doing herself. "Did you get ahold of Arran?"

"Nah. I was too worried aboot Snowball. I'll do it this week," Amelia said. She finished her last spoonful of cherry mocha ice cream. "Yum. Also, I want tae show you something at the flat. It was in McCormac's suitcase."

Was it something dangerous? Something to turn in to the police? "All right."

Amelia dropped her spoon into the empty bowl as she looked at Paislee. "I think you're pure brilliant at tracking down criminals. You should be a constable."

"No, *you* should be a constable." Paislee had no desire to do anything other than raise Brody and operate Cashmere Crush.

Amelia wiped her mouth with a small napkin. "I cannae. You see why it's impossible, with me family."

"They might be a challenge. Are you worried they won't talk tae you?" Not a big loss that Paislee could see. Same with her own mum.

But then there were her siblings. Siblings that wouldn't stay buried in her thoughts. Would they look like her, or Brody? Did they have the ice-blue eyes she shared with her mum?

Amelia smacked her palm to the table. "We've got tae check on the puppies at Mum's place too. I'm still upset they took the poor things. Michael learned tae be a bully from Mum and if they can see a way tae get what they want, they'll take it withoot a thought to hurting someone else. The idea of me having the puppies, and not them, made him mental."

"That's really sad."

"I know." Amelia pulled out her phone. "Nothing from Dr. MacTavish or Constable Payne. Sorry tae be such a lame duck."

"You aren't! I'm impressed that you've come so far." Paislee stood. "Should we go?"

"Aye."

They left the ice cream shop. Paislee's lips were frozen from the peppermint bark and this wicked cold didn't help.

"What's Sula's address?" Paislee asked.

"Sent it tae you," Amelia replied as Paislee's mobile dinged.

"Got it." She drove to Sula's two-story condominium. Amelia's place was average, while this was a tiny cut above. Had McCormac paid for it? What did Sula do for work?

"Hey!" Amelia said loudly, tapping the dash.

Sula was outside, yelling at a man with a tow truck. Paislee realized that McCormac's SUV was in the process of being attached to the ramp.

Amelia rolled her window down so they could hear.

"Lady, I'm just following orders." The driver held up a gloved hand.

Rolling it up again, Amelia seemed ready to fly from the Juke. "This isnae guid."

After she parked, Paislee and Amelia spilled out and Amelia stood next to Sula in solidarity.

"What's going on?" Paislee asked the driver.

"Taking the vehicle tae police impound," he said shortly. "That's all I know. You got a problem, call the police station."

"What?" Amelia hollered. "You cannae do that. It belongs tae my brother."

"I can, and I am." The driver didn't even look at Amelia.

Sula, shivering without a jacket, muttered at the driver with curses so inventive Paislee hadn't heard them before.

"I will be calling your boss!" Sula said. The man was impervious to her imploring green eyes or imperious tone.

"Please do," the driver countered. He handed her a sheet of paper with the details like the date, the time, the address, the license and make of the car. "Your copy."

Sula refused to take it.

Amelia stepped in and accepted the paper before it dropped on the road. "I dinnae understand what this is aboot."

The driver responded to a reasonable voice and said, "The police are takin' this vehicle for inspection. I dinnae ken more than that."

"I see. Thank you," Amelia said.

"Happy New Year," the driver replied and got into the cab, which had been running the whole time, and then drove off.

"I cannae believe this," Amelia said. "Impounded! Hadnae McCormac paid for it? I thought he was doing verra well with his sales job."

Paislee put her chilled hands in her pockets. It was cold outside.

Sula stepped toward her flat, her blond ponytail bobbing at her shoulders. "We cannae let the bastards get away with it," she said. "Come in while I call the station. I'll make tea."

Just in time before she turned into an icicle. Paislee and Amelia went into her flat. Thor was asleep on a cushion on the couch.

"How's your pup?" Paislee asked.

"Why?" Sula asked with suspicion. Rather than go toward the phone, she crossed her arms.

"Snowball was sick, so we had tae take her tae the vet," Amelia explained.

Sula made a sad face at Amelia. "Is she all right?"

"She's there overnight, and the vet is giving her medicine." Paislee watched Thor, who gave them a tail wag but didn't get off his cozy cushion. "We wondered if Thor was okay."

"So far, aye." Sula strode across the beige tile floor she'd made warmer with throw rugs. Her apartment was a little bigger than Amelia's, but the best draw was that it was on the ground floor. It had a back garden with sliding glass doors, the light making the interior brighter.

There were stockings on the mantel and an artificial Christmas tree flocked in white with blue and green lights. An angel perched on top.

Amelia followed Sula to the couch and examined Thor. "He's much bigger than Snowball. Dr. MacTavish thinks I mighta got the runt of the litter since she's so small."

"The paperwork says Thor is eight weeks," Sula said. "I wasnae at all sure aboot a puppy but I'm so grateful for this last gift from my soul mate." She sniffed and swiped a tear from her cheek.

"It's surprising how quickly they are in our hearts, eh?" Amelia shook her head. "Do you have information for Thor? Mibbe mine is wrong."

"Sure." Sula left them in the living room and went down a narrow hall. She returned shortly with a folder that had a generic picture of a dog on it, with a vet in a white coat.

"That's what mine looks like too," Amelia said.

"Let's read it together." Sula snuggled on the couch with Thor, and Amelia perched next to her. Paislee sat across from them on a chair.

Amelia perused the paperwork. "Microchipped. Dr. MacTavish. Eight weeks. Shots. Yep, it's the same."

"Did McCormac say anything tae you about where he got the pups?" Paislee asked.

"Something tae do with a receptionist at the car dealership he worked at it in Belfast," Sula said. "She'd told him aboot a breeder in Inverness who had puppies and it might be a jolly way tae find them homes while earning some extra money. A win-win, as who doesnae want a puppy for Christmas?"

A breeder with an influx of dogs in time for the holiday made her think of a puppy mill.

It couldn't be though . . . could it?

Paislee shook her head and focused on the issue at hand—making sure that the puppies from McCormac were healthy.

"I think Thor is fine, but I'm glad ye stopped by. Your mum had plans tae take the SUV today, saying that McCormac would want her tae have it." Sula's lip lifted as if she wasn't believing that for a hot minute.

"She did?" Amelia snapped photos of Thor's information to save to her mobile. "Mum can be . . ."

Greedy?

"Well, you tell her what ye saw here. It wasnae my fault that it's not here now." Sula grabbed Amelia's fingers and squeezed. "The police have it impounded."

"I will," Amelia assured her. "Sula, can you tell us anything aboot who might want McCormac, well, dead?"

"I've been thinking aboot this," the young woman murmured low, as if the walls of her flat were bugged. "And I bet it was the Irish mob."

Paislee sucked in a breath. "What?"

Amelia shook her head. "No way."

"Or a gang," Sula said, her eyes wide. "McCormac did time. You meet the wrong influences in jail."

"He turned a new leaf!" Amelia said, her hand to her heart.

"I know you want tae believe that, but . . ." Sula got up and dipped out of sight again, probably going to her bedroom that she'd shared with McCormac. When she returned, she gave Amelia the gold watch he'd been wearing. "Here."

Amelia studied it. "A Rolex. A knockoff?"

"I think it's legit," Sula said. "You should have it, Amelia. McCormac loved ye so much and he was verra proud of you."

Amelia's fingers closed over the watch, and she bowed her head.

"Thank you. That means so much right now," Amelia said.

"But whatever he was doing, was it above the law tae afford

such nice things?" Sula shrugged and tugged a diamond necklace from where it had been hidden behind her shirt.

Amelia gasped.

"I know," Sula said. "And I'm keeping this one too. Your mother doesnae need tae know a thing aboot it. Not the watch either. Let her keep the puppies."

"She's going tae sell them," Paislee said. The shine on the diamond was lovely. It wasn't a cheap knockoff either. "Sula, what do you think he was up tae?"

"I'm serious aboot the mob—laugh if you want tae, but McCormac said there was more money where this came from." Her hand closed around the jewel.

"You didnae ask?" Amelia wondered.

"No! Do I look stupid?" Sula shook her head. "I know nothing that could land me in trouble with the law, or the mob."

Paislee wondered if there was truth in her words. "How long have you and McCormac been together? That's a lovely gift."

"We'd dated a little before he went tae jail. I wrote tae him while he was away. Two years apart is nothin'," Sula said. "I have all the male attention I could want."

Amelia studied the gold watch in her hand.

"Were you exclusive?" Paislee asked.

"McCormac didnae know how tae be exclusive." Sula shrugged. "Again, I didnae ask too many questions."

Paislee wouldn't be able to live that way. She'd care a great deal if her significant other was cheating on her.

"Did you know McCormac was coming home for Christmas?" Paislee asked.

"No!" Sula said. "It was an amazing surprise. Did you, Amelia?"

"He texted around the middle of December." Amelia drummed her fingers to the folder. "But not aboot the puppies. Or the gifts. It is a beautiful necklace."

Sula smiled, pleased to have been chosen for something so special.

Paislee thought that it was sad. Sula loved McCormac while McCormac loved the ladies.

"Oops!" Sula stood. "I was going tae make us tea and call the station aboot the tow truck."

Paislee looked at Amelia, hoping that could be their cue to go. They still had to stop by the Henry home.

"We should get going," Amelia said. She patted the folder and scratched Thor under the chin. "I'll talk with Mum aboot the SUV, so she doesnae bother you, awright?"

"Thanks a million." Sula tucked the pendant under her shirt again. "I'll owe you one. She threatened bodily harm if I didnae give her the keys."

Amelia sighed. "Sairy. Will you let me know if Thor gets sick? It was kennel cough, and if they were raised together, he might get it, so just listen for a little wheeze in his chest."

"You're so sweet, Amelia." Sula touched Amelia's shoulder. "I see why McCormac loved you."

"He was my favorite," Amelia said with a downcast gaze. "I really hope that everything he did was aboveboard."

Sula scrunched her nose. "My expectations are not as high," she said. "However, he said that he checked oot the breeders in Inverness, as suggested by the woman in Belfast. Met the vet in the Highlands. *I* think he bought them all at a discount and then was selling them to make his money back. Except for the ones he gifted to us for Christmas. He must've started off with a lot more."

Amelia nodded. "That's not illegal. Risky, depending on how much he paid, but I guess money wasnae really a problem due tae his job as a luxury-car salesman."

"No." Sula smiled, seeming to be happy with their conclusions. "That must be right. I'll ask Dougie what he knows."

"Thanks," Amelia said.

"Shall we?" Paislee stepped toward the door. "Do your folks live around here, Amelia?" She was hoping to get the unpleasant experience over with.

"Yeah. In the old neighborhood where we all grew up." Sula gave an exaggerated shudder. "It was trial by fire between drugs and gangs."

"True," Amelia said.

Paislee reached the door but stopped when Sula said, "Me and Porche used tae be best friends back in the day."

"The Porche with the brother Hank, who slugged McCormac?" Paislee wanted to be clear who the participants were. Porche was an unusual name, but not that unusual.

"Same." Sula scowled. "Porche always thought she was so much better than me. Served her right for me tae take McCormac right oot from under her nose."

Chapter 10

Paislee didn't get a chance to reply as Amelia nudged her out the door with a wave of thanks to Sula. "Stay in touch," Amelia said, then shut the door. "Hurry."

With a press of her key fob, Paislee unlocked the Juke.

Once she was behind the wheel, she turned to Amelia. "That didn't sound very nice at all. I'm glad you got the watch, rather than your mum. You won't give it tae her, will you?"

"No. It was nice—and Sula is mostly, but when it comes tae McCormac, well, she was always a complete numpty."

Being in love could make people act like idiots. It was a common theme in romantic comedies.

Or murder.

Paislee stared at Amelia. "Your brother was shot in the chest. The heart."

Amelia's brows rose. "Not by Sula! She's afraid of her own shadow."

"All right." Though Paislee wasn't fooled by the sweet face and blond ponytail. "What about Hank, or Porche?"

"The physical fighting is more Hank's style," Amelia said. "Fists. I cannae imagine anyone being mad enough tae shoot, actually. Where would someone get a gun? They arenae just available on every corner."

Paislee started the car. "I don't know."

"Not even the constables have guns," Amelia continued. "Gangs. Irish mob? Sula sounded so serious. You dinnae mess with the mob."

"What is your parents' address?" Paislee looked at her friend, who was all sorts of panicked.

"*Och.*" Amelia stared at the watch in her hand. "Let's go back tae my place instead."

While Paislee would very much love that idea, it wasn't practical, and Amelia was without a vehicle and couldn't just change her mind later. "Don't you want tae see for yourself if the dogs are sick?"

Amelia's body sagged in the passenger seat. "Fine. I told the vet that I'd check. Thor looked great though, didnae he? He seemed bigger than Snowball. I am worried. And we told Sula we'd call my mother off. Mum can be such a bully. McCormac used tae protect me when they'd get pished and try tae use me as a punching bag."

"Ah, Amelia." Paislee couldn't imagine anyone hitting a child.

"Da would yell 'spare the rod, spoil the child' but never got tae the spoiling part." Amelia rubbed her nose. "But they're still family, even if they are eejits."

Amelia rattled off an address and Paislee put it in the GPS. Five blocks away.

"Where did Hank, and Porche, grow up?"

"We were all within a few blocks. I think Hank still lives in the family home. At least Porche and Sula moved oot."

"Sula is trying tae better herself. What does she do for work?"

"She's a stripper."

Paislee snapped her mouth shut.

Amelia laughed. "She makes verra guid money and doesnae do more than take her clothes off, according tae McCormac. It makes me sad tae hear her talk aboot loving him when I know he was just usin' her."

"For a place tae stay?"

"And the benefits," Amelia said.

Paislee hated that the comment made her blush.

"Turn here," the GPS directed.

The neighborhood was older and not as kept up as many portions of Nairn. Poverty hovered like a storm cloud.

"It's no wonder that McCormac, or my folks, skirted the law . . . there's been generations of Henrys makin' bad decisions."

"But you broke the cycle, Amelia. It is their choice too. What do you think about his involvement with the mob?"

"I cannae see it." Amelia glared at the gold watch, as if daring it to speak up and defend her brother. Maybe he'd bought it legitimately.

Paislee cruised to a stop before a row of attached homes, each two stories, with ten units. An older truck was parked in front of the address Amelia had given her.

"Michael's ride," Amelia said. "Now, just follow my lead. We'll be quick aboot it." Before she got out, she put the Rolex in the glove compartment of the Juke. "Mum might smell something nice."

They exited and Paislee locked the door, following Amelia, who knocked even though it was her childhood home.

The thin wood panel, warped, opened and Michael leered at them. "Brought your friend over," he said. "Yer pretty enough for a redhead. Might change me mind if you ask nice."

"Shut your gob," Amelia said, shoving into him.

He backed up, hands raised. He didn't lose the smirk.

Not in a million years.

The interior of the flat was dimly lit. No windows. Like Paislee's place, there were stairs to the right. Unlike her home, boxes and junk were piled high, and barely allowed walking room.

"Mum's in the kitchen." Michael led the way.

The house smelled like dog feces and Paislee worried that the dogs were sick.

Amelia's nose twitched but she didn't say anything, and she gave Paislee a warning look to let her handle things. She would know best how to get around her mother.

"Mum!" Amelia said brightly as they entered the kitchen. "Hey."

Dishes were stacked up in the sink, and dirty pots and pans defied gravity in their placement on the counter.

"Hey yourself." Letitia Henry poured cheap gin from a bottle to a mug. She didn't offer to share.

Everywhere Paislee looked there were boxes stacked, leaning against one another to keep them upright, without success. There wasn't a single holiday decoration or space to put one.

"Where's Da?" Amelia asked.

Paislee didn't see the puppies. The carriers they'd had were out of sight as well, so Paislee hoped they were tucked away somewhere safe.

"On his way home. Taking the train. Didnae realize we were gone till this morning." Letitia scowled at Paislee. "Paislee Shaw."

"Ma'am." Paislee kept her hands in her jacket pockets so she didn't accidentally bump into anything and knock over a stack—she feared it would be a domino effect.

"Mum, we were just at Sula's. The coppers took McCormac's new SUV. Towed it for impound."

"Bastards!" Michael said. "We tried tae see McCormac's body, but they arenae lettin' us yet. Bet they steal his cash from his wallet. How would we know what he's got in there?"

Amelia clenched her jaw, putting her shoulder to her brother. "Yeah. Mibbe."

Paislee bit her tongue but it was hard to not say anything. She wanted to know the puppies were fine and get out fast.

"Why are ye here?" Letitia asked. "Tae tell me aboot the SUV?"

"Aye." Amelia cleared her throat. "My dog was sick, and I was wonderin' how your puppies are faring?"

"Sick?" Michael frowned. "McCormac gave us sick dogs?"

"Mibbe not! Snowball—"

"That's a stupid name," Michael interjected.

"Snowball," Amelia continued, "has kennel cough so it's possible your pups might have it too. There's medicine for it and they will need tae be well before you can sell them. It's expensive but I can cover it."

Smart of Amelia to mention the cost.

"I dinnae like those dogs. Never have been a pet person," Letitia said. "Take 'em, Amelia, and hang ontae them for us until we can unload them. The mongrels were pissin' everywhere."

"Yeah." Michael scowled belligerently at Amelia. "I stuck 'em outside."

Paislee straightened, thinking of the cold weather and worried they'd not have proper shelter. "That's where they are now?"

Amelia punched her brother's arm. "McCormac got the brains. I hope they're okay and not frozen tae death."

"They smelled! Made a mess everywhere." Michael rubbed his arm.

"How long?" Paislee asked.

"Just now, so zip it." Michael glared at Paislee.

Amelia strode down the hall, leading the way to the back door. There was no porch, just a wooden landing. Both dog crates were there.

Michael had followed them. "We want the full amount when we sell them, Amelia. Dinnae think you can short us."

"I willnae," Amelia said. She bent down and peered into the crates. "Hey puppy. Paislee, do ye mind carrying the other one?"

"Not at all. Maybe we should go around the side of the building?" Rather than try the maze of the Henry living conditions.

"Aye."

"I'll be checkin' in," Michael shouted as they went down the stairs.

Amelia muttered something under her breath that was almost as inventive as Sula's curses had been, involving his genitalia.

They reached the Juke and Paislee opened the hatch to put the carriers inside. She opened the crate, and the pup licked her hand. The eyes were clear. "Oh, you are a cutie. But so tiny!"

Amelia said, "Let's go tae my place and assess. Hurry before Mum changes her mind. It would be just like her tae tease."

No other explanation was necessary, and Paislee shut the hatch and got behind the wheel. Amelia recalled the watch and put it in her pocket. Fifteen minutes later they were at Amelia's flat.

They each brought a carrier inside. Paislee took out the tiny pup in a pink collar, who shivered. She fit in the palm of Paislee's hand. Paislee wrapped the sweetie in her cashmere scarf to keep warm.

"How's the male?" Paislee asked.

"I've been calling him Robbie, and her Daisy," Amelia said, bringing Robbie to her nose. The pup gave her a lick and wagged his body.

"We were there just in time. I'm sorry that I said anything, but I was kind of in shock." The puppies were so small that things could have been very different right now.

"It's no bother." Amelia scratched Robbie under the belly. "Mum must've dropped Michael on his head."

Paislee didn't say anything to that. "Should we call the vet?"

Amelia considered this and shook her head. "I think they're fine other than cold. Obviously, a different litter."

"So, no germs exchanged?" Paislee suggested.

"I hope so." Amelia crossed the flat to the landline. "No messages from anyone. Isnae it like that, when you want news?"

Paislee smiled, cradling Daisy. "It seems tae be that way."

"I wonder how Snowball is?" Amelia got a dish towel from a drawer next to her sink and wrapped Robbie tight. His shivers eased.

Daisy was quite content in her cashmere. "You could call Dr. MacTavish."

"Do ye think he'd mind?" Amelia appeared worried.

"Not at all. That's his job."

Amelia laughed. "I'm an idiot." Sure enough, Dr. MacTavish answered right away—but he seemed annoyed that Amelia didn't trust him. He said Snowball was sleeping just fine.

Paislee sat on the couch with Daisy.

"The other puppies are also well. I'll phone in the morning," Amelia said. "Thank you!" She ended the call and scowled. "That wasnae comforting. I felt like I was bothering him. My brother paid ahead for a visit—do you think he's worried he willnae get money for takin' care of Snowball?"

"I think you should focus all of that mama-bear energy on these two munchkins and pick up Snowball in the morning."

Amelia sighed. "Fine." She tucked Robbie close to her chest and the pup almost purred with contentment. His ears pointed straight up.

"They are so adorable, but I'd worry that I'd step on one." Daisy was hardly bigger than Paislee's fist.

"Right?" Amelia switched on her electric kettle. "I could use some tea—how aboot you?"

Paislee checked the time on her phone. "How did it get tae be three in the afternoon?" She'd missed pizza for lunch and was hungry for dinner, whatever Grandpa whipped up.

"You cannae leave yet."

"Why not?"

"Because."

Paislee studied her friend closely, but Amelia wasn't meeting her eyes.

"What is it?" Paislee's shoulders tensed.

"I want tae show you something, but you have tae promise not tae overreact, or tae tell Payne or Zeffer."

Paislee shook her head. "I can't promise that!" She was a rule-follower. Boring. Safe. But now that Amelia had spoken, her curiosity was at high mast.

Amelia made them mugs of tea but left them in the kitchen.

"I have tae show you. You're the only person that I can trust." Amelia headed down the hall.

Paislee followed but she was very wary as she entered Amelia's bedroom.

"I let McCormac sleep in here while I took the couch for the two days he was with me," Amelia said. "I found this shoved under my bed."

Amelia placed the pup on the middle of the mattress, and Robbie waggled his little body. Paislee set Daisy next to him and the pair snuggled up immediately, two halves of one whole, the size of Brody's shoe.

Amelia pulled out a suitcase and sat back on her heels.

"It's not mine, obviously, and it wasnae locked." Amelia opened it.

Paislee brought her hand to her mouth. She had an icky feeling. "McCormac's?"

"Yeah." Amelia turned the case so Paislee could see it.

Stacks of money. No note. No clothes to cover the stash. Just cash.

"I can't believe it," Paislee said. Where on earth would he have gotten this kind of money?

Amelia stared at Paislee. "Me either. I need you tae tell me a few guid reasons why my brother would have all this cash."

Paislee shook her head, speechless.

Amelia blew out a breath. "That's what I was afraid of."

The mob connection that Sula suspected made more sense. "Whoever that belongs tae will want it back," Paislee said.

"I dinnae want it!" Amelia raised her hands, sitting back once more on her heels.

"What I mean is that you could be in danger, Amelia." She stared hard at her friend, who shook her head.

"I said no constables. No detectives. This belongs tae McCormac."

"I'm worried about *you* now." Her friend had overcome so much to be the decent young woman she was now.

Amelia slowly closed the lid and shoved it back under her bed. "I'll be fine."

Famous last words.

Chapter 11

"Fine. I hate that word," Paislee said. "It gets me intae a lot of trouble."

Amelia stood. "I'm sairy tae be a bother. I guess, well, I need tae give McCormac the benefit of the doot."

"A suitcase of money, though?" Paislee crossed her arms.

"Could be his savings. Could be what he needed tae buy the puppies tae sell. Could be what he earned from his car salesman commissions." Amelia picked up Robbie and tucked him under her chin. "What's the value for these designer puppies?"

"I don't know. When we bought Wallace, it was love at first sight in the pet shop window."

"Let's check it oot. Do some recon." Amelia, with the pup, left the bedroom and flicked off the light. Paislee quickly scooped Daisy off the bed and followed her friend to the living room.

Amelia brought out a laptop and sat on the couch, patting for Paislee to sit next to her.

"Should you see what the Pomeranians are worth?" Paislee asked, her back to the cushion.

"Aye." In the search bar, Amelia queried the average cost for a purebred Pomeranian and her mouth rounded at the figure listed. "Twenty-five hundred pounds."

"That's steep. Try Maltese."

Amelia put the breed in the search bar. "Two thousand, give or take. Not as much. What aboot the one that Sula had?"

"A Brussels griffon." Thor was cute in a shaggy-whiskered way.

"Whoa! This is pay dirt," Amelia said.

"How much?" Paislee patted Daisy, amazed at how trusting the tiny pup was in her hand.

"Four thousand. And they have health problems, so they're expensive tae maintain. I cannae believe it." Amelia shook her head. "It's the homeliest, in me humble opinion."

No puppy could actually be ugly, but Paislee conceded that Snowball was prettier. "What's the grand total in that suitcase?"

"I didnae count it, but they were hundreds."

Paislee stared at her friend, willing her to call Constable Payne. "McCormac would have had tae sell a lot of puppies tae get so much cash."

"It's got tae be from his car sales." Amelia chucked Robbie's chin.

"Sula wondered if he had tae front the money for the puppies and then sell them tae make a profit."

"Makes sense." Amelia slammed the lid to her laptop closed. "Mum willnae be happy that she has the Maltese that are the least expensive."

"Maybe don't tell her?" Paislee suggested. Her phone dinged for the second time.

"You're right. She doesnae even own a computer so she will have tae believe me. Mibbe. She's not the most trustin' woman."

"Michael?" Paislee glanced at her phone and shook her head. Her family was getting hungry and worried about where she was.

"He'd rat me oot in a heartbeat. But, he's lazy," Amelia said. "He might do a wee bit more research, though not much."

"Listen, I've got tae get home. Grandpa and Brody have both texted about dinner."

"I'm sairy tae have kept you away."

"Not tae worry," Paislee said. "Please be careful. Maybe hide that money?"

"I'm a mess," Amelia said, gesturing to the game system by the large telly. "I'm going tae play video games for the rest of the night. I have work tomorrow. Not havin' me car is really starting tae be a grind."

"When will it be fixed?"

"Next week," Amelia said. "Constable Payne is picking me up on his way tae the station."

"I'll drive you home after Knit and Sip," Paislee offered.

"Thanks. And thank ye, Paislee, for all of yer help today."

Paislee put the snuggly puppy next to Robbie on Amelia's lap with a bit of reluctance. "Welcome. Don't get up. I can let myself out."

Amelia waved as Paislee left, making sure that Amelia's door was locked. How much money was in that secret suitcase?

Not her concern. As Paislee drove home, she talked briefly with Hamish, who was an amazing son to make sure that his mother was set up to manage for herself when he was gone. Neighbors would check on her for him. It would be March before he went back again.

They had a loose date for Saturday night, and it was his turn to pick the restaurant.

She arrived home at half past five and parked in the carport. Snow would be a nice change to the cold. But they'd had snow for Christmas, which mattered most. She couldn't imagine spending a holiday in Key West.

What did they make instead of snowmen? Sandmen?

She hurried inside the house and breathed in the savory scents of rosemary and lamb. Fresh bread.

"I'm home!" Paislee called from the foyer. She removed her coat and hung it up.

"In the kitchen," Brody replied.

Wallace raced to meet her in the hall and gave her pants and shoes a diligent sniff as he detected interesting new puppies.

"Hey, boy." She scratched his head and walked to the kitchen, placing her handbag on her chair.

"Paislee, lass," Grandpa said, putting the casserole dish on a trivet on the kitchen table. "Perfect timing."

"We were goin' tae eat withoot you," Brody declared as if put out by her tardiness.

"That would've been fair." Paislee arched her brow at her son as a caution to mind his manners. "Sorry, Grandpa, I forgot the paper. I meant tae be home much earlier."

"What were you doin'?" Brody asked in a calmer tone. He was probably hangry and growing again.

"I was with Amelia. The puppies her brother gave as Christmas gifts are seriously valued at two thousand pounds or more. I thought McCormac had been exaggerating, but no. And Sula's is worth over four."

"But Thor was the ugliest," Brody said.

"He's called a Brussels griffon." Paislee washed her hands before joining them at the table.

"It's grand ye had a day with your friend," Grandpa said. "Dinnae fash—the paper will be delivered tomorrow."

"Ta." Paislee smiled at her grandfather with gratitude. "This looks really good. I had a granola bar for breakfast and ice cream for lunch."

"Nutritious!" Grandpa laughed.

"Not fair," Brody said with a slight pout, no doubt regarding the ice cream, but he recovered. "I think I'm tired of watching movies."

"I don't believe it." This holiday had been a wee break they'd all needed to recharge. "Are you ready for school?"

"Mum!"

"I'll take that as a no," Paislee said with a laugh. "What about you, Grandpa? You tired of movies?"

He squeezed his thumb and forefinger together. "A tiny bit."

"Who's up for a game of cards after we eat?" Paislee suggested.

"Me!" Brody yelled.

Santa had brought numerous family games. They were a lot of fun, with Brody being old enough to play and understand not only the rules but strategy.

After dinner, Paislee did the dishes. She was clearing the table and accidentally knocked her handbag over, spilling the letters from her mother onto the floor.

Eagle-eye Brody focused on the scrawled writing in marker and snapped it up. "Who's this from?"

"Never mind," she said, trying to get them back. Perspiration dotted her skin as if she had to avoid a collision from her past to her present.

Grandpa looked up from the stack of games with interest. "A boyfriend?"

"Boyfriend?" Brody dropped the letters to the table. "Yuck!"

"Not at all, Shaws." Paislee swallowed and tried to be nonchalant as she explained their origin. "Mum. In America."

"Your mum uses crayons?" Brody asked with a curled lip.

"No." Paislee scruffed the top of his hair. "Your gran, well." She took a deep breath. "Grandma Rosanna has two other kids besides me."

Grandpa stopped smiling to study Paislee, going so far as to remove his glasses.

"Their names are Josh and Natalie." She pressed her finger to the dancing pulse at her throat. "Natalie is nine, and Josh is eight."

"Whoa." Brody's jaw gaped. "I'm older."

"You're just now finding oot aboot them?" Grandpa stroked his beard.

"She'd mentioned them briefly . . . I didn't know if they knew about me." Paislee shrugged and placed her hand over her tummy as the lamb and tattie casserole she'd consumed whirled like a blizzard. "Seems they do."

"Am I related tae them?" Brody asked, confused.

Paislee realized that perhaps, in not really having a relationship with her mother beyond the occasional card on a birthday and Christmas, Brody didn't "know" his grandmother as anything beyond a faraway figure. It's not as if she'd sent gifts or cash to put in an account for Brody.

Her mum hadn't been interested when Paislee had confessed her pregnancy, and hadn't come back to Nairn in thirteen years. Brody had never met her mother. They'd had Gran, and now Grandpa. Faith that she'd done the right thing sorted, Paislee exhaled and faced Brody and her grandfather.

Grandpa's silvery brows arched to his scalp. He didn't get to be shocked. Paislee raised her finger at him. "You knew Rosanna. You know what she did." Damn her legs for trembling. She leaned against the kitchen table.

Grandpa compressed his lips and kept quiet; surprise, surprise.

"I want tae meet them!" Brody said.

"Em . . . I don't know. They live in America." That couldn't happen. It would upset her carefully balanced life here in Nairn.

"Let's invite them tae see the new kitchen. I'll share my room."

Paislee shook her head. "Calm down, Brody. My mum and I aren't close, all right?"

That tone must have reached something in her son's excitement, as he gave her a random hug. "Do ye miss her?"

Paislee didn't, really, but the appeal for contact from her siblings tugged at her heartstrings. She didn't answer.

"You gotta love her," Brody said, his arm still loose around her waist. "She's yer mum."

That wasn't an automatic. Was Rosanna Shaw as bad as Letitia

Henry on the sliding scale of motherhood? But, if she didn't say yes, she'd set a bad example. How to explain that not all mothers were the same? She and Brody had a relationship built on honesty.

"It's complicated," Paislee decided. She gave her son a squeeze of pure maternal love that he'd never had a reason to doubt and stepped toward the pantry for emergency chocolate.

"Can I read the letters?" Brody asked.

"Aye." Paislee found some dark chocolate sleighs and brought them to the table. "There aren't notes really, just their names and wishing us a happy Christmas. Asking us tae write back. Merry Christmas. They're American." She popped a bite into her mouth and let the bittersweet melt over her tongue and soothe her jangled nerves.

"Mum, we should go tae America." Brody picked up the card wishing Paislee a happy birthday.

Grandpa unwrapped a sleigh for himself. "Where do they live, lass?"

Was he thinking Florida, and his son Craigh? Paislee offered the envelope. "Arizona. Phoenix."

"Is that like here?" Brody asked.

"Why don't we look it up?" Paislee suggested. She didn't have a clue. Her mother had moved around quite a bit and Paislee hadn't allowed herself to care.

Brody brought the laptop to the table and opened it. "Phoenix, Arizona."

She and Grandpa read over Brody's shoulder as he said, "Phoenix is verra hot. It has desert and red rocks. It's famous for year-round sun."

"Completely different from Nairn." Grandpa glanced at Paislee.

"We should go," Brody said again.

Paislee thought of a million reasons why they shouldn't. "It's not a good idea."

"Why?" Brody closed the page.

"I have work." Paislee rounded the table and went to the tea station to heat the kettle. "You have school."

"What aboot summer holiday?" Brody insisted.

Exasperated, Paislee said, "We haven't been invited."

At that, Brody stopped badgering her. Then he asked, "Dinnae they want tae know me?" The idea that he had a family that might not want to know him was a foreign concept.

Her mother had deserted her at a critical time when Paislee could have used a parent. Her da had died when she was sixteen, in a boating accident. Her mum had left, the second Paislee had finished secondary school.

She'd fallen in love with an American, married him, and never returned. When Paislee had discovered that she was pregnant, her mum told her she had a choice to make. If it was up to her, Rosanna, she would not keep the babe. And, don't expect for her to take care of Paislee's kid. She'd done her time.

So, it was double the heartache to find out that her mum had two more kids after her suggestion to Paislee. She couldn't forgive that.

Grandpa tilted his head, not privy to her thoughts.

"If it wasn't for Gran, I would have been alone." Paislee cupped her mug to her chest.

Brody pouted, thinking of family he didn't know, near his age. "Can we call them, at least?"

Paislee remained at a loss. Call them? "I don't have their phone number," she said.

"You dinnae have yer own mum's mobile?" Brody asked in complete disbelief.

"Rosanna Shaw knows the landline here. Sorry, Rosie *Hartford* knows the number. It hasn't changed." Paislee blew on the hot liquid in her mug. "I told you it was complicated."

Brody read the envelope and the address. "We can find the number, I bet."

It was brutal that Brody wouldn't let it go. She could sense that Grandpa was on the side of building a relationship with them, though he didn't say so. Desperate, she said, "How about you write a letter tae them?"

She hoped that such a daunting task like writing would put him off, but instead, Brody went to the craft closet and brought out supplies.

"Let's make a card for them." Brody selected construction paper and markers.

"Grand idea," Grandpa seconded.

"Really?" Paislee said, hurt.

"Family," Grandpa countered.

Paislee sat at the table and tugged the laptop toward her, putting her mother's first and last name and the address in the search bar, doing a reverse lookup online. She was able to find a phone number. Her mouth dried when she found her mother's social media pages.

"This is her," she said, staring at the screen. It was like a ghost had sprung to existence and her brain was about to short-circuit at all the information. Her mother was strawberry blond, with the same ice-blue eyes as Paislee. Trim. Happy. The influx of images made her angry and sad both. This woman had had a full life that didn't include her—by her mum's choice.

"Lemme see!" Brody jumped up. He leaned into her side to share her chair and she breathed in the scent of his shampoo. This was real.

Grandpa peered over Paislee's shoulder. "Ah. She hasnae changed much. Are those her bairns?"

Paislee's siblings had light brown hair. Natalie had blue eyes and Josh brown. Her mother looked youthful. Happy.

When Rosanna had left Nairn, she'd been miserable. Crying all the time about the loss of her husband. It didn't matter that Paislee had also lost a father.

"How old is she?" Grandpa asked.

"Forty-nine." Paislee's heart thudded as if overworked, and she'd just turned thirty.

"Nineteen when she had you."

Paislee scowled at Grandpa over her shoulder. "Yeah. I was *eighteen* when I had Brody."

Brody zoomed in on the pictures of Natalie and Josh.

"I meant, that Rosanna was verra young. She still is," Grandpa said. "Could be she was verra emotional aboot Bruce's death. It hit us all hard."

Paislee couldn't forget that her grandparents had lost a son. The pain of that would be too much to bear. "I suppose."

"Mibbe ye could take that intae consideration as you comb through your memories. I'm not sayin' what Rosanna did was right, Paislee"—Grandpa put his hand on her shoulder and squeezed—"but perhaps ye could look at what happened with compassion?"

Paislee shook her head. "She ran, Grandpa."

"Ran?" Brody asked.

She swallowed.

"What I mean is that after my da passed away, I was still in secondary. Grandma Rosanna went a wee bit mental and left me."

"Left you?" Brody's nose turned up in disapproval.

"I moved in with Gran."

Brody hugged Paislee tight. "And had me."

"You are the biggest blessing in my life," Paislee told her son, meaning every word. She wouldn't do a thing differently.

"Mibbe you are yer mum's too." Brody studied the picture on social media of his grandma and his aunt and uncle at a fall fair in Phoenix.

That would be so not true. How to get beyond this conversation?

"Listen. Let's write a letter tae them, all right? Let them know who you are, and I'll mail it with some pictures." Paislee stared into his astute brown eyes. "I don't know that I'm ready for a phone call."

"Okay." He slipped from her chair to return to his own seat. "I love you, Mum."

"Brody, lad, I love you." What wouldn't she do for her only child?

They spent the rest of the evening playing board games and didn't discuss America once.

Chapter 12

Paislee was glad to sleep in on Thursday morning, as they'd stayed up late playing cards, listening to music, and laughing. No talk of America, no talk of McCormac's demise, or the sick pup.

When she'd been Brody's age, Paislee recalled simmering tension in their home. She blamed Grandpa for questioning her memories. Had her mother been unhappy? Had it been caused by her da's death, or had it been a constant?

The smile, relaxed and happy, on her mother's social media pages wasn't something she'd seen before.

The fact that her mother had social media blew her away. It never had occurred to her until yesterday that she could find Rosanna Shaw Hartford.

She needed Lydia, so sent her bestie a text over tea, around ten.

Mum's on social media. Rosanna Hartford. And I have two siblings younger than Brody.

Her phone rang.

"You're kidding!" Lydia said. "Hang on, I'm pullin' her up."

"And good morning tae you too," Paislee said with a laugh.

"I'm at the office already. Made a brilliant sale yesterday. Also, showed Zeffer around. His lease will be up in February. I asked him aboot McCormac, what happened that night, but the man can keep a secret like a bank vault. I think the DI might be loaded."

"One awful subject at a time, please." Paislee went to the pantry and dug through the boxes for some chocolate biscuits. It was going to be that kind of day.

"Well, Rosanna hasnae really changed, has she? And that's your brother and sister? They're supercute, Paislee. Adorable. Cannae be mad at faces that sweet."

"I'm not!" Not at the bairns. Her mother's choices weren't their fault, but she couldn't have one without the other.

"What brought this on?" Lydia asked.

"Went tae the post office yesterday about the mail and the letters were there. One of the kids had written in marker that smeared, so the address was hard tae read."

"Natalie is the spitting image of you," Lydia said. "With those gorgeous eyes."

Paislee sipped her tea to swallow the biscuit that had gotten stuck in her throat.

"Her status says married," Lydia continued. "Why no pictures of her husband?"

"I don't know." Paislee got up and refilled the mug with hot water, the teabag good for another cup, peering out the kitchen window. The sky was gray, the chestnut tree visible. Grandpa was still in his room, and Brody in his. They'd better enjoy this lazy morn because Monday the Shaw family schedule started in full force.

"I'll find him, dinnae worry," Lydia promised.

"I wasn't!" Paislee returned to the table, her shoulders heavy.

"You have a stepdad. And siblings. You got a letter?"

"Two. Brody saw them when they fell from my handbag."

"What does he think?"

"He wants tae meet them," Paislee said. "But he has no idea how Mum can be."

"It's been over twelve, almost thirteen, years." Lydia stated that fact as if testing the water to see how Paislee felt about it.

"Mum looks happy, eh?" Her nose stung and she rubbed the tip. "A lot happier than when she was here."

"I hear that tone, Paislee Ann."

"What tone?"

"You're aboot tae cry. It's okay. Should I come over?"

"No!" Paislee sniffed and patted the ache in her chest. "You don't know."

"I know you as well as I know meself. I remember when Rosanna left and wasnae supportive of you having Brody."

"That's a nice way tae say that she suggested I not fall intae the same *trap* she did, motherhood at a young age."

"You have every right tae be upset, but mibbe it's time tae forgive. You havenae forgotten, so it's not like you ignoring her is makin' her go away."

"Until yesterday, I didn't know if her family even knew about me, Lyd." Her stomach clenched. She sipped her tea and broke off a piece of biscuit.

"That must have been a shock."

"It was." Paislee couldn't stop herself from picturing Josh and Natalie, perhaps here at the table, with Brody.

"Why didnae you call?"

"Just busy. Amelia's car is in the shop. Her puppy was sick, so I drove her tae the vet in the Highlands."

"Has she mentioned any progress on McCormac's murder?"

"No. She thinks Payne might be giving her the runaround. I met her mum. It's a miracle that Amelia didn't get stuck in that life. Her da is a hoarder and has boxes everywhere. They want tae sell the puppies rather than keep them. They aren't really pet people, so I think it's a good idea."

"What's wrong with the puppy?" Lydia asked.

"Kennel cough. Snowball is staying overnight for medicine at the vet. I should call Amelia and see if she needs a ride."

"Poor Amelia!"

"Right? Well, she has the two puppies for her mum and brother tae keep her company. Michael put them outside in the frigid cold because they were messy. They could have died."

"Eejit." Lydia sighed. "We still on for tonight?"

"Aye. I have a hundred coin purses tae make for Ramsey Castle. Can't believe how popular they are. Easy tae do for a nice profit." She didn't sound so different from McCormac wanting to make money.

Paislee was tempted to tell Lydia about the suitcase of cash but didn't. If Amelia wanted to share over knitting tonight at Cashmere Crush, she would.

"How's Corbin?"

"Amazing. He's so different than his siblings. Corbin told me that since he's been with me, he can see how the family might appear from the outside looking in. A bit full of themselves, is what he meant, and he apologized again for not stickin' up for me. It will never happen again, and it hasnae." Lydia paused and said, "Sometimes you have tae give people another chance."

"If by *people* you mean my mother, well, I will tell you what I told Brody—we can start with a letter and go from there."

"I cannae imagine you not having Brody, so she was wrong. A thousand percent."

"She was. Maybe still is."

"That's the other line—gotta run! Love tae all the Shaws!" Lydia ended the call and Paislee rose to get another teabag after all.

Grandpa stood at the threshold of his door, partially open. From the look on his face, he'd heard her part of the conversation with Lydia and understood what it meant. Her mother had wanted her to get rid of Brody.

Paislee glanced toward the staircase to make sure they were alone. She didn't hear Brody stirring upstairs.

"I believe women have a right tae choose," Paislee said firmly. "Brody was my choice. Gran supported me and that decision, despite my mum, despite my reputation as a single mother, despite me not having many friends—and none that knew what I was going through. Gran taught me the skills tae take care of myself, and Brody. I love her so much. When I think of a mother, that's who is in my heart."

Grandpa enfolded Paislee in a hug. "I'm sairy. I should learn tae butt oot when it's not my business."

He poured himself a mug of tea and helped himself to a chocolate biscuit, dipping the sweet cookie into the tea before popping it in his mouth.

"It's okay. It's just not easy. I want Brody tae know he has family. Can I trust Mum? Does it matter? I won't set Brody up tae get his heart broken."

"As you said, a letter is probably the best way tae start." Grandpa lifted his mug and winked at her. "Or not. Things get lost in the mail all the time."

Paislee laughed, glad that Grandpa had her back.

He shuffled down the hall to the front stoop and brought in the paper. The first thing Paislee read for was an update on McCormac Henry's death, but there wasn't a mention. Paislee looked at Tesco sales, Grandpa read the local news, and separated the comics for Brody.

Amelia sent a text that wee Daisy had the sniffles and she'd tried to call Dr. MacTavish to see how Snowball was doing but he hadn't answered.

Paislee shared Dr. Kathleen McHenry's number to Amelia as a backup for Daisy.

"I still can't get over how much the dogs are worth," Paislee said. "Amelia doesn't want tae believe that her brother fell off the straight and narrow path, but I wonder. He was very slick, so it makes sense he'd excel as a car salesman. Or a puppy salesman. How many dogs would you have tae sell tae make it worthwhile? A car seems more lucrative tae me."

Grandpa grabbed a pen and scrap paper. "What kind of commission? Ten dogs at four thousand pounds at ten percent would only be four hundred, twenty percent would be eight. Eight hundred times ten is eight thousand so isnae chump change. He's a guid salesman."

"Eight thousand is decent." But it didn't equal the cash in the suitcase. Didn't pay for the SUV or diamond necklace or Rolex.

Her phone dinged a text message from Hamish, who wanted to know what her plans were for the day. When she told him ice-skating, he warned her to be careful. She would, but also, she'd been skating since she was a wean.

She checked the time. Ten thirty.

"I'll wake Brody up at eleven. Ice-skating starts at one and we will be home at four thirty. Then I'll go tae Knit and Sip tonight."

"He must be growing again," Grandpa said.

"No!" Paislee shook her head. "I just bought him new clothes." Doc Whyte had predicted Brody would be six feet or more.

"It's the way of things, no sense in being upset aboot it."

"All right, Grandpa, that's enough wise advice for one morning."

That afternoon a very tired Shaw family returned from a fun day on the ice. The indoor rink allowed for all-year skating without the blustery wind.

After a quick shower to warm her bones, Paislee shared a meal of hot chowder with Brody and Grandpa before heading to Cashmere Crush with her bag of knitting projects. The coin purses were fast, and she'd add the metal clasp later. She brought a tin of macadamia nuts and chocolate-covered pretzels to share, along with a bottle of sweet tea.

Paislee arrived before any of the others and parked in the back of her shop, climbing the cement steps. Once inside, she flipped on the lights, seeing a shadow at the front window. She hurried across the polished cement floor to unlock the door.

Amelia was waiting, having walked from the Nairn police station. Her friend's lips were as blue as her eyes, her customary backpack on her shoulder.

"Hey!" Paislee pulled her in and looked down Market Street. Nobody else was around, though the Lion's Mane pub across from them had a full lot of cars. It was too cold to linger.

"Hi." Amelia stomped her feet but there was no snow or dirt on them. It hadn't snowed since New Year's Day.

"I could've picked you up." Paislee had driven by the station on her way.

"It's fine. I needed tae cool off. Zeffer was giving me side-eye all day. Thinking that I know more aboot McCormac's life than I do." Amelia sounded very put out.

"That's not fair."

Her cheeks flushed. "Och, he may have caught me tryin' tae hear what he was saying tae Constable Payne and didnae like it."

That didn't sound good. "You don't want tae be fired!"

"I love me job, but I love my brother more." Amelia put her backpack on a chair and dug out crackers, whisky, and a ball of black yarn with bamboo knitting needles.

"Did you tell Constable Payne about the money in the suitcase?" Paislee arrayed her items on one of the tall tables and put Amelia's contribution next to it.

"No. And you willnae either."

"I won't." Paislee waited a beat. "Any updates about what happened tae McCormac?"

"It's a bleedin' mystery. I did hear them talking aboot McCormac's Mercedes. They were looking for something, and of course, I wondered if it was the cash."

That made sense. When Amelia didn't continue, Paislee changed the subject. "How's Snowball?"

"Dr. MacTavish called back, and he promised that I can pick her up tomorrow, but the cough is bad and contagious, so if I was tae bring her home it might make the other dogs sick." Amelia poured herself a glass of whisky. "I cannae do that tae the wee things."

"That's really sad. And how is Daisy?"

"The same. I asked Dr. MacTavish if he could phone in medicine. He cannae without an examination, so I'm tae keep him apprised of how things are goin' with Daisy. I might be bringing her in tomorrow in exchange for Snowball." Amelia scowled. "It's been a bad day. Mum has no idea how much trouble she's causin' with her phone calls tae the station complaining aboot the lack of progress regarding McCormac. Like I can do anything that I havenae?"

"That puts you in a bind," Paislee commiserated.

Mary Beth arrived next, then Blaise, Meri, and last, Lydia. Mary Beth was dressed in jeans and a red shirt with poinsettias embroidered on the collar.

"I dinnae want the holidays tae ever end." Mary Beth placed a basket of iced sugar cookies on the table. "Who's with me?"

"I'm tired of Christmas carols." Blaise patted Mary Beth's arm, then pulled out a new project she was working on in bright sunshine yellow. "I'm ready for spring."

"Spring!" Lydia raised her hand. She unwrapped a warm cheese dip with assorted cut vegetables.

Meri shrugged. "I'm a winter person through and through." She rounded the tall table to find a space for a shepherd's pie she'd brought. "Paislee?"

"I love the holidays too, but I'm ready for different music on the radio." She smiled at her friends, somewhere in the middle.

Blaise cracked open a can of fizzy water. "Mark your calendars for Burns Night—Shep's making a traditional Burns supper at the house, and you're all invited, bairns too. We've got something special for the kiddos."

January 25th was when the poet Robert Burns had been celebrated for centuries with haggis, poetry, singing, and dancing. It was even a school holiday. "I'll check with Grandpa, but Brody and I will be there." Blaise's husband, Shep, was a golf pro and taught golf at the local course. They'd moved from Inverness to Nairn and fit right in.

Meri, a more recent addition than Blaise, gave Amelia a hug. "How are you doin', pet? Any news aboot McCormac?"

"I'm so sairy, Amelia—I completely blocked the tragedy from my mind." Mary Beth wrapped Amelia to her ample bosom. "Is there anything I can do?"

"No, but thank you," Amelia said. She stepped back from the hug, her eyes welling though the tears didn't spill.

"Arran told me he's willing tae help in any way. I think he feels responsible, being there with McCormac at the end," Mary Beth said.

"He's not at all!" Amelia's eyes rounded with shock. "I've been meaning tae call him tae thank him, actually, but I've been rather blue."

"Understandably so!" Blaise said.

"I'm sairy too, love." Lydia filled a tumbler with whisky, Amelia's drink of choice, and handed it to her. "It's a shame. I'm sure the constables will find who is responsible."

"I hope they do, but I was at the station all day and didnae see any progress." Amelia nodded her thanks at Lydia and accepted the whisky. "I heard Zeffer and Payne murmuring aboot McCormac's Mercedes that they'd impounded. Zeffer saw me near the office door, so he's not pleased."

"It's not wrong tae want answers aboot what happened tae your own brother," Mary Beth declared.

"If the DI isnae talking tae ye, then of course you're going tae be curious," Meri agreed. "They should know that and include you."

"DI Zeffer was commenting tae Payne how Henrys have been smugglers for centuries and he wondered if McCormac was bringing drugs from Ireland."

"Drugs?" Paislee shook her head.

The unwavering support and friendship of these ladies meant Amelia wouldn't be alone through this misfortune and they'd all do what they could. Paislee was grateful for the love in this knitting circle.

"Thank you all." Amelia sipped from her tumbler, her shoulders not as high with tension as they had been.

Paislee's phone dinged and she read a message from their missing member, Elspeth. "Elspeth can't make it but will see us next week. She's training with the guide dog instructor and Susan's dog, Rosie. I hope the instructor helps them work together rather than being at odds."

"Elspeth is a verra guid sister," Lydia said. "Not many people would welcome someone into their home who was crabbit all the time."

According to Elspeth, Susan's mood swings were the root of their disagreements, though they all knew how hard Elspeth tried, which seemed to just make things worse.

"We enjoyed speaking with Susan verra much at your open house, Paislee," Mary Beth said. "She's quite educated, did you know? She lost her vision due tae a rare eye disease, poor dear."

"Her dog, Rosie, was verra well-behaved at the party," Meri said. "And I've just gotten tae know Susan a wee bit. She seems nice."

"Then the dog is working," Lydia said with a wink.

The ladies all brought out their projects and talked over the holiday activities they'd been busy with, and Paislee's new kitchen was the first topic.

"Paislee," Mary Beth said, "I love the layoot of your kitchen!"

"It's a dream, honestly. If you ever need Lydia tae design something for you, I highly recommend her. I have the cutest little tea station." Paislee lifted her bottle of sweet tea in a toast to Lydia. "*Sláinte.*"

Lydia raised her glass of pinot grigio in return. "My pleasure."

"My favorite part is the window over the sink, which gives a view of the back porch and a portion of the garden." Even though Scotland deserved its reputation for dreich weather, natural light made a difference to Paislee's mood. "I had no idea what I was missing."

"I thought you'd say it was the new washer/dryer combo that actually dries your multiplying socks." Lydia laughed with delight.

Paislee finished a coin purse, setting it aside to be assembled with the clasp later. "Lydia, I like the way clothes smell when they're outside on the line tae dry, but I admit it was splendid tae have the tablecloths from the party washed and dried like magic overnight."

Her friends chuckled, except for Amelia, whose lower lip trembled.

"I'd like some elves tae do my laundry," Meri quipped. "If we're makin' wishes."

Amelia stabbed the knitting needles into the ball of yarn in her lap as she burst into a torrent of tears. "I wish that me brother was still alive. I wish me dog wasnae sick. I wish . . . I wish that McCormac had *truly* turned over a new leaf."

Chapter 13

Friday morning, Paislee's last for sleeping in during this holiday break, she was awakened by a series of texts and phone calls. Her phone was on silent so that she could sleep, but a sixth sense of some kind made her sit up and reach for her phone on the night-stand.

Amelia?

She'd just dropped the lass off at ten the night before, the knit-ting circle commiserating with Amelia about McCormac's possible but unproven misdeeds, and it was now . . . well, eight. Eight wasn't the crack of dawn. Her shoulders lowered and she shot off a text.

Are you all right?

An immediate reply: **Come over! I think someone tried to break in.**

Call the police.

Can't.

Paislee deep-sighed and dressed on hyper-speed. She stuffed her hair under a cap, brushed her teeth, and grabbed her keys, hoping that she didn't wake her family. She wished she had some means of self-defense, but not only did Scotland ban guns, even pepper spray was illegal. Criminals in London carried around jars of acid as weapons rather than knives, because the consequences weren't as severe if caught.

Once in the car, which didn't want to go anywhere, it was so cold, Paislee shivered and regretteded she hadn't had time for tea. Oh well. She arrived at Amelia's place, which was quiet, as most people were still on holiday until Monday.

The Juke was just getting warm when she had to dash out and into the lobby. The place was old, with no security guard. Two cameras were on opposite corners of the ceiling. Paislee was having adrenaline-inducing memories of when Lydia's flat had been broken into, the door off its hinges. Constable Payne had been instrumental in helping them.

The exterior of Amelia's door looked okay—no marks on the wood around the frame—so Paislee knocked. She'd knitted the green wreath on the door. "It's me!"

"Thank heaven!" Amelia unlocked the knob and pulled Paislee inside. Her friend was pale, hair spiked, and dressed in an oversized sweatshirt, jeans, and boots. The TV to the left was on low; the Maltese puppies, out of their crates, yipped in greeting. They shared a dog bed beneath the dining table, blocked in the kitchen by various assorted tubs and bins.

"What happened?"

"Someone rattled the knob. My car is at the shop, so I wonder if whoever it was thought I wasnae home." Amelia shrugged and curled her fist. "I pounded back at them and said I'd called the police. I heard footsteps, but not clear enough tae say whether male or female."

Paislee closed the door behind her, and Amelia locked it. A candle gave the flat the scent of evergreen the artificial tree didn't provide.

"Tea?"

"Yes, please."

Paislee stepped over a mesh crate and entered the wee kitchen, the living area softly lit by the Christmas tree lights and the glow of the telly. Amelia's game console was on, the headset resting on the arm of the couch.

"What time did it happen?"

"Midnight." Amelia flicked on the electric kettle. "I couldnae believe it. I was playing the game and kinda heard something, but I had my headphones on, so I wasnae sure. Tae anybody outside it would sound quiet in the flat."

"Right. Brody's headphones have been a lifesaver. I don't want tae hear guns and fighting all the time."

Amelia half smiled. "It's a way tae escape. Honestly, I'm just glad that they went away."

"But what if they come back? Whoever tried tae break in is probably after the money in your brother's suitcase. And just might be the same person who killed McCormac, right?"

Amelia winced. She poured Paislee a mug of hot water and offered a tin of tea bags.

Paislee chose a breakfast blend for the caffeine hit.

Amelia went with a green tea, the scent lemony. Her expression was defensive as she said, "We dinnae ken that."

"No, but it's a good guess." Paislee wrapped her hands around the mug for comfort. "How's Daisy today?"

"Still sniffly, and now Robbie is too." The big-eyed pair looked up from their bed at the sound of their names.

"Oh no! Could it be the kennel cough?"

"I left a message with Dr. MacTavish. On his voicemail, his hours are listed as ten tae six. He'll probably call back at ten, but I'm so frustrated by his lack of availability." Amelia bent to pet Robbie, then Daisy before straightening again. "I'd rather pay oot of pocket for a vet with better hours than use the certificate from McCormac."

"Should we take them tae Dr. Kathleen? She opens at eight and she's only ten minutes away." It was half past eight right now.

"Yeah. I think we should." Amelia placed her mug on the counter. "I'll dip intae the suitcase money if I must in order tae pay for the vet bills. I wish I would've taken Snowball tae your veterinarian too."

"You thought you were doing the right thing. Snowball will be okay." Paislee wasn't sure about that at all, actually, but there was nothing to be done about the decision in hindsight. She had a bad feeling about the whole setup. Maybe because her vet was so amazing that she had a high standard for pet care. It was a responsibility not to be taken lightly, as your pet might live for fifteen to twenty years, or more.

Amelia put the pups in their crates. "Do you mind driving us over?"

"Not at all," Paislee said, blowing on her tea so she could have a quick sip. "Don't you work today?"

"I called oot at the station." Amelia shrugged into her down coat. "I cannae concentrate on anything and I'm tired of gettin' the cold shoulder from Zeffer."

Paislee hadn't taken her jacket off and dared another sip, the tea stinging her lips. "Should you bring their paperwork?"

"Guid idea." Amelia grabbed the folder McCormac had given her that contained the puppies' health and breeding records.

Paislee carried Daisy's crate and Amelia got Robbie's. Her friend locked up the apartment and they took the stairs down to the lobby because they were closer than the elevator.

"Thank you, Paislee," Amelia said.

"Happy tae help." Paislee drove to Dr. Kathleen McHenry's animal clinic. It was now nine in the morning and when they entered, Diana Gould, the receptionist, greeted them with a welcoming smile.

"Hi! Paislee, who do you have there? Doesnae look like Wallace at all—too small a carrier." Pretty Diana had blond hair, brown eyes, and a nose piercing.

"You're right, Diana, this is Daisy"—Paislee lifted the carrier—"and my friend Amelia is carrying Robbie. They are purebred Maltese puppies she was gifted for Christmas."

"How adorable!" Diana checked the computer. "You didnae have an appointment?"

"No." Paislee eyed the door separating the front lobby from the back offices. To the far left of the exam rooms was a kennel where they boarded animals for extended stays, or if they needed to be kept overnight after surgery. "I was hoping the doc would be able tae squeeze them in."

"Why dinnae you sit doon, and I'll go check?" Diana gestured to a table against the wall with a red machine for hot drinks. "Help yourselves tae coffee or tea."

Diana disappeared through a swinging door. The space was cozy and had linoleum tiles on the floor, hard plastic and metal chairs along the wall, and below the drinks station, shelves of canned dog food.

Paislee and Amelia had just sat down when Diana returned, brimming with positivity. She had to be in her early twenties. "Dr. Kathleen can see you right after you fill oot the paperwork."

Amelia handed over the certificates with the vaccinations they'd had and the microchip information. "This might help?"

"Thank you! I'll scan this intae the system," Diana said. "Why dinnae you go on back? Room two, Paislee, since you know the way."

"Thanks!" Paislee pushed through the swinging door, careful of Daisy's crate. Amelia looked around the space with interest as she carried Robbie's by the handle.

Dr. Kathleen McHenry was in her fifties, trim and energetic. She loved animals so much she had Noah's ark tattooed on her forearm—having a brilliant sense of humor, she'd added the national animal of Scotland: the unicorn. "Paislee! Nice tae see you."

"And you. Dr. Kathleen, this is my friend, Amelia. She's taking care of some pups that aren't feeling well."

"Hi there," Dr. Kathleen said to Amelia. She took Daisy out of the carrier that Paislee had placed on a central exam table and crooned, "What is the problem, little love?"

Daisy's eyes were rimmed in yellow, her nose runny. At the kind voice, she tried to perk her droopy ears.

"She's not well." Amelia put the carrier holding Robbie next to Daisy's. "My other puppy, Snowball, has kennel cough."

"Where is she?" The vet used her stethoscope to listen to the wee furry chest.

"With Dr. MacTavish the last two nights." Amelia's voice broke. "I miss her."

"Where is his clinic located?" Dr. Kathleen soothed Daisy, who was very relaxed in her competent hold.

"The Highlands." Amelia's concern for the puppies was clear in her expression.

Dr. Kathleen handed Daisy to Paislee and next took out Robbie. The puppy gave a tiny sneeze. He had the same symptoms. "How long have you had them?"

"Since Christmas." Amelia counted back. "Not even two weeks. My brother McCormac bought them for us."

"And did you request puppies as a present?" the vet asked sharply.

"No." Amelia blushed at the question.

"It's a particular peeve of mine that puppies and kittens are lauded as the perfect holiday gift when so many are returned because they werenae wanted in the first place." Her stern tone caused Robbie to whine.

Paislee winced, and Amelia stepped back from the table.

Dr. Kathleen peered into Robbie's eyes and ears. "Breeders are notorious for making sure they have extra puppies for sale around the holidays. Is your brother a breeder?" Her brow arched.

"No, ma'am." Amelia shook her head. "A car salesman, who was offered a chance tae make extra money selling puppies. We think. He was killed on Hogmanay."

"I dinnae bite," the vet said in a softer voice. Her gaze scanned Amelia with empathy. "There is no specific test for kennel cough, but it is highly contagious, and they are showing similar symptoms. I'd like tae keep them overnight tae give them fluids and antibiotics."

"All right," Amelia said.

This was in line with what Dr. McTavish had done, so Paislee relaxed regarding his actions. Maybe he could work on his bedside manner . . . then again, if he had a bias against puppies and puppy mills, like Dr. Kathleen did, well, she could give him more leeway before making a judgment.

Diana, who'd been listening as she brought in the paperwork to the vet, said, "McCormac Henry is your brother?"

"Aye." Amelia scowled at the pretty girl's wavering voice, understanding that Diana must have "known" McCormac in some manner.

Diana sniffed as a mascara trail ran down her cheek. "I cannae believe he's gone."

"What are you talking aboot, Diana?" Dr. Kathleen put Robbie in the carrier. "You knew her brother?"

"I guess you dated him?" Paislee asked.

"Aye," Diana said.

"Dear heavens," the vet exclaimed as her young assistant fell apart. "Diana, do you need a moment?"

The sorrowful lass fled with bowed shoulders.

"My brother has that effect on the ladies," Amelia explained with a wry smirk. "I never understood it."

"Quite normal, as his sister." Dr. Kathleen reached across the carriers to briefly squeeze Amelia's hand. "I'm sairy for your loss. I too lost a sibling when we were in our teens. Time makes the grief more manageable."

"Thank you." Amelia blinked tears from her eyes.

"Will the pups be all right?" Paislee asked.

"I will do my best tae get them well. Most cases of kennel cough are not deadly but when the pups are already compromised, it increases mortality. Let's talk tomorrow." The vet read the paperwork. "They are darling Maltese. The paperwork says eight weeks, but my guess is they are only aboot five."

Speechless, Amelia put her hand to her mouth. "Snowball is also tiny."

"They should have been with their mother longer, but as I said, I'll get them fluids and medicine."

"Thank you so much." Amelia peered at the puppies with teary eyes.

"What are you going tae do with them?" Dr. Kathleen glanced over the folder.

Amelia bit her lip. "Daisy and Robbie are actually gifts for my mum and brother. They want tae sell them."

"Shame," Dr. Kathleen stated. "But, better than living with someone who doesnae want them. Puppies for Christmas should be banned."

Amelia blinked. "I didnae ken."

"It's not your fault," the vet said sadly. "However, I am always going tae be on the side of the animal. I'm on the board of many nonprofits for that reason alone. Educating the public is key."

"When I get Snowball back, I'd love it if you'd be her doctor." Amelia clasped the vet's hand.

Dr. Kathleen nodded. "All right. Let's get these two wee pups sorted."

"Should I pay now?" Amelia asked.

"You're a friend of Paislee's?" The vet looked at Paislee.

"Aye," Paislee said. "A good one."

"Tomorrow is fine."

Paislee and Amelia thanked Dr. Kathleen profusely as they left. Diana never came out of the bathroom. Stepping onto the lot, Paislee sucked in a brisk shock of air.

"Dr. Kathleen is great," Amelia said. She stuffed her hands into her pockets. "I see why ye love her. She just gives it tae ye straight."

Breath plumed from their mouths as they talked on the way to the Juke. "She's the one who really helped with Wallace," Paislee said. "Told me tae get a trainer so that we would all be happy with-in the family. Scottish terriers can be stubborn and want tae rule the roost."

"Wallace? But he's so well-behaved."

"Thanks tae the trainer," Paislee hit the fob and unlocked the car. "How big will Snowball get?"

"I dinnae ken." Amelia opened the passenger side and hurried in. "But I'll keep the trainer in mind."

"Now where tae?"

"My place." Amelia glanced at Paislee as Paislee started the Juke. "I want you tae hang ontae the suitcase, all right?"

Paislee reached across the console and patted Amelia's arm. "Afraid you're going tae spend it all?"

Not in the mood for a jest, Amelia shook her head. "No. I just dinnae want it at my house. What if it was my mother and brother who wanted tae come in last night? I wouldnae put it past Michael, greedy sod, tae make sure McCormac didnae leave anythin' of value."

"Sure." That way if her family wanted it, Amelia could hon-estly say she didn't have it.

Paislee headed toward Amelia's.

"I willnae worry aboot it, then," Amelia said. "Mum always knows when I'm hiding something."

Paislee found Amelia and Letitia's relationship interesting, and recalled Brody saying that one had to love their mother. "Do you love your mum?"

Amelia snickered. "Uh, yeah. She's a terror, but she gave birth to me, so . . . Why do you ask? Cannae see the appeal of a maternal tyrant? What's your mum like?"

"It's not that," Paislee promised. "Mine lives in America—Phoenix, Arizona. She sent a holiday card. For the first time, my two younger siblings signed it."

"That's wonderful, eh?" Amelia settled back and crossed her ankles. "How old? Could be fun tae take them tae the pubs."

Her lips twitched as she clarified, "Josh and Natalie are younger than Brody."

After sucking in a breath of surprise, Amelia said, "That's different, but still. Family is family. So, you go ice-skating instead of drinking. Better for you anyway."

"I suppose." Paislee tapped the steering wheel as they waited at a traffic light. "She wasn't supportive. I worry all the time with Brody that I'll make a colossal mistake."

"What?" Amelia exclaimed. The light turned green. "I'd have loved tae have a mum like you, Paislee. You're fair and give boundaries. Lots of hugs. Brody knows he's loved. You didnae have that?"

Paislee pressed her foot to the gas pedal, appreciating Amelia's words. Adding another prayer to the constant stream to the Above that she didn't mess Brody up too bad, she explained, "Not from my mother, but my gran. She was my rock and now she's my angel." She gave a quick glance upward.

Amelia drummed her thumb on the console between them. "It's silly since I've only had Snowball such a short time, but do ye mind taking me tae Dr. MacTavish's clinic right now? I miss the little furball, and since Mum's pups are with Dr. McHenry, it will be safe tae bring her home. Just dinnae let me forget tae give you the suitcase when you drop me off."

"No problem." Paislee was thrilled to bring Snowball home. Amelia and her pup would be in more available hands with Dr. Kathleen.

The address in the Highlands was remote. Despite it being a Friday, when Paislee turned into the car park, not even Dr. MacTavish's SUV was in the lot. Like before, the place had a vacant feel. A lot of offices closed until the Monday following New Year's, so she covered her rising alarm with justifications.

Parking before the clinic, Paislee and Amelia climbed out of the Juke and looked at one another. The air held a strange disquiet.

Paislee knocked. No answer. She shivered and rubbed her arms.

"Wasn't there a sign on the door that read *Dr. MacTavish*, with the hours?"

"Yeah!" Amelia stomped her booted feet and even pressed her hand to the door where it had been. "Where'd it go?"

It was eerie that there was nary a car in this complex. The tire prints for Dr. MacTavish's vehicle were slowly melting. He'd had a Mercedes SUV, but an older model than McCormac's. "Should we call the police?" Paislee asked. It was the correct question to ask but Amelia didn't answer.

"This is unbelievable." Amelia raced around the building. Snow had frozen but there'd been nothing fresh on the ground since New Year's. The snow had evaporated off the sidewalk, leaving no trace of their footprints from several days ago.

Paislee followed Amelia and saw her friend peering over a garbage bin. She slowly straightened. "Empty. An operating business should have trash. Especially a veterinarian's clinic."

Behind the offices was a stand of pine trees. Evergreens. This was the mountains and very secluded. There would be cattle and sheep, so it made sense for a veterinarian to be in this location. There weren't any neighborhoods nearby. Paislee preferred the sounds of town to this total silence.

"This cannae be right." Amelia's cheeks flushed with fear. "Where is my dog?"

Paislee crossed her arms, wondering at the same time, "Where is the veterinarian?"

Amelia's expression twisted in panic. "I've got tae find Snowball. McCormac gave her tae me, and I've lost her. How could I have done such a rotten thing? This is an awful dream."

"It's not a dream at all," Paislee said. "And not your fault."

"You're right," Amelia said. "It's a bloody nightmare."

Amelia cried and Paislee gathered the young woman to her, patting her back. "Sweetheart, can we please call the police?"

"No." Amelia sniffed and backed away from Paislee, shaking her head. "No, we really cannae."

"Why not?" Paislee regretted the exasperation in her tone. Nairn Police Station had competent officers sure to get to the bottom of this missing puppy situation.

"I think"—Amelia blinked her big blue eyes—"McCormac's been lyin' tae me after all. And if so, I might be in trouble with the law."

Chapter 14

Paislee didn't think that Amelia's fears were rational—but she also remembered what it felt like to have the efficient police breathing down your neck when you were under suspicion.

"If we can't call the officers, what do you want tae do?"

Amelia took a deep breath and calmed down. "I need tae find oot who killed my brother. I've been focusing on the puppies and keeping them healthy, but I've gotta switch gears."

"How so?"

"Can we talk in the car?" Amelia's body shook with shock and cold. "With the heat on?"

Paislee's coat was made for the weather, her scarf and cap made of cashmere, which kept her warm. "Of course." They walked around the building to the empty lot. Paislee studied the tire tracks and decided to take a picture of them before they melted. If Amelia changed her mind to enlist the constables' aid for her missing Snowball, it was proof that there'd been another vehicle here. Sometimes her hunches mattered.

Paislee hopped in, started the Juke, and cranked the heat. "What's the plan?"

Amelia's chin jutted. "Discover what McCormac was doing so that I can clear my name, and find his murderer."

"Have you broken the law?"

"Not exactly," Amelia hedged. "But how do ye think me keeping the Rolex and suitcase of money secret will go over at the station? I didnae steal it. Did McCormac? I've got tae find oot, which means evading Zeffer and Payne for a few days. You shoulda heard how they talked aboot the Henrys. Like we were trash. If me brother legit made that money, and it's a possibility between sellin' puppies and his car commissions, my parents would benefit. If he didnae," she held up her hand, "I promise tae turn it all in."

"For the record, I think you should talk with Constable Payne." Warm air from the vents heated the interior. Paislee drove away from the vet's clinic. "If not him, then Constable Monroe."

"I cannae! I've told you why." Amelia's knee bobbed in the passenger seat. "The officers dinnae trust me. It's a terrible feeling tae show up at work and know that you've been the topic of discussion."

"Did you lie tae the police?" Paislee needed to know the truth before she would commit.

"No. My sins are more of the omission variety, but you know them all." Amelia raised her palm. "I swear."

Paislee believed her friend. "If you feel like you're being treated unfairly, Arran Mullholland has offered his assistance—no charge."

"That's sweet of him." Amelia glanced at Paislee. "Please help me, Paislee."

"All right. I wonder if following McCormac's money trail will lead tae his killer?"

Amelia's knee stopped jouncing. "Over the years at the station, I've noticed how constables will start with facts. Time lines. Known associates of the victim. Possible motives. Then, it's like crossing things off the list."

"I can see that. Do you want tae make a list?"

Amelia pulled out her phone and opened a notes app. "Yeah."

"What do we know?" Paislee kept her attention on the trees on either side of the road in case a deer jumped in front of the Juke.

"McCormac died at midnight on Hogmanay. He was shot and the sound was covered by the blare of the fireworks."

Nodding, Paislee said, "I thought I felt something brush by me, and then I got a hint of singed fabric. It might have been the fabric of his shirt. Also, he'd hit the bandstand hard. Stumbling. I thought he'd been drinking."

"You might have just been missed by the bullet, Paislee." Amelia turned very pale.

Paislee kept her friend on target. "We're okay. This is about McCormac. We know he was in a fist fight at ten p.m. with Hank Walsh. His ex, Hank's sister Porche, was also there."

"But they left after the fight," Amelia said. "I didnae see them come back."

"But would you have noticed, in the crowd?" There had to be hundreds of revelers at the park.

"Possibly not." Amelia wrote down Hank and Porche.

"What other friends did McCormac have here?"

"Dougie Selkirk, Sula's brother."

Paislee slowed around a sharp curve. The trees were beginning to thin, and a farmhouse was visible from the road. "Did he meet the guys first, and then start dating the sisters, or was it the other way around?"

"Dunno. The lasses always liked him. Him and Porche hookin' up was a big deal when we were younger because Hank and Mc-Cormac were best mates. Blood brothers. Then, Porche got her hooks intae McCormac and that came between them."

"Too bad. Did Hank and your brother ever make up?"

"Naw. And then McCormac went tae jail, where he was communicating with both Sula and Porche—he told me letters as well as in-person visits. When he was released he skedaddled tae Belfast for a fresh start."

"Was Hank mad that McCormac was two-timing Porche with Sula? Mad enough tae kill him?"

"I want tae say no." Amelia shook her head. "But someone bloody well did."

"Tell me about Sula and Dougie."

"Sula was always waiting in the wings, and didnae mind Porche's leftovers. Dougie, being younger than everyone, didnae run in the same crowd. They've gotten closer since McCormac has been oot of jail."

"And Lyla, Dougie's girlfriend? Did Dougie know about her hooking up with McCormac?"

"Dougie and Lyla arenae serious. It's possible they shared."

Paislee shuddered at the cavalier attitude. "How much time did McCormac spend in jail?"

"Two years. The letters he wrote tae me, Paislee, broke me heart. He seemed sairy for his crimes." Amelia drummed her fingers on her knee. "He was here in Nairn for a while, before leaving for Belfast, where he's been for the past year. He'd come home tae visit when he felt like it—the drive is long, around eight hours, but not impossible."

Paislee stopped at a stop sign. A large lorry filled with hay was coming the other way. The driver waved and smiled. She smiled back. Her home was a friendly place, most of the time. "When did McCormac start flashing money around?"

"That's new in the last few months." Amelia looked at Paislee with an earnest expression. "That's why I believe he'd earned his stripes as a luxury car salesman. My brother could be verra charming."

Paislee knew firsthand that he could also be a pig, but she didn't share with Amelia about the cheeky kiss he'd given her. McCormac might have insulted anyone, and these days people were quick to anger and could respond with violence. "So, he's been out of jail for a year?"

Amelia tilted her head. "Yeah."

"And you credit his move tae Ireland for his decision tae keep his nose clean so far as illegal activities, as well as his success."

"I do." Amelia brushed her hair off her forehead. "McCormac told me he would never go tae jail again. He promised me that he'd behave. Staying here in Nairn stifled him. Tae change, he had tae leave."

"Did he always stay with Sula while in Nairn?"

"No. He had lots of ladies that he was with. Lyla. Or this Diana lady at Dr. Kathleen's! Sula didnae always know when he'd come for a visit." Amelia shrugged. "It's not my business tae tell her otherwise. McCormac would usually stop by me flat tae say hi."

Paislee couldn't live that way. "McCormac and Porche?"

"McCormac promised me that he'd stay away, but I was never brave enough tae ask him," Amelia confessed. "I heard she'd moved oot of the old neighborhood tae Inverness."

"Less than thirty minutes away, so close enough tae run home if she needs tae, but independent."

"I guess so." Amelia stared out the window as the street became more congested with traffic. "I dinnae like Porche, and I hated how she was with McCormac. She tied him up in knots."

"What about Hank?" The outskirts of Nairn had homes and businesses interspersed. "What does he do for work?"

"He's a brilliant auto mechanic. Mum used tae say he could fix anything so long as he wasnae strung oot. Problem is that he's usually high."

"Do you hang out with these guys too?"

"No. I mean, I'm polite if I see them but we dinnae have anything in common anymore." Her mouth tightened. "Once I started working at the station, that definitely got me oot of being invited tae some of the parties from the old neighborhood."

"Sad?"

"Big no." Amelia grinned at Paislee. "I have my gaming friends and my knitting friends. I am much happier as an adult."

Paislee sighed. "Just wait until you hit thirty."

"Three years away!" Amelia crooned. She'd been to Paislee's birthday bash and teased her about being *so much* older.

Laughing, Paislee said, "Back tae the list. Who else did your brother visit while home?"

"Me. Michael and Mum. Da. He didnae hang oot with his old friends because they were trouble. He didnae stay long, ye ken?"

"Did McCormac have any close mates in Belfast that you could contact and find out more about his life there?"

"Girls, most like." Amelia typed the question into her notes. *Mates in Belfast.*

"You have phone numbers or emails for any of them?"

"No. McCormac didnae do social media either. He tended tae stay oot of the public eye. Besides, it was always Porche in his heart." Amelia shrugged. "You cannae help who you love."

"That sounds like you've been in love before." Paislee glanced at Amelia, staring pensively at her mobile.

"Yeah. Long time ago. Ginny left Nairn at sixteen. She asked me tae come with her tae London where she had a cousin who would take her in." Amelia traced the case on the phone with her fingertip. "Her parents were worse than mine. I didnae go."

Paislee's heart ached at the losses her friend had suffered. "Do you regret it?"

"Sometimes." Amelia peered at Paislee, then looked away. "Ginny died soon after she left. Chances are I would have been in the car with her, and then I'd be gone too. She was a wild and reckless driver," she said sadly.

"You've been through so much, Amelia."

Amelia studied Paislee closely. "You ever been in love?"

"No. Not even once." The truth and nothing but the truth. The son she'd conceived on a wild night was her whole life. It had been her choice to raise him despite the naysayers and gossips. The awful advice from her mother. Gran had been at her side, teaching Paislee how to stand by her decision while taking her place in the community with her head high. She'd taught Paislee to ignore mean comments. There was no shame in God's eyes and everybody else could fall into the River Nairn.

"What aboot Brody's dad?"

"Nope." Paislee kept the tone short. She wasn't going to elaborate.

"Well, Hamish wants tae change your mind," Amelia said. "He cares for you a lot."

"I'll tell you a secret—we kissed the night of the ceiling crash." Paislee cruised through a yellow light. "I think it's a sign from Above that I'm meant tae be single until Brody's grown."

Amelia's eyes rounded in surprise. "I dinnae agree with that. Och, poor you, poor Hamish. Life is damn messy, isnae it?"

"Yes, for sure. But good too." Paislee switched lanes as she neared Amelia's flat. "Grandpa turned out tae be amazing and that was a big messy surprise."

"I like Angus Shaw verra much."

Paislee did too. "So . . . who else can we add tae the list of folks who knew McCormac that we can question? Has tae be local, as I don't fancy a road trip tae Ireland, and your car is at the mechanic."

"Dr. MacTavish. His name is on the veterinarian paperwork, so McCormac must have known him. And now he's vanished. What if he's been taken oot of the picture, like my brother?" Amelia smacked her phone to the console.

"Write down MacTavish . . . I hope he's not in danger. Taken out of the picture makes me think of the Irish Mob, as Sula suggested. It seems more like he disappeared—but where did he go? Does he have anything to do with the suitcase of money?"

Amelia bowed her head as she typed into the app. "I could never be a constable. There are too many questions and it's near impossible tae find answers."

"I think you can trust Zeffer and Payne, about your brother."

She lifted a doubtful brow.

"I really do."

"Fine. Let me check in with the station and test the waters," Amelia said. "Before I lose my nerve." She put her mobile on speaker.

Constable Payne answered the phone. "Nairn Police Station."

"Hey, it's me. Amelia."

"Hmm. Hello." The tone went from cheery to flat.

"I was wonderin' if there are any updates aboot McCormac's death?"

"No." Constable Payne gave a heavy sigh. "Amelia . . . dinnae worry aboot coming intae work for a few days. It might be best if you took a leave of absence until we find who killed your brother."

"A leave of absence?" Amelia clutched the mobile. "Why?"

"This is verra difficult for me tae agree with, but the fact is, your mum and brother are being questioned today and it's best if you're not in—just until this case is solved."

"Questioned? Why?" Amelia's voice rose. "They were in Glasgow when it happened!"

"Were they?" Payne snorted like a frustrated horse. "I have pictures of your brother driving on New Year's Eve along the A9. Matches his plates and everything. No question. You told us they wernae in Nairn."

Paislee glanced at Amelia, whose mouth pursed as she calculated the driving time from Glasgow to Nairn . . . three and a half hours, give or take.

"Oh?" Amelia squeaked. She was giving Payne's story credence but didn't know how to defend it.

Paislee felt awful for Amelia. "Ask why?" she whispered so that Constable Payne wouldn't hear her.

Amelia nodded. "Payne, what motive would they have tae kill McCormac? I cannae believe it."

"Money, Amelia," Payne replied. "Your brother had come intae a lot of it. He and Michael had a big fight overheard by the neighbors. Michael wanted him tae pay for the house, but McCormac said it would be a waste of cash, throwing guid after bad."

They had to find the origins of the suitcase filled with cash.

Amelia swallowed and brought her fingers to her throat. "Mum mentioned the argument tae me, but it wasnae worth killin' over, I promise you that!"

"Paid leave of absence," Constable Payne said quietly. "You've proven yourself here at the station with your solid work ethic, but I'd hate tae put you in a situation where ye might feel compromised. Anybody would."

"Anybody with criminals in their family, you mean," Amelia retorted.

Paislee watched as a shield seemed to cover Amelia, a guard against Payne and their decision to give her leave from her job. The lack of trust from her coworkers.

Amelia might understand it, but it still hurt. "Nobody in my family owns a gun."

"Sadly, they are easy enough tae acquire." Payne continued. "It was a small handgun and could have been hidden in a jacket or gloves."

"I woulda seen my mum and brother at the park! They were-nae there." But her tone wasn't sure.

"Amelia, we will call you once the murderer is apprehended."

"You cannae do this! Dinnae shut me oot."

Constable Payne hung up.

Amelia and Paislee looked at one another in shock before Paislee returned her gaze to the traffic that zipped along the clear roads. Did Payne really suspect Michael and Letitia Henry of killing McCormac for money?

"What will I do?"

"Paid leave of absence, Payne said." Paislee gripped the wheel of the Juke and calculated the extra income she'd earned from the castle. "You are welcome tae work more days at Cashmere Crush if you want a distraction."

"Really? Paislee, that's . . . thank you."

"I'm the lucky one. You're great with customers and I don't have tae train you." She could make inroads on her inventory. How long, anyway? A week or two?

They reached Amelia's building as Amelia's phone rang again. "Dr. MacTavish!" She pressed the answer button. "Hello? We were just at your place of business, and nobody was there. I want me dog," Amelia said. "Should I phone the police?"

"No, no. I planned tae open at eleven because we were there late with an emergency. Amelia, we need tae keep Snowball one more night. She's responding well tae the medication, arenae you, pet?" A puppy barked in the background. "You cannae take her now and risk infecting the others."

"It's too late. My other two puppies are at Dr. McHenry's. Sick."

"I cannae apologize enough for this mistake," the vet said. "I will call you tae arrange a time for pickup, but it'll be another day or two. Please be patient."

Paislee supposed that the building might be so well insulated that the puppies couldn't be heard from the outside. It was possible they'd just missed him.

Amelia sighed. "You give me no choice."

"Have a nice day," the vet said before he ended the call.

"Did you hear her? Snowball even sounded sick." Amelia put her phone on the dash. "This has been a terrible beginning of the year. It's got tae get better, eh?"

"Aye, it does. It will. Want tae go back tae the clinic?" Paislee parked in the lot and turned off the engine.

"Naw, but thanks. I feel awful for wastin' yer time today. Come on up for the suitcase? Now I dinnae have any dogs at all," Amelia groused as she got out.

It did feel strange to have three and then none. Paislee followed Amelia to the flat on the second floor, taking the stairs rather than the elevator as it was closer.

They went inside Amelia's place. The sparkly Christmas tree in the corner was the only sign of merriment. Their mugs of tea were cold . . . she'd prefer something stronger.

"Do you have anything else of McCormac's, like a backpack or a wallet?" Paislee asked, going with Amelia to her bedroom. "Anything that might hold a hint tae his actions?"

Amelia flipped on the light. "No. I thought his suitcase would have clothes. Mibbe Sula has those? She had his watch."

Paislee entered, this time looking around the neat if plain room. Framed canvasses of comic figures drawn in black ink hung on beige walls. Monsters being vanquished by superheroes.

"This is so good," Paislee commented, pointing to the art.

"You think so?" Amelia shrugged. "I doodle a little."

"Like the holiday puppies on the Cashmere Crush window. You're talented."

Amelia waved the compliment away. "We willnae get McCormac's personal effects until the coroner and medical examiner are finished with his body. The things he was wearing and had on his person." Her teeth clenched.

Paislee went along with the change of subject, thinking of what the steps had been when her da had died and then her granny, both buried in the churchyard. "Are you and your family religious?"

"Nah. Christmas kinda thing at the Church of Scotland."

"Will McCormac be buried, or cremated?"

"Dunno. We never talked aboot those kinds of things. He was thirty, Paislee." Amelia brought her thumb to her lower lip. "Mum and Da will decide, once the constable gets his head from his arse, and realizes that my family didnae kill McCormac."

Paislee understood her anger but also why the officers were behaving in such a manner. "Money is a common motive for murder and unfortunately family or someone you know is the likely perpetrator."

"I ken that verra well, working at the station." Amelia slumped on the bed. "But I dinnae anymore. I've been part-time since I was eighteen, then moved tae full-time when a position came open. Inspector Shinner gave me a chance despite my family. It nearly did me in when he arrested McCormac for stealing car parts. McCormac was twenty-six, and I was twenty-three."

"Car parts?" Paislee's brain put two and two together. "Did you say that Hank was a mechanic?"

Amelia straightened. "Yeah. That would be a handy skill tae have, wouldnae it? Stealing parts tae put in vehicles tae make them a viable commodity. What if McCormac did the time for a crime they'd committed together?"

"Why would he?" Paislee asked. The McCormac she'd met was all about McCormac.

"Not unless he got something oot of it, and from the way Hank was so mad, it was like McCormac had done him wrong somehow. Personal, not just Porche." Amelia tapped her chin in thought.

"Should we talk tae Hank?" Paislee suggested.

"*I* should," Amelia said. "You'd stand oot in the old neighborhood like a sore thumb."

"You can't go by yourself."

Amelia sighed. "Mibbe Sula is free. I'll give her a ring."

"Don't be hasty, all right? Let's come up with a plan." Paislee's brain loved to solve a puzzle. Right now, the pieces floated around in her mind: McCormac's flaunting of money, the fight with Hank, jail time. McCormac's ladies. His own family.

"You're probably right." Amelia's shoulders shook.

"Hon!" Paislee gave her a hug.

"My co-workers dinnae trust me, and it really hurts," Amelia sniffed. "Mum and Michael lied tae me, Paislee."

"Maybe you should make an appointment with Arran and let him know what's happening? He's an incredible solicitor and he's offered already. He once helped me out of a bind."

"You?" Amelia scooped her hair back over her ear.

"It was around the time that Grandpa showed up in my life. Anyway, Arran can be trusted," Paislee promised.

"I'll think aboot it. We've got tae find oot where this money came from. I dinnae believe McCormac worked with the mob. Sula's ridiculous. My biggest fear aboot this suitcase is that Mum will ferret it oot of me. Michael would spend it in an instant. Can you imagine what the constable would say tae this?" Amelia shivered as she reached under the bed and pulled the valise free. "This could be McCormac's life savings or seed money for the next puppies. I know how the legal system works and even if this is legit, it could still take years before the inheritance is cleared in court."

Paislee was uncomfortable with Amelia's decision but understood it. "What will you tell your family about the leave of absence?"

"As little as possible." Amelia raised her hand. "Trust me. Brevity is best with the Henry crew."

"Let's talk tae Hank about McCormac, and Sula—we should see how Thor is doing . . ."

Paislee's phone rang, Bennett Maclean's name showing, and she answered with surprise. Why would Brody's best friend's dad be calling? "Bennett?"

"Paislee, I'm at the park with Brody by the bandstand. He slipped and hurt his arm."

"I'll be there in ten minutes!"

Amelia followed her with the suitcase and tossed it in the back of the Juke, covering it up with a blanket Paislee kept in the hatch.

"Guid luck with Brody," Amelia said. "I'll see you tomorrow at ten."

Paislee waved, but her mind was on Brody, and wondering if Doc Whyte was open for business.

Chapter 15

While Paislee'd been helping Amelia with the sick puppies, Bennett had offered to pick Brody up so that he and Edwyn could run off some energy. Grandpa had okayed it, as Paislee would have if she'd been home. The boys played football for a good portion of the year, so bad weather put a cramp in the physical activity.

She arrived at the park, where her son was trying to keep on a brave face for Edwyn's sake, but she could tell by the way he kept his arm to his side that he was in pain. Bennett felt terrible but Paislee didn't blame him in the least. Accidents happened when one had boys who were active.

"It hurts tae move it," Bennett said. He and Edwyn were both lean in physique with blond curls and green eyes. "A trip tae the hospital?"

"Doc Whyte is open, so we're going there," Paislee said. For once Brody didn't argue about visiting the doctor.

"Call tae let me know, okay?" Bennett asked.

"Of course. Bye now," Paislee said. She was glad that the roads were clear as she may have gone a wee bit over the speed limit.

Brody kept his eyes closed and moaned to himself for the ten minutes it took to reach the office. Each bump, Paislee winced for him.

Doc Whyte hurried Brody in. Luckily, Brody had only sprained his arm, rather than a break, as she'd feared.

"Sprains are often more difficult than a break because with a break there's a cast tae protect the injury. We'll try a soft sling, but if you move too much, Brody lad," Doc Whyte said, "we'll do a cast anyway."

The white-haired doctor gave Brody a quick jab in the arm for pain management.

Brody looked at the drawer where the nurse kept the lollipops with hope in his brown eyes.

"Dinnae suppose you're too old for one of these?" The doc got one for Brody, one for Paislee, and slipped the other into his own pocket.

Gran had always said you needed a good mechanic, a good priest, and a good doctor for a happy life. Cheese pizza and ice cream also helped.

The next morning was Saturday and Paislee planned to be at work at ten. Brody had promised to stay quiet at home with Grandpa and watch movies. Edwyn might come by with a new video game if they didn't roughhouse. Would he be able to play with the sling?

Paislee, after a hearty breakfast of eggs, Lorne sausage, and a morning roll, wished her family a good day and went to the car. The silver SUV glistened with a fresh coat of frost and her gaze went to the back.

Amelia's secret suitcase full of cash!

Her stomach clenched. The money and the suitcase had been out all night, just under a blanket. Sure, the car was locked but that didn't always stop a determined thief. She said a little prayer that nothing had happened to it and opened the hatch.

Whew.

Wrapping the suitcase with the blanket, Paislee brought it inside and up to her room. Downstairs in the foyer she heard Brody ask, "Mum?"

"Yes, it's me. Sorry. Forgot something." She poked her head into the kitchen and waved at Wallace, Grandpa, and Brody. "Bye!"

She arrived at Cashmere Crush, thinking she would have a slow day and maybe she and Amelia could work on the list of people who might have had a reason to kill McCormac.

Instead, they were busy nonstop with happy holiday shoppers wanting to spend their gift money.

She'd incentivized by selling gift certificates at a ten percent discount to the buyer, with a cute, crocheted gift bag for the recipient. Just a little bit fancy for the holiday. It could be spent at this location or the Ramsey Castle gift shop. A lot of people didn't know about the new shop and Paislee was happy to spread the word, just as Cinda did for Paislee.

Dr. Kathleen called Amelia to tell her that the pups were ready to go home. Paislee offered to drive her friend at four when they closed for holiday hours.

At four thirty, Paislee parked in the lot across from the veterinarian's clinic. The streetlamps illuminated their way.

They entered and Diana greeted them with a bashful smile. "I'm so sairy for my breakdown a few days ago. It's not like McCormac had made me any promises."

Amelia thawed at her confession. "My brother was verra guid at evading commitment."

Dr. Kathleen came out with the pups, one in each hand.

"These two cuties are on the road tae recovery," the vet said. "I'll send you home with medicine."

"I fell in love with Robbie," Diana said. Her nose piercing flashed in the overhead light. "You'd mentioned that they might be for sale?"

"Mibbe," Amelia said. "That would be up tae my mum and brother."

"We looked up the going rate for purebred Maltese and it was around the two-thousand-pound mark." Diana winced.

"The papers are all there," Amelia said. "Microchipped and everything. They'd want a guid deal."

Dr. Kathleen blew out a concerned breath. "Aboot that, Amelia. I didnae find a chip in either pup."

"No?" Amelia rocked back.

"I'm sairy, but no." Dr. Kathleen handed Daisy to Paislee while Amelia took Robbie. "So," the vet said, perching on the edge of the reception desk, "I looked up the veterinarian, Dr. MacTavish, in the Highlands as you said."

Paislee's stomach clenched.

"Yes?" Amelia's shoulders hiked.

"There is no such doctor, or veterinarian, of that name." Dr. Kathleen wore a grim expression.

Paislee stepped closer to her friend as her knees buckled.

"What? But I've been talking tae him. Right, Paislee? Paislee's met him too!"

"Aye. We went yesterday tae pick up Snowball, but there was no answer and the building seemed vacant. We were worried, but then he called back and said that he wasn't there because of a medical emergency the night before." Paislee cringed. "It sounded legit."

Amelia turned green around her mouth and eyes. "He snarkily said that I shouldnae expect them tae be there at all hours especially during the holiday and that Snowball needed tae be with them another night, and then we heard a little pup bark."

Dr. Kathleen fumed and crossed her arms.

"That's right," Paislee said. "It seemed shady but then somehow okay when he was talking."

"How awful!" Diana said.

"It is!" Amelia said. She patted Robbie. "What can we do?"

"Call the police," Dr. Kathleen suggested.

Paislee put her hand on Amelia's arm. Was it time to actually spell things out for the police, who'd put Amelia on the bench when she could have been an asset?

Amelia shook her head in denial. "There has tae be a reasonable explanation."

Diana and Dr. Kathleen exchanged glances.

"Have they found oot what happened tae your brother?" Dr. Kathleen asked.

"No." Amelia cooed to Robbie, stroking under his chin.

"Could it be connected, somehow?" Diana let the sentence, and suggestion, hang.

"I dinnae want tae talk aboot it anymore," Amelia said. "How much do I owe you?"

The bill came to two hundred pounds and Amelia paid for it with a card. It wasn't too bad for an overnight. The news from Dr. Kathleen would take some getting used to. No microchip. No actual veterinarian. It was definitely time for Amelia to talk to Arran if she didn't trust the police.

"Let me know if Robbie goes up for sale, would you?" Diana asked as they left.

"I will pass the message on tae Mum," Amelia said.

They tucked the two carriers with the pups inside the hatch of the Juke and drove toward Amelia's flat.

"I need my car," Amelia said. "I called tae see if I could get it sooner, but they are waiting for a part."

"That's the worst. I don't mind driving you."

"I know that if we go up tae the Highlands veterinarian clinic the guy willnae really be there. It's been a sham. I dinnae know *why*, though." Amelia glanced at Paislee. "It's not like I gave him money or my credit card. Just my dog."

"I don't either."

"I want Snowball. What if they hurt her?"

Paislee hadn't thought of that. "They have no reason tae do that."

"I dinnae understand any of this," Amelia said in a sad voice. "I was so excited when McCormac came home for Christmas. What a

surprise! But he didnae tell my folks at all, and I just got a few days'
notice. Then he showed up with this shiny new Mercedes, his fancy
watch, and cash."

"Did he have the dogs already?"

Amelia tilted her head. "When he arrived at my place for two
nights, he didnae have the dogs, and then he was at Sula's. I think
he came back with the pups on Christmas Eve. Handed them oot
like Father Christmas—only Mum and Da were in Glasgow, with
Michael."

"Should we talk tae Sula? Why wouldn't he stay at your parents'?"

"You've seen that dive. McCormac was probably someplace a
lot nicer and realized that we grew up in a rat's nest."

Paislee sighed. "I think you should tell Constable Payne about
the pups and the fake veterinarian."

"Why? What would they do? Shame on McCormac for falling
for a scheme." Amelia brought out her phone. "Not surprising, if
there was quick money tae be had."

"We can give Payne, and Zeffer, the information. Maybe they
can track the guy down from the phone number that you've been
calling."

"I want Snowball back. That's all."

"You might need tae be more forthcoming with the police."

"I cannae. We need tae figure oot what's going on, Paislee.
Why did Mum and Michael lie tae me aboot being in Nairn for
Hogmanay? It makes it look like I've been covering for them by
telling the constables they were in Glasgow. Mum texted me New
Year's Day saying she was in Nairn, as if she'd just arrived, and
wanted tae see me." Amelia's face turned an awful red. "It was a lie
because they must have come home the day before."

"I think it's time tae bring in Arran."

"You're right. Monday morning. I dinnae trust the police to
have my family's best interests. Payne must have cleared Mum and

Michael, or I'd have heard otherwise. It's been crickets from them both." Amelia dialed the number for the fake vet. No answer. She left a strident message. "I know you're up tae something! I want my dog back or I will go tae the police!"

They reached Amelia's flat, and Paislee parked. The lot was very well lit with tall streetlamps on each corner.

"I probably shouldnae have done that," Amelia said.

Paislee placed her hand over Amelia's. It had been desperation talking. "Do you want tae come over? I can make up a bed on the couch downstairs. It's pretty cozy. Or we can see if anybody is at Lydia's yet—maybe you can stay there. What if someone tries tae break in again?"

"I'm fine," Amelia said. "Not a peep since it happened, so it had tae be a mistake. I was probably overreacting, and it was some-one with too much tae drink trying tae open the wrong door."

The ladies got out and retrieved the dog carriers.

Once upstairs, Paislee realized the time and squealed when she got a text from Hamish wondering where she was at for their din-ner date.

On my way!

"I have tae go. Totally forgot dinner with Hamish!"

"You always have something going on. I'm glad you didnae cancel. Hamish is a guid man, and he likes you a lot."

Her thoughts were frazzled. "Please do me a favor and stay here. Don't get ideas of tracking down Snowball, all right?" She took Daisy out of the carrier as Amelia freed Robbie.

The pups raced around the kitchen, glad to be home, or at least not in a kennel.

"Video games for me tonight, after digging around online a bit on my brother and what McCormac might have been up tae in Belfast." Amelia sighed heavily. "How can I save myself from being implicated in McCormac's activities? Everybody has either ignored my calls or lied tae me."

Paislee gave Amelia a hug. "Be safe."

"I'm not going anywhere. You have fun. I'll see you on Monday morning and go over what tae say tae Arran."

"Perfect."

Paislee petted the pups goodbye and rushed out the door.

She dialed the landline at the house and Grandpa picked up. "Hi! Forgot about dinner with Hamish, so I'll be later than I thought. You guys all right?"

"Aye, right as rain. Edwyn is here with a new game and the boys are upstairs. I said I'd order pizzas, but Brody wanted a ham and cheese toastie instead. Strange lad."

"You know they're living great if they've had too much pizza."

Grandpa chuckled. "Give me regards tae Hamish."

"I will. See you later—thank you."

Paislee parked at the Pickled Mermaid Pub and climbed out, grabbing her bag and wishing she'd had time to fluff her hair. She went inside where Hamish waited for her on a bench by the hostess stand. "Hamish, how are you?"

"Paislee!"

They smiled at one another, and she studied him closely. He was so handsome, with his dark brown hair and eyes. He wore a belted leather jacket that he'd loosened as he'd waited for her.

"I'm sorry for being late," she said.

"So long as you didnae forget." Hamish helped her with her coat.

She ducked her head.

Hamish brushed her hair back. "Did ye then?"

"In my defense, I was helping Amelia with the puppies her brother got for the family and they're sick, and the vet that he was using isn't even a vet, and . . ."

"Hold that thought." Hamish smiled at the hostess. "We'd like a private table tae catch up if we may. Something quiet and oot of the way."

"Good idea." Paislee felt slightly embarrassed at the verbal velocity of her greeting.

Hamish tucked his hand in the crook of her elbow, and they followed the hostess to a back table for two against the wall. Romantic candlelight shimmered on the sconces.

He held her chair for her and scooted her in before taking his own.

The hostess smiled. "Can I take your drink order before the waiter arrives?"

"Water is fine with me," Paislee said.

"Tae start," Hamish agreed.

When the hostess left, Hamish winked at her and rolled his hand in a gesture to say that she should continue where she'd left off.

"It doesn't matter," Paislee said, laughing at herself. "There's a lot going on. How are you? How's your mother?"

"On the mend! And Brody's arm?"

"Just a sprain and not a break, like your poor mum's leg, so that's good. He and Edwyn are at the house with Grandpa, playing video games."

Hamish clasped both her hands and squeezed. "I've missed you," he said.

The waiter arrived with two glasses of water and told them the specials. "Fish and chips or steak pie."

Hamish put his hand to his stomach and Paislee missed the warmth of his fingers. "I'm verra hungry—I've been catching up on laundry and havenae gone for the messages, so no groceries at my house. Canned soup." He stuck his tongue out. "Haddock for the fried fish, you said?"

"Aye. And steak pie."

"Paislee?" Hamish asked before ordering for himself.

"Fried haddock and chips sound great," she said.

"I'll have the same." Hamish reached again for her hands as the waiter rushed off.

"We'll have tae see if they are as good as the Lion's Mane pub,"
Paislee said. "I've only been here a few times."

"It's near the house so I come often for the chowder special."

"So, laundry all day?" Paislee scrunched her nose.

"School is on Monday, and I feel like I havenae had a break."

Paislee smoothed her thumb over his knuckles. "Because you
haven't. You've been helping your mother, like a dutiful son."

"I adore her," Hamish confessed. "But she's reverted tae being
bossy and I keep reminding her that just because I'm back in my childhood bedroom doesnae mean she can tell me what tae do. Two
weeks is my limit."

Paislee laughed. "You deserve a break."

His eyes peered into hers. "I hope I can convince you tae have
a weekend away with me in spring as a reward for my dedication."

Paislee froze.

A weekend away?

That would mean . . . well, it would mean that their relationship might be taking the next step.

"I don't know what tae say. That sounds faster than slow."
Paislee forced herself not to immediately release his hands.

Hamish's eyes flashed. "You caught me."

"That wasn't the deal." Now, Paislee slowly tugged her fingers
free.

"You know what?" Hamish smoothed the top of his pristine
hair. "I'm sairy tae rush you. You've been so busy with the holiday
and Brody's arm that you've probably hardly thought aboot me, but
you've constantly been on my mind."

Paislee bowed her head. "McCormac's death has been front
and center. Amelia is going tae be full-time at Cashmere Crush
until the police find out who killed her brother."

"What happened?" Hamish's gaze warmed with concern.

"She was advised tae take a leave of absence. Her brother Michael and her mother lied to Amelia about being in Nairn on Hog-

manay. Amelia told the constables that they couldn't be persons of interest as they were in Glasgow, which wasn't true."

Hamish's mouth gaped. "Suspects? Could they have done it? The Henrys have a notorious reputation."

Paislee wished she hadn't come to dinner, but it was too late to go home now. She'd told him about the murder, of course, but it hadn't been a priority as he'd been in the trenches with his mother.

It was possible they were on entirely different pages.

Chapter 16

Paislee didn't sleep well after dinner with Hamish. He wanted to go away for a weekend, which would mean more than just kisses.

She had a child, for heaven's sake, but she still felt like the Virgin Mary. Hamish must have sensed her reticence as he hadn't brought it up again. They'd had a delicious dinner and caught up on the news since he'd been away.

He'd wanted to come and see the new kitchen, but she put it off for another day—they'd gone to their separate cars after a quick kiss goodbye that she blamed on the frigid weather.

Now at seven in the morning, Paislee was up with a strong cup of Brodies tea. She moved the stool by the little tea area so that she could look out at her back garden. The trees were winter bare, but a busy squirrel nattered at her from a limb.

Gran, what is the matter with me? Have I been so long out of the dating game that it doesn't matter anymore?

Amelia texted at eight thirty with a panicked message that she knew who had tried to break in. She asked Paislee to come help her.

Who?

Dougie. Just come.

Dougie? Sula's brother? **On my way!**

Paislee looked around her kitchen for any type of weapon and settled for a whistle in the event of danger. She dressed in warm boots, and a coat with a hood. The sky was a dismal gray.

She left a note on the counter by the electric kettle for her guys and went outside.

Edwyn had spent the night last night and the boys had been in the middle of a battle between the elves at midnight. She imagined they'd sleep late. At twelve, they were capable of getting their own breakfast.

She remembered to bring a hot to-go mug of her tea, so she'd fend off frostbite in the Juke as it warmed up.

Paislee arrived at Amelia's to find Amelia fully dressed and waiting for Paislee in the lobby of the building.

"Hi! Are you sure it was Dougie?"

"Aye. Dougie Selkirk tried tae break in! I heard him an hour ago, rattling the door." Amelia scowled. "He hasnae figured oot my car is in the shop. Eejit. I saw his car drive away when I ran ootside."

"Could he be after the suitcase full of money?" If they were such good mates he might have known about the cash.

"Mibbe." Amelia shook the small bat in her hand. "He'll be sairy he messed with me."

"Now, now." Paislee didn't condone violence and showed her friend the loud whistle she'd put in her pocket. "This situation has taken a dangerous turn. It's time tae alert the police."

Amelia lowered the bat. "Nah. I called Sula, but she's probably still sleeping because she didnae answer. She works late anyway."

"What did you call *her* for?"

"Dougie's phone number and address. What does he know aboot McCormac? They were tight since my brother was oot of jail. Listen, you gotta back me up. I am going tae deny anything aboot the money if he asks."

"Understood." Paislee gestured toward the exit in the lobby. "What now, since you don't have Dougie's address?"

"I am not a victim. I dinnae like being played one bit. I want tae go tae the vet's clinic in the Highlands and rescue Snowball."

Paislee shook her head. "I don't think it's a good idea."

"I'll rent a car if I need tae, or take an Uber," Amelia said. "It's important." She held Paislee's gaze with pure determination as if she was channeling one of her gaming heroes.

"All right." Paislee would rather be on hand to help than have her friend go alone. "I'll drive. I just don't want you tae be disappointed if Snowball isn't there."

"The fake vet has tae be somewhere, right? He's not a ghost—we both saw him. Spoke tae him. Had a conversation on the phone."

"We did." Paislee's immediate plan was to calm Amelia down. She'd never seen her so riled up. It was terrible to be out of control.

"Let's go." Amelia led the way and pushed the door open.

They stepped out to the car and got in. The heavy gray sky started to drop big fat drops of snow that wouldn't make the curvy drive to the vet's shop in the mountains an easy one.

"I owe you, Paislee. If you ever need anythin' from me, you have it. Okay?"

"Sure." What a sweetheart. "But this is what friends do for each other."

"The knitters are me first foray intae female friends. My gaming mates are guys," Amelia said. "The lads are worse gossips than the women any day."

"I had no idea—well, I'm glad you've joined our group." Paislee drove carefully toward the clinic as the flakes came down so fast they blurred the windshield.

"How is Brody's arm?"

"In a sling, and he's got Edwyn over, so they're fine. Grandpa will make breakfast or not. He's home if there's an emergency." Paislee had a wee bit more freedom. She'd never thought she'd use her free time to track down a missing pup.

"He's a guid lad. Edwyn too. How was your date with Hamish?"

Paislee's emotions regarding the evening were in flux. "We went tae the Pickled Mermaid and had the fish and chips, which weren't as tasty as the ones at Lion's Mane."

"I've been there." Amelia patted her stomach. "Verra nice steak pie."

"That was the other special," Paislee said.

"How's his mum?"

"Good. He's ready tae get back tae work at Fordythe on Monday." Hamish happened to be the youngest headmaster the primary school ever had. Paislee didn't mention that he wanted her to go away for a romantic weekend. For most people that would be the natural evolution of a friendship.

What is wrong with me?

The drive to the clinic took an extra ten minutes because of the snow. There were no vehicles in the car park. No lights on—not even streetlamps. The sun was covered by gray clouds. Paislee pointed her headlights toward the building.

Amelia put her hand on the door. "I'll pop oot tae see if it's open."

"All right. I'll wait here." Paislee figured it would be closed. She had the idea that the fake vet, for whatever reason, had something to do with McCormac's money and it was up to them to find out how they were tied together.

Amelia slipped out of the SUV and dashed across the cement, her boots skidding on the fresh snow.

Her friend hunched over the doorknob and gave it a twist. Her body blocked Paislee's view but instead of coming back defeated, Amelia had gone in!

Paislee turned off the engine and hurried inside the front office. The lights were on but no Amelia. No doctor. No Snowball. Not even a dust bunny under the desk that wasn't there. Nothing on the wall either.

"Amelia?" Paislee called.

Her voice echoed in the empty room.

"Back here!" Amelia said.

Paislee pushed through the swinging door to see Amelia, red-faced, going through the drawers of the desk that had been in the reception area. On the corner was a nondescript plastic spray bottle that smelled like white vinegar. Lots of folks used it as a natural cleaner. The exam table and shelves were gone. It had been stripped.

"Snowball isnae here. There are no rooms or kennels behind here—it's a closet." Amelia tossed a cheap disposable mobile phone to the desktop. She dialed from hers and the phone rang. "It was a setup—all of it."

"What about fingerprints? We should be careful."

Wincing at the realization that she shouldn't have touched anything, Amelia cursed. Her expression crumpled, devastated. "Where is *Snowball*?"

"We should call the police, Amelia." Paislee crossed her arms in the chilly room.

"Not yet. I need tae talk tae my mum and brother first and find oot why they lied tae me. What else do they know aboot McCormac's activities? What if that knowledge can help me find Snowball?" Amelia's chin trembled. "I'll tell Arran everything tomorrow like we agreed. We might need a solicitor."

It was difficult but Paislee forced herself to imagine that she was in Amelia's shoes, even though it didn't feel right. She was amazed at how careless MacTavish had been. "I can't believe he just left the door open."

Amelia shyly showed Paislee a lock pick. "It wasnae. Another reason not tae involve the constables. I havenae lost me talent for breaking and entering. Payne and Zeffer were right that I dinnae belong at the police station."

"I don't agree." Paislee was proud of how her friend had risen from challenging circumstances.

"You're too nice." Amelia sniffed the spray bottle. "Vinegar. I doot if there are any prints left. He probably cleaned it all doon, even the burner phone. Still, I wasnae thinking."

"Burner phone?"

"A cheap device that ye buy with a certain number of minutes, no mobile plan necessary. Untraceable and inexpensive." Amelia's lip curled. "Let's go before the weather gets any worse. Sairy for wasting your time."

"You haven't—we found out more information tae add tae the list."

"I'll add the info in the car after I message Mum and suggest a meeting."

"Do you want tae drop in?"

"It might be easier tae get answers face-to-face." Amelia shot off a text. "Just offered tae bring a bottle of gin that I've kept in the cupboard with their name on it. I hate the stuff."

Amelia preferred whisky. "You have a bribe on hand?" Paislee asked.

"She and Michael have been ignoring me. I'll do whatever it takes." Amelia wrapped the burner phone in her knit cap.

"Fair."

Amelia's phone dinged. "Ha! Snagged my prey with the gin but they want tae come over tae my flat and check oot their investments—the puppies, greedy sods." She shook her head.

"Will you be okay?" Paislee asked with trepidation. Would her family harm Amelia? Had they killed McCormac for his money? What if Amelia was next?

"I'll be fine," Amelia said.

"Forgive me if I'm overstepping," Paislee said, leaving the back room for the main office. "But until we find out if they're behind McCormac's death, I'd be wrong tae leave you alone with them. Constable Payne knows for a fact that they were in Nairn on New Year's Eve. That McCormac and Michael argued over cash."

"You want tae stay?" Amelia carried the knit cap like a small shopping bag. "That's sweet of you. You'd have tae be quieter than you were at Mum's."

"All right. I don't suppose asking them if they're guilty would work?"

"You wouldnae have lasted a day in the old neighborhood."

Amelia exchanged the lock pick in her pocket for her phone and showed it to Paislee. "I took a video of both rooms. The constables will eventually be involved, but right now, my priority is my family. Then Snowball, then the station."

"Listen, I think Arran can help you more than you realize, especially if Payne or Zeffer lean hard on you." Paislee ushered Amelia before her, toward the door.

"Tomorrow," Amelia promised.

They left the building, Amelia locking it behind her. The snow was falling so heavily that an inch had already accumulated on the top of the Juke. Paislee swept the snow off her door and opened it. "It's so pretty but makes the roads slick."

By the time they arrived at Amelia's flat, forty minutes had passed and Paislee's palms were damp with nervous sweat.

Michael and Letitia had already arrived and waited in his truck with the windows fogged.

"Smoking," Amelia said as she hopped out. "Hopefully just tobacco." She tapped on the driver's-side window and her brother lowered it a crack.

"What took ye so long?" Michael shouted.

"The weather, numpty. We were up in the Highlands."

"Och. I didnae ken."

"Come inside then." Amelia stepped toward the entrance of the apartment building.

Paislee followed. Letitia leaned heavily against Michael as they hurried across the lot and made it inside. From the lobby, the foursome took the elevator up to the second floor rather than the stairs. Letitia was already breathing heavily from the trek.

Amelia opened the door to her flat and Paislee entered. The scent of oranges, cinnamon, and pine escaped, and the interior was pure holiday cozy; the lights on the Christmas tree flashed, the pups curled up on a round dog bed in the kitchen together. The mishmash blockade of boxes and crates kept the wee ones on the linoleum with their food, water, and puppy potty pad.

Letitia lumbered in before Michael, then Amelia, who shut and locked the door behind them.

"What's going on?" Letitia asked. "Why werenae you at the station yesterday, Amelia? I let that Constable Payne know what I think of his whole shoddy operation."

Amelia winced. "I work at Cashmere Crush on Saturday."

"So you say." Michael sneered as he scanned the puppies with a curled lip.

"Why would *I* lie?" Amelia demanded.

The pups woke and wagged their tails but were too sleepy to get off the dog bed. It had been a long two weeks or more for Daisy and Robbie.

"How are they?" Letitia pointed at the pups with her thumb but didn't cross over the barricade of the calf-high boxes.

"Better, but they still need medicine. I can show you how tae do it." Amelia crossed to the kitchen and placed the knit cap with the hidden burner phone next to the orange bottle on her kitchen table. "Three times a day and you cannae be late or miss a dose."

"I'm not doin' all that!" Letitia said, putting her hand to her chest.

"You said *you* would," Michael said.

This had been Amelia's plan all along. She knew how to work around her family. Smart girl.

"Can I get you some tea, or gin?" Amelia asked.

"Bring oot the bottle, lass," Letitia instructed.

"This couch looks comfy," Michael said, heading toward it. "Hey, what's this gaming system?"

"Dinnae touch it. It's broken." Amelia passed him a tumbler and the gin bottle with some soda water to make his own drink.

"Paislee?" Amelia asked.

"Just tea for me. I'm driving."

Letitia snorted and plonked down onto the couch at the opposite end from Michael.

Paislee brought a chair from the kitchen to sit in the living area near the Christmas tree. She wanted to hold one of the puppies but didn't dare call attention to them, like how cute they were. Out of sight, out of mind.

"Thanks," Letitia said to Amelia as she filled a tumbler with gin and added a splash of soda. "Where's yours?"

Paislee watched the way they studied Amelia and understood when Amelia went to get a mug. She made herself a drink, then handed Paislee a cup with a tea bag.

"*Sláinte!*" Michael said, taking a big drink.

"So, you mentioned you were at the station yesterday? I havenae heard nothin' aboot McCormac," Amelia said. She slouched but didn't sit on the couch between them. "Not a thing."

"That big officer, Constable Payne, he was all right, but that other fella, DI Zeffer, he's verra intense," Michael said. "Like he'd enjoy nothing more than tossin' us in jail."

"Intense is a good way tae describe him," Paislee agreed.

"What did you think of him, Mum?" Amelia asked.

"I dinnae like the law, never have, never will." Letitia slurped and winced. "The police dinnae have no business poking around the Henrys. And that Constable Monroe?" She gave an exaggerated shiver.

"You're right, Mum. They dinnae. Why didnae you tell me that you were in town earlier? It looks like I lied tae my boss when I said you were in Glasgow." Amelia's jaw clenched.

"Is that why yer in a snit?" Letitia scoffed.

"I am not." Amelia gritted her teeth. "I want tae find oot what happened tae McCormac, but my own bosses dinnae trust me."

"The coppers are trying tae find the killer," Michael said. "They asked a lot of questions aboot what McCormac was up tae in Ireland. We dinnae got a clue. He was closemouthed aboot his setup in Belfast."

"McCormac didnae tell you?" Amelia asked. She looked especially hard at Michael.

"Nah," Michael said. "We told that DI Zeffer how McCormac liked you best—if he shared with anyone it would be his sis."

Amelia bowed her head as her knuckles tightened on the handle of her mug. "Why'd you do that?"

Paislee could see how that wouldn't be helpful in keeping the officer's trust.

"He stayed with you, right?" Michael pressed. "Not with us."

"Two nights," Amelia protested. "Then he was with Sula or one of his other lasses. Lyla somebody."

Letitia slurped her gin again. "Dinnae forget Porche."

"Mum, him and Porche are over. Have been for a long time," Amelia said.

"I know what I saw." Letitia shifted on the couch.

"When?" Amelia asked.

"Time before last, October?" Letitia's sharp brown gaze glittered with mirth. "McCormac showed up all of a sudden and snuck over tae Hank's house while his mate was at work. Him and Porche were shagging for hours before Hank came home and in slinked McCormac tae our place like an alley cat."

Michael smiled into his glass. "Lucky bastard."

Paislee thought she detected pride in both Michael and Letitia's voices. If Brody ever treated women like that, she'd smack him on the back of the head.

"No, he wouldnae go there." Amelia sounded hurt. "Porche broke his heart and stomped on it."

Letitia arched a brow. "McCormac loved that girl. He'd do anythin' for her, anythin' she asked tae prove it."

Amelia stared into her mug. "You're right. I guess I really didnae know McCormac that well after all."

"How can ye?" Letitia scoffed. "I'm his mum. You cannae keep secrets from your mother. It's not possible."

Paislee bobbed the tea bag in her cup, hoping that for Amelia it *was* possible, or they'd be in trouble regarding the suitcase chockfull of cash.

"The police suspect Michael, Mum." Amelia sounded very tired. "Possibly you, though it was Michael driving the car. And now me." She scuffed the floor with her boot, maintaining her slouch.

"Not anymore." Letitia lifted her mug with a sly expression. "At this verra moment they should be over at Hank's place and dragging him tae the station tae answer a few questions."

"Let him get a feel of what we Henrys have gone through," Michael said.

Paislee's heart ached for Amelia, the one Henry trying to be her best.

"Och, no, Mum. What have ye done?" Amelia asked.

Chapter 17

Paislee observed Letitia with astonishment, wondering if she'd understood correctly. "You set up Hank?"

"Could be he really did it," Letitia said, obviously proud of her deduction. "Didnae Hank punch McCormac on Hogmanay?"

"Amelia told us aboot it, but we heard the tale from plenty of other witnesses too," Michael said.

"I saw it myself," Paislee said. "But then Hank and Porche left, and I didn't see them again."

"It was crowded, eh?" Michael asked. His expression suggested that perhaps he'd gotten one over again somehow, in this game of who might have killed McCormac.

"Aye." Paislee narrowed her eyes at Michael. Payne had mentioned an argument between Michael and McCormac. What time had the Henrys arrived on New Year's Eve?

"And you'd probably knocked back a few drinks," Letitia said. She tapped her temple with her free hand, the other clutching the tumbler of gin. "Cannae trust what ye saw. What is that phrase, something aboot withoot a doot . . . cannae pin nothin' on a body withoot proof."

"I wasn't drunk," Paislee stated firmly. "I prefer a hot cider or cocoa on a cold night."

"Probably thinks she's too guid for that." Michael sneered.

"I had two drinks," Paislee said, then lowered her tone because it sounded like she was explaining herself. "It was busy though. And the snow was intermittent, making things cloudy."

"The Walshes could have been right in front of you, and you wouldnae have known, it was snowing that hard," Michael said.

Paislee's nape tingled. "You sound like you were there at the park, Michael."

Letitia scowled at Michael. "Eejit."

Michael tossed back his drink.

Amelia stepped toward her brother and the mug trembled in her hand. "Were you at the park New Year's Eve?"

"So what if I was?" Michael countered. "Dinnae have tae explain anything tae you."

"*Why* were you there?" Amelia demanded.

Paislee wanted to know too.

"Does Payne know?" When Michael didn't answer, Amelia shifted her focus to Letitia. "Were you there too?"

"*I* wasnae," Letitia said righteously. "I was playing cards with Louise and Jack next door, as I told the constable."

Amelia scowled. "And let me guess, they're under the impression that Michael was with you."

Letitia gave a small shrug of indifference. "He was, for a bit."

Paislee, annoyed by Michael's smugness, decided to press his buttons. "Hard tae believe you could pull off such a scheme in that kind of weather, Michael."

"I took an Uber, so my car was parked at the house." Michael explained the brilliant plan. "Looks like I was there. Jack and Louise get so pished they willnae remember what time I left or came back after a liquor run."

Paislee glanced at mother and son on the couch, surprised they didn't go up in flames beneath the heat of Amelia's glare.

"Why. Were. You. There?" Amelia placed her mug on the low table. "Dinnae lie tae me, Michael. I've had enough of you both."

"I'll tell you, sis. I wanted tae know what McCormac was up tae, flashing around so much cash," Michael said.

"He was a luxury-car salesman," Amelia stated. "Why is that so hard for you tae believe?"

"Why cannae you see the truth, lass?" Letitia asked. "You're blind tae McCormac's faults. It's not smart. Leaves you open tae attack."

"He drove the kind of vehicle that he sold," Amelia said. "He had a nice watch and gifted us all designer puppies for Christmas. He was successful, Mum. Michael. Why wouldnae you want tae believe that he was doin' this honestly?"

Letitia stood, sorrow on her face. She stepped around the table and gathered Amelia in a hug. "Dinnae be daft, pet. You'll only get hurt."

Paislee oddly agreed with Letitia.

After a moment, Amelia nodded and backed up from the embrace. "Why would McCormac risk going back tae a life of crime? He hated jail. Was he involved with the Irish mob?"

"Och, that would be in over his head, eh?" Letitia poured gin into her mug, skipping the token soda, and sat again. "Dinnae *think* the mob is behind it. McCormac wanted money, plain and simple."

"He wasnae the kind tae want flash for flash's sake," Amelia argued. "As a lad he was aboot the thrill."

"What changed for him?" Paislee asked, thinking aloud.

The Henrys all looked at her as if they'd forgotten she was there.

"Guid question," Amelia said. "What forces someone tae change?"

"Prison?" Paislee suggested. "He never wanted tae be poor again."

"He and Sula grew close," Amelia said. "Sula feels like he realized she would stick by him no matter what. She even brought up marriage, which would take money."

"Love," Paislee said.

"Not for Sula," Letitia scoffed.

"She's all right," Michael said. "I've seen her dance. Pretty enough. But McCormac wouldnae have ever gotten serious with her, because of her job. Double standard tae sleep with her, but what can ye do?"

Paislee didn't answer that question. McCormac had made enough money to splash it around. "Who else was he seeing?"

"Like, hooking up with?" Michael asked.

"Yes." So far, she counted four: Diana, Lyla, Sula, and Porche.

"Depended on the week, really," Michael said with pride. His brother's skill with the ladies must not have been something Michael had mastered. Considering his extreme lack of charm, it was no surprise.

Letitia chuckled. "He was always handsome. Charming. Like your da," she said.

Amelia grimaced.

Michael winced.

Yes, there was jealousy there along with the pride. Though Michael was older, it had been McCormac who had the luck.

Then again, McCormac was now dead and had been shot in the chest, in the heart. Perhaps not so lucky after all.

Michael had time and might yet find someone to be his mate. So long as they didn't have red hair, she thought with a grateful shiver.

Amelia paced the space between the kitchen and the living room. "So, you decided tae come home on New Year's Eve tae *spy* on McCormac," she said.

Michael spluttered.

"Watch yer tongue, lass," Letitia cautioned.

"It's true, though. Did you approve of this idea, Mum?"

"Money's tight around the holiday," Letitia said, not admitting to anything.

"McCormac had plenty. Why shouldnae he share with family?" Michael continued. "It's only fair. I wanted him tae help with the house."

"What's fair," Amelia said in a calm voice, "was that he was earning money for himself. I'm torn up because if it wasnae by legal means, that puts me in a verra tough position at the police station."

"It's why he didnae tell you, pet," Letitia said.

"Did McCormac say that?" Amelia pressed.

"No, but he wouldnae have had tae." Letitia drank her gin. "A mum knows."

The puppies started to whine, and Paislee glanced at them as wee Daisy toddled to the puppy potty pad. Robbie whined louder at Daisy's retreat.

Letitia clapped her hand to her ear and scowled at Amelia. "I hate that sound. I willnae put up with it."

"You need tae stash them outside. Or in the loo?" Michael mimicked the pained look on his mum's face.

"No." Amelia studied the puppies then turned back to her family. "It's time for their medicine, anyway. I can show you how tae do it?"

Michael raised his hand. "Naw. Thanks."

"Fine. They stay where they are." Amelia puffed out her chest and straightened her shoulders. "I have tae really wrap my head around what you're sayin', regarding McCormac and Porche and his means tae bring in money."

"It's best tae just accept him how he was," Letitia said.

"What do you think McCormac was doing?" Paislee asked.

"You with the cops?" Letitia curled her lip. "Or just nosy?"

Paislee sipped her tea, suddenly grateful that her mum was in America. "I own a yarn shop."

"Hardly worth it," Michael said.

"True. I'm always on the edge of financial ruin." Paislee wouldn't want them to think she was a success in any way, or they might want a loan.

"You'd best not skip oot on paying Amelia her wages, or I know people who will have a talk with you," Letitia threatened.

"Mum!" Amelia said, enraged.

"I pay her on time," Paislee promised. What a strange example of motherhood. "Well, what do you think McCormac was up tae? You know him best, after all."

"Hank was his partner in crime," Letitia said. "Since they were kids. That's what I told Constable Payne. I reminded him of the fistfight New Year's Eve and complained that my McCormac was tryin' tae do right, but Hank was draggin' him back doon tae the dirt."

It wasn't a terrible conclusion, Paislee thought.

"Could be true," Michael said. "It was enough for the coppers tae back off of me and Mum. Told us not tae leave Nairn, but whatever."

"Did you tell the constable you came back early tae spy on McCormac?" Amelia said.

"No. Tae play cards with the neighbors," Letitia replied. "If they ask you, you go along with that, now."

"And why didnae you tell me aboot McCormac? The truth?" Amelia asked.

"I talked with you," Letitia said, "aboot his wealth and you were just so happy for him tae be successful that I admit a part of me was also hopeful."

"I dinnae understand," Amelia said. Amelia added a splash of soda water to her mug, skipping the gin she hated.

Letitia looked at Paislee. "You have bairns?"

"One child. A son."

"Then you understand."

"What exactly?" Paislee didn't want to agree with anything until she knew the full story, as she had a wary respect for Letitia.

"Even though it seemed like McCormac had returned tae a life of crime, I'd hoped he would prove me wrong. Like Amelia."

Paislee nodded.

"What do you mean, Mum?" Amelia asked.

"You are a guid lass," Letitia said. "If you could make the right choices, there was hope for McCormac. That he could too."

Michael shuffled on the couch, obviously uncomfortable at his mother's comments. He was not on the *good kid* list.

Amelia swiped a tear from her cheek. "I wanted that too, verra much. But if his windfall wasnae by legal means, what might Mc-Cormac have done for huge amounts of cash?"

"I dinnae ken, pet," Letitia said. "It's possible he was involved with Hank, as McCormac went to Hank's a lot, though he coulda been there to be with Porche."

"Porche lives in Inverness!" Amelia said.

"And dinnae she have a car?" Letitia sipped from her mug with a raised pinky. "Just as fancy, too . . . a posh Mercedes."

"Who are his mates?" Paislee asked. "Besides Hank or Dougie Selkirk, we know of Sula. Lyla. Diana."

"Who's Diana?" Letitia asked sharply.

"A receptionist at Paislee's vet's clinic named Diana, who had a relationship with McCormac," Amelia explained. "Blonde—ye know the type."

Letitia shrugged. "What about mates in Belfast?" Paislee asked Letitia and Michael.

"Dunno," Michael said.

The puppies yipped. Paislee stepped over the barricade to see what was wrong so that Letitia didn't get upset by their noises.

Daisy had returned to the dog bed after her foray to the potty pad and had joined Robbie, who was now sideways with Daisy's paw on his nose. Nothing wrong but whingeing.

Paislee scooped Daisy up and snuggled her close.

"You want tae buy her?" Letitia called from her seat on the sofa.

"I have a dog already. It's a lot of responsibility." But oh, Daisy was tempting.

"I'll cut you a deal," Letitia said.

"I really can't, but thank you." Paislee breathed in the sweet scent of a puppy, remembering when Wallace had been so small. Well, never this small, which was a problem.

"Diana, the woman at the vet's clinic, might be interested in Robbie," Amelia said quickly.

"How much?" Letitia rubbed her thumb and forefinger together.

"The pup cannae be sold until he's healthy," Amelia said. "And I didnae offer a price because I figured you'd want tae do that."

Michael nodded. "You're right. I did some research on the purebred Maltese, and I could get two thousand pounds."

"That's the high end," Amelia cautioned. "Dinnae spend it before it's in your pocket."

"Like I would!" Michael complained.

But, Paislee thought he seemed like the type who might spend it a million ways before it was actually a done deal. She wondered why Amelia didn't tell them about the fake vet.

"I'll need Diana's information," Michael said. "How long before Robbie's ready tae leave the nest?"

Amelia considered this and said, "Three weeks."

"What?" Michael rose in a hurry. "That's ridiculous."

"Sit doon," Letitia cautioned.

"She's hustling me." Michael sank to the cushion.

"It's the best way," Amelia said. "If you sell a puppy and something happens tae it, you'd have tae give the money back."

"Not bloody likely," Michael said. "We dinnae know a thing aboot them sick dogs. Just like McCormac tae screw us over. Where's yours?"

"Snowball is still sick." Amelia sighed. "Do you think McCormac could have been stealing again? Maybe instead of car parts, he'd advanced tae home robberies?"

Letitia shrugged, tight-lipped.

"Makes sense." Michael nodded. "You know your hero McCormac had ratted oot Hank, which is why he got only a two-year sentence for theft?"

"I didnae!" Amelia placed her hand over her heart. "McCormac snitched?"

"Aye," Michael nodded.

"But Hank never went tae jail like McCormac." Amelia's blue eyes were wide with surprise.

"Is that why Hank punched him?" Paislee asked. A wee clipe was not something to be proud of in any circle.

"I want tae talk tae Hank," Amelia said. "We have tae talk tae him."

Paislee stroked Daisy's tiny nose and then put her back next to Robbie, who made room for his littermate on the dog bed without any more grumbles.

What would it be like to have another furry member in the family?

Paislee walked back to her chair to focus on finding out more from Letitia and Michael. "Would that be wise, Amelia, confronting Hank?"

"I think you should stay oot of it, love," Letitia cautioned. "Take care of the pups and be a guid girl. The fuss with McCormac will blow over and you'll be back at work in no time."

"I cannae believe my ears," Amelia said.

"It's a lot tae ponder," Letitia said. She finished her drink, then turned to Michael. "Well, we should go check on your da."

"He's having a rough time of it, since losing his job," Michael said to Paislee.

"That was four years ago," Amelia said, with no audible pity for the man.

"Family," Paislee said. "People do things tae provide for the ones they love."

Michael grimaced. "I thought McCormac should do more, which is what we'd had a row aboot. When he didnae agree, I thought he should let me in on whatever scheme he was doing."

Amelia sucked in a breath. "New Year's Eve?"

"Aye." Michael shrugged. "I offered tae step in and learn the ropes. He could stay in Belfast if he liked, and I could concentrate on local expansion."

"Doing *what*?" Amelia asked.

"Doesnae matter," Letitia said. "It was obviously a money-maker."

Amelia expelled a breath of frustration.

"Did you talk tae McCormac that night, Michael?" Paislee asked. She tried to picture him holding a gun and shooting his brother out of jealousy.

"Nope," Michael said. "I missed the fistfight. It was just Mc-Cormac and Sula, with your lot"—Michael gestured to Paislee—"and the fireworks had started. Next thing I know he was already dead."

Chapter 18

It was no wonder that the police officers required cold, hard facts, because lies made stories as slippery as metal knitting needles. Paislee stayed with Amelia as her friend said goodbye to her family.

As soon as the door was shut, Amelia shook her head in disbelief. "They lied tae me and the constables. Michael is jealous and greedy, but I just cannae believe he'd kill McCormac, or I'll go mental. Total breakdown."

Paislee patted Amelia on the arm.

Michael was a dobber . . . did that equal killer? He was jealous of his brother and jealousy was often a motive for murder.

"Your mum loves you in her own fashion, so I don't see her taking any of her children out of the picture." Paislee hated to go there but felt her friend should be on guard against Michael. "Michael wanted a piece of the money pie and had an argument with McCormac about funding the household budget, which McCormac refused tae do, despite your da's lack of work."

"Because Da's a lazy sod," Amelia declared.

Paislee didn't comment. "Neither of them seems tae know *how* McCormac was making that money. Right now, they need you tae take care of the pups, so I think you're safe."

"Sound logic." Amelia exhaled hard and plopped onto the

couch. "It's why I didnae tell them aboot the fake vet and their puppies not being worth as much. I've bought Daisy and Robbie a few weeks. I hope Snowball is all right."

Paislee studied Amelia's wan face. The poor lass was in shock. "What about calling Arran?"

"It can wait until tomorrow. Mary Beth doesnae need me tae disturb her family on a Sunday. I have a feeling this is going tae explode into a bloody mess."

"And then there's Hank." Paislee had thought it would be a good idea to talk with the man before she'd discovered that Letitia had set him up, and that McCormac had ratted him out to do less time. Why hadn't Hank also gone to prison? Now, it might be dangerous. If Hank was involved or guilty, hopefully he'd be in jail.

Amelia straightened and rubbed her eyes. "McCormac snitched on him, which just isnae how you do things in Nairn. Hank had a right tae be mad."

"Even if he is a thief?" Paislee wanted to know the ground rules.

"Thief isnae the same level as murderer," Amelia said.

"True." Paislee read the time on her phone. Almost noon. She texted Grandpa, checking on the boys. Maybe she could bring home ice cream or take them all to Scoops to see how the new ice cream venue stacked up. "I should—"

"You cannae leave me, Paislee!" Amelia slowly got to her feet. "I have tae find oot who is behind this awful scheme. No puppy, no brother, no job. I cannae trust anybody but you."

"You didn't do anything wrong." Paislee tried to operate in a fair manner, but she was aware the world didn't always work that way. Amelia might be sacked from the station because of her family. "You should add that tae your list for Arran in the morning."

"I have a new plan." Amelia scanned her phone. "Still nothing from Sula yet, but I say we go there and talk with her in person— we can drive by Hank's on the way. They're in the same neighborhood as my family. Get Dougie's address and find oot what he wanted from me last night. That's a lot of cash in that suitcase, and surely somebody knows aboot it."

Grandpa texted that everyone was watching movies and staying quiet because of Brody's sprained arm. He'd made cheese and bacon toasties for a snack. At the rate they were eating both boys should be growing, and Paislee might need a third job.

Chuckling, she sent a reply that she was spending time with Amelia, so if they needed her just let her know. She added a thank-you emoji.

"Okay," Paislee said. "Sula's via Hank's. Maybe we can grab some lunch?"

"Sure." Amelia patted her stomach and stuck out her tongue. "Something tae go with gin for my brekkie. I'll get the pups settled. That was a close one, eh? With Mum and Michael, aboot when they could be sold? Michael was right on that amount."

"You were quick on your feet," Paislee said.

"I know the Henrys, and if it takes an extra step they willnae do it," Amelia said with a shrug. "Which is why murder is off the table. It's too complicated. Somebody *planned* tae kill my brother at midnight."

It made a little bit of sense, but Paislee wasn't sold on Michael's innocence. She stepped over the barricade to the kitchen and petted Daisy before putting the tiny pup into the crate.

Amelia noticed with a good-natured smirk. "Are you sure you're not interested?"

"Positive," she replied. But, she was completely on the fence. Daisy was a sweetie. Then she thought of the two thousand pounds and let the fleeting wish go.

Money was dear after the holiday and paying for the house repairs. Plus, the brakes on the Juke. And now Grandpa's point of keeping her son in groceries.

Someday, when she had extra to spare, she'd consider another pup. There were times when being responsible really wasn't fun, and heaven knew that when Paislee had gotten Wallace it had been a heart decision, not a financial one. Gran had died and Wallace had eased that ache just a wee bit.

Amelia's phone dinged with a notification, and she read the message before shrugging into her coat. "Mum's home. She warned that the roads are slick."

Paislee opened the door and studied the exterior handle. "You're sure you saw Dougie?"

"Aye, the weasel." Amelia joined her at the threshold. "What are ye lookin' at?"

"Wondering about fingerprints." Paislee sighed. "A moot point after we've all touched the knob." She stepped into the hall.

Amelia joined her. "Let's start with Hank, then Sula, then Dougie. Gather information, as Constable Payne likes tae say."

The pair went down the stairs to the lobby of the building and out the door to the Juke, covered in several inches of snow. Snow had accumulated to her mid-calf since this morning.

"It's not letting up, is it?" Amelia said. "Are you okay tae drive?"

"Sure! Been driving in this stuff all my life. Just have tae go slow and watch out for other people, who might not be as cautious." That particular bit of advice had come from her da.

"I dinnae like it," Amelia confessed, "but luckily, it's a straight shot tae the station from here. And Cashmere Crush."

"Yes, true."

Amelia cursed aloud. "Missing Snowball, and McCormac, is awful enough. What if I dinnae get my job back?"

"Don't borrow trouble," Paislee cautioned. And that was Grandpa. What if she'd been raised by a family as crooked as the Henrys, and not the Shaws? Would she have the strength to find right over wrong?

"I'm a planner," Amelia said as she opened the passenger side of the Juke. "Plan A, plan B, and C . . . sometimes all the way tae Zed."

Paislee swiped her bare hand over the window and door handle. "Brr. Forgot gloves in all the excitement of the day."

"I have an extra pair." Amelia dug into her interior pocket and offered Paislee a set of gloves that could be bought inexpensively, but they would do the job of keeping her fingers warm.

"Thank you." Paislee started the engine and turned on the wipers and the heater. The smell of fresh snow had a crisp tang that she associated with holidays, sledding, and ice-skating. "Should you try Sula again?"

"Nah. Let's surprise her. I got tae thinking aboot that necklace and if McCormac stole it for her." Amelia pressed her hand to her stomach. "Makes me sick."

"You think she'd know it was stolen?"

"That's what I intend tae find oot, honestly." Amelia sighed. "Lass had me feeling so bad for her . . . it better not be a con too."

Recalling Sula's tears, Paislee agreed. "All right. What is Hank's address?"

Amelia shared it to Paislee's GPS and Paislee plugged it in. She already had Sula's from the day the Mercedes was impounded. All within several blocks of one another, though Sula's was on the nicer edge.

"I keep thinking aboot Hank and what made him so angry that he'd punch McCormac like that. The obvious answer has tae do with my brother being a snitch. It's been a year since he moved tae Ireland and mibbe this is the first time Hank has seen him. And then tae have my mum tell the constable he had reason tae kill him." Amelia's cheeks turned red. "We'll just drive by tae see if he's home."

"Isn't there supposed tae be honor among thieves?" Paislee teased.

"In my game world, yeah," Amelia said. "You get high marks for integrity."

Paislee made a right, and then a left, driving slowly past the row of adjoined housing that had seen better days, despite the fresh layer of snow. Old vehicles parked in an abandoned lot, missing tires or metal, or glass. Some skeletons were missing all three.

"Anythin' of value would be sold," Amelia said as they slowed. "The junkers are left tae rot."

"It's so sad tae see them."

"Aye. What's even sadder?" Amelia ruffled the top of her short hair. "During the spring it'll be a playground. It's amazin' that more of us didnae need tetanus jabs."

"You're kidding!" Paislee wouldn't let Brody near that junk-yard.

"Mum woulda told me it was me own fault for not being care-ful and dinnae be an eejit next time."

Tough love. It was still love. Her own mum had abandoned her to Gran.

"Should I park?" Paislee was practically at a crawl. "It's the one on the end, right?"

"Yeah. See that car under a tarp? And the tracks are fresh. Bet he just got home from the station." Amelia rubbed her hands to-gether, the mittens muffling the sound. "He's got tae be cursing the Henry name."

"Is he the only one tae live here?" There weren't any Christmas decorations or lights on his door, though some of the other flats were decorated.

"I think his folks have passed." Amelia gritted her teeth. "Porche moved tae Inverness, but according tae Mum that hasnae stopped her from returning when she feels like it, tae see McCormac."

Paislee glanced at Amelia.

"I hate Porche because she treated McCormac like her toy. He promised me after she broke his heart, and he wanted tae *die*, that he would stay far away from her. Another lie, obviously."

Paislee yanked her gaze back to the traffic—there were no other cars on the road, but the street was slick.

A shadow appeared at the window overlooking the street. Someone moved the blind and noticed that Paislee was going at a crawl.

The figure disappeared and suddenly the door opened and

Hank, the man that she'd last seen on New Year's Eve, raced down the two steps to the street, slipping and sliding, off balance, as he barreled toward the Juke.

Alarmed, Paislee stepped on the gas, but the tires spun, and she quickly lifted her foot to keep from spinning around in circles.

Hank slammed his hands to the bonnet and Amelia sucked in a breath.

"What are you doing here?" Hank shouted, his face a dangerous shade of crimson.

Paislee put the car in park. The last thing she wanted was to accidentally run the angry man over. Even if he had killed McCormac. His temper made it easy to believe that he could make his way through the holiday crowd with the intent to kill an old frenemy.

"Just stay calm," Paislee advised. "Once he relaxes maybe we can ask some questions from inside the Juke."

Amelia hopped out and Paislee's stomach clenched.

"What are you doing?" Amelia didn't answer, so Paislee turned off the engine and climbed out too, grabbing the keys like a weapon. What good would her whistle do?

"Amelia Henry, are you trying tae ruin my life?" Hank shouted. Snow piled on his head, turning the brown hair to white.

"I'm sairy, Hank. You know I'm not!" Amelia reached out to touch his bulky arm. Muscles strained his shirt from chest to biceps.

"What are ye doing here?"

"On our way tae visit Sula." Amelia stared up at the man who appeared to be a giant next to her petite frame.

His cheeks grew ruddy with emotion. "Your mother told the constables that I'd punched McCormac on Hogmanay—a punch, aye, but I'd not shoot anybody. Even if the bastard deserved it, eh?"

"Why did you?" Paislee asked.

"None of yer business." Hank's brow furrowed. "Who the hell are you?"

"A friend of mine." Amelia spoke to Hank in a calm tone—not her first foray in calming a wild man, she'd bet. "Paislee Shaw. She owns Cashmere Crush on the corner of Market Street. I work there on Saturdays."

"McCormac said you worked at the police station." Hank sneered as if Amelia was working in a whorehouse.

"It's true. Got the job when I was old enough because Inspector Shinner had a heart, though he'd caught me shoplifting. Told me I had a choice in how I wanted tae live my life—it was right embarrassing when he arrested McCormac for stealing car parts." Amelia puffed up with anger. "He went tae jail, but you didnae. Why is that?"

Paislee was impressed that she'd gone on the offensive rather than apologize for her brother snitching.

"Couldnae prove I was there," Hank said. "Still cannae, which is why the coppers had tae let me go just now. I havenae been a part of that scene in years. McCormac went tae jail, aye, and I know he ratted me oot for less time. He was gone, so I cleaned up my act."

"Then why'd ye skelp McCormac?" Amelia asked. Her tone held curiosity but not blame, and Hank responded.

"He tried tae rope me into a crazy scheme and wasnae having it when I said no. Porche tried tae intervene but she's no better than McCormac. We should've set a better example for you bairns growing up." Hank's jaw clenched. "My aunt's son was killed, and he was the same age as me. I didnae want tae die or do time. Left me a clear choice."

"I'm sairy for your loss," Amelia said.

"I'm sairy for yours." Hank ruffled the snow off his hair. "Let me know when you have a service for the poor bloke. I'd like tae be there. For better or worse, we were best mates once."

"I will." Amelia gave Hank a hug, the bigger man dwarfing her.

"And tell yer mum tae lay off, would ya?" Hank raised his hand in farewell then dashed back inside his home, slamming the door.

Paislee and Amelia got into the car.

"What do you think?" Paislee asked. "Is Hank sincere?"

"Aye, I believe so." Amelia leaned into the passenger seat. "An-

other truth: McCormac should have gotten cleaned up but didnae."
She smacked her palm to her forehead. "I should have asked what
the plan was!"

"We can ask on the way back, if we don't find out anything
from Sula," Paislee suggested. It was now almost one in the afternoon. Tomorrow was a return to their routine, and she was ready
for it.

"Okay."

Paislee pulled up Sula's address and arrived in minutes. A fancy
Mercedes SUV, similar to what McCormac had driven, was in the
car park.

"Is this the car you saw?"

"Aye. If he's here, then we dinnae have tae track him down."

That would be a bonus after all of the running around they'd already done today, Paislee thought. Also, too easy. They exited and
went to the door.

Amelia pounded on the door.

"Hello?" Sula answered their knock with a confused expression. Fresh from the shower, her hair was damp, and she wore no
makeup. Yoga pants and a baggy shirt.

"Hi! I was hoping I could talk with you. Aboot . . . McCormac," Amelia said. Probably smart not to go blaming Dougie or
they might not be let in.

"Sure. I mean, I guess . . . you're already here, and you brought
yer friend." Sula stepped back. "Paislee, how are you?"

"Fine, thanks." Paislee inched over the threshold.

"My car is in the shop, so she's been a dream and drivin' me
around while I try tae figure oot what's going on with my brother,"
Amelia said, on Paislee's heels to the foyer. "The puppies, the lies,
the fancy jewelry."

Sula paled, showcasing dark shadows under her eyes.

Amelia forced her way past Sula, dragging Paislee along with
her to the end of the short hall.

"Why not come in?" Sula asked sarcastically.

The interior of the flat was brightly lit, the flocked Christmas tree flashing merrily. Thor was on a cozy dog bed and lifted his head to woof a hello.

"Did you get my messages?" Amelia asked.

"I did." Sula's lower lip protruded.

"And?"

"What do you want me tae say?" Sula arched a brow. "I dinnae ken how McCormac was making his money."

"I'd like tae talk tae Dougie." Amelia crossed her arms and planted her feet. She wasn't going anywhere.

"Dinnae be that way," Sula said. "I know McCormac loved you. I want tae help find who did this tae him as well."

"Start by being honest with me," Amelia said.

"What do you want tae know?" Sula touched the diamond pendant.

"Was McCormac on the straight and narrow?"

"You're being naïve, Amelia," Sula chided.

Amelia blushed hard and glanced toward Thor. "I want my dog back. Can you make that happen?"

"Huh?" Sula wore a genuinely confused expression.

"Snowball." Amelia spoke slowly, anger in her words. "My dog is gone. And I want tae know why Dougie has tried twice since McCormac died tae break into my flat."

Paislee studied Sula's reaction and was surprised when Sula sighed. "You've got it all wrong, Amelia. It wasnae Dougie. It was me."

Chapter 19

"I beg your pardon?" Amelia asked. She leaned backward in shock and Paislee put her arm around her shoulders to support her.

"Let's sit doon and I can explain." Sula passed by Amelia and Paislee. "I was just making some tea. Would ye like some? I have herbal or fully caffeinated."

"I'd love a cup," Amelia said. "And answers!"

Sula looked at Paislee in question. Her brows were much darker than her blond hair and Paislee suspected that Sula must dye it, to keep McCormac happy?

"Me too," Paislee said. "Anything with caffeine. I'm addicted."

Sula smiled at Paislee's enthusiasm. "I love it so much but I'm going tae be cutting back."

"Nerves?" Paislee asked. She sometimes got jittery on her third or fourth cup of strong tea.

"No." Sula hurried forward. "Long story. Have a seat?" She gestured to the table for four in the kitchen. It was a smaller square table covered with a holiday plaid cloth, and an unlit candle in the center, surrounded by fragrant pine boughs.

Thor trotted over to his mistress, and Sula patted the sable Brussels griffon on the head. "I had no idea how much I would love this dog," she admitted. "They steal your heart!"

"So, you understand why I want Snowball back," Amelia said, staying on track.

"I have no idea what you're talking aboot. Tell me what happened." Sula was able to put together the tea, with biscuits, and converse at the same time in the open layout.

Amelia explained everything up to the fake veterinarian and the visit to the empty clinic this morning. "Nothing was in that room, Sula. Well, other than the burner phone on the desk. Like this bloke was mockin' me. I dinnae like it."

Sula looked faintly ill. "I cannae believe it. There has tae be an explanation."

"Yeah, there should be. But," Amelia said as she accepted her steaming mug and opened a tin of assorted teas, "I'd like tae start with why you were tryin' tae get inside my flat. You didnae see my car, so what? You thought you could just come on in?"

Sula's cheeks turned red with embarrassment.

"You're right. I didnae realize that your car was in the shop. My bad—it's why I'll never truly be good at this life of crime," Sula said quietly.

"But you were trying it out?" Paislee asked. "For size?"

Sula snickered and fixed herself a lemon zest tea, adding a spoon of brown sugar. Paislee didn't need anything added but selected a chocolate biscuit. Her stomach was running on empty.

"Not quite like that." Sula dunked a thin cookie into her mug and chewed the softened biscuit. "I love nice things. So?"

"Sula!" Amelia exclaimed. "That's no answer."

"Sairy." Sula leaned toward Amelia, then eyed the ceiling. "It's just that, I'm not proud of myself, all right?"

"Noted." Paislee sipped and her stomach eased. Sustenance and answers at last.

"I think there was a mistake with what McCormac had left here when he'd slept over a few nights," Sula said.

"I dinnae understand." Amelia stared hard at Sula, not letting her go.

"Amelia, it's like this—your brother and I were going tae run away." Sula's gaze flickered with uncertainty, which Paislee found odd.

"You don't have tae run anywhere," Paislee said. "You're both single. Have jobs. You don't answer tae anyone."

"Not exactly," Sula said. She started to cry.

Amelia stood and patted her shoulder. "What is it?"

"I miss him so much!" Sula sniffed as tears hit the tablecloth.

"You didnae even live in the same country," Amelia said somewhat sharply.

Sula raised her head, her response immediate. "We talked all the time. It's almost eight hours from Belfast tae here and sometimes we'd meet halfway. Your brother has . . . a healthy sexual appetite."

Amelia scrunched her nose. "Ew!" She abruptly sat down.

"Anyway, I knew I had tae keep things exciting," Sula said. "I didnae mind."

Paislee was curious, despite herself, but she kept quiet. This was between Sula and Amelia.

"That still doesnae explain why you were trying tae get into my flat." Amelia leaned back in the chair.

Sula blinked then murmured, "Did McCormac leave anything there for me?"

Paislee kept her mouth shut. Could this be about the suitcase at last? Amelia didn't give so much as a flicker of her eyelid away.

"No," Amelia said. "Like what?"

"I dinnae know exactly." Sula shrugged. "I'd hoped tae look around."

"You are not welcome tae snoop in my flat, understood?" Amelia said.

"Got it." Sula rubbed her stomach. "I've been a mess. I mean, I cannae really continue my work anymore."

"Why not?" Paislee asked. "Too heartbroken?"

Sula tapped the table. "It just willnae be a guid fit, now that I'm carrying McCormac's baby."

Amelia sputtered tea. "What?"

"I'm pregnant." Sula cried some more. "It's my fault that he was doing extra besides his sales job. I wanted money tae quit dancing and raise our little family, just us."

Paislee heard the sincerity in Sula's tone. "McCormac knew, then?"

Sula looked at Paislee with an arched brow. "Of course, he did."

"Were you planning on the babe?" Amelia asked, zeroing in on the key question. "Together?"

Her eyes welled. "No," Sula said. "Accidents happen and I couldnae be happier." She sobbed and bowed her head.

"Stop—it cannae be guid for the baby for you tae cry so much." Amelia seemed horrified.

Sula dabbed her cheeks, her breaths catching. "All I've done is cry, so this little wean is probably used tae it. I wanted tae get married and move somewhere we could both have a fresh start."

Amelia appeared very doubtful. "McCormac agreed tae get married?"

"No." Sula kept her head lowered.

"Well, I know you're telling the truth," Amelia said. "McCormac was anti-marriage or commitment."

"Does anybody know?" Paislee asked, dipping her head toward Sula's tummy. "Besides you, I mean."

"No. I took a home pregnancy test on New Year's Eve. It's just been a few months."

"I'm in shock," Amelia said. "I thought I'd come over here and convince you tae help me find my Snowball, not find oot that McCormac was going tae be a daddy."

"Life is strange, eh?" Sula sniffed and reached for a napkin to blow her nose.

"Agreed." Amelia drummed the tabletop. Her expression ran the gamut and settled on confusion.

Paislee turned her attention to Sula. "So. Have you told the constables this baby news?"

"It's none of their business!" Sula said.

No, then.

"I'm not sure if I should be congratulating you or not," Amelia said.

"I'm happy aboot the babe," Sula said with a heavier sob.

"Congratulations," Amelia whispered, her brow knit.

"If you can tell us what McCormac was intae, how he made so much extra cash, then we can leave you alone," Paislee said softly. "I apologize for intruding on your privacy at a time like this."

Sula dragged in a rough breath. "I'll tell you what I know but it's not much. My brother Dougie is staying here with me, so that I'm not so sad aboot losing McCormac."

"Does he know about the babe?" Paislee asked.

"No. He'll think I'm a slut, and getting what I deserve. Now I'll be a single mum, just like our mum." Sula's words held the weight of judgment by her peers and family.

"I'm also a single mum. If you want tae do it, there are resources available. I'll help you."

Sula drew back in surprise. "You dinnae know me."

"That doesn't change the offer," Paislee said. "This is your choice. You don't deserve any judgment for it."

A partial smile graced Amelia's face. "I'll be an aunt. Wait until Mum and Da hear—they'll be grandparents!"

"No!" Sula said immediately. "Dinnae say anything, please. Not yet. I want tae be farther along." She dropped her hand to her stomach.

"All right," Amelia agreed.

The three drank their tea in a very heightened state of emotion.

"I really hope that what McCormac left for me, er, us, wasnae packed into the SUV they impounded," Sula said.

"Why is that?" Paislee asked.

"It will be long gone, eh?" Sula looked at Paislee as if Paislee wasn't very bright. "Cops will help themselves."

"I suppose. And you have no idea what it could be?" Why not press ahead if Sula didn't think her that smart in the first place.

"We were going tae have a fresh start. *Money* makes that possible." Sula finished her tea and bit into another cookie.

"Where was this influx supposed tae come from?" Amelia asked. "The dogs?"

"The puppies were a side hustle," Sula said. "McCormac got most of his money from the car dealership he worked at in Belfast. At least, that's what he told me."

"A side hustle?" Amelia asked, her gaze intent. "But, legit."

"What is it with you?" Sula asked. "What difference does it make?"

"It matters tae me," Amelia said, bringing her hands to her heart.

Sula fluttered her fingers as if Amelia's feelings didn't count.

"Explain tae us again how you thought he made the money from the puppies," Paislee said.

"Dougie would be able tae tell you better than me." Sula smoothed the diamond. "I didnae really pay attention."

"But Dougie knew aboot it?" Amelia asked.

"Aye, for a piece of the pie. He was learning the trade."

"Must've been a big pie if McCormac was willing tae share," Paislee said.

"I guess." Sula ran her fingers over the nubby fabric of the tablecloth and glanced down the hall. "I hate tae wake him up. He's been working overtime with McCormac gone."

"Doing what?" Amelia asked.

"I already told you that I dinnae know the details." Sula narrowed her eyes at Amelia.

A door banged and Paislee jumped, startled.

A masculine voice cursed, then strode down the hall, turning at the kitchen. "What in the hell is going on? It sounds like a damn hen party."

"Dougie!" Sula said, not getting up, and not seeming to be overly worried by his outburst.

Her brother wore a solid red sweatshirt over plaid sweatpants with drooping pockets, his feet bare. His hair was messy, and his face wrinkled by sleeping hard.

"What is going on?" Dougie demanded. "And does it have tae be so damn loud?"

"It's our fault," Paislee said, not cowed by his grumpy demeanor. She'd learned with Grandpa, and Brody, how to ignore a male temper tantrum.

"Sairy!" Amelia said, not sounding at all contrite. She'd had brothers.

"Dougie, can I make you some tea?" Sula asked. "Lunch?"

He entered the kitchen all the way and leaned back against the counter, crossing his arms. "That depends on if these birds are staying. I cannae sleep with all of this racket."

"Actually," Sula said, "they're here tae talk tae you."

"Me?" He thumped a fist to his chest.

"Aboot McCormac and the jobs you did for extra money." Sula crumbled a bite of cookie on a napkin.

"You the cops?" Dougie asked suspiciously.

"No, eejit." Sula shook her head. "You dinnae recognize Amelia, McCormac's sister? Her friend Paislee?"

Dougie squinted. "Not withoot me contacts in." He stepped closer to Amelia with a nod, and then Paislee. "Didnae ken you were a redhead."

What did this crowd have against red hair? "Hi. Yes, we met New Year's Eve at the park."

"I know. That night cannae ever leave my head." Dougie tapped a fist to his temple and winced. "I wish I could knock it oot."

"What did you see?" Amelia asked. "We havenae had a chance tae talk since it happened. I'm trying tae find oot so that I can go back tae work."

"Eh?"

"I answer phones at the police station," Amelia said. "They've put me on a leave of absence."

His body language bristled at the word *police*.

Paislee couldn't imagine being so afraid of the local law enforcement—then again, she didn't have any shady side hustles.

The two were related, she was sure.

"I dinnae ken anything," Dougie said.

Amelia smacked her knee. "Funny. Not buyin' it either. I know McCormac approached Hank aboot the scheme in Belfast, and that's why Hank punched him that night."

"I thought it was over Porche," Sula said quickly.

"That tramp?" Dougie sneered. "They werenae an item. McCormac was a player, sis, and doesnae deserve yer tears."

"Mum said she thought McCormac had seen Porche while here in October. I guess you were unaware?" Amelia said to Sula.

Sula's lower lip trembled. "We had an understanding," she said.

Dougie clenched his jaw. "Lasses, I'm tired. What can I answer for you so that you will leave, and I can go back tae bed?"

"How did McCormac make his money?" Amelia asked, point-blank.

"Besides his commission? The extra was the puppies he sold. He bought a litter for a discounted flat fee and sold them individually for an inflated price." Dougie sounded bored.

It really made Paislee mad, so she was glad when Amelia stood. "My Snowball is missing. I know that the vet Dr. MacTavish is a fraud."

Dougie lowered his arms, but he couldn't hide that he knew, though he tried to play it off. "What do ye mean?"

"You knew," Amelia pressed, getting into Dougie's space. "It was a scam?"

"Mibbe."

"That's as good as a yes," Paislee said.

Sula arched a brow at Paislee. "You should stay oot of it."

Paislee bit her tongue. It seemed that Sula maybe knew more too.

What would Sula do to protect her unborn babe?

As a mum, there was no length too great for her to help Brody.

"I just want Snowball back," Amelia said. "I dinnae care aboot the rules broken or the phony vet, do ye understand?"

"Where can we find her?" Paislee asked. She'd made no promises not to tell the constables everything about the puppies.

"Tell me what your job was . . . did you steal the puppies?" Amelia jabbed Dougie's chest.

"No! No, we didnae." Dougie spread his arms to the sides. "McCormac did not."

"Then explain," Amelia said.

Dougie bowed his head. "Can you back up? I need tea if I'm going tae be interrogated like this."

While they waited for him to fix a mug, Paislee wondered if he was buying himself time to think of a plausible story. Amelia didn't return to her seat, but moved so she blocked the hall from the kitchen.

The puppies were bought at a discount and then it was up to McCormac to sell them. Again, while shady, not illegal.

"Where did he buy them?" Paislee asked.

Sula kicked Paislee's shin. "Give him a minute!"

"Ouch!" Paislee rubbed the knot on the bone.

Dougie joined Paislee and Sula at the table with a mug. He sipped. Amelia glared. Paislee did her best to ignore what would surely leave a bruise.

"Where, Dougie? I just want my puppy. I dinnae care aboot the fake microchip, or the fake vet, or the fake certificates," Amelia said.

Dougie slurped and then selected a chocolate biscuit.

"I want my dog." Amelia was unrelenting. "It was the last thing that McCormac ever gave me. Will ever give me."

"He bought them in Inverness," Dougie said at last.

"Wonderful! What is the address?" Paislee asked.

Dougie cursed as he squirmed on the chair. "I dinnae know it."

Amelia edged closer, her hands on her hips, fury in every pore. "If you dinnae tell me right now, I'll tell Mum you know more than you do, and she'll take care of you. Letitia Henry has her ways."

"No need for that." Dougie raised his cup. "I can drive you there!"

Chapter 20

"How can you not know the address?" Amelia demanded. "Did ye use GPS? If so, it will be in your past trips."

Dougie grabbed another cookie. "It's supposed tae be a secret, right? So, McCormac gave me verbal directions. Had tae memorize 'em but I dinnae recall exactly."

"It's a fact," Sula said. "Dougie's memory is rubbish."

"Thanks, sis." Dougie scowled at Sula, who ignored it.

"How long will it take?" Paislee asked, thinking of her family at home. Inverness to Nairn in good weather, less than thirty minutes each way. This wasn't good weather. She could see from the patio window that the snow had continued its flurry.

Dougie also looked out the window. "Dinnae ken. Longer with the storm."

Paislee sighed, kissing her afternoon goodbye. But, it was for her friend, so she kept quiet.

"Mibbe we should wait for tomorrow?" Dougie suggested.

"No way," Amelia said. "I want my dog."

"I dinnae ken where Snowball is!" Dougie protested.

"You might not," Amelia said, "but whoever you guys bought the puppies from could point me in the right direction. Do you know this fake MacTavish?"

"No," Dougie said.

Sula petted Thor. "You have tae help them, Dougie. I promise tae make your favorite lamb stew while you're gone so it'll be ready when you're home."

Dougie's shoulders lowered. "Fine. But I want rolls too."

"Whoever marries you will need tae know the way tae your heart is through your stomach," Sula said with a chuckle.

"I'm not gettin' married," Dougie said.

"You sound like McCormac," Amelia said.

"We were mates." Dougie finished his tea and rinsed the mug in the sink, the pockets in his sweatpants dragging them down to his hips. "I'll get dressed. We're leavin' in five minutes. If you're not ready, you're not going."

"Is he always so controlling?" Amelia asked as the man left.

"My fault," Sula said with a shrug. "It takes me an hour tae get my hair and makeup done. Not that it matters anymore, with McCormac gone. I'll be alone for the rest of me days. Who will want tae raise another man's bastard?"

"That's a little harsh," Paislee countered.

"I've seen it myself." Sula patted Thor. "How can I start over here in Nairn? The gossip will begin the minute I start tae show."

"It's difficult but you just have tae ignore it," Paislee said. "Think of you and the life you're carrying inside of you. Nothing else matters."

"I might move anyway, perhaps tae Edinburgh. It's not far from Dougie but I could begin fresh in the big city."

"That's not a bad idea," Amelia said. "What will ye do for work?"

"Salesperson?" Sula sighed. "But all I know is exotic dancing. Please dinnae mention it tae him. I'll have tae find the right time, but I know he'll come around."

"Ready?" Dougie shouted halfway down the hall.

Paislee and Amelia both jumped up, grabbing bags and coats. Paislee brought both mugs and saucers to the sink.

Dougie had his hand on the front door's knob.

"I'll wash the mugs," Sula said, fighting a smile. "You'd better hurry."

"Thank you!" Paislee said.

Amelia clasped Sula's shoulder. "Let's talk more."

"Later," Sula whispered, averting her gaze.

They went outside and Paislee's nose stung from the cold. Her SUV as well as Dougie's were covered in snow.

He stomped his booted feet. "You should come with me. No way can you follow in this weather."

"Good idea," Paislee said. That way they could talk on the drive and possibly learn more about McCormac.

"Thanks, Dougie." Amelia brushed snow from the car handle as Dougie clicked the fob to unlock it.

Paislee climbed behind Amelia, who sat in the passenger side.

"This is a verra sweet ride," Amelia said. "Is it exactly like Mc-Cormac's?"

Dougie turned on the vehicle and patted the dash. "Yep. Got a great discount by buying it in Belfast and it's amazing for the Highlands. Got tae admit I'm curious as tae how it does in the snow. I've only had it a few months."

After buckling up, Paislee sent Grandpa and Brody both a text that she was driving with Dougie and Amelia to Inverness and would be home later than she thought.

They both responded with a thumbs-up emoji and Grandpa added a message to be careful. The storm was turning into a blizzard.

Paislee hearted the message and watched the snow come down. Instead of a hot chocolate at home with her knitting, this journey to Inverness was for Snowball and Amelia.

"I'm glad you're driving," Paislee confessed. "This is a tank. Lydia's Corbin has something similar."

"He interested in a new one? I can get him a deal. McCormac was going tae introduce me tae his boss, see aboot getting me a job."

"In Belfast?"

"Aye. I might be taking over for him." Dougie glanced at Amelia in the passenger seat. "Sairy, Amelia, tae talk aboot him so soon."

"Why would you leave your family?" Amelia asked. "Your sis and your mum."

"It's brilliant money."

"You're not as good a salesman as McCormac," Amelia said bluntly.

Dougie ignored the dart fired by Amelia and patted the dash. "These babies sell themselves."

"What will happen tae McCormac's car, do you think? Was it paid for, or part of his job?" Paislee leaned forward to look between them.

"I dinnae ken. We were mates but he didnae tell me everything." Dougie glanced at Amelia, then Paislee. "I know Sula thinks McCormac left her money."

"So?" Amelia asked. "He didnae."

Dougie said, "You know anything aboot it?"

"Nope." Amelia kept her gaze on the road ahead. Traffic was heavy on the A96 to Inverness. "Do you think McCormac hid it somewhere? Like his car?"

Dougie shrugged. "I broke into the police yard and checked oot the SUV in impound. There was nothing tae be found, so maybe the coppers already got it. If it's bought and paid for, your folks might inherit it."

"Cannae see Mum driving this," Amelia said sadly. "Or Da. Michael maybe."

"Michael would love it." Dougie shifted on the seat. "I've met him a few times. Seems like the kinda bloke who might need tae compensate for something."

"You broke into the police impound yard?" Paislee wished she could hide the shock in her voice, but it was too late.

"Yeah, so?" Dougie's upper lip curled in derision.

Amelia exhaled loudly. "What if you'd been caught? Sula would be devastated if anything happened tae you, too."

"I wasnae." Dougie tightened his grip on the wheel as the tires slid slightly.

"You dinnae have tae be mean aboot Michael. Did you know that he wanted tae talk tae McCormac aboot joining your puppy scheme?" Amelia asked. "Tae help cover expenses at Mum and Da's house with Da oot of work and all."

Dougie snorted. "No, but I can imagine that it wouldnae have gone well. No offense, Amelia, but your brother is an eejit."

"He's the only one I have left," Amelia growled, "so I suggest you try harder tae be nice."

Dougie turned on the radio to rock music to avoid further conversation. Paislee wrote down the turns as they happened, just in case she needed them later.

These days getting places meant plugging in an addy to the nav system and having GPS direct you, but Paislee could imagine McCormac wanting it to be a secret. They arrived in downtown Inverness.

"Is it nearby?" Paislee recognized her location. Inverness was all about the Loch Ness monster, and a popular Nessie adventure ticket booth was across the street. She'd been here plenty of times with Brody. She didn't believe the monster was real, but Nessie certainly brought tourist money into the city.

"I need tae get petrol. Wasnae expecting tae go on a long drive today." Dougie pointed to the dash. "It's not guid tae stretch beyond the warning light." He slipped out of the car.

The Juke didn't have any fancy signals that showed when she was down to the last ten miles, like this did. It could be a spacecraft with all the dials, knobs, and extra conveniences.

"What do you think?" Paislee asked Amelia.

Amelia traced the dash. "Aboot what part? I'm a wee bit peeved over his dismissal of Michael. Yet, he has a point."

Dougie climbed back in, ending the conversation.

According to the time on her phone, what was normally a thirty-minute journey had taken forty-five. Paislee recognized the itch at her nape as discomfort. She enjoyed being in control behind the wheel. She had to trust Dougie, who didn't recall the exact address of where the puppies had been bought but was hoping to return there by memory. *Och*.

"How do you know where tae go from here?" Amelia asked, as if picking up Paislee's thoughts. "I hope that Snowball is okay. What if they arenae feeding her? Or petting her? What if her kennel cough isnae gone? What kind of medicine was that fake doctor going tae give her, anyway?"

"Calm doon!" Dougie said. "I think I was supposed tae get off on a different exit. The one before this—but I needed tae fill up and forgot."

Amelia steamed. "That's ridiculous."

"You're ridiculous!" Dougie said. "I told you I didnae know for sure. Let me backtrack."

Paislee bit her tongue to keep her opinion to herself. Dougie drove back toward the highway.

"Hey!" Paislee tapped the window, recognizing a woman with long flowing mermaid-blond hair in a pink winter jacket. Had she been at the petrol station? "Is that Porche?"

Dougie slammed on the brakes. "Where?"

Amelia smacked him on the shoulder. "She lives in Inverness, dobber. Could be. Doesnae matter—take me tae the house where ye bought the puppies."

"All right, all right. But this is the last time I'm doin' you a favor, Amelia. For McCormac's sake."

The "favor" ended up being two hours of driving around neighborhoods. Paislee gave up trying to keep track of it all.

"Take us home," Amelia said at last.

To Dougie's credit he was willing to keep trying. "I'm really sairy, Amelia. I can hear Sula now yelling at me. I should have written it doon even though McCormac didnae want me tae."

"You should have," Amelia agreed. "How are you going tae make any more money if you cannae bloody find it?"

Dougie tapped the wheel. "I'll have tae wait for the boss to call me, and I promise I'll ask aboot Snowball, all right?"

"That's your system?" Amelia cried. "Tae sit and wait?"

"Yeah." Dougie drove toward Nairn as the snow began again.

"Is MacTavish the boss?" Paislee asked.

"Dinnae know him." Dougie shrugged. "McCormac said the less I knew the better, just in case things went sideways. I doubted he thought somebody might kill him."

That afternoon, in Nairn once more, Paislee dropped Amelia off at her flat. Sula had met them at the door, but when she didn't see Snowball, she'd retreated.

"Arran's office doesn't open until ten. Would you like tae work tomorrow at the shop?" Paislee asked. "It might keep your mind off things, and I can catch up on knitting projects."

"That would be great. Thank you." Her friend dragged herself from the car to the lobby and went inside. The plan to question Dougie, and Hank, and Sula, had gotten her no further in finding Snowball, or her brother's killer.

Paislee drove home and arrived at half past five. She was starving and hoped there were still leftovers from New Year's Day in her fabulous fridge. She parked in the carport and dashed inside her home, pausing in the foyer to take in the peace of being in her own place.

"I'm home!" she called.

Wallace darted from upstairs to greet her with a body wag, racing down the steps on agile feet.

Brody was next, his hair stuck up on one side as if he'd been napping. His sling was crooked.

"Hi! How are you feeling?"

"Fine. Tired from staying up all night playing video games. Mum, you should see this new monster mash from—"

Paislee crushed his good side to her for a hug. "I'm glad. You can tell me about it over dinner. What shall I make?"

Grandpa came out of his bedroom, hair also mussed from a nap. It was a nice lazy way to spend an afternoon. "Dinner is in the oven, lass. Found a recipe for tarragon chicken that I thought I'd try."

"Wonderful!"

"It's warming, so ready when you are." Grandpa patted down his hair and put on his glasses.

"I am a lucky woman." She hung up her coat and kicked off her boots, following Brody and Grandpa down the hall, grinning at the pictures that Lydia had chosen for the wall. Her bestie knew her so well.

"The table's even set!" Paislee said. "Let me get everyone their drinks, then."

"Milk for me," Brody said.

"Tea." Grandpa opened the oven door, using mitts to bring out a bubbling golden dish that he placed on a trivet in the center of the table. Zeffer's holiday bouquet still smelled beautiful, the white-and-red candy cane lilies lovely and fragrant.

Paislee poured the beverages, including tea for herself, then joined them at the table.

"I've had nothing but biscuits today since breakfast and I could eat a horse."

Brody snickered and sat down, a lock of auburn hair sweeping his freckled forehead. "Gross."

"It's just an expression," Paislee assured him.

Grandpa served them and then sat down. "I'm famished, so hope this is guid and not rubbish."

"It couldnae be," Brody assured him. "You're great at putting together the best flavors. No offense, Mum."

"None taken." She took her first bite of the savory chicken in a golden gravy with wilted green herbs. "Wow."

"Mind blown!" Brody said. His arm in the sling was resting on the table. The chicken was cut into bite-sized pieces, as Grandpa was aware that Brody had to eat one-handed. He dropped his fork and splayed his fingers toward the ceiling.

Once dinner was done, Paislee happily did the dishes as Grandpa and Brody talked about America. Phoenix, specifically.

Brody finished his letter to her mother. "You promise tae mail it?"

"I do!" Paislee turned so her back was to the sink. If it was important to her son to have a relationship with her mother, and his aunt and uncle who were younger than him, then she would make it happen.

Amazing what a person was willing to do for the ones they loved.

Brody went into the living room to watch a show he liked, and Grandpa stayed to chat over a cup of tea.

"How was the day?" Grandpa asked.

"Long! I wished I was here, but Amelia needs me right now. She's missing Snowball and torn up over McCormac."

"Poor dear."

"If you'd like another day tae yourself, Amelia is coming tae work tomorrow, since the officers don't want her at the station."

"Sure! I'll make some of the homemade flies that Brody gave me for Christmas. Fishing season has tae come eventually. Was thinking of ice fishing but these bones are too old for that."

"Ice fishing?" Paislee shivered. "I don't blame you if you wait for spring." She turned to make sure that Brody wasn't paying attention. "Amelia is worried that something might have happened tae her pup." She explained about the fake vet and about how Dougie just kept driving around.

Grandpa lowered his gaze to his mug, a smile flitting around his mouth. "Seems implausible, lass."

He was right. "I mean, how could Dougie not know where he'd been tae pick up those puppies? But at the time, with the snow, and Sula asking him tae help us, I thought he was just an extreme numpty."

Grandpa laughed outright at that. She loved talking to Grandpa because he had a no-nonsense side that didn't let her get too far off track.

The more she thought of the wasted afternoon, the more she felt like a fool. "I think Amelia and I were given the runaround for two hours."

Sula was very sly, and she wondered if the drive had been Sula's idea.

Chapter 21

Monday morning, Paislee awoke before her alarm, her mind on Amelia and puppies everywhere, like the children's animated film, *One Hundred and One Dalmatians* showcasing the villain, Cruella de Vil.

She got up and dressed, peeking at the suitcase under her bed, and was tempted to count the money.

How many puppies had McCormac sold to afford that nice Rolex, assuming he hadn't stolen it? The truth was that so far it seemed Amelia's brother's only crime was walking a fine line on being a decent human.

And while that was hard to accept, it wasn't illegal.

That money under her bed could really help the Henry family, especially since Sula was pregnant with McCormac's babe. Who would get the cash? What did McCormac think of being a father? Had he been honest with Sula about starting over somewhere new? Unanswerable questions.

Paislee sent a text to Amelia asking if she needed a ride to work that morning.

A thumbs-up emoji was the immediate reply. If only the rest were as easy. She'd collect Amelia after dropping Brody at school.

Paislee, quiet as could be, went downstairs and prepared her list

for the day. She missed being at her cozy yarn shop and enjoyed the
security Cashmere Crush provided.

She'd created it, stocked it, and grown the shop to a reliable income. "Getting closer tae Aberdeen Angus, Gran," she said with a
small smile. The fanciest beef one could buy.

"Who you talking tae, Mum?" Brody asked, wiping his eyes
with his good hand. His poor arm was sideways in the sling, which
could be removed for ease of showering.

"Just saying a few things tae Gran."

Brody's eyes widened and he looked around. "Is she here? Like,
a ghostie? Is she mad aboot the kitchen?"

"Not like that, silly. I feel her." Paislee placed her hand over
heart. "Here."

Brody snickered and opened the back door so that Wallace
could go out. The black fur was stark against the fresh layers of
white snow as he dove over the stairs to the yard . . . and it was still
falling.

"That's mental, Mum." He gave her a one-armed hug that
melted her heart and made her skip over the mental part. "I miss
her too. That's why I think we should meet your mum, if she wants
tae come here."

Paislee took advantage of this sweet moment to stroke his hair.
They were finally nose-to-nose and it had happened literally overnight. Tears welled.

"What?" Brody pulled back in alarm.

"Nothing." Paislee turned to the cupboard with the bowls and
got two down for cereal. "We just bought you new clothes and
you've grown overnight like a weed." He wouldn't appreciate her
being mushy. Every second of this time mattered and she scrambled
to find her footing as she realized he was on his way to being a
young man.

"Cereal?" he complained.

"It's back tae school for us. Back tae our routine." Paislee
pulled out juice for him and grabbed the orange marmalade. Butter.
Toast in the toaster.

He chose cereal from the pantry, the tender moment gone. "I hate cereal."

"Would you rather have oatmeal?" Paislee countered. It was the one thing her son truly loathed, and it didn't matter how she'd tried to doctor it up.

"No!" He grinned big. "Cereal is great. The best. I wish you'd let me have sugar cereal."

"You're really pushing it this morning," Paislee said. "You get plenty of sugar in your jam."

"I eat it at Edwyn's house." Brody sat and poured from the box. "Three bowls sometimes."

Grandpa came out of his room, slipping on his glasses. His thick new robe they'd gotten him for Christmas wasn't belted and the ties hung toward the floor.

"Mornin'!" he said.

"Why are you so cheery?" Brody wanted to know.

"I get another day off." Grandpa rubbed his hands together, looked at the table. "The paper here yet?"

"I haven't checked," Paislee said. She opened the back door to let Wallace in, getting the towel from the porch to dry his short furry legs and underbelly. She filled his bowl with kibble, and turned to see Brody toss him a piece of toast. "Hey!"

"What? He's hungry."

"You know what will happen if he gains any more weight? It will hurt his back—do you want him tae go on a diet?"

Brody burst out laughing. "Wallace on a diet. He's not fat! He's fluffy."

The dog raced around the kitchen as if being chased—maybe by Gran's ghost, Brody suggested. This made her son laugh even harder. Of course, that brightened Paislee's mood in the best way.

She was even smiling when Grandpa returned with the paper, soggy because snow had slipped into the plastic.

Grandpa removed it from the cover and spread it out over the counter to dry.

"Why do you get a day off and I dinnae?" Brody asked, getting up to snag the comics. The section was dry.

"Amelia is working at the shop today," Paislee explained, selecting a piece of toast for herself. She spread butter on it from a standing position. "We need tae be on time so that I can pick up Amelia after dropping you off at school."

Brody lifted his injured arm in the sling. "This is lame. Do I have tae wear it? The kids will make fun of me."

"Nobody will make fun of you," Paislee said. "It's cool."

Grandpa covered a surprised chuckle that Paislee would even try to convince him of that.

"No, it's not." Brody sighed and slurped a bite of cereal.

"Mibbe you could ask Jenni tae help you," Grandpa suggested.

Brody perked up. "That's a guid idea."

Paislee arched her brow at her grandfather, who focused on reading the slightly damp business section of Nairn's paper.

They were out the door in plenty of time. The Juke didn't want to start but did, Old Reliable, and Paislee drove very slowly on the way to Brody's school. The energy of the kids outside after the break was high, as if they hadn't seen each other in years.

Jenni was there, in the cap and scarf Paislee had made. The cutie waved at Paislee and admired Brody's sling.

Paislee gave a disgruntled sigh but waved back, then drove to Amelia's flat. Amelia waited in the lobby and darted out as soon as she pulled up.

"Nice and toasty in here!" Amelia buckled up. "Thanks for the ride."

"My pleasure."

"My car will be done at the end of the week. I already called first thing this mornin' tae see if they could make it more of a priority. Tried tae tell me that it would be next week, but I wasnae having that." Amelia offered Paislee cash. "You cannae drive me around all the time."

"Keep it." Paislee sent her a smile. "I don't mind."

"Well, I do. I like tae be independent." Amelia placed the backpack she used like a handbag at her feet.

"My gran would also say that sometimes we just need tae accept a helping hand with thanks," Paislee said.

"I wish I'd met your granny."

Amelia was Protestant and Church of Scotland, while Gran had been Catholic, otherwise they might have known one another.

"She was an angel on earth." Paislee turned left toward the shop. "How are the pups?"

"Verra well, actually. I like Dr. Kathleen a lot. Once Snowball is home, I'll use her as a vet."

Paislee smiled with encouragement though it wasn't looking good for finding Snowball, with no leads at all.

"Be sure tae tell Arran and Constable Payne about the puppies."

"I am two steps ahead," Amelia said with a chuckle. "I also called Payne this morning but had tae leave a message, so I told him aboot the burner phone and sent him the video I took of the empty rooms."

Paislee was so relieved that a weight immediately lifted off of her shoulders. "I'm so glad!"

"You were right that Arran's office doesnae open until ten, but I'll set up an appointment first thing. It's so hard tae be patient," Amelia said. "I'll be on pins and needles until the constable calls me back."

"You're doing what you can and that's all anybody can expect of you." Paislee parked behind Cashmere Crush. "I hope it's a slow day so I can knit inventory for the shop."

It was nice to have the business at Ramsey Castle, but it meant more luxury items to knit for stock there.

"Just tell me what I can do tae help," Amelia offered.

Exiting the vehicle, they went up the snow-covered cement stairs in the back and inside, Paislee flipping on the fluorescent light.

The polished cement floors glimmered—an easier solution than tile or hardwood and simple to keep clean.

"Home away from home," Paislee said with a satisfied smile. She hung up her coat and switched her snow boots for leather flats, then went to the counter with the register, tossing her bag on the shelf.

"Want me tae unlock the front?" Amelia divested her winter apparel and revealed stylish pants and a flannel shirt over a Henley. Black sneakers adorned her feet.

"Sure."

Amelia's help today would be invaluable as she knew the customers, and the product, and knitted herself. They worked in companionable silence, allowing Paislee to finish more of the coin purses that just needed the metal clasps attached.

At ten on the dot the front door opened, and Dr. Kathleen McHenry entered. The woman's smile widened when she saw Amelia there too.

"Amelia! So guid tae see you, lass," the vet said. "I've been curious as tae how the puppies were getting on."

"Guid as new, thanks tae you." Amelia smiled.

"I was happy tae help—and do the job I was trained tae do. I was verra angry at the imposter pretending tae be a veterinarian." Dr. Kathleen shut the door behind her. "I'm here tae spend my gift certificate that Paislee gave me for Christmas."

"Do you knit?" Amelia asked.

"No, no. I leave that tae the professionals." Dr. Kathleen went to the rack of bespoke sweaters, scarves, and caps. She admired the knitted dog harnesses and leads, then slippers, and cashmere socks.

Paislee hadn't known what the veterinarian would like so had decided on the gift certificate so she could choose. She'd given one to Eddie the mechanic as well as Father Dixon.

"If you'd ever like tae learn, I'd be happy tae teach you," Paislee said.

"I highly recommend our Thursday Knit and Sip group." Amelia leaned her elbow on the high-top table.

Dr. Kathleen caressed a soft vest in a thick fisherman's braid. "No, thanks. Och, did I say that too fast?" She laughed. "I have other jobs when I'm not working at the clinic."

"Like what?" Paislee asked.

"I'm on the board tae maintain veterinarian practices—it matters tae me that animals receive proper care. It's a sad fact that puppies are given at Christmas tae people who dinnae want them, and is it the fault of the pup? No!" Dr. Kathleen answered her own question.

"No," Paislee and Amelia agreed.

"I was one of those people, but now that I dinnae have Snowball, I'm heartbroken," Amelia said. "I want her back."

"Where is the dog?" Dr. Kathleen vibrated with righteous anger.

"I dinnae ken." Amelia pushed away from the table toward Paislee.

"Was she microchipped?" the vet asked.

"Supposedly, but then again, Daisy and Robbie had also been chipped but werenae." Amelia's sigh was heartfelt.

"Poor dear. That's rotten."

"Right?" Amelia walked to the front door and stared out the window.

Dr. Kathleen brought the vest to the counter with a caress of the wool. "This will be perfect tae keep me warm and my arms free. There are times I need gloves up tae my elbows. Coos. Sheep."

Paislee admired the brown-and-gray merino wool garment. It had been a popular pattern, and this was the last one. "I'm glad you found something you like."

"I'll be back. I didnae realize you had so many gifts tae choose from. I thought you were mostly yarn," Dr. Kathleen said. "I will spread the word aboot your hand-knit items."

"Thank you."

The vet turned from the counter and faced Amelia, who had paced from the window and back to the register with nervous energy.

Amelia arched her brow in question.

"I am a blunt woman," the vet said.

"As am I," Amelia said. "What is it?"

"It's aboot your brother, McCormac. The one who was shot."

Paislee wrapped the vest in tissue, then tucked the gift in a Cashmere Crush gift bag.

"Do you know why he was shot?" Dr. Kathleen shifted her weight from one hip to the other.

"No," Amelia said, "but the police are looking intae it."

The vet squinted her eyes, her mouth twisted as if she was undecided. Finally, she said, "I hear different schemes at the board. Aboot puppy farms and the dangers of forcing a young dog tae be pregnant over and over, until she dies from it. I'm sairy tae be brutal."

Amelia's nose flared but she nodded. "Go on."

"The puppies are often sold too young. They arenae weaned or nurtured before being taken from their mum." Dr. Kathleen's mouth was a flat line across her unhappy face.

Paislee and Amelia exchanged a glance. Could that be what McCormac had participated in?

"My brother bought puppies from a breeder in Inverness. He paid a flat fee for the litter and sold the individuals." Amelia raised her hand. "At least, that's what was told tae me by someone also involved."

"I see." Dr. Kathleen absorbed this new information like a sponge.

"What is the scheme?" Paislee asked. "Or is that it?"

"No. There is another piece tae the puzzle." The vet scowled, her sigh exhausted. "The breeders will rent a space for a month or two tae conduct business, and then move on. It makes it verra difficult tae catch a moving target."

"Oh!" Amelia brought her hand to her mouth.

"I wish I had a picture of this fake vet who scammed yer brother," Dr. Kathleen announced. "I'd spread it all over the internet."

"I fear McCormac was in on the scam," Amelia said with a whisper.

"And you arenae of that fabric." Dr. Kathleen stated this as fact. "I can tell a woman of integrity."

Amelia's cheeks pinkened. "I dinnae agree with his actions, but he's my brother. I still loved him."

"And he was killed, too. I'm sairy." Dr. Kathleen studied Amelia's face. "Do ye think you could pick the imposter from a lineup?"

"Mibbe," Amelia said. "Paislee saw him too."

Dr. Kathleen's eyes narrowed. "I'd like tae get the word on the street aboot him."

"He had brown hair. Thirties. Blue glasses. A mole on his chin." Amelia tapped hers where the fake doc had had one.

"All things that could be part of a disguise. Or not." Dr. Kathleen blew out a disgusted breath.

"A disguise?" Had anything regarding the vet seemed fake? Like a toupee? His brown hair had seemed natural to her. And who'd want to fake a mole? "Amelia, can you sketch him?"

"That would be a tremendous help, if so," the vet said.

"I'll try, but no promises." Amelia held up her hands. "I draw comics, not real people."

"These frauds will go tae great lengths tae make that crooked pound," Dr. Kathleen said. "I'll send oot your description in an email alert tae the other vets in the area, in case they also have a sick puppy who isnae in the system."

Amelia sighed. "On behalf of my brother, I am so verra sairy."

The vet drew back in surprise. "Lass, you are not your family. Thank goodness we all get tae make our own choices. My father was a gambler who lost everything on a desperate bet. I grew up knowing what I would never do—sometimes our greatest lessons are learned by not wanting tae follow in our family's footsteps."

The vet left with the vest and a reminder to Paislee that Wallace was due for his annual checkup.

"I adore her," Amelia said.

"She's right, you know. We get tae choose our behavior." Paislee had been so lucky to have her gran's guidance.

Amelia's mobile rang. "Constable Payne!" She took the phone to the back, expecting an update, but immediately returned and put the device on the counter.

"Well?"

"No news." Her face flushed with emotion. "Seems he's not happy that I didnae tell him sooner aboot the fake vet and agreed with Zeffer that a leave of absence was a guid idea."

Amelia was hurting. "Call Arran!" Paislee said. "It's after ten, and I know he can help."

Chapter 22

Paislee stayed in the back all morning, knitting another merino vest to replace the one she'd just given to Dr. Kathleen. Amelia was able to handle the slow foot traffic and sketch a drawing of the fake vet, but not to her liking. During her lunch break, Amelia walked to the station to give Payne the burner phone wrapped in her knit cap and returned in a sorrowful mood. She had an appointment with Arran on Tuesday to discuss what was happening.

Now it was two in the afternoon and Paislee was working on a scarf, something she could finish quickly. Music played softly in the background. Amelia wasn't one to sit around doing nothing and so was sweeping the floor.

Though people stomped their feet before coming in, debris from the snow tracked in on their boots. Note to self—buy a sturdy mat for the shop like the one at home.

The door opened and Paislee smiled as Lydia entered. "Lyd!"

"Hey." Her best friend often dropped in to chat for an afternoon break. "I have fresh-baked lemon muffins!"

Amelia waved at Lydia as she paused, leaning against the tall broom. "Hi!"

"It's not Saturday," Lydia said in confusion as she checked her phone. "No. Monday. But dinnae worry, I have plenty tae share."

Her friend was very stylish in a red suit made to fit her tall, slender frame. Her hair was cherry red, like Santa's outfit. Her gray eyes were expertly made up with a smokey smudge along the upper lids.

"I love it when you bring treats—stress baking, or happy baking?" Paislee asked, to clarify what mood she should be in.

"Relieved-to-have-the-holidays-over baking. Notice lemon is a springy flavor," Lydia said. "Who ordered all of this blasted snow?"

Lydia placed the bag of muffins on the high-topped table where Paislee was working. Paislee gladly put her project aside.

Lemon was one of her favorite flavors. "I don't mind it," Paislee said.

"Me either. I like tae snowboard." Amelia put the broom away and joined them. "Should I heat the water for tea?"

"No tea for me," Lydia said. "But I'll take a Pellegrino if there's one in the wee fridge."

"Let me look," Amelia said. "Paislee?"

"Tea. I'm boring," Paislee said. "Thank you!"

"Where is Angus?" Lydia asked, taking off her coat and putting it across a stool.

"He's at home for an extra day of vacation. Amelia isn't at the station for a few days, so I figured she could handle customers and I've been able tae knit. I'm at a hundred coin purses for Ramsey Castle, complete with clasps."

"Perfect. But, why not at the station?" Lydia opened the bag.

"Constable Payne and DI Zeffer think I might interfere with my brother's murder investigation." Amelia brought a bottle of Pellegrino to Lydia, and mugs of tea for her and for Paislee.

"What?" Lydia handed them each a muffin with a Christmas tree napkin. "That's nonsense."

"I agree that it's ridiculous." Amelia sat on a stool, her mug before her. "If I didnae need the job, I'd tell them tae stuff it."

"Blasted rent," Lydia said.

Not that Lydia had to worry, but she understood the heart of the problem, Paislee thought, as she often did.

"It's uncomfortable," Amelia said. "Paislee has been verra sweet."

"Nah," Paislee protested. "It's what friends do."

"What's new with the case?" Lydia asked. "If you dinnae mind talking aboot it."

"Not at all." Amelia twirled the muffin on her napkin. "But there isnae much tae tell."

Paislee broke off a moist piece of lemon muffin and put it in her mouth as the zestiness of the lemon overtook her senses. "Amazing, Lyd. Just amazing. If you ever decide tae quit the estate business, you should consider baking."

"It's a hobby," Lydia protested, her expression pleased.

Amelia took a bite and grinned. "Who needs real estate?" She laughed. "Just kidding. You are verra guid at what you do." After a pause she said, "Hey, would it be reasonable for McCormac tae get rich selling high-end cars?"

"Salespeople get a decent commission," Lydia said. "But I dinnae know his company. I think you should ask his boss."

"In Belfast?" Amelia turned over the sketch she'd been working on and jotted that down. "Guid idea tae contact his company. I dinnae even know if they've been informed that McCormac is dead."

"Dougie, Sula's brother," Paislee told Lydia, "wants McCormac's job."

"What an awful thing tae think aboot on top of his death," Lydia said with compassion.

"A hundred percent." Amelia sighed.

"What are you drawing?" Lydia asked, reaching for the note and sketch.

"It's nothing. I told Dr. Kathleen I'd try tae draw a picture of the fake vet, but I cannae get it right." Amelia pushed it to Lydia.

"Is this similar at least tae what he looks like?" Lydia asked, looking from Amelia to Paislee.

"Glasses, mid-thirties, mole on his chin," Paislee said. The rendering Amelia had done seemed close enough, but Amelia wasn't pleased.

Lydia gave it back.

"I just feel over my head," Amelia said. "My brother wasnae aboot flashy things before."

"Before . . ." Paislee prodded.

"Before he went tae jail." Amelia shrugged. "Before Sula. When he was with Porche she just made him a worse daredevil. Sula told us flat oot that she likes fancy things. She had her brother drive us around where he thought mibbe he and McCormac had picked up the puppies from the breeder."

"Where?" Lydia asked.

"Inverness." Amelia reached for her tea.

"That's a big city," Lydia said. She sipped her Pellegrino.

"I know." Paislee sighed. "I think Dougie was giving us the runaround. He drove us all over the place and still couldn't remember where the breeder was at."

"You think he was conning us?" Amelia cried. "Why didnae you mention this earlier?"

"I do. I'm sorry." Paislee clasped Amelia's hand. "I didn't say anything because what good can it do?"

"I dinnae always remember things," Amelia said, "so why not forget directions? Sula told him tae help us. She's the boss in that family since their mum isnae quite well."

"I could be wrong. I mean, it was snowing really hard." Paislee tried to be fair.

"Snow changes landmarks," Lydia said.

"True." Paislee finished her lemon muffin, tempted by a second. "Amelia, we should tell Lydia what Dr. Kathleen said. She might have some ideas."

"Okay!" Amelia tilted her head. "Dr. Kathleen read aboot a puppy breeding scheme where the breeders use short-term rentals tae move around quickly so they dinnae get caught."

"That's bizarre," Lydia exclaimed.

"As bizarre as this whole puppy and murder thing?" Paislee asked.

"You have a point." Lydia wadded her napkin into a ball.

Amelia turned the note about Belfast and McCormac's boss around to add some features to her sketch of the fake vet.

"What's the name of this imposter?" Lydia pulled up her notes app.

"Torrance MacTavish," Paislee said. "He had a certificate on the wall. Though the office was bare, there were bags of dog food on a shelf. A desk, phone. Cleaned out when we came back."

Shaking her head, Lydia said, "All an elaborate ruse."

"Yeah. And we were caught in it," Amelia said. "My brother had tae know. So, he was part of it."

"What did McCormac get from the plan?" Lydia asked.

"Money. Legitimate background for the pups would bring in more cash," Amelia said. "The certificate of their purebred status, their proof of vaccination, and the microchip. The setup has tae be on the move, or they risk being busted."

"Was any of it true?" Lydia typed on her phone using her manicured fingernail like a stylus.

"I dinnae ken." Amelia paced. "I just know that when we took the other puppies who were sick tae Dr. Kathleen, she said she couldnae find the microchip though it was on the paperwork."

"For either pup?" Lydia asked.

"Correct. Same Maltese litter. Snowball was a white Pomeranian, and Sula has a sable Brussels griffon."

"Same setup?"

"Aye," Paislee said. "A folder with paperwork that looks reputable."

"What do the police think?"

"This morning I told them aboot the puppies and the fake vet," Amelia said. "The officers consider my brother Michael a person of interest. I wanted tae believe that McCormac had changed, but he hadnae."

"I'm sairy," Lydia said. She touched Amelia's arm.

"It's all right." Amelia shook her head. "Actually, it's a nightmare. But, what can we do? I'm all ears for a solution."

"Arrest them?" Lydia lowered her phone to look at Amelia.

"I didnae think they were breaking the law," Amelia said.

"Just being a poor example of humanity." Lydia scowled.

"It hurts." Amelia pursed her lips. "I cannae change it, so I need tae move forward. I want my dog, Snowball. I dinnae care aboot the rest."

Lydia crossed her ankles. "Let me see what I can do."

"How so?" Paislee gazed at her magical best friend.

"Well, I'll start with a property check on the address where this vet was supposedly located. It will give us the name of the owner anyway. They might help us connect tae the next thread."

"That's a great idea," Paislee said.

Lydia tapped her temple. "I have them occasionally."

"More often than that," Paislee said.

"How's Brody's sprained arm?"

"He was nervous about school and being teased, then Grandpa suggested that he ask Jenni for help and our Brody had a different attitude. He likes her. She better not break his heart. I don't want tae get in trouble for scolding a young lady."

"I'm right there with you," Lydia said. She loved Brody like he was her own.

"Brody's a guid kid," Amelia said.

"He's too young!" Paislee grabbed Lydia's wrist. "Oh my God. This morning we were seriously the same height. The. Same. Height. I thought I was going tae pass out."

Lydia patted Paislee's fingers. "That's quite a grip with those fingers of steel."

"Sorry!" Paislee released her. "Jenni's a sweetheart. Met her dad, Drew Ross. He's a nice guy."

"He is," Amelia said.

A customer came in and browsed the shelves of yarn. Amelia went to speak with the woman and helped her select five skeins of bright yellow yarn.

"I guess everyone is craving spring," Lydia said quietly.

"I suppose. Thanks again for the muffins. Do you think you can find the person who owns the building, for real? Amelia is desperate tae save Snowball."

"I dinnae blame her," Lydia said. "People go crazy aboot their fur babies."

"Well?" Paislee batted her eyes at Lydia.

"Paislee, when it comes tae property, I am as talented as you are with your knitting." Lydia blew on her knuckles. "I'll start looking as soon as I go back tae the office."

"Thank you, so much."

"Anything for a friend, isnae that what you always say too?"

Paislee hated to have her words lobbed back at her that way. "I do."

Later that evening, Paislee dropped Amelia off with a promise to see her at noon the next day. Her friend had an appointment with Arran in the morning. She justified the cost of an extra employee during the week because of the inventory she was able to crank out.

"See you!"

"Bye," Amelia said, shutting the car door.

Brody had gotten out of school at three, so she'd run to get him, and then dropped him at home. She'd gone back to the shop and worked until six.

At this rate, she'd have many of her partial projects completed.

Once home, she discussed the school day with Brody. The house smelled like cumin and garlic from the chili Grandpa had on the hob. Grandpa listened in with a pleased smirk about all of the accolades placed on Jenni.

The lass was a saint.

"She's a winner," Grandpa said.

Paislee cleaned up afterward, still in a cheerful mood when Lydia called.

"Hey," Paislee answered the phone.

"Hello!" Lydia replied, sounding excited.

"What's going on?"

"Did you forget I said I'd look up who owned the building?"

"Of course not." Paislee put away the spray cleaner. "I didn't want tae nag you if the search had been a bust."

"Challenge accepted, and I believe challenge delivered."

Paislee sat on a kitchen stool, eager to hear. "What did you find?"

"It took me a while because there was a lot of red tape. Like, this person wants tae stay hidden," Lydia said. "Probably for tax purposes."

"Okay . . ." Paislee flipped on her electric kettle. "Who?"

"Jamison Torrance MacTavish."

"Doctor?" Paislee recalled that Dr. Kathleen hadn't found a doctor or vet.

"Not a veterinarian either. Just a failed businessman who has already filed bankruptcy twice and he's only forty. I found a picture. Glasses."

"Mole on his chin? He looked young when we met him, so I thought thirties."

"Yes. We can only hope that his misdeeds will catch up with him," Lydia declared. "What are you going tae do with this information?"

Paislee realized that it wasn't her decision to make. "Thank you so much, Lydia. I'll start by calling Amelia."

"Mum!" Brody shouted. "I soaked my sling!"

* * *

At half past eleven that night, Paislee woke from a dead sleep, remembering that she'd forgotten to call Amelia. She sent her friend a text about *Jamison* Torrance, as well as a reminder to watch for Paislee around noon. She sent a good luck emoji about the meeting with Arran and went back to bed.

Chapter 23

Paislee arrived at Cashmere Crush Tuesday morning just as Jerry McFadden parked his lorry to deliver her yarn.

"Happy New Year!" Jerry jumped from the front of his truck and strode around to the back, selecting two boxes.

"Hi!" Paislee unlocked the back door and kept it open as Jerry brought in a variety of merino wool skeins. Always the beige, with the sage and cocoa brown a close second and third.

Once he was inside, Paislee shut the door. "I wanted tae apologize for the other day," she said.

Jerry shouldered a box to the counter, his mustache quivering. "No, I'm sairy. I was so excited by meeting Freya that I was overly enthusiastic. She teased me, understanding that you'd just run tae the store in your coat and wellies and mibbe then wasnae the right time for an introduction."

Paislee grinned at the pure joy he exuded. "I'm happy for you, Jerry."

"I've never been in love," Jerry said. "The instant I saw Freya Duncan on the goat farm, our eyes met, and I was gobsmacked."

"I can't wait tae meet her."

"Her eyes are cornflower blue, her hair soft and silky. She's trim because she works so hard managing the farm. She makes cheese," Jerry said. "The best cheese I've ever had."

Paislee dipped her head. This was a lot like Lydia had sounded when she'd met Corbin. She'd never been in love like that. What she felt with Hamish was attraction, aye, but not feeling like she'd been hit by a truck.

Maybe it wouldn't be in the cards for her, which considering how dafty it made folks, that was fine.

She focused on Jerry as he continued, "And she's a vegetarian. I cannae believe it. Can you imagine a day withoot lamb or beef?"

"Does she eat fish?"

"Aye, thank God, otherwise we wouldnae be able tae share a meal. I tried a tofu burger." His mouth scrunched beneath his thick mustache. "It was awful. I managed tae swallow it doon because of the delicious cheese she'd made."

"Veggies are good for you." Paislee counted the yarn inside to make sure the order she'd placed was correct and then wrote out a check for him.

"So, what do you think of a double date?"

"Huh?" Paislee peered up at Jerry in surprise, sure she'd misheard him about a date.

"You and Hamish, me and Freya."

"Well, let me think about it. Brody sprained his arm so I'm not sure . . ." She handed him the check, disliking how she was tongue-tied.

Jerry didn't need to know that Paislee was uncomfortable because Hamish wanted a weekend away, and that would take things to the next level.

Sex.

Dear God. Of course. She glanced at Jerry, who practically glowed with satisfaction. She squeezed her eyes shut, not wanting to think of Jerry and Freya. Having sex. Her face flamed, and she couldn't hide her traitorous redhead skin.

"Are you okay?" Jerry squeezed her upper arm.

"Fine!" Paislee fanned her face with a trifold menu for the Lion's Mane pub. "Just hot in here is all, compared tae outside."

Jerry scooted the second box away from the edge of the counter. "How did Christmas at the castle go over?" He rubbed his fingers together in the universal sign for money.

Grateful for the subject change, Paislee said, "I'll need tae increase my cashmere order from the farm."

"Freya loves cashmere too. I'd like tae buy a scarf for her, in cornflower blue." Jerry went to the shelves of yarn to admire the luxurious cashmere skeins. "The color of her eyes."

"I'd be happy tae make her one." Jerry hadn't had a serious relationship in a long while.

Jerry pulled a skein free and studied the hue. "Her eyes are bluer than this, but I suppose it will be close enough." He placed the soft yarn against his cheek. "Do ye think she'd like it?"

"She'd be mental not tae, Jerry. From everything you've told me about her she doesn't seem crazy at all."

He grinned and brought the skeins to Paislee, taking out a hundred in cash. "Is this enough? She's worth every penny."

Paislee returned the bills to him. "Let me create it first, and then you can pay—I don't know how many skeins it will take."

A knock sounded on the front door. "Thanks, Paislee. I'll just look around at what else you have. I've never had the occasion tae buy gifts for a lady and I want tae spoil Freya."

With a warm heart, Paislee unlocked the front door. Grandpa and Amelia weren't due until noon, and it was just half past nine. She didn't officially open until ten, but sometimes Elspeth dropped in after walking with her sister Susan to work.

But, it was cold even to walk six blocks, the distance Elspeth lived from Market Street. And now they had Rosie the labradoodle to consider.

She opened the door with a smile that she wished she could rescind as a scowling Zeffer, dressed in a fancy blue overcoat, had his hand raised to pound again.

"Happy New Year," the DI said. His frown suggested he didn't mean it, unlike the flowers he'd brought to her home just a few days ago.

"And you," Paislee replied cautiously.

He walked inside, past her, and saw Jerry perusing the soft jumpers stacked in a basket. "Mr. McFadden."

"DI." Jerry nodded and headed toward the back of the shop. "Paislee, just let me know what I owe for the scarf. Cheers!"

"Bye, Jer." Paislee chuckled as her friend practically floated out of sight, a rush of cool air giving away his quiet exit.

"What's up with him?" Zeffer scuffed past the high-top tables.

"He's in love," Paislee said.

"Poor bloke." Zeffer examined the interior of Cashmere Crush. "Anybody else here?"

"No. Grandpa and Amelia will be in at noon, but right now it's just me." Paislee tried not to roll her eyes with impatience. It was obvious that they were alone.

"Amelia? Thought she just filled in on Saturdays."

"Since you won't let her work at the station she needs hours here," Paislee said, arching her brow before he could arch his.

"She's getting paid leave," Zeffer said. "We made sure of it so she wouldnae be caught short."

Paislee walked to the counter and unpacked the skeins of yarn from the boxes Jerry had delivered, to price and shelve. "Can I help you with anything, DI?"

"Have you ever been in love?"

Paislee shook her head. "No. You?"

"A long time ago," Zeffer admitted. "That awful phrase, puppy love, hit me hard. I was fourteen, she was seventeen . . . it went nowhere."

Paislee studied Zeffer to see if he was serious—he was, so she said, "An older woman. Ooh la la."

"Aye." Zeffer pumped his arms as if gliding along the ice. "I thought I could win her over with my impressive skating skills, but I lost oot tae a gent who could drive."

"Fair. Well, I'm sorry for your heartbreak. It's only been,

what"—Paislee thought his age to be around hers, thirty—"sixteen years?"

"It's been a long haul." Zeffer smoothed his natty lapels. "I threw myself intae work."

"At fourteen?" Paislee sensed they were walking a fine line between joking and truth.

She knew one sure way to get Zeffer back to being the Zeffer she understood, not one who shared stories of his past, or brought flowers just to be nice, but who was in charge of keeping Nairn safe . . . She wasn't sure she wanted to break *this* spell.

"It's a long story." Zeffer stared right back at her.

Tension simmered.

Paislee couldn't take it. "Why did you impound McCormac's brand-new Mercedes?"

Zeffer stepped back and disappointment seemed to flash in his seafoam-green gaze. "Did Amelia tell you aboot that?"

"We were there when it happened that morning. Sula Selkirk, one of McCormac's girlfriends, thinks he might have hidden money, or something, in the SUV; money that she wanted in order tae leave Nairn and start over." Paislee remembered what Amelia had overheard Zeffer saying to Payne about smuggling and the Henry family.

She didn't share that Dougie had broken into the police yard to see for himself but hadn't found anything. Drugs would have been confiscated for sure. Money, if it wasn't the stash under her bed in the suitcase, would have been too.

How did one go about smuggling? Special compartments in the engine maybe . . . or part of the body of the SUV. A gifted mechanic, such as Hank Walsh, might know just how to create a special secret hidden space to hide whatever stash.

"And McCormac was on board with this runaway plan?" Zeffer asked coolly. "Him and Sula?"

"Sula loved him, but Amelia doesn't think that McCormac loved her in that way, so I'm not sure." Paislee counted the rolls of yellow yarn and made a note to order more.

"Are you investigating, Paislee?" Zeffer sounded controlled but furious.

"No!" She whirled to face him, then put the register counter between them.

"Paislee, dinnae lie tae me."

"I'm not . . . Amelia's car is in the shop, and McCormac died right at our feet, Zeffer, so of course we want tae find out what's going on. I've been driving her around—honestly, it's more about the puppies than McCormac being shot."

"Now I really dinnae understand." Zeffer crossed his arms on the high-top table to watch her closely. "You have me in a proper state of confusion."

"McCormac gave designer puppies as gifts tae his girlfriends and tae his family," Paislee rushed to explain. "We talked tae Dougie, who was helping McCormac in the puppy scheme. The money was good—they'd buy a litter from a breeder at a flat rate and then sell the pups individually."

Zeffer was mad enough to unbutton his jacket. She wouldn't have been surprised to see steam wave off of his body to strangle her.

"It's not illegal tae sell puppies," Paislee said.

"It's a problem if McCormac was selling a puppy as a purebred if it's not," Zeffer said. "We've had multiple conversations with Michael Henry as tae the origins of the pups."

"Michael claimed not tae know anything but still wanted in on the plan . . . he considered it easy money. It's why he and Letitia came back early from Glasgow, tae talk with McCormac."

"You cannae tell me Amelia didnae know what her brother was doing," Zeffer said.

"She didn't. I promise!" Paislee continued, "Amelia believed McCormac had turned over a new leaf and was selling custom luxury Mercedes in Belfast."

"I cannae believe you've been keeping all of this from me."

Paislee was stung by the accusation. "It's not true. I haven't seen you, for one thing. For another, I don't have tae gossip about my friend tae you. Amelia wants her puppy Snowball back and I'm going tae help her find the wee thing."

"Snowball?"

"Cute white Pomeranian. Supposedly purebred. The fake veterinarian, Torrance MacTavish, is actually Jamison Torrance MacTavish, the owner of the building where he'd had the pretend clinic set up. Bare bones and gone now."

"Why am I not aware of this?" Zeffer scanned his mobile then dropped it in his jacket pocket.

"Amelia told Payne." Paislee shrugged. "She even gave him the burner we found."

"I dinnae want the pair of you poking your noses into this investigation." Zeffer splayed his palms on the table. "It's more dangerous than you can understand."

"Amelia would never have killed her brother." Paislee had to make him believe that.

"I dinnae think she did," Zeffer said.

That was a good start. "Her mum and brother either."

"On that, I'm not so sure." Zeffer rubbed his jaw, wheels churning.

Paislee raised a finger. "Michael thinks he's clever but isn't; Letitia is very sly, and she wouldn't have killed the cash cow. McCormac said he wouldn't give them money, but maybe they were in Nairn tae change his mind."

"Or he didnae change his mind, so one of them shot him. And you've formed these opinions because . . ." Zeffer drawled.

"I told you!" Paislee snatched glimpses of the calmer detective as she reached for the stack of coin purses in the Ramsey tartan and put them in a yarn box to take to the castle. "I've been spending time with Amelia, and her family."

Zeffer nodded speculatively. "Torrance MacTavish is the fake vet?"

Paislee wrote the name down on the back of a receipt paper. "*Jamison* Torrance. He's a failed businessman with two bankruptcies and probably desperate for money, at least according tae what Lydia found online."

"Thanks." Zeffer pocketed the information. "I would kick myself if I left here withoot asking if there is any other information aboot the case you might know."

"The puppy breeders? Fake vet? Sula's . . ." Paislee clapped her hand over her mouth.

"What aboot Sula?"

Well, Paislee hadn't promised to keep that secret and it provided motivation. "She hasn't told anyone but she's pregnant with McCormac's baby." What if McCormac had decided he didn't want a baby or to settle down? Sula had been in the crowd with them. A gun might be easy to hide in a dog blanket.

Zeffer's mouth firmed. "Planned?"

"Accident."

"I bet." Zeffer tapped his chin. "I've had run-ins with Sula Selkirk before, at the strip club."

Paislee nodded. She'd be willing to believe that Sula had gotten pregnant on purpose to try and hold on to her philandering man. It never worked in the movies or books. "McCormac, according tae everyone who knew him well, was in love with Porche Walsh. Maybe Sula had enough?"

"Love is a crazy business," Zeffer said. "What else?"

"My veterinarian for Wallace, Dr. Kathleen McHenry, looked up this supposed vet, Torrance MacTavish. His legal name is actually Jamison Torrance MacTavish. Dr. Kathleen alerted us that the puppies in her care didn't have the microchips as stated on the certificate, which made her research MacTavish. She told us that there was no vet in the area by that name."

"Why did she have them?"

"The puppies Amelia was watching for McCormac's mum and brother were sick. Snowball had a wee cough, which was why Amelia took her pup tae MacTavish. We had no idea it was a con. There were actual bags of dog food and pet supplies on the shelves, which weren't there two days later." Paislee nibbled her lower lip. What else could she share?

"And?"

"Dr. Kathleen is on the board for fair animal practices when it comes to breeders in it only for the money."

Zeffer waved his hand for her to continue.

"She told us about a new scheme where the breeders are using rental properties, like for the week, or month, so they can move around without getting caught."

Zeffer blinked in surprise. "That's new. It's a shame that human beings can be so crooked."

"But not all are." Paislee sighed. "I have tae believe that there are equally as many good people, or more, than the bad."

"That's naïve," Zeffer said.

"It's not the first time I've been called that." Paislee shrugged. "There are worse things."

"I'm afraid tae ask . . . Is that all?"

"Yes. I believe so. Zeffer, Amelia gave the burner phone to Payne yesterday. She came back from the station just gutted that she's not allowed tae be there."

"The Henry family has been shady for centuries, Paislee, and while Amelia is a shining example of overcoming a rocky beginning, she would do anything for them. Can you deny it?"

Paislee knew he was right, to a point. "She wouldn't break the law . . ."

"No. But she'd be tempted. Why put her in that position?" Zeffer exhaled. "I had personal business in Stonehaven, or I would've been here sooner. I should know better than tae leave town. Please do not go anywhere today other than where you need tae be."

"I'm going tae pick up Amelia at her flat—she had an appointment with her solicitor this morning—and bring her here, if that's all right with you?" Her back was up, she couldn't help it.

"Fine." Zeffer didn't comment on the solicitor remark. "Have Amelia stop in at the station when she arrives."

"She's supposed tae be working."

"What aboot a break?" Zeffer spread his arm to the side.

"That will be up tae her," Paislee said.

Zeffer left with a curt wave. Paislee was tempted to lock the door after him but that wouldn't serve any purpose when she had so much to accomplish.

Instead, she cranked the music, finished packing the coin purses, and then began knitting the cornflower-blue cashmere scarf for Jerry's Freya.

At quarter till noon, she put a CLOSED FOR LUNCH sign on the door and went to pick up Grandpa, and then Amelia. The weather was too cold for either of them to walk.

Grandpa hopped in looking well rested and cheerful. Black glasses, silver-gray hair under a cocoa-brown cashmere knit tam. Snow boots, lined trench coat. Stylishly dressed for the winter weather. "Hey, Paislee!"

"Hi, Grandpa. We're going tae swing by tae pick up Amelia."

"All right. How are things today?"

She told him, perhaps complained to him, about Zeffer and what he'd said regarding Amelia's family. The impounded Mercedes SUV.

A figurative lightbulb dinged on over her head and she pulled to the side of the road so fast she lightly rammed a snowbank.

"Lass, what is it?"

"Zeffer said that the Henrys have been smugglers for hundreds of years. The police impounded McCormac's car. Over-breeding puppies for profit is wrong, but hardly jail worthy. What if, Grandpa, McCormac was smuggling puppies from Belfast?"

Chapter 24

"Puppy smuggling has tae be illegal." Paislee couldn't be more ramped up about the idea, and angry too. Was that even a thing? Dr. Kathleen would need to know about this right away to send a warning out to her network of veterinarians.

"How?" Grandpa asked. "The ferry on either side would have checkpoints from Ireland tae Scotland."

"I don't know the particulars." Paislee, the Juke still in park on the side of the road, squeezed the wheel, certain they were on the right track. "I have no idea how tae transport puppies. Bins? Crates?"

"McCormac might not have declared that he was carrying pups at all." Grandpa adjusted his glasses. "Hence the smuggling. If the authorities dinnae ken tae look for something, why would they?"

"You're right. They would be hidden away." Paislee carefully joined traffic again toward Amelia's. "Hank Walsh is a brilliant mechanic. Do you think his talents segue into building hidden compartments?"

Grandpa flinched. "Tae hide puppies? You told me that Hank said McCormac wanted him tae do a bigger scheme—could this be it?"

Her mind spun with possibilities. "I can't wait tae find out how the appointment with Arran went this morning. I bet you Amelia will be blown away by the puppy smuggling conclusion."

"Will ye tell Zeffer your idea?" Grandpa removed his tam and dropped it over his knee. The gray afternoon was dreary but Paislee's hope that they were close to finding Snowball banished the blah atmosphere.

"Yes! I will . . . but I want tae talk with Amelia first. What if Arran has cautioned her in some way regarding the case?"

"Smart," Grandpa said. "You're verra good at putting these things together."

"With your help," Paislee said. "We make a good team."

Grandpa tugged his ear lobe. "Mostly listening on this one."

"It counts." She parked at Amelia's flat, peering into the lobby. No Amelia. It was ten after noon and they'd agreed that Paislee would be here at twelve and Amelia would dash out. Or at least, the text message from last night had gotten a thumbs-up.

"Strange," Paislee said. Her nape itched. "Amelia's usually on time."

"What if she's running late with her appointment at Arran's office?" Grandpa suggested. "When did you talk tae her last?"

"Yesterday, when I dropped her off." Paislee dialed Amelia's mobile number but there was no answer. "I'll call Arran's office tae see if she's still there and we can pick her up, so she doesn't have the cost of an Uber."

Grandpa settled back in his seat as Paislee called via Bluetooth. The receptionist answered. "Mullholland Law Agency."

"Hi! It's Paislee Shaw. Is Amelia Henry still there, by chance? She had an appointment with Arran this morning." She chuckled. "Poor lass's car's in the shop so I'm giving her a ride but she's not here at her flat."

"Morning, Paislee," the woman said. They'd met briefly when Paislee had needed Arran's services. "Amelia hasnae been here. Should I put you through tae Mr. Mulholland?"

"Aye, thanks."

Paislee looked at Grandpa and saw her concern reflected in his brown eyes.

Amelia would never miss an appointment like that, not when her and her family's safety was on the line.

"Paislee?" Arran spoke calmly. "How are ye?"

"Fine." She repeated what she'd told the receptionist, and ended with, "So I thought we'd run by tae get her."

"Amelia didnae show," Arran said, "when I'd moved things around tae fit her in. I'd warned Amelia that her family's history provided unjustified bias, regarding her position at the station. I worried that perhaps I'd been too frank and scared her."

"She's a straight shooter," Paislee said. "I think she would have appreciated that, actually. Arran, have you heard of puppy smuggling before?"

"That's a left turn I didnae see coming," Arran replied in a dry tone.

"How much did Amelia tell you about the fake veterinarian and the possible scheme of selling puppies with falsified certifications?"

"Didnae mention it," Arran said. "Only focused on keeping her brother oot of jail for possibly murdering McCormac."

Paislee quickly summarized all they'd discovered and the information she'd put together in the last hour since her talk with Zeffer.

"That is verra interesting," Arran said at last. "Let me do some research and I'll get back tae you. It makes more sense for McCormac tae have been killed tae cover up something bigger than a puppy mill. Smuggling is a whole different ball of wax. Touch base in an hour?"

"All right. I'm at Amelia's now. Bye!"

Paislee and Grandpa exchanged a look. Grandpa said, "He's quite a savvy solicitor, Arran. He didnae disregard what you told him, which tells me it's a verra real possibility."

Exhaling, Paislee unlocked the doors of the Juke. "Amelia is probably just running late and overslept or something. She's been under a lot of stress. I'll check on her."

"I'll go too," Grandpa said. He unbuckled his seatbelt and tugged his tam over his ears.

"You don't have tae." Paislee patted the dash. "Stay inside where it's warm."

"I'm coming," Grandpa insisted. "I wish we had something with us." He eyed the building. "No security. Never thought I'd miss that perk at Lydia's place."

Grandpa also felt danger, but she knew telling him to wait would be a waste of breath. She grabbed her phone and had 999 on speed dial. In the four months they'd lived there it had been reassuring to be greeted by the guard.

"Let's go." Paislee didn't question that they both were thinking of the worst possible outcome. It wasn't the first time they'd been in danger, and it was best to take precautions.

There was a chance that Amelia was probably still sleeping after a late night of gaming. She'd taken the news of MacTavish being a failed businessman with acceptance and determination to find the imposter and get her dog back, supposedly with Payne's help. What didn't track was her missing the appointment with Arran when it could provide legal protection for her family.

"I wonder if she's with Constable Payne?" Paislee said. "She'd hoped he'd help her look for Snowball."

"That has tae be where she is." Grandpa's shoulders relaxed as they entered the lobby in Amelia's building. Not only was there no guard, but the security cameras had also been disconnected, as evidenced by the wires dangling free.

The elevator took them to the second floor and Paislee hurried toward Amelia's place. "If she's not here, I'll call the station. Zeffer was looking for her this morning as well. She might not even have her phone turned on for notifications if she's with the police officers."

They rounded the hall. "Puppy smuggling," Grandpa said, "is something I just cannae fathom. It's quite the setup tae create the certificates of vaccinations and pedigree. How much do you think those puppies are worth withoot all the hoopla?"

"Not nearly as much. It was a gamble tae pay for a litter and hope that he could sell them all. I wonder if that's why McCormac gave them tae his family, Lyla, and Sula as gifts?"

Grandpa shrugged as they neared her door. "I think he was showing off, like the Rolex and the lasses. The brand-new Mercedes SUV."

"You're probably right. Even if McCormac couldn't have gotten thousands of pounds, he'd have made a minimum of five hundred or more for each of them if he needed tae unload them." Paislee winced at the words coming out of her mouth. She was a pet lover and hated to sound so cold.

"Here we are." She stopped before the green knitted Christmas wreath on Amelia's door. She knocked and the door slid inward. "Oh no."

"Not again," Grandpa said. "Grab your phone but let me go first."

Paislee hip-checked him so he didn't scoot past her. "Don't touch anything. Amelia? Amelia!" She heard a yip from the kitchen to her right that could be Daisy, Robbie, or Amelia. "I'm coming in!"

She could imagine Zeffer reading her the riot act. On the other hand, she knew CPR, and if Amelia was in trouble, she *would* help her friend.

"Amelia?" Paislee scanned the room. The Christmas tree was knocked over, the angel on its side, the lights off.

The telly had been smashed with a game controller in the center of the large screen. The game system was destroyed. Amelia's phone was on the low table.

This was anger, not a robbery. "Amelia?"

"Careful, lass, the puppies are loose." Grandpa gestured to the pups out of their crates and cowering beneath the felled Christmas tree. Two little noses twitched. They were too scared to make a noise.

Paislee nodded in their direction. "Stay with them, okay? I'm going tae check her bedroom."

She continued down the hall. Pictures were knocked askew, the bathroom door kicked open, the bedroom door off its hinges. The picture Amelia had drawn was on the floor. The mattress was slit into shreds, and off the box spring.

"Somebody was looking for the money," Paislee said.

"What money?"

She wasn't surprised Grandpa had followed her and had her back, literally.

She sighed. "I promised I wouldn't say anything, but this is out of control. Amelia found a suitcase of cash under her bed after Mc-Cormac died that she thinks he stashed there. Sula is looking for it."

"Does Zeffer know?"

"Amelia was working with Constable Payne," Paislee said. "It wasn't my story tae tell."

"I understand, but I dinnae ken that Zeffer will," Grandpa said.

He had an awful point. Paislee turned and faced her grandfather. "I better call him."

"Rather than just emergency services? Strangers might be nicer," Grandpa ventured.

"Aye. I really hope that Amelia is at the station with Payne and Zeffer," Paislee said. "This break-in must be related tae the case."

Paislee dialed Zeffer, who answered, "DI Zeffer here."

"It's Paislee . . . er, Shaw," she said with a stutter. Of course, he would know who she was—they were one another's nemesis. "Have you seen Amelia this morning?"

"No."

Grandpa rubbed his arms as if cold, in regard to Zeffer's tone.

Paislee nodded and asked, "Is Constable Payne there?" She could talk to him instead.

"Sitting in my office," Zeffer replied.

Blast. Paislee had no choice but to deal with the DI. "I'm at Amelia's tae pick her up for work at the shop, but she's not here."

"And?"

Paislee could be as detached. "The place was broken intae. The puppies are out of their crates and scared. Amelia is not here but her phone is on the table. Where is she? What if she's been hurt, like McCormac?"

"I told you not tae butt intae this investigation. Dinnae move a muscle," Zeffer instructed. "We're on our way and will be there in ten minutes." He hung up.

Paislee bristled with anger, fear, and annoyance. "I know I'm going tae be in trouble, but I didn't do anything," she said to Grandpa. She put her phone in her jacket pocket.

Maybe Daisy and Robbie recognized her voice because all of a sudden, they both yipped and yowled from the living room, so she ushered Grandpa before her down the hall. What if the puppies were hurt by the fallen tree?

"That sounds terrible," Grandpa said. "Hope they're not injured."

Paislee and Grandpa carefully crossed the lounge to the Christmas tree on its side. Daisy saw Paislee and, still yipping, she roly-poly crawled bravely toward her. The distressed pup was caught by a knitted ornament and Paislee bent down to release her.

Daisy, so sweet, but scared to her marrow, trembled while wagging her tail in greeting. Robbie whined and shivered under a branch, not daring to follow his sister. With tears in her eyes, Paislee sat cross-legged on the floor and scooped Daisy toward her heart.

"I dinnae think this is what Zeffer had in mind," Grandpa said, "when he didnae want you tae move."

Paislee looked up at Grandpa from her spot. "Daisy and I are old friends now."

Grandpa kneeled next to her to pet the scared Maltese. Robbie, beneath the branches, broke free of his fear to sniff Grandpa's fingers.

Paislee pulled her phone from her pocket. "I'm really mad that anybody could be so cruel. Where is Amelia?"

"Who killed McCormac?" Grandpa asked. Robbie was the size of his hand, yet he was so gentle as he let the pup nibble on his thumb.

"Sula was looking for the money," Paislee said. "But would she hurt the puppies?" She didn't think so.

"MacTavish?" Grandpa suggested. "He has the most tae lose in this scheme."

"Could be," Paislee replied. "His personality is a risk-taker. Maybe Amelia got too close tae uncovering the smuggling plan, so he nabbed her."

"She didnae know aboot it." Grandpa patted Robbie.

Paislee took comfort from Daisy as the pup relaxed in her cashmere scarf on her lap. "I bet Lydia can find MacTavish's home address. Maybe Amelia tracked him down somehow and confronted him about Snowball. I'd sent her his real name last night."

"That's sound logic. Snowball has been Amelia's focus all along." Grandpa picked up wee Robbie and the pup snuggled close to his chest.

Paislee dialed Lydia, who answered on the first ring. "Paislee, how are you, love?"

"I could be better! That awful man, Jamison Torrance MacTavish, can you find his home address? Amelia's flat was broken into, and she's gone. Her phone is here, but she's not."

"Aye—the police?" Lydia didn't miss a beat.

"On the way. Should be here any minute. The pups are terrified. What if Amelia was so close tae catching this guy that he took her?" McCormac dead. Shot in the heart.

Her pulse hummed out of control. Amelia had to be safe.

"Stay calm, Paislee. Let me call you right back."

"Okay." Paislee was speaking to a dial tone.

"She must need both hands?" Grandpa suggested.

Paislee gave him a tepid smile. "What do you think of Daisy?" She brought the scared pup to her cheek. A wheeze sounded in her chest, like what Snowball had. The cough had gotten worse despite the medicine. "We need tae get these guys tae Dr. Kathleen."

"They are so small I'd be afraid tae step on them," Grandpa said. He pushed his glasses back up the bridge of his nose.

"I keep reminding myself of that, but Daisy's really sneaking close tae my heart."

Grandpa petted Robbie and looked around the apartment. "Place was tossed."

"Yeah. The TV and game stuff broken, not stolen. Her phone left behind."

"It makes sense that it would be the fake vet trying tae silence Amelia from blowing his cover rather than a robbery." Grandpa shifted on the floor so that Robbie would be comfortable in the crook of his arm.

Her phone rang and she answered, putting Lydia on speaker.

"Hey!" Lydia sounded excited. "MacTavish has several rental homes in Inverness."

"Several?" Paislee asked. Her hope suffered a blow that they'd be able to go directly to MacTavish's to save Amelia.

"Perfect for the puppy scheme," Grandpa said.

"You're right, Angus." Lydia retained her pleased tone, which Paislee didn't understand. "I did a little undercover work and a re-peat renter by the name of Porche Walsh caught my attention."

With a gasp, Paislee said, "Hank Walsh's sister, and the love of McCormac's life." She wondered how it all fit, with more pieces just added to the puzzle.

"Get this: Porche rents by the month. I was able tae look at her

rental paperwork—dinnae ask how—but she put doon her employ-
ment as a veterinarian assistant," Lydia said.

Whatever started to gel in Paislee's brain was gone as Constable
Payne and DI Zeffer arrived.

"Gotta go—but thanks, Lyd. Uh, forward me . . ."

"I just shared all three addresses with you," Lydia said. "Be
safe!"

Paislee and Grandpa stayed seated on the floor as Zeffer, Payne,
and Monroe entered Amelia's flat and took in the destroyed items.

"What did ye touch?" Zeffer asked.

"Not even the door—it was already open. The puppies are sick
and need the vet. We've got tae take them tae Dr. Kathleen."
Paislee feared for the wee pups.

Zeffer, in his stylish blue jacket, raised his hand. "Once we're
done here."

Paislee nodded, knowing it wouldn't take long for the professionals to assess the situation and return.

"What were they looking for, tae slice the mattress and knock
things around?" Zeffer asked.

"Don't be mad," Paislee began.

"I hate it when you tell me that." Zeffer narrowed his eyes at
her. "Spill."

"It could be the suitcase full of cash—but, tae be clear, Amelia
only found it after McCormac died. She didn't know what tae do
with it, as it could be legitimately earned income that he'd stashed
tae go away with Sula, so she asked me tae hold it. Sula mentioned
money for their secret getaway."

"Sula Selkirk confirmed her pregnancy yesterday in an inter-
view at the station," Payne said. "Dougie wasnae there." He joined
Zeffer and the pair stood shoulder to shoulder. Monroe snapped
photos in Amelia's bedroom.

"I hope you didn't tell her I told you!" Paislee got to her feet,
helping Grandpa next, as they each held a puppy.

Zeffer squinted. "Give me some credit for getting information, all right? We asked aboot her relationship with McCormac, and I recalled how utterly distraught she was at the hospital, and how McCormac's life had ended so young with no family tae carry on his legacy. She told me then that she was pregnant."

Paislee adjusted the small weight of Daisy in her arms. "I thought Sula might be involved because she'd been searching for the money, but it makes more sense that Torrance MacTavish is the one who has Amelia. We need tae hurry and find her. Her phone is here—she wouldn't leave it on purpose."

"Taken?" Zeffer exclaimed.

"Obviously," Paislee said, not backing down.

"Why do you think so?" Payne asked.

"Amelia just wanted Snowball, but MacTavish didn't return her dog. She could blow his cover and ruin his stream of money." Paislee met the constable's gaze and was rewarded with his slight nod.

"Could be." Payne read the notes off his tablet. "The burner phone, the video Amelia shot of the empty clinic, it's a classic setup for a pop-up operation. Nobody there tae actually answer the phone."

Paislee, with her free hand, took out her mobile. The new phone was at thirty percent battery. "As you know, Lydia helped me find the owner of the property and she just sent three different rental addresses in Inverness that he owns."

"Three?" Payne asked.

"Which one does he live in?" Zeffer sounded fired up, like Paislee had been.

"I don't know . . . she didn't say. I could ask her," Paislee offered.

"I'll do the asking," Payne said. "You've done enough."

Grandpa nudged her arm and murmured, "Smuggling."

Paislee exhaled and dove right in. "Also, a frequent renter is Porche Walsh. Her brother Hank Walsh is a handy mechanic. I was wondering if the puppies could be part of a smuggling operation."

Zeffer exchanged a look with Payne. Paislee knew she'd scored a hit.

"I don't know the address, because Dougie didn't know it, but I can show you where he started in Inverness," Paislee said. "I'll do my best tae remember the route, but it was snowing so hard. We have tae try."

Zeffer nodded. "Angus, you drive the Juke home, Monroe and Payne, you handle things here, and I'll take Paislee tae Inverness." When he noticed her mouth rounded to protest, he added, "After dropping the pups with the vet."

Chapter 25

Grandpa settled Robbie into his carrier as Paislee gently placed Daisy in hers, truly worried for the poor wheezing puppies. Payne, Monroe, and Zeffer murmured together as they stepped outside of Amelia's flat to the second-floor hall.

"Will you be all right?" Grandpa spoke softly so as not to attract the officers' attention in the event they came back inside.

Zeffer was probably giving last-minute instructions. Paislee zipped the carrier closed as the puppy curled around in place with a sigh. "I'll be with the DI so what could go wrong? I'm more worried about you. Maybe we can skip opening the shop today."

Grandpa cooed to Robbie and the pup wagged his tail. "I'll be fine. Elspeth should already be there, eh?"

Paislee checked her watch. One in the afternoon! "Good point. Will you call Arran and let him know what's happened?" They were supposed to touch base, but she had no answers.

"Besides"—Grandpa gripped the handle of the carrier—"making me own flies is awright, but I miss the customers who come in tae shop."

"And Elspeth?" Paislee teased.

"She's a dear."

The pair had a sweet flirtation that would never go anywhere, which suited them both fine. If only Hamish hadn't pressed.

Daisy had given up her curled pose to lick Paislee's fingers through the mesh.

"Daisy is attached tae you," Grandpa said.

"Don't say that—Daisy is so adorable that it wouldn't take much tae fall all the way in love with her."

"Well, she's for sale, right?" Grandpa headed toward the door the officers had left ajar.

"Not at a price I can afford," Paislee said. "Who knows what will happen once this is all said and done?" She had no clue what the protocol would be for puppies smuggled in from Belfast compared to a local greedy dog breeder.

Zeffer peered around the open door. "What's takin' so long, Shaw family?"

"Coming, coming." Paislee blew Daisy a kiss and put the warm feelings she had for the pup aside to focus on finding Amelia. She carried Daisy's carrier and Grandpa held Robbie's as they left Amelia's building. Zeffer opened the door for them, and they stepped into the winter cold.

Zeffer's SUV was already running, and so she put Daisy in the back, then settled Robbie next to Daisy. The interior was toasty warm.

Paislee then gave Grandpa the keys to the Juke. "Brody's off at three this week so if you don't mind picking him up? He can't stay after because of his sprained arm."

"Aye." Grandpa tipped his tam, and climbed into the Juke with impressive agility that belied his age.

Paislee got into the front seat of Zeffer's blue SUV. It was clean and neat, with not a single sweets wrapper or wadded-up napkin.

"Where tae?" Zeffer asked.

She told him the location of the veterinarian's clinic. "You should come in and talk tae Dr. Kathleen about this puppy scheme. She's a champion for fair animal practices and can alert the other clinics about fake vet MacTavish."

"Are you sure you dinnae ken which address in Inverness would be closest tae where Dougie drove you around, for the breeders?"

"I don't. Dougie said McCormac wanted it tae be a secret—I wish I did."

Zeffer rubbed his smooth-shaven jaw. "I hoped tae drop you off at the clinic."

Paislee frowned. "And just leave me there? Rude. It's important for you tae hear what Dr. Kathleen might say. She's very knowledgeable." Come to think of it, Diana, the receptionist, might know Porche. Every little bit of information helped.

The DI exhaled but finally nodded. "Fine."

The vehicle was a safe space for her to question the DI because he couldn't penetrate her psyche with his cool, somewhat dismissive gaze. "So, were you already thinking that McCormac might have smuggled those puppies from Ireland? It wasn't drugs or jewelry?"

Zeffer turned left, following the audible directions of the GPS. "Where do you get these crazy ideas?"

He wasn't denying it. "You impounded McCormac's car," Paislee said. "Hank was furious enough tae punch McCormac that night. McCormac wanted him tae be part of a wild scheme . . . maybe in creating a way tae hide those poor pups somehow on the journey from Belfast tae Inverness."

Zeffer tapped the wheel. "Mibbe. We interviewed Hank and he didnae say exactly. Amelia wondered if he'd been upset by Porche and McCormac still hooking up, but he didnae care—they deserve each other, according tae him. He slugged McCormac because McCormac wanted him tae pick up breaking the law as they had before McCormac went tae jail. Hank is walking the straight and narrow path."

"So, Hank is probably not involved," Paislee said. "He seemed genuine when he and Amelia were talking, saying that the older kids should've set a better example in the neighborhood."

Zeffer stopped at a red light. "You are verra observant."

"Letitia Henry called me nosy."

Zeffer chuckled.

Paislee settled back, appreciating that the seats in the SUV were heated. The Juke's were not. "I just don't understand why people can be so mean. Why put innocent puppies in danger? Money can't be that important."

"Tae some it is. It means success, after the basics, like food and shelter."

"Those are big deals," Paislee admitted. "I would understand food and shelter a lot more than flashy cars or jewelry. But tae hurt a living creature? No way."

"Your family raised you tae know the difference between right and wrong." Zeffer glanced at her. "Also, you never went withoot a meal."

"True." Paislee chose not to take that as an observation about that extra weight around her middle, but for the hardship it would be if a person hadn't eaten. "My da managed a hardware store and Mum was in customer service at an office. They didn't have college degrees, but they worked hard and paid their bills. You're right that we never went hungry. Family was very important." Thanks to her granny. She looked out the window at the passing cars.

"Was?" Zeffer homed in on the single word like Gran on a grammar check.

"Mum left after my da died. Who just ups and leaves their daughter tae move across the world?" Paislee heard the strident tone of her voice and swallowed.

Zeffer didn't comment but she could tell that he was listening—not being judgmental. She shared a tiny bit.

"I guess it's on my mind because Mum sent a Christmas card, and my siblings, both younger than Brody, signed it. It's the first time I realized that she'd told them about me." Paislee looked toward Zeffer. "I had no idea."

"Ouch." He kept his gaze on the snowy road.

"Yes, it hurt." Paislee laced her fingers together over her knee.

"What are you going tae do aboot it?" Zeffer routinely checked his mirrors and Paislee felt safe in the SUV despite the fact she wasn't behind the wheel. They came to a stop at a red light.

"Brody saw the card and is interested in the fact that I have a mum and siblings. He has an aunt and an uncle that he's older than. Tae him it's funny. I'm still a little, a lot, angry about the whole thing." Paislee dug into the side pocket of her handbag for a tissue and dabbed her stinging nose.

"Did she ever explain?" The light turned green, and Zeffer stepped slowly on the pedal so that the tires didn't spin on the snow.

"Years ago, Mum said she was hurting about my da. She loved him so much that his death nearly killed her. She left the day after my graduation."

"Does she know aboot Brody?"

Brody had been conceived that night. "Brody is my choice. She made it clear that she thought I was making a huge mistake by keeping him. We definitely didn't talk much after that. Then she finds this guy and starts all over again. Some love she had for my dad."

"Some people shouldnae be parents. I'm one of them. I never wanted kids," Zeffer shared. "I am content tae pour my efforts intae my career."

"Why is that?" Paislee asked.

"That's a story for another day. Here we are." Zeffer's mobile rang as he parked at the veterinarian's clinic.

Paislee could see that the caller was Constable Payne, but Zeffer answered and held the phone to his ear so she couldn't hear.

"Got it. Keep me posted." Zeffer hung up.

"Well?" Paislee unbuckled her belt, filled with questions. "Did they find Amelia?"

"No." Zeffer also released his seatbelt. "Payne, thanks tae Lydia, has MacTavish's home address—here in Nairn." A tinge of excitement laced his voice.

"Can we go?" Paislee asked.

"No. Payne and Monroe will handle it."

They exited the SUV and Paislee retrieved Daisy's crate and Zeffer got Robbie's. Paislee opened the door, and they entered the vet's clinic.

Diana smiled in welcome, her eyes lighting at seeing the puppies again. "Robbie and Daisy! Where's my wee laddie?"

"This one's Daisy." Paislee put the crate on the corner of the desk and Diana peered inside. "They're still sick."

"That happens sometimes. Let me get Dr. Kathleen." Diana's gaze went to DI Zeffer. The man had style, even carrying a wheezing pup in a crate. He nodded.

"Good! I was hoping tae speak with her," Paislee said. "About the MacTavish situation." She wasn't sure what Diana knew so kept the sentence vague.

"Be right back." Diana disappeared but there was no time for Paislee and Zeffer to converse before she returned with Dr. Kathleen on her heels.

"Paislee, you've brought the pups! Not tae worry if they're still coughing. Sometimes it takes longer for medicine tae kick in." Dr. Kathleen's voice was reassuring. "Did Amelia ever find Snowball?"

"No, and now Amelia is missing."

"What?" Diana and Dr. Kathleen said in unison.

Zeffer dipped his head at her. Was that a warning? Well, her friend *was* missing. He always wondered how she got information—this was how. Give a little, learn a little.

Paislee lifted Daisy out of the crate and petted the quivering pup, who calmed beneath her gentle touch. "Amelia was supposed tae work with me today at noon, so I went tae her flat. She wasn't there—it had been broken intae. The pups were terrified beneath the tipped-over Christmas tree."

"Oh no!" Daisy coughed. Dr. Kathleen took the pup from Paislee and examined her eyes and ears. "It sometimes requires a double dose depending on their situation. The puppies cannae tell us, so we must uncover what clues we can. This one worries me, with a heart murmur. She might outgrow it, but she'll probably be verra tiny and whoever does buy her will need tae understand the medical costs involved. This is the sad side effect of puppy mills."

The vet looked at Paislee and Zeffer. "You must find Amelia. How can I help?"

Zeffer's phone rang and he turned to answer it.

"Who is that handsome hunk in a designer coat?" Diana murmured.

"He's a DI assigned tae McCormac's murder case," Paislee explained.

Diana blinked tears free from her lids, but they didn't spill over.

"You can do so much better," Paislee said, then her face flamed. "I'm sorry! You're so pretty and kind, and smart. I don't understand McCormac's appeal."

"I've told her the same." Dr. Kathleen placed an empathetic hand on her shoulder. "Is there anything that we can do?"

"It's a slim chance, but I wondered if either of you knew Porche Walsh?" Porche had put her job down as a vet's assistant, and she had to be working with MacTavish. "She's a veterinarian's assistant, so perhaps you'd run in the same circles."

"Not well." Diana glanced at Dr. Kathleen, who nodded with encouragement. "Porche approached me over drinks on Hogmanay aboot whether Dr. Kathleen would be willing tae earn extra money by signing off on blank veterinarian certificates. Said she was a vet assistant and flashed a diamond engagement ring. I was so shocked that I immediately said no. I should have gotten more information, but I just reacted."

"You did the right thing," Dr. Kathleen said. "I only wish you'd told me sooner, rather than just this morning."

Diana ducked her head.

Zeffer joined them. "What did I miss?"

"Porche Walsh, the woman renting homes by the month in Inverness, approached Diana tae see if Dr. Kathleen wanted tae earn some extra cash by signing off on the puppy health certificates." Paislee wished she could still hold Daisy but realized it was best if the dog remained with Dr. Kathleen.

"We would never condone such a thing," the veterinarian said.

"I've put together an email tae warn my associates of this latest travesty."

Zeffer tilted his head. "Have you heard of puppies being smuggled from Ireland?"

Diana's eyes rounded in surprise. "Ireland? Like, McCormac's Belfast?" The assistant plopped to her seat, unable to stand—though she didn't lose her grip on Robbie.

"We are in league with the special investigations unit of the Scottish Society for the Prevention of Cruelty tae Animals," Zeffer said. "Dealers from Ireland are behind the majority of pet trafficking."

"Smuggling." Dr. Kathleen's forehead scrunched in disapproval. "That's quite an endeavor, and unfortunately even worse for the puppies than irresponsible breeders. I'm aware of gangs in Belfast but I thought they'd been shut doon."

"Dealers are like the Greek monster, Hydra," Zeffer said. "Chop one head off and two more grow. According tae the latest data, almost three hundred dogs have been recovered in the last few years." He squeezed his finger and thumb together. "A small percentage."

"These people create a disposable income withoot morals or integrity." Dr. Kathleen blew out an angry breath. "The pups are the ones hurt. They come tae Scotland sick already and so they pass away. Can you imagine spending money on a pet for the family only tae have it die in your arms?"

Paislee blinked quickly, commiserating with how painful that would be.

The vet continued, on a rant, "The puppies are kept in cramped and unsanitary conditions, which might lead tae parvo—which can be lethal, or campylobacter, a bacterial infection that can be passed tae humans."

"I cannae believe McCormac would be part of such a thing," Diana said.

"How often did he come from Ireland tae visit you?" Zeffer asked.

"Once a month, give or take," Diana said.

"Were you aware that he had other girlfriends?" Zeffer asked.

"Aye." Diana stroked Robbie's silky fur.

"We have his vehicle coming across on the ferry from Belfast twice a week," Zeffer said, reading from his tablet. "Sometimes three."

Was he bringing puppies each time? Paislee calculated that it would be eight or more trips per month, not once. Poor Diana. Poor Sula. Maybe even Lyla could be pitied.

Zeffer pocketed the device. "Did McCormac ever suggest that Dr. Kathleen take part in the falsification of certificates?"

"Not him, just Porche." Diana sighed. "I thought McCormac and Porche were over, romantically speaking."

"My educated guess is that it was only a matter of time before McCormac pressured you," Zeffer said. "A few of his other female acquaintances are also in the veterinarian biz."

Diana hugged Robbie to her, then looked at Dr. Kathleen. "That's awful. I wouldnae—you know I would not!"

"I know," Dr. Kathleen said. "DI Zeffer, how can we help you close doon this operation run by MacTavish and Porche?"

Zeffer smoothed his lapels, his tone serious. "Send oot that warning email so that nobody else falls prey tae the scheme. The police are involved, so if anybody has information, they should call the station."

Diana stood and gestured with one hand to Zeffer. "Do you think MacTavish killed McCormac? Does he have Amelia?"

"We are following the leads. If you hear from anybody else who might have been asked tae participate, please let me know," Zeffer said. He reached into his inner jacket pocket and placed two business cards on the desk.

"We will," Dr. Kathleen said. "I'm delighted tae work with the police on this. It's criminal."

Zeffer didn't say anything, but Paislee could tell by the narrowing of his eyes that he wanted to go. She gave a half smile to the best veterinarian ever. "Thank you so much, Dr. Kathleen. I'll pay whatever they need tae be well."

"I'll be worried sick aboot Amelia." Diana dropped a kiss to the top of Robbie's head. "Tell us when she's safe?"

"I will—thank you for sharing what happened, Diana." Paislee headed toward the exit, which Zeffer opened for her. She stepped out into the brisk air. "Was that Payne on the phone?"

"Yes. He went tae MacTavish's home but nobody's there. I let him know aboot Porche Walsh contacting Diana for a connection. Could be other vets in the area are also working with them."

"MacTavish isn't even a vet! He's just a player." Steam fogged from Paislee's breath. Who might have Amelia—to keep her quiet? No, her mattress had been slashed, which meant MacTavish knew about the cash.

Zeffer unlocked his SUV, and they got in. "Tell me aboot the money you mentioned at Amelia's flat. A suitcase?"

"Okay." Paislee buckled up and pulled out her phone to calculate the monetary amount at stake with McCormac coming from Ireland eight times per month. A litter of puppies could be anywhere from three to five. Five at two thousand average income, ten thousand, eight times per month, eighty thousand a month.

"What are you doing?" Zeffer asked, his tone abrupt.

"Listen tae this!" Paislee read the astonishing figures aloud. "Eighty thousand a month can buy a lot of luxury items and is more in line with the suitcase of money McCormac left under Amelia's bed."

"She should have told us," Zeffer said. "How much?"

"Neither of us counted it." Paislee glanced at Zeffer. "It's a gray area. Amelia believed that McCormac was legitimately earning money, so kept it until she found answers."

"Why do you have it?" Zeffer asked. "Did she realize she was in danger?"

"No!" Paislee shifted on the seat. "Amelia was worried her mother would find it and spend it." She shook her head. "Her brother went tae Ireland tae live a clean life. I suppose that if you're already a teensy bit crooked, a temptation like that would be tough tae ignore."

"A teensy bit?" Zeffer started the car and signaled to the road. "McCormac Henry was twisted through and through. I just hope that what he's done doesnae get Amelia killed. That would be a real tragedy."

"I thought you didn't like her?"

"I like her fine!" Zeffer checked his mirrors and changed lanes. "I dinnae trust her in the station during a criminal investigation involving her family. Different story altogether."

"She wouldn't hurt anybody."

"I know that. But she would cover up for them."

Paislee sighed and focused on the plan at hand. "I'm glad Lydia found three rental possibilities. Driving around with Dougie had been a total waste of time."

"Can you remember any landmarks?"

"Yes. We stopped for petrol at a station across from one of the main Loch Ness monster ticket centers downtown. We spotted Porche, but knew she lived in Inverness, so it wasn't strange tae see her there. That's when Dougie said he'd gotten off on the wrong exit."

"Not bloody likely, eh?"

What did Zeffer mean? "We didn't know Porche was working with MacTavish as his vet assistant until today."

"What if Porche was giving Dougie a message? They probably know each other," Zeffer said. "Then what happened?"

"Dougie and Porche *do* know each other, he never said they didn't, but the connection was through McCormac, her ex, and the fact they'd all grown up in the old neighborhood. After he'd filled up, he took us back tae the previous exit that he said he'd over-shot."

"This was the day of the big storm?" Zeffer seemed to be putting things in order.

"Aye. The snowfall that day was practically a blizzard, so it was possible he had missed the exit. He'd promised his sister, Sula, that he would drive us around tae try and find Snowball."

"Not the suitcase of money," Zeffer said dryly.

"No. I doubt he was aware of Sula and McCormac's plan tae leave Nairn for a new beginning." But he'd heard Sula talking about money. "Or that she was pregnant. Besides, Dougie has his own special edition Mercedes and wants tae step into the luxury-car sales position in Belfast."

"This is the first address that Lydia sent," Zeffer said as they exited the A96.

Paislee recognized the area right away. "There's the petrol station, and the Nessie ticket booth."

"It would be convenient," Zeffer said.

"Let's drive by." Paislee put her hand to her thumping heart in alarm. "How are we going tae know who is inside?"

"Knock," Zeffer answered wryly. It started to snow again. He put on the wipers. "Blasted winter. Makes it harder when the day is over at half past four. Lots of criminal activity happens at night."

They reached the rental address but the place looked empty and forlorn.

"I'll go." Paislee hopped out as Zeffer called her back inside the car. She wasn't in any danger. Snow had built up to her calves in the driveway and covered the steps and porch. The home had a vacant feel, but she knocked anyway. The DI opened the driver's side door and stood to watch her.

A nosy neighbor with gray hair and glasses stuck her head out the front door, a thick shawl around her shoulders. "Help you?"

"Hi!" Paislee smiled and waved as if she was campaigning for public office. "I'm looking for my friend, Porche Walsh? I'd hoped tae see her puppies."

"I called tae complain aboot the constant racket, that I did. Havenae seen her or those dogs since," the woman snapped.

"That's the one." Paislee lowered her hand.

"It's criminal that just anybody can have pets," the woman said, then slammed the door before Paislee could ask where Porche might have gone.

"Thank you," she said to the closed door.

"Friendly type." Zeffer covered his twitching lips with his knuckles when she got back in the car. "Next time, stay here."

"It was obviously an empty house." Paislee focused on the positive. "We're on the right track, Zeffer."

House two was vacant with not a hint of occupancy, and no neighbors home on either side. She was losing hope that they'd reach Amelia while it was still daylight.

At the third strikeout, Paislee had to think again. *Where are you, Amelia?*

Chapter 26

"We have thirty minutes before it gets dark," Zeffer said. They'd pulled over at a convenience mart where Zeffer had bought himself a coffee and a tea for Paislee.

Disappointment stung.

"I sent Lydia a text letting her know that we struck out with those addresses," Paislee said. If she expected accolades she was reprimanded instead.

"What did Payne tell you?" Zeffer took off the lid as they sat in the SUV, and blew on his coffee to cool it. "He'll talk with Lydia and manage the questions."

While the DI had run in for much-needed caffeine, of course Paislee had alerted Lydia. It's what she would normally do in *any* knotty situation.

Pulling a pack of gum from her handbag, Paislee offered Zeffer a piece. He declined. She chose a stick of peppermint and chewed while she waited for her tea to be less than third-degree-burn hot.

"I've been thinking," Paislee said.

"Uh-oh."

Paislee quirked a brow at him. "What do you know of Sula? She wanted that money and believed that McCormac had left it by mistake with Amelia. It's an entire suitcase of hundreds. Would she let that go? McCormac is dead. That could be her escape plan."

"Payne wants tae question Sula again. He's apprehensive aboot how she'd avoided looking him in the eye." Zeffer risked a tiny sip and winced. "He's got the instincts tae be a DI someday."

Her phone dinged and she read her bestie's text. "Lydia, bless you. She has a fourth rental possibility."

Zeffer carefully put the cap back on his hot coffee and placed his phone in the dashboard mount. "Where?"

Paislee shared the address to his mobile and heard the notification ding.

Lydia sent another text and Paislee sucked in a breath, accidentally swallowing her gum. She choked and drank her hot tea to get the glob down.

"What's wrong?" Zeffer asked, concern emanating from his gaze. His hands were on the wheel of the SUV, but he didn't want to go if she needed the Heimlich maneuver.

"Not wrong, DI." Paislee knew this was important. "Lydia said the renter is Sula Selkirk!"

Zeffer rammed the car in gear, the tires spinning on the snow. "Buckle up!"

Paislee spilled tea on the way to the cup holder, her fingers burning a wee bit, then fastened her seatbelt. They were going to find Sula, who would lead them to Amelia, and Snowball. "Why would Sula rent a place in Inverness? Maybe a love nest for her and McCormac?"

"Or she's in on it," Zeffer said.

"Sula loves animals, so she wouldn't hurt the puppies." She might be greedy, but that was a character flaw that could be improved on, compared to murder.

Paislee perched forward, alert. Not Sula. Sula had been devastated and shocked by McCormac's death. Not Hank. Not Michael. *MacTavish* had to have killed McCormac that New Year's Eve. Maybe McCormac was getting sloppy by gifting so many puppies to his friends and family and whoever was in charge of the operation wanted him shut down.

Evening skies darkened as they raced the clock.

Zeffer made a right turn.

"There!" Paislee pointed to a small, white one-story house with two vehicles in the drive. "That's Dougie's SUV that Sula borrowed before, when she was trying tae break intae Amelia's flat. It's exactly like McCormac's. And that's MacTavish's SUV, also a Mercedes but it doesn't look as new."

"There's a third on the side of the house," Zeffer said as they slowly drove by before he pulled in behind the brand-new Mercedes. The home was on a cramped lot—the houses on either side were dark, as if their owners were away. The picture window in the front was covered by closed curtains. Two stairs reached a porch. "You're sure Dougie didnae know aboot Sula being pregnant?"

"When we were at Sula's, the day of the storm, she told us it was a secret from Dougie because he'd be furious . . . He knew how McCormac felt about marriage, as in, against it, which meant Sula would be a single mum like theirs had been. In his words: a slut."

"Family can be brutal."

"Meaning tae be protective." Paislee thought of Letitia Henry's style of motherhood. "What if Sula borrowed the SUV again?"

"All Mercedes." Zeffer put his vehicle in park, blocking Dougie's SUV. The windows were tinted and the chrome polished. "There's a big Mercedes-Benz dealer in Belfast and it checked oot that McCormac worked there. It might be the connection tae MacTavish, and the puppy scheme."

Paislee texted Lydia about Paislee's theory that MacTavish was the New Year's Eve killer.

"Maybe Sula rented the place tae try and entrap MacTavish for killing McCormac. She claimed not tae know details of what McCormac or Dougie were doing, but how is that possible?" Paislee shifted on the heated seat. "And you might be right, Zeffer. McCormac told Sula that he was approached by a coworker about the opportunity tae make extra money."

"We dinnae jump tae conclusions, Paislee." Zeffer read a message on his mobile. "We gather facts. Payne just arrived at Sula's." What sounded like fireworks went off behind the house, the unexpected noise alarming. "Stay here—I mean it." Zeffer grabbed his phone and turned off the engine. He looked at her with consternation. "I'll be right back." With that, he slipped out, careful not to slam the door.

Paislee didn't want to stay behind! However, unlike the deserted feel of the vacant homes, this situation held danger, so she would do as Zeffer asked.

Lydia responded to Paislee's text with a social media picture of Jamison MacTavish in Edinburgh on Hogmanay with a bunch of mates, time-stamped midnight—blowing her theory that he'd shot McCormac.

Paislee stared at Dougie's Mercedes and noticed that the panel on the side had an indent and smudged fingerprints. The smugglers used compartments to convey the pups. Dougie had never denied wanting to take over for McCormac at the Belfast dealership. Sula had mentioned the Irish mob. How involved were the Selkirks?

It was plausible that Dougie, who had supposedly left the park that night to take Lyla home, had killed McCormac to put himself as the top man for the position. There was no honor among thieves. Perhaps the siblings were in on the scheme together.

The interior of the SUV turned cool. She stared at the house and property as the light faded.

Her phone rang. Not a familiar number. "Hello?"

"Paislee? Where is Zeffer?" Payne asked.

"We're at the fourth rental house Lydia found in Inverness, rented by Sula Selkirk. She must have borrowed Dougie's SUV again, because it's here. We're parked behind it. Zeffer said he'd be right back, but it's been a few minutes." Paislee was getting concerned.

"Send me the address," Payne said curtly.

Paislee did. "Got it?"

"Aye. Paislee. Quickly bring me up tae speed."

"Sula wanted the money that Amelia had from McCormac, so she tried tae break into Amelia's flat. Now she's here—I hope with Amelia and Snowball."

Payne cursed. "I'm outside Sula's now. In *Nairn*, Paislee. Sula isnae at that rental. It's probably Dougie. Zeffer's not in sight?"

"No." Her skin chilled from the inside. "We heard fireworks behind the house."

"Paislee, I'm going tae be frank with you right now and I need for you tae stay calm. I just saw Sula Selkirk and she has a black eye. Dougie discovered the pregnancy test she'd hid in the bin and got so mad that he punched Sula, knocking her oot for several hours. He wanted the money she thought McCormac had, and went tae Amelia's this morning tae get it—with a gun. She hasnae heard from Dougie since."

"That's horrific." Paislee counted to five and kept her panic under control—her teeth chattered from the cold. "Are you on your way?"

"Aye. But there's a wee problem. There's been a huge crash on A96 and there's no traffic gettin' through anytime soon."

Zeffer might have expected Sula inside the house, but it was Dougie, and Dougie was armed. Dougie was angry.

Another explosion sounded and Paislee realized that it wasn't fireworks. It was a gun. She'd never heard one before now, but it wasn't the same as the fireworks. She feared Zeffer might be in trouble. Unlike regular police constables, who were not armed, the DI, as a detective, carried a weapon. Had he fired it at Dougie? Or worse, had Dougie fired at him?

"I just heard another sound. It must be a gun," Paislee said. "What should I do?"

"Stay in the car."

Her skin chilled. Zeffer wasn't coming back. "It's cold, Constable."

Payne cursed again.

"What about the local police?" Paislee asked. "Can they come?"

"I'll try them, but they're verra busy with the crash. It's a bad one, Paislee. A lorry on fire."

"What about a police helicopter?" Paislee asked. She'd seen those on the telly.

"It will be covering the crash." Payne sighed, heartfelt. "This cannae get any worse. I need for you tae just stay in the car. Be patient."

"It's getting dark." She realized that her battery was low. Her phone was new, so she didn't worry as much, but the screen began to flicker.

"There should be an emergency kit in the back of the SUV. It'll have a blanket—but you need tae be verra quiet. I wil—"

The phone went dead. Black. With all the talking she'd been doing, and the pictures, the battery had died. Now what?

Paislee crawled into the back of the SUV and poked around, finding the emergency kit, with a blanket and a flare. Matches, and a first aid kit. There was also a tire iron. She gingerly tugged the metal rod free and hefted it in her hand. She pocketed her torch and returned to the passenger seat.

What was happening inside the home?

There wasn't going to be help for some time.

Another shot sounded, and then she heard a howl of pain. Dog? Human? Paislee thought of Zeffer. Of Amelia. She couldn't sit in the car not knowing—her active imagination was on overdrive. She had to see what was going on and if she could help. Tire iron in one hand, she quietly slipped from the passenger side of the SUV, not daring to close it all the way in case it automatically locked.

It wasn't dark yet but there were mere minutes before twilight ended. Paislee patted the flashlight in her pocket. She hunched by the large front window, covered with curtains, and walked to the side of the house. The third Mercedes, also new, had pink hearts and stickers with fuzzy puppy paws on the back window with *Porche* in fancy script.

Paislee was glad for the square window that had the blinds partially open. She stood on her tiptoes and made out a view of the kitchen. The cold metal of the tire iron chilled her palm. Modern white cupboards, a table. No people or dogs. She sighed. Now what?

A trodden path led around the back, multiple footprints melting the snow to the grass.

The next window along the side was too tall, so she dragged a broken plastic crate beneath it and climbed up to peek in. A beige couch with blankets tossed along the armrests. Discarded winter coats in a pile. A fireplace. Dogs penned behind a gate that wasn't as tall as her knees. White fur—Snowball?

She shifted her gaze and gasped. Dougie had a gun trained on Zeffer's forehead. That close there would be no mistakes. If he shot, Zeffer was dead. Her stomach clenched and she quickly scanned the lounge. Dougie also had Amelia, who he'd tied to a wooden chair, as were Porche and MacTavish. MacTavish was bleeding from his arm; his head lolled to the side.

Porche was sobbing as she tried to jerk her hands free. "Let me go, Dougie! Did you kill Jamison?"

Dougie's skin was flushed crimson. "Shut up! Gimme me the money, Porche, or you get the next bullet."

Zeffer had his hands to his sides, cool and seemingly unruffled by the danger. His black winter coat might be good for the weather but wasn't bulletproof. Dougie was trying to force Zeffer to a chair to be tied up, but he wasn't cooperating, and his legs were braced. Zeffer probably realized that if he gave in to Dougie, it would be game over.

Her mouth was dry, her palms damp.

How to stall for time until Payne and the other police officers arrived on the scene? Scratch that. Sirens blared in the distance; the smell of burning petrol and rubber from the crash on the motorway wafted toward her. There was no guarantee of assistance.

"Why'd ye come here, man?" Dougie waved his free arm, the other hand trembling as he gripped the gun and stared at Zeffer. "It's your fault I shot MacTavish. Sneakin' in here."

"Let me have the weapon," DI Zeffer said. "Nobody else has tae get hurt."

"I ain't leaving withoot the cash," Dougie bellowed, maneuvering Zeffer so that he could also glare at Porche. "I'll kill this copper, Porche. I killed McCormac, do you understand? I got nothin' tae lose here. Give me the money so I can leave!"

"I dinnae have any money," Porche shouted back, fear making her voice quake. MacTavish remained out cold. "McCormac and I werenae together. I'm with Jamison, and that's what I told McCormac too. You didnae have tae kill him."

"Yes, I did! He knocked me sister up and wasnae going tae marry her, or even stick around. I willnae bloody well stand for that."

Paislee hoped the shouting and accusations would pull Dougie's focus from Zeffer's forehead. While the DI was trained to handle this situation, she was not. His expertise didn't stop her heart from thudding with dread. Dougie, sweating, was at the breaking point with nothing to lose. She climbed down and raced to the front of the rental home, staring at the SUVs and the porch. She hefted her tire iron.

She crept up the stairs on tiptoe and tried the front door, but it was locked. How to get Dougie to come outside?

His fancy Mercedes was sure to have a car alarm. Taking a chance, Paislee hopped off the porch and swung the tire iron to the front headlight with all her might. The smash sounded very loud to her ears—but not as loud as the alarm that blared from Dougie's SUV.

Heart thumping, Paislee leapt to the porch and ducked beneath the window out of sight. Her grip on the tire iron was firm. She had no idea if the distraction would work. She didn't want anything to happen to Zeffer or Amelia.

Would Dougie investigate?

The front door opened, and Dougie came out with the gun at Zeffer's temple. She stayed low so she wouldn't be in the line of fire and thwacked the tire iron against Dougie's ankle. His leg buckled, which was all that Zeffer needed.

Within seconds, he had flipped Dougie to the porch and his knee jammed in his lower back. Cuffs snapped over Dougie's wrists.

Paislee allowed a relieved tear to fall but sucked in the rest. "You're all right," she said.

Zeffer nodded gruffly. "Thanks tae you." He looked at the blaring SUV and noticed the lack of other police officers. "Please tell me you called for backup?"

Paislee straightened, her body trembling with spent adrenaline. "Aye. Payne can't come right away because of the accident on the motorway. I heard shots—dumb tae think I could mistake the sound for fireworks."

"You dinnae ken, until you do." Zeffer hauled Dougie to his feet, tucking the weapon he'd retrieved into his waistband, and then yanked his own gun from his ankle holster.

"That's where it was," Dougie said. "You lied and said you didnae have one."

"Yep." The DI turned to Paislee. "What in God's name were you thinking?" The tone was controlled despite the words.

With a gulp, Paislee explained, "That if I provided a distraction, you'd be able tae act and take Dougie down. You're trained tae be a hero. I saw Amelia and Porche tied up." Her teeth chattered. "MacTavish. Is he dead?"

The DI didn't answer as he patted Dougie down.

Paislee pushed the front door so it opened wider. Snowball saw

Paislee in the shadows and barked in greeting. "Can I untie Amelia?" She moved down the hall, the tire iron still in her hand.

"Paislee?" Zeffer asked. He stayed on the porch.

"Yes?" She stopped and turned to face him. Her stomach whirled with nerves. Dougie, head bowed, was struggling against the handcuffs, but he wasn't getting free from Zeffer.

"You dinnae need that." The DI nodded to her weapon. "It's okay now. I'm verra glad that you didnae stay in the car."

Paislee didn't know what to say, so she dropped the tire iron in the hallway and hurried to the lounge. A dozen or more puppies were barricaded behind a dog gate. MacTavish breathed heavily but was alive. After a lot of tugging, she untied Amelia, who immediately rose to her feet. She'd leave Porche and MacTavish in their seats for Zeffer to deal with.

No doubt, they'd be questioned thoroughly regarding their shady activities.

"Are you okay?" Paislee asked Amelia.

Amelia nodded and rubbed the skin at her wrists. "Snowball has been here with MacTavish the whole time. Dougie said MacTavish was going tae sell Snowball in the next round of puppies. Even though she had kennel cough, she's a beautiful specimen." Amelia glared at MacTavish. "Why not get double the money for her, eh?"

MacTavish groaned.

At her name, Snowball jumped over the dog gate and her back legs knocked it over, freeing the dozen puppies that had been penned.

The beautiful white Pom pawed with joy at Amelia's shins, giving licks to Amelia and Paislee both.

"You saved the day, Paislee," Amelia said. She sank to her knees on the floor, accepting the puppy adoration with laughter. Snowball's pals wanted in on the love too.

"No. Zeffer did."

Zeffer . . . when she'd seen him in danger, her mind had insisted she save him even if it wasn't smart.

It wasn't practical.

It made no sense.

But knowing that he was all right without a hole in the middle of his forehead, well, it was worth the yelling he was going to do at her later.

Amelia saw her looking down the hall as Zeffer returned to the lounge, Dougie in cuffs, and tried unsuccessfully to hide her smile.

Chapter 27

"These are too tight. Take 'em off," Dougie demanded, shaking his cuffs.

"Nope." Zeffer pulled out a set of zip ties and helped Dougie to the seat Amelia had been in, fastening Dougie's ankle to the chair leg so the DI could be hands-free without worrying his prisoner would attempt to escape.

"Ouch! She broke me ankle!" Dougie shouted, glaring at Paislee.

Zeffer poked the swollen skin visible above Dougie's sneaker. "Sit still. They'll have an ice pack at the Inverness police station." The DI glanced at Paislee. Amelia had moved to the couch, Snowball in her arms and the other puppies next to her. Paislee held one that reminded her of Sula's Thor—so ugly it was adorable. "How many are there?"

"Twelve, not including Snowball," Paislee said. The pup in her arms gave a wheeze. "They're sick! We should have Dr. Kathleen examine them."

"Call her," Zeffer suggested.

"My phone ran out of battery and died."

Zeffer closed his eyes and then opened them to stare at her. "You dinnae have a phone?"

"No, but I'd updated Constable Payne before it went kaput. He said Dougie had punched Sula out cold, so Sula couldn't be here at the home she'd supposedly rented."

"Know anything aboot that?" Zeffer asked Dougie.

"Nope. I'm innocent."

Porche barked a laugh. "Doubtful."

"I heard you say you killed McCormac. You threatened tae kill DI Zeffer." Paislee glared at Dougie. "Kidnapped Amelia. Punched your sister. Far from innocent."

"Just tell me where the money is," Dougie called to Amelia. "You gotta know. McCormac stayed with you. He trusted you."

Amelia patted Snowball and didn't acknowledge Dougie. This man had shot her brother.

"Where are the constables?" Porche asked. "I want off this chair. Untie me, Red. Who the hell are you, anyway?"

"Paislee." Paislee didn't move to free the woman. "There was an awful accident on the motorway, requiring emergency services and the police. Constable Payne will be here as soon as possible. He contacted the local Inverness police." She studied Zeffer, who watched Dougie closely. "Is your phone working?"

Zeffer shook his head. His skin flushed. "Dougie smashed it. I was outside and he snuck up on me. Brought his heel down on the mobile as I was mid text. Not my proudest moment."

Amelia peered up from her spot on the couch. "You got him though, DI."

He waved off her words.

Paislee knew Zeffer'd be a lot harder on himself than anybody else would be. "You've got him in cuffs and the situation under control." She looked at Amelia. "Your phone is at your flat. What happened this morning?"

"Dougie showed up and I stupidly let him in, thinking it was MacTavish who had killed McCormac." Amelia sighed.

"My fault since I sent you the info Lydia found that Jamison Torrance MacTavish was the imposter's legal name. I'm sorry."

Paislee scratched the homely pup behind the ears. MacTavish moaned but didn't rouse.

"I dinnae care what happened. Untie me and let me oot of here, Amelia," Porche shouted. "I didnae do anything wrong."

Amelia gave Porche her palm. "When Dougie knocked, I let him in like an idiot. He shoved me intae the table and broke my TV and gaming console. The Christmas tree. Tore up the mattress. I wouldnae have told him where the money was for anything."

In that second, Paislee realized that holding the suitcase for Amelia could've been dangerous. It never occurred to her that the contents would be anything more than McCormac's puppy money.

"Shoulda told," Porche said. "I could've died." She jerked her chin toward MacTavish. "Dougie shot Jamison."

"This Henry doesnae snitch." Amelia tapped her heart. "I hoped Dougie would make a mistake."

Dougie strained against his restraints. "But I didnae, lass; I knocked you oot and loaded you in the SUV like dirty laundry."

"Dirty laundry." Paislee stared at Dougie. "Do you work for the Irish mob?"

"Shut your trap, Dougie," Porche said, leaning toward him with a scowl.

Zeffer listened with interest.

"I heard through the window, Porche, that you and McCormac had broken things off—why is that?" Paislee asked.

Porche scrunched her nose, her heart-shaped face not so pretty as she told Paislee what she thought of the question in words that would have made her granny blush.

Amelia started to laugh. "You protest too much, Porche. I think you still loved my brother as much as he loved you."

MacTavish raised his groggy head, his blue glasses askew on his nose. "I need a hospital."

"And a *real* doctor?" Amelia's tone was cold. She looked at Zeffer and Paislee. "When we got here, Dougie tied me up. He and Porche argued aboot the money. MacTavish threatened tae cut him oot of the smuggling scheme—they planned tae set McCormac up tae take the blame when they moved since Inverness was now compromised for the pop-up. Dougie went pure mental and decided tae tie them both up too. Not sure what his plan was after that."

"Nobody has the damn money!" Porche shouted at Dougie. "You got greedy, and ruined everything."

Dougie paled.

"You shot my brother," Amelia said. "It's unforgivable."

He didn't answer.

Paislee heard the sirens coming as did the puppies, whose ears perked. Zeffer straightened.

"The day you drove us around, lost," Paislee said, "did Porche talk tae you? Tell you tae waste time in the storm?"

"Aye," Dougie said, happy to implicate his cohort in crime. "Met up at the petrol station."

"I was there tae buy a coffee," Porche said with a roll of her eyes.

"How did you transport the puppies?" Paislee asked. "Without hurting them?"

"Shut your gob," MacTavish said, finally waking up enough to realize that there was trouble brewing, besides his injured arm.

It had to be in the body of the SUV somehow. "I hope you impound Dougie's Mercedes—probably all three of them," Paislee suggested. "If they came from Belfast. I have a photo of Mac-Tavish's SUV track outside the fake clinic."

"You need tae mind your own business, Red." Porche stared at Paislee in a calculating manner.

Zeffer scrubbed his jaw, but his eyes twinkled. "You were verra calm, Amelia," the DI commended.

"All credits tae my video games. I learned tae watch for the right moment tae act. I thought I saw a shadow—you, Paislee—and that's when Snowball alerted. Then we heard glass breaking and Dougie brought Zeffer oot tae see what was going on."

"Paislee provided a brilliant distraction," Zeffer said. "Took a tire iron tae the headlight of the SUV, and then Dougie's ankle."

"Police brutality!" Dougie said.

"I'm just a concerned citizen. And Zeffer had Dougie down so fast my head spun." Paislee patted the puppy who was asleep in the crook of her arm.

Just then the front door opened, and the Inverness police arrived in bright yellow jackets. Zeffer introduced himself as he motioned Paislee toward the couch with the puppies. After a few moments, while he sorted the chaos, Zeffer joined them.

"Hey. Here's my keys. I want you both tae go sit in the car and wait for me tae drive you back." Zeffer handed the keys over. Their fingers touched and her skin tingled.

She looked away but couldn't stop the redhead blush. "Should I call Dr. Kathleen about the puppies? I know she'll help and she's familiar with the situation. I can charge my phone from your charger once the engine is on."

"DI?" An officer called for his attention. "What should we do with the others?"

"Go ahead," Zeffer said, striding away to assist with the arrests.

Paislee and Amelia peered at the whingeing puppies. "We can't just leave them here."

"No. They could get hurt or overlooked," Amelia said.

As stealthily as possible, Paislee and Amelia found two plastic bins, minus the tops, and piled the bottoms with blankets, then puppies.

They headed out of the house with their bins and had reached the porch when one of the constables called out. Amelia gestured toward Snowball. "She's mine."

With a nod, the constable returned to his coworkers. Jamison Torrance MacTavish and Porche Walsh were not happy about being under arrest and were demanding a solicitor.

They passed Dougie's SUV, the car alarm off now, and Paislee showed the indent of the panel to Amelia.

"Should I try tae open it?" Amelia asked.

"Better not." Paislee opened the passenger door, noting that it was still slightly open. She slid the bin of frightened puppies on the seat, then got behind the wheel to start the car and plug in her phone to call Dr. Kathleen. "When you return tae the station you can ask Zeffer for the details."

"Aboot that . . ." Amelia said. She positioned her bin of puppies on the floor in the back seat, petting them and trying to keep them calm.

The car started like a champ and Paislee plugged her phone into the charger on the console. It blinked to life.

"Paislee, I've been thinkin' and wondered if I could work for you full time rather than at the station?" Amelia held her gaze.

Amelia was wonderful in her sales position at Cashmere Crush. The customers liked her, and she knew her yarn. "Care tae explain?"

"I know Payne and Zeffer were just doin' their jobs, but I dinnae think they have my best interests at heart. I'll take a pay cut if necessary. I dinnae have a lot of expenses." Amelia smirked. "I can always sell my brother's Rolex. I'll turn in the suitcase—I dinnae want anything tae do with puppy money."

Paislee mentally went through her incoming projects but then tossed all logic aside and nodded. "We'll make it happen, Amelia. My luck has finally turned around."

Once her phone reached twenty percent, she dialed Dr. Kathleen's office. The vet picked up after several rings.

"Hi! It's Paislee—I have Amelia, Snowball, and a dozen puppies with a cough related tae the case we were discussing. Can we bring them tae you?"

"I was just on my way oot, but I'll gladly stay," Dr. Kathleen said.

"The smugglers have been arrested," Paislee said. "This is the tip of the iceberg and will probably lead tae the breeders."

"Well done." They ended the call. Paislee realized she had a million missed texts from Lydia, Grandpa, and Constable Payne.

She quickly replied that she, Amelia, and the puppies were safe, but they couldn't talk yet—home soon.

Zeffer exited the house and Paislee scooted from the driver's side. She met Zeffer in the headlights and pointed to the panel on Dougie's SUV.

He brought a finger to his lips and didn't say anything until they were all inside and the doors to his vehicle closed and locked. He saw the puppies and started to protest.

"We talked tae Dr. Kathleen, and she can take them right now—she's waiting for us," Paislee said. "You know they'll get great care, poor things."

Zeffer exhaled. "Fine. Let's see it through. You have a guid eye, Paislee. Puppy smugglers use fake bumpers, or dashboards, or false compartments, tae get the pups across. Tire wheels even. Not all survive. Now. Can we just concentrate on these lucky dozen dogs?"

Amelia, holding Snowball, nodded. Paislee grinned.

"Thank you," Amelia said.

"Dougie's gun will be a match for the bullet we found in the wood of the bandstand." Zeffer dipped his head to Amelia. "I'll start the paperwork tae get you back in the office."

"That's okay. I quit." Amelia patted Paislee's arm. "I'm going tae work for Paislee."

Zeffer's jaw tightened. "I'm sorry tae hear that, Amelia. You are a guid employee."

"With a bad family?" Amelia challenged.

"It's complicated." Zeffer looked right at her.

Amelia's jaw firmed. "Inspector Shinner never made me feel like I was *less than* because of my last name. You might want tae consider that."

"I apologize." Zeffer was very sincere. "It was not our, my, intent. I stand by the decision made because we couldnae be one hundred percent sure that you wouldnae protect your family."

"You have me there," Amelia said. "I would have. But also, I wouldnae break the law. After we drop off the puppies, let's grab the suitcase of cash at Paislee's."

Zeffer blew out a breath. "You're verra lucky that we willnae charge for obstruction, Amelia."

"I thought that money was legit. We helped solve my brother's murder and saved the puppies. You can keep the cash and we'll call it even." Amelia sat back and snuggled with Snowball.

It took forty minutes to reach Nairn because of the aftermath of the crash, and the weather. Paislee was able to text everyone an update while Zeffer was on the phone with Payne—using his headset so they couldn't listen.

As they unloaded the puppies, with Zeffer promising Dr. Kathleen to crack down on pet smuggling, Paislee hugged Amelia to her.

Friends—family by choice. What wouldn't you do for those you loved?

Epilogue

The following day, the Henry family had a huge spread on the front page of the paper.

Grandpa slurped tea and chuckled. "Amelia Henry is being lauded as a hero."

Brody ate a bite of cereal with berries and jumped up to read the page over Grandpa's shoulder. "That's brilliant! How many puppies were saved?"

Paislee slathered butter on her toast. "The twelve that we took from the house where Amelia was held after Dougie kidnapped her, and then Porche squealed on MacTavish, and they uncovered two other houses with a hundred puppies." She couldn't stop smiling that the pups had been rescued.

"Yer name is in here too, Mum, and Cashmere Crush," Brody said.

"What does it say?" Paislee lowered her butter knife.

Grandpa held up his hand and brushed cereal crumbs from his shoulder. "Sit doon, lad, and I'll read it aloud." He shook the pages and cleared his throat.

Paislee winked at Brody as he sat back down, Wallace at his heels just in case he dropped something else. They had thirty minutes before they had to leave.

" 'Puppy smuggling ring routed by local Amelia Henry, whose

family has been in Nairn for generations. Her brother, McCormac Henry, was murdered on Hogmanay by a member of the Belfast crew, Dougie Selkirk. The puppies will be available for adoption once cleared by Dr. Kathleen McHenry. Contact Amelia at the number listed below for more information. She's put a stop tae the fearsome Henry reputation—one of her grandparents was a known pirate—tae take her place as an example in our community. She was assisted by her guid friend Paislee Shaw, who owns Cashmere Crush on the corner of Market Street.' "

Paislee couldn't stop a giggle from escaping. "Zeffer won't be happy with that," she said.

"I wish I could be a pirate," Brody lamented. "How'd you help, Mum?"

"I'll tell you the same thing I told the police—Amelia's car was in the shop, so I drove her around when she needed it." She held up her palm and concentrated on her toast.

Brody accepted that and finished his breakfast, not at all hindered by his arm in a sling. "I told Jenni and Edwyn I'd be early today."

"And when were you going tae mention that tae me?" Paislee swallowed her toast.

Brody grinned. "I forgot. We gotta hurry!" He raced upstairs.

Paislee shook her head. She saw the letter her son had written to her mum and siblings next to the landline and put it in her purse. She met Grandpa's curious gaze with a shrug. "Not sure what this will mean for us, but I'm going tae reach out tae my mother."

Grandpa covered her hand with his. "It's the right thing tae do, lass."

"I hope it doesn't bite us in the . . ." She glanced at the place where their swear jar used to be before the big ceiling crash. "You know."

Grandpa discreetly fed a corner of his toast to Wallace. "Aye, I know." His brown eyes grew somber as they often did when he thought of his only child still living. "But where would we be withoot family?"

Acknowledgments

Thank you to John Scognamiglio and the team at Kensington. I am so appreciative of all the different pieces you manage to create this book, from the editing, to the cover, to the marketing and more behind the scenes. I feel like together we make art, which is rarely a simple thing.

Thank you to Evan Marshall, agent extraordinaire, and thank you to Sheryl McGavin. Your talents amaze me. I am so grateful for our friendship—family by choice.

Christmas Stocking Project

Sheryl McGavin

Abbreviations:

CC	Contrasting color
K	Knit
MC	Main color
P	Purl
PSSO	pass slipped stitch over
Tog	together

Materials:

Worsted weight yarn, about 316 yds total

When doing 3 colors—MC (which includes cuff, toe, and heel and 1 stripe) will be about 168 yds, and add about 74 yds each of the other 2 stripe colors (CC1 and 2). In the picture, green is the MC, white is CC1, red is CC2

Straight knitting needles, sizes 7 and 9

3 stitch holders

2 markers

Yarn needle

Instructions:

CUFF

Using size 9 needles and MC, cast on 50 stitches loosely

Work in K1, P1 ribbing for 4 inches, 50 stitches

LEG

Change to size 7 needles

Row 1: with CC1, knit across

Row 2: Purl across

Rows 3-4: With MC, work in stockinette stitch (Knit 1 row, purl
1 row) for 2 rows

Rows 5-6: With CC2, work in stockinette stitch for 2 rows

Rows 7-90: Repeat Rows 1 through 6, 14 times

Row 91: with CC1 knit across

Row 92: Purl across

LEFT HEEL

Note: When instructed to slip a stitch, always slip as if to purl.

Row 1: Slip 16 stitches onto stitch holder (this will be for the
Right Heel), slip 18 stitches onto a second stitch holder (this
will be for the Top of Foot). With the MC, slip 1, knit
across, 16 stitches

Row 2: Purl across

Row 3: Slip 1, Knit across

Rows 4-15: Repeat Rows 2 and 3, 6 times

Short Rows (to form corner of heel): P2, P2 tog, P1, turn; slip 1,
K3, turn; P3, P2 tog, P1, turn; slip 1, K4, turn; P4, P2 tog,
P1, turn; slip 1, K5, turn; P5, P2 tog, P1, turn; slip 1, K6,
turn; P6, P2 tog, P1, turn; slip 1, K7, turn; P7, P2 tog, P1,
turn; slip 1, K8, turn; P8, P2 tog: 9 stitches

Slip remaining stitches onto stitch holder

RIGHT HEEL

With Right side facing, slip the 16 stitches from Right Heel stitch
holder onto needle

Row 1: With MC knit across

Row 2: Slip 1, purl across

Rows 3-14: Repeat Rows 1 and 2, 6 times

Short Rows: K2, slip 1 as if to knit, K1, PSSO, K1, turn; slip 1,
P3, turn; K3, slip 1 as if to knit, K1, PSSO, K1, turn; slip 1,
P4, turn; K4, slip 1 as if to knit, K1, PSSO, K1, turn; slip 1,

P5, turn; K5, slip 1 as if to knit, K1, PSSO, K1, turn; slip 1,
P6, turn; K6, slip 1 as if to knit, K1, PSSO, K1, turn; slip 1,
P7, turn; K7, slip 1 as if to knit, K1, PSSO, K1, turn; slip 1,
P8, turn; K8, slip 1 as if to knit, K1, PSSO: 9 stitches

GUSSET AND INSTEP SHAPING

Note: Continue with color pattern established in the leg, alternating between the 3 colors every 2 rows.

Row 1: With MC, pick up 7 stitches on inside of Right Heel, knit the 18 stitches from stitch holder, pick up 7 stitches on inside edge of Left Heel, knit 9 stitches from Left Heel stitch holder: 50 stitches

Row 2: Purl across

Row 3: With CC2, K14, K2 tog, K18, slip 1 as if to knit, K1 PSSO, K14: 48 stitches

Row 4: Purl across

Row 5: With CC1, K13, K2 tog, K18, slip 1 as if to knit, PSSO, K13: 46 stitches

Row 6: Purl across

Row 7: (continue alternating color pattern) K12, K2 tog, K18, slip 1 as if to knit, K1, PSSO, K12: 44 stitches

Row 8: Purl across

Row 9: K11, K2 tog, K18, slip 1 as if to knit, K1, PSSO, K11: 42 Stitches

Row 10: Purl across

Row 11: K10, K2 tog, K18, slip 1 as if to knit, K1, PSSO, K10: 40 stitches

Row 12: Purl across

Row 13-36: Continue to work in Stockinette Stitch (Knit across, then Purl across, change color and repeat the 2 rows) in established color pattern

TOE SHAPING

Row 1: Change to MC, K7, K2 tog, K1, place marker, K1, slip 1 as if to knit, K1, PSSO, K14, K2 tog, K1, place marker, K1, slip as if to knit, K1, PSSO, K7: 36 stitches

Row 2: Purl across

Row 3: *Knit to within 3 stitches of marker, K2 tog, K1, slip marker, K1, slip 1 as if to knit, K1, PSSO, repeat from * once more, then knit across: 32 stitches

Row 4: Purl across

Rows 5-10: Repeat Rows 3 and 4, 3 times: 20 stitches

Bind off all stitches

FINISHING

With right sides together and beginning at the toe, sew seam to within 2" of the top edge; then with wrong sides together sew the remaining seam. Fold cuff over.

For the hanging loop you can braid three 6" lengths of yarn together or crochet a chain, fold it in half to make a loop and stitch the ends of the loop to the seam at the top of the folded cuff.

Visit our website at
KensingtonBooks.com
to sign up for our newsletters, read
more from your favorite authors, see
books by series, view reading group
guides, and more!

Become a Part of Our
Between the Chapters Book Club
Community and Join the Conversation

Submit your book review for a chance to win exclusive
Between the Chapters swag you can't get anywhere else!
https://www.kensingtonbooks.com/pages/review/